The Light Who Binds

By Lilo Abernathy

I0607196

Bluebell Kildare Series
Book 2

COPYRIGHT

Title: The Light Who Binds
Author: Lilo Abernathy
Editor: Shauna Ward

Dedication

Readers

Thank you so much for all of your encouragement and support since I first published *The Light Who Shines*. Many of you connected with me on social media and were a constant confidence boost as I struggled to learn everything a new author doesn't yet know. For that, I'm ever grateful.

In the next year, I hope to deepen my friendships with those of you who have already reached out to me, and I also look forward to meeting more friends along the way.

I'm especially grateful for my all of my wonderful readers who left feedback on various websites in the form of blog posts, recommendations, and reviews. You can't imagine how I hung on to every bit of feedback in the beginning, just hoping people would like the story. And you did. And I could hardly believe my eyes. I still read every one of your reviews, and they all truly matter to me.

Your combined efforts made *The Light Who Shines* a resounding success for a debut novel from an independent author. So in thanks, I give you the second installment in the *Bluebell Kildare Series*, and I hope you'll enjoy it just as much.

Truly, this wouldn't have happened without you, so this story is for you.

Lilo

TABLE OF CONTENTS

ACKNOWLEDGEMENTS

irst of all, I'd like to thank you, Shauna Ward, for your editing assistance, which is so necessary to enrich my stories and make them ready for the world. I've learned so much from working with you, and I know I could never have done this without you. Gina Fiserova, I thank you for your excellent critical eye in finding ways to tighten the story and make it more believable. And Stephanie Shultz, your final proof is the icing on the cake, giving it the polish it needs to compete with traditionally published authors.

To E.B. Hood, Kayti Niki Raet, and Virginia Sellers, I'm so grateful for your assistance to enliven the fight scenes and ensure I wasn't doing anything technically idiotic, which I was bound to do without your help. Virginia, I also thank you for your assistance with the Prophecy of the Illustrissima; as you know, poetry is not my "thang."

A special thanks to my beta readers: Jean Lombardo, Charles Lombardo, Joy Eileen, Anne Marvin, Carol-Ann Hill, Duffy Walters, Tracie Webb, and Joan Baker. I so appreciate your time and honest commentary, all of which helped me improve upon the story.

I can't possibly close these acknowledgements without extending my appreciation and admiration to Kirsi Salonen for providing the gorgeous book cover illustration and to Kristin Sallee for modeling as the face of our beautiful heroine.

Most importantly, I'd like to thank my readers for purchasing this book and continuing this journey with me. I hope this book is all you expected and more.

SUMMARY

This story is not intended as a stand-alone novel and would be difficult to understand without first reading *The Light Who Shines*. For those of you who are moving straight from *The Light Who Shines* to this book, reading the following summary isn't necessary.

I've created this summary in deference to my wonderful readers who have been waiting patiently for this story. This covers some important definitions and the key threads and mysteries from *The Light Who Shines* that will be picked up in this book. It's organized into topics so you can easily skim through if you wish.

BREEDS OF PEOPLE

The world is known to be populated by three different breeds of humans: Norms, Gifted, and Vampires.

NORMS

Regular people who are neither Gifted nor Vampire.

GIFTED

The Gifted are people who have magical gifts. Usually they only have one gift, such as the ability to see auras or to portal from one location to the other. There are endless ways someone can be Gifted. All Gifted people have a mark, which is not always visible because it may be under clothes, under hair, hidden between toes, etc.

DAYLIGHT VAMPIRES

When the concentration of Vampire blood in a Norm or Gifted person reaches fifty percent, that person goes through the change. If they survive, they become a Daylight Vampire, and their soul holds Lilith's mark. They're no more evil than regular people; however, they do require human blood to survive, and they suffer from blood cravings. Unlike Dark Vampires, they can walk in the sun, bathe in holy water, and stand on Holy ground. They're also virtually indestructible, as they can regenerate limbs, cannot contract illnesses, don't require sleep, and possess super strength, speed, and senses. They move so fast that at their highest speeds, they appear as a blur to the human eye. Their one weakness is their blood craving because if they kill in bloodlust they forfeit their soul to Lilith, and their body remains on earth as a Dark Vampire. Killing in bloodlust simply means killing a blood donor while drinking their blood, whether voluntarily or involuntarily. There is a great risk of Daylight Vampires killing in bloodlust when they're fighting a hated enemy, when they're starving, or during times of extreme passion.

DARK VAMPIRES

Once a Vampire turns Dark and becomes soulless, they lose their sanity—some more slowly than others. They have a veracious appetite and will kill at every opportunity. They can be killed with an oak stake, with holy water, by standing on Holy ground, or by the sunlight. Since a Vampire must kill in bloodlust to become a Dark Vampire, all Dark Vampires are considered evil and can be killed without repercussions. Additionally, since they're soulless, they aren't considered people. They simply become things.

CURSE OF VAMPIRISM

Once someone is turned into a Vampire, whether willingly or not, the only way they can truly die is by first becoming a Dark Vampire. At that point, their soul will go to Lilith on the Plane of Fire. Therefore, all Daylight Vampires are destined to the Plane of Fire. The only thing they can hope to do is to hold on to the desire to live. But the blood craving forever eats at them, tempting them mercilessly.

There is much prejudice and hatred between some breed members. This is called breedism. Both the Gifted and Daylight Vampires are distrusted, but the Gifted are the primary breed persecuted by Norms because the Daylight Vampires are so strong and powerful.

Timeline of This Alternative Universe

At approximately 1600 A.D. by our calendar, the first Vampire was made. This began year one of the Red Ages (R.A.), named for the tremendous bloodshed during this era. This is the point at which the world of the Bluebell Kildare Series splits from the reality we know and live in. In this world, the Red Ages continue to this day.

The Red Ages are divided into three distinct time periods:

Deconstruction Era
(0 R.A. to 1300 R.A.)

Vampires first came into power and society started to deconstruct.

Bloody Era
(1300 R.A. to 1500 R.A.)

Civilization completely fractured, and the Norms and Gifted were driven almost to extinction. The Bloody Era ended in 1500 R.A. when the Great Peace Pact (Great Pact) was made among the breeds. Daylight Vampires realized they must kill Dark Vampires to preserve their food source because the Gifted and Norms were going extinct. They made a pact with Norms and Gifted to hunt Dark Vampires and keep their own numbers in check in exchange for willingly offered blood.

Reconstruction Era
(1500 R.A. to Present)

After the Great Pact, the Norms and Gifted populations started to flourish again.

The Bluebell Kildare Series begins in the year 2022 of the Red Ages. This equates to 3522 A.D. by our calendar. Society is not as far advanced in some ways as it is in our reality because of the huge setback caused by the Deconstruction Era. It is more advanced in other ways due to the use of magic.

EARLY HISTORY AND IMPORTANT PLAYERS

SHAINA, SORCHA, AND MOR

The Light Who Shines begins with the story of Shaina and Sorcha on the Isle of Erin (Ireland), which takes us back to year 1 of the Red Ages as Mor awakens Shaina to warn her that the villagers are coming to burn her as a witch. Shaina cannot escape with her baby, Sorcha, so she gives the baby to Mor. Mor escapes with Sorcha to the relative safety of the woods, while Shaina is caught and given a witch's trial. As she dies, she curses the Great Demon Lilith for her demise.

TORLOCH (PATERSUCO)

Torloch is Shaina's husband and the reason the villagers believed her to be a witch. Torloch, sick with blood cancer, used the Grimoire to call the Great Demon Lilith from the underworld. He tried to bargain with her to save his own life, but she twisted his wish to her desires and cursed him to become the first Vampire, embedding her mark on his soul. He is also called Patersuco, which literally means "Father of the Vampires."

MAGICAL ARTIFACTS AND OBJECTS

GRIMORIUM CANTIONUM SPIRITUALIUM (GRIMOIRE)

In Latin, this translates to The Spell Book of the Spirit and Soul. It's a powerful book that holds the knowledge to call Demons and spirits from other planes. The Grimoire can't be unlocked without a two-part key consisting of an amulet and a stone eye. All three items were secreted away after Torloch used the book to call Lilith and strike the bargain that created the Vampire breed. At the end of The Light Who Shines, we know that Blue has the amulet hidden in the church's bell tower. We don't know the locations of the Grimoire or the eye.

THE BELLADONNA NECKLACE

The evil Tobias Blackwater placed this necklace on Blue's neck when he captured her. He claimed the necklace would subdue any potential magical gifts she might have—but curiously, Blue's gift only became stronger when she wore it.

CHIMERATOR

This is a charmed ring that allows you to see someone's image and hear them speak to you. It has a cover that flips open to reveal a shiny stone, jewel, or pearl, and the visage appears on its surface. Some chimerators can project an image into the air. When someone calls, the ring tightens around your finger to notify you.

ADVERSARIAL GROUPS OF PEOPLE

DILECTUS DEO
(BELOVED OF GOD)

A group of religious extremists who view all Gifted and Daylight Vampires as evil beings.

BLACKWATER'S GROUP

At the end of The Light Who Shines, we know that Tobias Blackwater had been searching for the amulet, and he wasn't acting alone. Tobias dies, but his group is an open threat. Tobias was Gifted; so this precludes his group from being Dilectus Deo. We don't know much about who they are, except that they exist and clearly want to harness the power contained in the Grimoire.

CHARACTERS

This is a partial list of characters, focusing on those with open threads or mysteries from *The Light Who Shines*.

BLUEBELL KILDARE
(A.K.A. BLUE)

Blue is our heroine. She was stillborn, born with an umbilical cord wrapped around her neck. Her father used his gift of healing to try to bring her back to life as her mother, who could see souls, called her soul back into her body. Blue's parents were killed by Dark Vampires in an alley when she was just a babe. When the Dark Vampires uncovered Blue, her aura (or soul's light) burned them as they would be burned by the sun, and she survived the encounter. A Daylight Vampire found her and brought her to Father O'Brennen who in turn put her in the Green Tree Orphanage. Blue's childhood at the orphanage was painful. Her gift of empathy allowed her to know things that normal children would not, and so the children were cruel to her, verbally and physically abusing her. As an adult, she works as a Homicide Inspector for the Supernatural Investigation Bureau, whose goal is to ensure interbreed peace and security. Because Blue has dealt with hate her whole life, she supports this goal with all her heart.

JACK TANNER

Jack is a Daylight Vampire and Blue's boss. He was turned well over five hundred years ago, just before the Great Peace Pact. He knows what the Bloody Era was like and he's not proud of the way his breed behaved during that time. He clearly has feelings for Blue, but what in the world is holding him back?

VARG

Varg is a wolf who mysteriously appeared in an alleyway as Blue was being attacked. He protected her at that time and has continued to protect her ever since. We don't know where he came from, but we do know he heals extremely fast, can grow in size, and can escape any locked area. Varg is loyal only to Blue.

DRAGOMIRA
(THE DRAGOMIR)

Dragomira is the enigmatic woman who owns the Dragomir Magical Artifact Shop. We know her eyes glint yellow and change colors, she speaks with a wild melodious voice, and can open cabinets with a spin of her hand, but we don't know exactly what she is.

Dean Schmidt

Former Officer Dean Schmidt, out of prejudice, anger, and jealousy, attempted to rape Bluebell Kildare in an alley. Blue escaped the worst of the attack with the help of Varg, who tore Schmidt up badly. Then, under threat of death by Jack, he was forced to resign from the police force. The last we saw of him, he was terribly injured from his encounter with Varg and was joining the Dilectus Deo. He is an evil loose end that has yet to be dealt with.

Anna Marie

Anna Marie was a housemother at the Green Tree Orphanage years ago. She was forced to leave when it was suspected she placed an enchantment on Blue as a child. The reason for the alleged enchantment remains a mystery.

Illustrissima

Dragomira refers to Blue as the Illustrissima, but we don't know yet what that means. At the very end of *The Light Who Shines*, Jack says he needs to tell Blue who she is—and that mystery is left to be explored in this novel.

PROLOGUE

MOR

WINTER, YEAR 1, RED AGES

It's getting closer. Bolder. It's been tracking me for three days now. I run as swiftly through the forest as my starved body can, holding wee Sorcha tightly in the sling wrapped about my torso. Low-hanging branches and brush tear into my forearms, but I pay no mind as I roughly push them aside.

I glance back and don't see the beast. But I know it's there. Invisible, and silent, it stalks us. My mind's eye sees many things my real vision cannot. Flashes of images that make me shudder. Hungry eyes watching, waiting. Fangs descending.

A bird squawks at my intrusion, and I stumble in exhaustion. Fear rips through me as I remember how Shaina's fall ensured her death. An injury to me now would do the same. But I catch myself. My years of running over the moors as a youth have served me well.

The Sea Caves must be within one day's travel from here, perhaps less. I'm so tired, but I dare not rest. This morning I awoke to the vision of the man-creature leaning over me while I slept. His fangs were extended as he stroked my hair and stared hungrily at my neck. No, I cannot sleep again. Not tonight, for tonight he may not walk away.

With resolve, I push through branches and shrubs, following the river to the sea. I stop for a moment at the bank and scoop handfuls of water into my parched mouth. Then, tenderly, I expose Sorcha's little mouth and dribble water onto her tongue, hoping desperately that it will keep her alive.

Her sweet, round face lolls pathetically in the crook of my arm, a pale ghost of the rosy baby she had been just a few days prior. Her eyes remain lifeless, and my heart clenches. If I don't reach the Sea Caves soon, her chances will be ended. The sinister chill of the wind wraps around us, trying to claim her, and I have no more warmth to offer than my own body. With grim determination, I set off again at an exhausted trot.

Darkness falls, and the moon hangs high and bright atop a shield of mist. The glowing orb is ambivalent to my worry about being easier to track, but at least it gives light to walk by. The fog thickens with each passing hour as I move steadily toward the sea. Serpent-like, it twists and writhes, then billows up in alarming gusts, enveloping us in its pearly, biting embrace. Despite my chattering teeth, I take solace in the icy wind because it means we must be getting closer.

I see a nearly imperceptible movement from the corner of my eye. A dark shadow hovers on a tree limb high above, out of place in the misty forest. Then the fog shifts, and the shadow disappears in a smear of white like the rest of the world. But I know what it is.

So this is it, then. I have come so far, but the beast will get me before I reach safety. The fear and panic that have been building within me for days have finally driven me to my wit's end. I will stop this now.

"Show yourself!" I shout. "Let me look upon the face that will end my life and the life of this innocent child."

The shadow leaps from the trees above me, and the man—no, the beast who used to be a man—stands before me now. Tall and powerful with long fangs cutting into his lip. Dirty and ragged, the tattered remnants of clothes hanging off him. Then he speaks, and his voice is that of a man. "I have no wish to harm you. I've seen what happens to those who kill to ease their craving."

His sharp eyes pierce me.

I don't believe him, and though I tremble in fear, I bite back. "Then why do you stand over me while I sleep and gaze at my neck with longing? Why, even now, do your eyes flit to the lifeblood pulsing there?"

He turns away in shame. "Because I hunger. I have not yet eaten since I was turned. The pain is nearly unbearable."

"Why do you stalk me, then?"

He moves in close and grips my arms, fingernails digging into my gaunt shoulder blades. I gasp at the shock of his touch.

"Because your blood calls to me," he snarls in frustration.

"Is it my blood you want, or my flesh?"

His brow wrinkles in confusion. Then he drags his nose over my neck, inhaling the scent of my skin. Fear racks my body, but I stand frozen in place, trembling beneath his hands. He gives my jaw one long lick. The baby hangs silently between us.

"It is your blood I hunger for."

Then, in a flash, he's ten feet away, where the mist is thick and his features indistinguishable.

"How long?" I ask.

His voice travels softly through the silvery haze. "What do you mean?"

"How long before you give in to the hunger and slay me?"

"I don't know. Soon, I fear."

The stark honesty of his reply shakes me to my bones. My knees collapse beneath me and I sprawl backwards on the damp earth, clutching Sorcha to my breast. "Must you end my life? Can't you take some blood, enough to ease your pain, but leave enough for me to live? I must get this child to the Sea Caves, to the Dragon tribe. She's ill and starving. She hasn't woken once today. Already, I fear it's too late for her."

He moves forward and regards Sorcha with concern. "You think I could stop? None of the others did."

"Did they try?"

The question hangs heavy in the air between us while his eyes dart from my neck to the motionless baby pressed to my breast and back again.

Suddenly steel bands grasp my shoulders, sharp daggers pierce my neck, and my body arches in an instinctual scream that's absorbed by the unsympathetic forest. His mouth undulates relentlessly, like a baby at a teat. I feel my lifeblood flowing inexorably toward his mouth, but surprisingly, the pain is minimal. Before I can struggle against his strength, I'm overcome by a profound exhaustion, heavy as a leaden blanket, which forces me against the earth. My vision grows dim as it tunnels ever narrower. Then the last prick of light blinks out.

CHAPTER 01

THREE DEATHS

BLUEBELL KILDARE

JULY 7, 2022, RED AGES

Lightning streaks across the twilight sky casting a brilliant glow on the building before me. Stone gargoyles loom above me, their eyes seeming to gleam and blink, their great amphibious wings, arched for flight. A slow roll of thunder fills the air as though the bowels of the earth are opening.

I behold the formidable oak doors of the Dragomir Magical Artifact Shop, wondering what mysteries lie inside. Oh, I know many spells, charms, and magic secrets reside within the artifacts, but those aren't the unknowns I seek tonight. Tonight, I anticipate learning secrets about myself.

From behind me, the warmth of Jack's chest radiates into my back, and Varg leans into my thigh. A measure of calm returns to me. Whatever news awaits me, at least I have friends at my side. I straighten my spine, lift my chin, and remove the remaining space between me and my future, pushing the heavy oak doors open to boldly stride in.

As I enter the shop, eddies of dust coalesce from the swish of the doors into a whirlwind at my feet. I'm instantly comforted by the familiar shelves of aged magical texts stacked on bookshelves and delighted by the glass-doored cabinet stocked with magical artifacts. I was last here just a few months ago, but I feel like an entirely different woman now.

Dragomira stands behind the counter and lifts her head with a weary expression, but a fierce glint fills her warm, brown eyes. She is not Dragomira right now. No, she is the Dragomir. Her movements, as fluid as rippling water, trace a path across the room as she quietly deadbolts the door behind us.

With a wave of her hand, she beckons us into her back room. A small fire flickers in the fireplace, casting dancing shadows across the walls. Jack and I take a seat in wing-backed chairs next to the hearth, while Dragomira, still curiously silent, pours three drinks from a beautiful decanter sitting on an ornate wooden table amidst the chairs. She places one in my hand in silent command, watching as I taste it. The shock of whiskey burns my throat and slides warmly to my belly. She sets a glass in front of Jack and keeps the last for herself.

As Dragomira takes her place, I notice again how strikingly beautiful she is. Her hair cascades in long, tumultuous brown waves against her olive skin, and her deep-set eyes gleam with life. Sitting back in her chair, she directs her scrutiny toward me. "Welcome, Illustrissima," she begins. "I'm sure you have many questions."

Her harmonious voice rolls through me in a soothing wave. I forget myself for a moment and tilt my ear to enjoy its song. Then I gather myself and say, "I do. Let's start with the name Illustrissima. Why did you give this name to me?"

Dragomira blinks. Then she regards me steadily and answers, "I no more gave you the name Illustrissima than I gave you your blue eyes. It is a Latin word that has many meanings: the Shining One, the Bright One, the Lustrous One, the Famous One, the Distinguished One." She waves her hand as though all of that is inconsequential. "You are all of these things. You simply *are* the Illustrissima."

I take a slow sip of whiskey. "You can see my light."

The Dragomir's eyes flare with a glint of yellow in acknowledgement.

"How?"

She contemplates the fire for a moment before responding. "I am also many things. I have magic . . . gifts, you might call them, which allow me to see things that would normally pass unnoticed. However, what I have been most as of late is a scholar." She looks at me intently again. "Tonight, your time would be better spent allowing me to share what I've learned about you."

She's right; after all, Jack and the Dragomir have kept me waiting on this information for months now. "Yes, why don't you," I answer curtly.

The Dragomir raises her eyebrows and Jack gives me a warning glance, but I am not so easily cowed.

She nods and settles back in her chair. "Let's start at the

beginning. I've told you the story of Patersuco and the inception of the Vampire race. As you know, it didn't take long for him to kill in bloodlust and turn Dark, as corrupt as he was, but he had already started creating children. And so the curse spread."

"What I did not tell you was that Patersuco was survived by his wife. Shaina lived in the village, and before the first winter of the Red Ages had passed, several of the townspeople had died at the hands of Patersuco and his Vampire progeny. The villagers turned on Shaina and burned her as a witch."

I shudder at the thought of that pain, thankful I wasn't there to feel it.

"Yes, these were rough times, Illustrissima. We have very few written accounts from that time, but from what we know, Shaina was Gifted. Like you, she was an Empath. The villagers tied her to an ash tree and used oak branches to burn her alive."

"Both these trees have deep, old magic. Ash acts as a bridge between worlds, and oak provides strength. Somehow, the combination of the rage of the villagers, the strength of the oak, and the power of the ash all fed Shaina's pain, creating a force strong enough to open a pathway from Shaina to the Great Demon Lilith. As she burned, Shaina was able to reach across to the Plane of Fire and lay a powerful curse upon Lilith."

"What was the curse?"

Dragomira leans back, and her eyes glaze as her mind transports to another place and time. The firelight flickers, and shadows play artfully on the curve of her cheekbone. Then her husky whisper fills the room.

"Lilith, I call on you to hear me.
By my blood, you will be destroyed.

A light will come—
a light that shines through your evil;
a light that calls you to answer for your deeds;
a light that binds you as I am bound and burns you as I burn;
a light that rips you asunder and destroys your darkness.

Lilith, hear me.

I call to you.
By my blood, you will pay for what you have done.

Lilith, by my blood, you will be destroyed."

As these words wash over me, tendrils of fear sink into my flesh and thread through my soul. The curse grabs something deep and dark inside of me, and I start to shiver. I reach out for my drink and take another burning sip.

My voice comes, breathless but laden with protest against the implications of Dragomira's story. "And you believe I am this light? You've proved no connection."

She takes another drink of whiskey, a deep pull this time. I'm not sure if it's the fire reflecting off them, but her eyes seem to swirl with yellow in their depths.

"Three times Shaina called Lilith's name that night. Three times she demanded that Lilith listen. Three times she said that retribution would be by her blood. This cinched the curse. But what you need to know most is that while Patersuco's son was sacrificed, his twin sister survived. Her name was Sorcha."

"Still, how does that relate to me?"

She raises one dark eyebrow at me. "When Shaina said 'by my blood,' she meant her lineage, not the blood that flowed through her veins. You are Shaina's only remaining descendent, through Sorcha."

I stand rapidly, knocking into the table and causing it to rock furiously, my glass of whiskey threatens to spill. The table eventually comes to a rest, but I do not. I fling myself across the room and pace as the thoughts roil around in my brain. Despite the cacophony of questions on the tip of my tongue, one thought rises urgently above the rest.

They think I'm supposed to destroy Lilith!

I spin around to see both Jack and Dragomira watching me with grave concern.

Jack sits tensely on the edge of his seat as though ready to leap to my rescue. The light glints off his cropped golden curls, and he reminds me of a fierce golden angel ready for vengeance. Every hard plane of his body speaks of coiled strength and lethal abilities. I've felt those enticing planes beneath my fingertips just a few times, and I'm honest enough with myself to admit I want more.

Dragomira says, "There's more."

Jack and Varg growl simultaneously, and I guess the more she's talking about isn't quite the more I want.

I swipe my drink from the table and knock back the rest. The liquid scorches my throat and traces a fiery path down to my belly, providing a momentary distraction. With a huff, I sit down again and cross my arms. "Just tell me all in one shot, please. I'd like to process this once, not five times."

Dragomira deliberately refills my glass. I consider this a bad omen. She begins again, this time watching me intently.

"Shaina was close with a woman named Mor who had the gift of sight. She warned Shaina that the villagers were coming for her. Still, they could not escape in time. When Shaina saw that she couldn't outrun them, she entrusted Mor with Sorcha.

"Mor watched the burning from the safety of the woods, and it is she who documented the events of that night. Afterward, she took the babe to the Dragon tribe, a clan who lived in the Sea Caves nearby. While she was there, she had a vision. That's what brings us to you."

Dragomira lifts her hand and a roll of parchment flies off the mantle and into her palm. She passes it to me, and I carefully unroll the aged hide. Quietly, I read aloud the ancient script that promises to reveal my fate.

The DARK ONE spreads her plague across the land.
Rivers run red and earth soaks black with blood.
Man will fear the Cursed and greatly decline.
When they hide like rabbits, the end is near.
The DECEIVER will dance in her triumph.

There is one way that Man can rise again:
trust their enemy
live as one people,
or all will perish.

If they succeed, the DESTROYER will rage;
mourn her loss of souls,
plot her artifice,
move forth with vengeance.

*Beware! The **PRETENDER** has many ways.*
Need changes to greed;
love corrupts to hate;
hope buckles to fear.

Foes renew and the Great Pact is broken.
*When Man wrongs Man, the **BEAST** has all but won.*
Yet one last path still remaining for Man,
Yet one last path to deliver the Cursed.
*The scion of Shaina's blood will shine **BRIGHT**.*

*The **BRANDED ONE** will thrice-fold be guarded:*
blade preserves body;
bone benefacts mind;
Cursed entrenches soul.

*The **LUSTROUS ONE** will thrice-fold be fitted:*
light her palisade,
justice her design,
love her instrument.

*The **ONE WHO IS KNOWN** will thrice-fold meet death:*
once in trade for life,
once that is taken,
once that is given.

*The **LIGHT WHO SHINES** will shatter the darkness.*
*The **LIGHT WHO SHINES** will deliver the Cursed.*
*The **LIGHT WHO SHINES** will assail the **DARK ONE**.*
*The **ANNIHILATOR** will be destroyed.*
*The **ERODER OF SOULS** will be rebirthed.*

Be steadfast, for the end is uncertain.

The edges of the aged parchment nearly crumble under the force of my grip. I loosen my shaking hands, and color flows back into my knuckles. Varg, sensing my stress, leans heavily against my knee. He places his snout in my lap, raises his eyebrows and blinks his ice blue eyes. I wrap my fingers in his long fur, gaining strength from his comfort.

I turn my attention to Dragomira and Jack. They clearly knew the prophecy, as their faces are not filled with questions; instead, a great solemnity surrounds them like a thick mist. Dragomira seems weary but resolute. Jack's eyes burn with an unnatural shine, and fear and pain wisps around him in an eerie dance. Most telling of all are the tentative vines of hope intertwined with his concern.

Once more, I fill the dark silence. "The first stanza refers to the beginning of the Red Ages. The second stanza clearly describes the creation of the Great Pact."

An unhappy agreement with my interpretation weighs their expressions.

I study the parchment for another moment. "We have no way of knowing if the third and fourth stanzas have occurred yet. The beginning of the fifth stanza says that the Great Pact will be broken."

My hands tremble at the thought of that. It is not an event I wish to see in my lifetime. The image of Daylight Vampires taking blood at will and Dark Vampires going unchecked by Daylight Vampires horrifies my very soul.

Dragomira prompts, "And what does the end of the fifth stanza predict?"

Suddenly, I feel older than the darkness of the sky and more burdened than the ground beneath the mountains. "It predicts my birth and says I am the last hope."

I lay my hand on Jack's arm. "The last hope to free the Vampires from the curse."

His jaw clenches, and his body becomes taut. Shame wraps around him as guilt leaks from him like wine through a sieve, filling all corners of the room.

"Jack?" I ask.

He glances at me briefly, then stares straight ahead. "You should go over the rest."

The parchment, all but forgotten in that singular moment, still remains in my hand. I wrestle my eyes away from him and examine the next set of stanzas. "I can see how the Lustrous One could refer to me, but what about the Branded One and the One Who is Known"

Dragomira responds, "Recall that Illustrissima means Famous One and Distinguished One. To say someone is known is equivalent to saying they're famous. Remember, there was no technology in those days—no phones, cars, or news stations. People's circles were small. If someone was widely known, they were famous."

"But I'm not famous, and I'm certainly not branded."

Jack grimaces further. "You are famous. When the slaves were found in Blackwater's house, the Dilectus Deo staged protests across the land. Of course, you were missing at the time, so your name was spoken in every other broadcast. The Dilectus Deo cast aspersions on you, said that you were involved in the crime rather than a victim. You were a topic of much debate."

"You're also branded. Your birthmark is no ordinary mark. To be marked like that is to be distinguished. It connects you both to the name Illustrissima and to the prophecy."

It feels as though the noose is tightening further. I can't imagine that I'm special enough to be the savior of the breeds. Every scrap of my life has been a fight for even the smallest amount of respect, so to be cast in this light, as though I'm important . . . I just can't grasp it. But, clearly, they believe it.

"So you really think that I'm the Illustrissima, and I'm supposed to deliver the Vampires from the curse?"

Jack replies softly, "You don't have to do anything. I'm not sure that the entire Vampire breed is worth your life."

"Jack, it isn't just the Vampire breed at stake," I point out. "According to the prophecy, the fate of all mankind hangs in the balance. That's a large prize for destroying Lilith. If this is true, then it's lucky that I've already died twice and I only have once more to go."

Their heads snap toward me, four shocked eyes taking me in as though wings have suddenly sprouted from my back.

I narrow my gaze as I take in their befuddlement. I was sure they would have known.

"I was stillborn," I explain, "and with a combination of my father's healing skills and my mother calling to my soul, much the way you did, Jack, I came back to life. That's the first death, which was in exchange for life. The second death, the death that was taken, was at Blackwater's hands. That leaves a third death: one that must be given, though I have absolutely no idea what that means. And I'm not saying I believe the prophecy, but how does one go about giving a life and killing the Great Demon, anyway? I'm certainly not killing anyone in sacrifice."

A wry smile slides across Dragomira's face. "If I knew, and if it were within my power, I assure you it would already be done. I can tell you though, it's no coincidence that the amulet found its way into your hands. This is ultimately a war between you and Lilith, and somehow the Grimoire is involved. I wouldn't be surprised if that necklace of yours played a part as well."

I lightly finger the Belladonna necklace, which drapes down my breasts and shoulders like a piece of archaic chainmail. "Can you remove it? Do you know how?"

Dragomira stands in obvious dismissal. "Come to me tomorrow evening, and I will see. Now, I have other things to attend."

CHAPTER 02

SEEKING WISDOM

BLUEBELL KILDARE

JULY 7, 2022, RED AGES

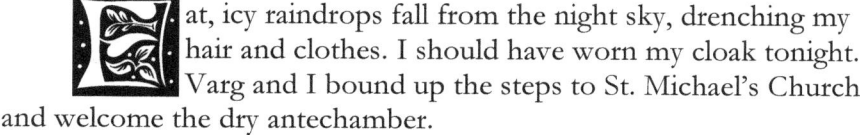at, icy raindrops fall from the night sky, drenching my hair and clothes. I should have worn my cloak tonight. Varg and I bound up the steps to St. Michael's Church and welcome the dry antechamber.

I hope Father O'Brennen is still up. Though I'm not religious, he's always been there for me. When my parents died, he encouraged my grandparents to take me in, but they were too full of hate for the Gifted, so he placed me in the Green Tree Orphanage. The housemothers would bring us here for Sunday mass, and I would escape to the bell tower, happy to be alone. When I came of age, Father O'Brennen let me live rent-free in an apartment next door until I got my first job. Above all, he's always been a counselor to me, someone to just listen when I need a sounding board. I certainly need both now.

I find him in the kitchen, standing by the beige tiled counter with a cookie in his mouth. A few crumbs fall to the gray slate floor as he chews. Father O'Brennan is of average height and build, his graying hair capped with a small bald spot. But his most stunning features are his deep-set, dark gray eyes that are so expressive, so wise, and so filled with compassion.

"Father O'Brennen," I call from the arched doorway, leaning slightly so Varg can poke his head in next to me.

He jumps up guiltily.

"Having a midnight snack, are we?" I tease.

An abashed smile fills his gentle face. "Caught red-handed, I suppose. Come on in, Blue. I'm glad to see you looking so well. Would you like some cookies?"

"I'd love some."

He opens the cookie jar, grabs another plate, and pours me a glass of milk.

"Mmm, chocolate chip," I say through a mouthful of cookie. "My favorite."

He chuckles, then pulls out another jar and hands a cookie to Varg. "That's peanut butter for him. So, how are you, Blue?"

"Fit as a fiddle." I peer down at my cookies and pick at the corner of one until it crumbles. "But I've had a bit of a shock over some things I learned today."

His eyes soften. "Well, sometimes it is best to unload your worries. So why don't you share the burden with me?"

I smile at his gentle kindness. "Remember how you told me I was stillborn and my mother called my soul back into my body?"

"Of course," he says, studying my face.

I peer intently at my plate again. "Well, the same thing happened to me again in the crypt with Blackwater. Jack found me because my soul's light was burning so brightly, he said it was shining straight past the moon. He called my soul back into my body and gave me Vampire blood to bring me back to life."

"I see."

I glance at Father O'Brennan. His forehead is furrowed in grave concentration.

I push forward through the rest. "Well, that isn't nearly all of it. Today, I spoke with Jack and Dragomira. You may know her as the owner of the Dragomir Magical Artifact Shop."

Father O'Brennen gives a little murmur of acknowledgement.

"Apparently, a prophecy from the beginning of the Red Ages foretold of my birth, and somehow I'm supposed to fight the Great Demon Lilith and destroy her." I keep going now, avoiding his gaze because otherwise I'm afraid I won't get it out. "I'm called the Illustrissima. It means 'the Light Who Shines.' The prophecy says the Great Pact will be broken, and I have to destroy Lilith to save mankind and deliver the Vampires from their curse.

"It says a lot of things in threes—like I'll be thrice guarded and have three weapons. It also says I'll have three deaths."

I pause now, conscious of how ridiculous it all sounds, expecting to see disbelief or scorn on his face. Instead, his solemn eyes gently hold mine as he places his hand on my shoulder. "That's a heavy burden to bear."

"Yes, it is. I'll do what I can, of course. But I have no idea what I should do now."

"If this is your calling, it will find you," he responds. "When the time is right, I'm sure you'll know what to do. Just trust in the Lord and follow your heart."

"Well, you know, I'm not very happy with the way he runs things, so the Lord and I aren't exactly on speaking terms right now."

Father O'Brennen smiles at me gently. "I know that. I'll pray for you, if that helps."

"Thanks, Father. It does. So, can you tell me anything about the number three? It struck me as odd that everything in the prophecy was supposed to be in threes."

He gets that dreamy expression that he gets during mass sometimes. "Three is a very important number in the Catholic Church. It signifies unity, completion, and perfection, and as you know, the Trinity is comprised of the Father, Son, and Holy Spirit. In broader Christianity, Jesus was crucified and entombed for three days before he arose. It's a strong number, significant in Pagan mythology and other religions, as well. Some mythological gods were considered to be triple-deities and were said to have three different aspects. For instance, the goddess Badb was also known as Macha and Anand. Ancient Druidism was comprised of three specialties; the Bards who were the memory of the tribe, the Ovates who were natural healers, and the Druids and Druidesses who were shamans or directors of the rituals.

"Those who believe in the Lady of Light say she came to earth once at the beginning of the Red Ages to teach Daylight Vampires to feed without killing, then a second time to usher in the Great Pact. And it's said she's promised to come to earth a third time at the end of the Red Ages to guide us to peace. I think it bodes well for you that things will come in threes."

How interesting. "Do you believe these other Gods really existed?"

He smiles. "I believe in only one God. But I think you have to consider what "existed" means. If a group of people believe in a god and worship him or her, doesn't that god exist for them? Over man's history, many gods have been worshiped. Some people believe those gods truly did exist and when man stopped believing in them, they lost their divine powers and faded away. In my faith, I believe those were false gods and idols and whether they truly existed is not of consequence."

"I have one more question, Father."

"I have open ears."

This question has confused me the most. "Why me, Father? Why do you think all this is happening to me?"

Father O'Brennen eyes droop in deep empathy. "You've had a hard life, Blue. No doubt. But don't most heroes have to rise above hardship and misery?"

CHAPTER 03

DOUBLE TROUBLE

BLUEBELL KILDARE

JULY 8, 2022, RED AGES

Warg and I step inside the warehouse, but before I have a chance to take in my surroundings, a sharp blow to my knee has me crashing toward the mat. I hold my hands out, desperately trying to keep my face from smashing into the floor.

As I break my fall, another force slams into my back, pushing my head inexorably toward the mat. I resist. My arms strain with every bit of their strength and tremble with exertion, but I'm no match for the force behind me.

My elbows collapse and I'm knocked flat so hard that my breath is stolen away. I gasp for air as my attacker takes my weapons and yanks my arms behind my back.

Still determined to escape, I kick my legs backwards. To my delight, my aim is true. I hear a soft groan, and then a man's voice requests, "Can you remove your beast? He's wrapped his fangs around my neck."

I grunt into the mat. "It depends. Will you let me up?"

The tense voice says, "Yes, I only intended to teach you a lesson about being caught unawares."

"Seems you've been caught unawares, too," I retort. "Varg, stand down."

The heavy weight lifts off me, and I rise to face my attacker. Wang stands tall and sleek with well-defined abs and biceps. In contrast, his round face appears soft and sweet, especially when his dimples make an appearance. Right now, the corners of his soft lips rise in an impish smile.

His partner Yao appears at his side. Yao is the complete opposite of Wang. He reminds me of a Samurai in build; he's of average height but solid all over. He wears a full beard, a sleeveless shirt, and the same style of flowing black pants that Wang does.

Wang and Yao are two world class warriors who Jack commissioned to train me. In addition to being partners in battle, they are also lovers, inseparable since they first came up against each other as undefeated champions of their regions in the annual Cathay Tournament. I was too young at the time to remember it, but it's said they battled non-stop for over twenty-four hours before the tournament was finally called a draw.

Since the Dark Vampires wiped out most of humanity in the Bloody Era of the Red Ages, the majority of Earth is sparsely populated. The families who escaped to the New World fared better than the Old World, because the Vampires were slower to arrive here. So we recovered much more quickly after the Great Pact. However, in the Old World, the continents of Christendom in the West, Cathay in the East, and Africa to the south were all devastated. The few peoples remaining from those continents were true survivors, strong and swift in battle, who passed down a warrior culture to future generations.

Wang and Yao, having been raised to the Eastern warrior arts on Cathay, went on to compete in and win tournaments all over the world. When Yao and Wang retired, they moved to the New World. Sometimes they disappear from the public eye for months at a time, leaving the media speculating that the pair is working private assignments.

When Jack said he was going to find a trainer for me after I failed to fend off Tobias Blackwater's assault, I thought he was going to sign me up for a boxing class at a local gym. Instead, he hired the two greatest warriors of Cathay. He arranged everything, provided this warehouse, put them up nearby, and gave them an unlimited budget for training equipment. So their sole focus is finding ways to torment me.

Wang hands me my knife and gun. Embarrassed that he was able to get them from me so easily, I take them back. He immediately goes into lecture mode.

"You have a wonderful advantage with your gift, but you must wake up!" he says. "Your five senses are dull. Your sixth sense is sleeping most of the time. We'll be watching for when you're not alert. Remember, if I were your enemy, you'd be dead right now—beast or no beast."

I sheathe my knife and lift my chin in determination. "Then you have your work cut out for you, so let's get started."

Yao agrees a little too enthusiastically for me. "Yes, we'll run six miles today."

"Six miles! You've been adding about two blocks each day and suddenly you're adding a mile?"

He steels his face. "It took you two months to run five miles easily. Now you have a strong base, so you'll progress faster."

I bow my head in acceptance and walk toward the locker to stow my weapons for the run.

Yao stops me. "This time, bring your weapons. You won't always have my protection when you run."

With a scowl I snap my holster back on, but I can't fault his logic.

A minute later we're flying down a mountain trail. Yao likes to go downhill first so I'm already exhausted by the uphill portion of the run. It's just another cruelty he inflicts. Er, I mean, it's just another tactic he employs to increase my stamina. But for now, this blessed beginning part is my favorite. We run down the east side of the mountain, thick with the shifting fog of early morning. The pink wash of dawn filtering through the mist is a glorious sight to behold.

"Stop," Yao commands.

I immediately turn in a tight circle to my right and start uphill a few steps, letting my momentum fade until I come to a complete stop. Teaching me to stop while running at an ungodly pace downhill was one of the first lessons Yao taught me. Use the mountain, he always advises. It took just one good tumble to teach me that lesson.

"Run," he commands, and I dutifully obey.

He has this thing about strengthening the heart, and supposedly stopping and starting quickly helps. He says the most valuable muscles in running are your heart and your diaphragm.

Yao yells for me to return. I grit my teeth and circle again to run back up the mountain. Three miles uphill is no easy feat, but he claims the most important strength you need is your determination. I suck it up and push my legs to continue despite their burning protests.

"Breathe through your nose! Use your diaphragm," he yells from behind me.

You would think I'd remember that rule after swallowing goodness knows how many bugs, but my instinct is to gasp for breath. Yao says it's inefficient breathing, and I can tell he's right. I snap my mouth closed and breathe the crisp dawn air through my nostrils.

Varg zips past me, ducking under trees and gliding over brush, ignoring the path entirely. He loves the morning runs, the evil beast.

During the last mile my thighs feel as though they're on fire, but Yao's constant yammering from behind me keeps me going. "Use your arms and your sides to help pull your body along," he commands.

When I start to slouch, Yao advises, "Keep your head up, and be aware of your surroundings."

When I focus too much on the path, he commands, "Stop staring at the ground! Your enemy is not underfoot." This one is difficult for me because we're running uphill, and the ground is before me, but I get his point. You can't see your enemy if your eyes are glued to your feet. Learning to keep my knees soft so I can take the impact of uneven ground was one of the hardest lessons.

We make it to the final stretch of the run. Varg stands on top of the ridge behind the warehouse watching us approach, as though to say, "Hah! I beat you." Spawn of Satan.

When I reach the top of the mountain, Yao has me walk the perimeter of the warehouse three times to slow my heart rate. I don't know why he allows me this cooling off period when he makes me stop and go so quickly during the run, but I'm grateful for the short reprieve. He handles all my basic strength and endurance training while Wang concentrates more on fighting and weapons. Naturally, that means I hate Yao more than Wang—but when Wang has me pinned to the floor, it's hard to decide who I loathe most

Ready to turn myself over to Wang's gentle abuse, I push through the warehouse doors again to reveal the expansive training room, but first, Yao has a few words for me. "You thought you weren't able to do six miles," he says. "What did you learn?"

I spit out through gritted teeth. "That I hate you, and I was wrong."

He smiles broadly, stretching his beard to gigantic proportions. "Yes, and it's fine to hate me as long as you learn that perceived limitations of your body can be overcome with a strong mind."

Wang stands in front of me, eager for his chance to torment. "Today we begin a new challenge: you will complete half of your practice blindfolded."

"Blindfolded!"

Wang grins, throwing those two gorgeous dimples into his baby-faced cheeks. "Yes, since you can sense souls, your ability to fight in the dark will be a great advantage."

He spends the next forty-five minutes painstakingly correcting my posture and my movements as we run through a series of forms for Taekwondo and Jiu-Jitsu. After doing a set with my eyes open, he hands me a blindfold and makes me repeat it in the dark.

"In the past you've used your eyes to balance. Now you'll learn to feel your center of gravity," he advises.

At first I'm off balance, but as he corrects my posture by touch, I slowly get the feel for it, and a small feeling of pride wells up inside me.

At the end of the hour, Wang announces that I'm to wrap up my session with shooting practice. That sounds like a nice, relaxing break, but Yao wants me to spend thirty minutes rollerblading on the ramps after that to increase my balance and core body strength, followed by arm work on the obstacle course. I groan my objections, but I know I have no choice.

I take a deep breath. This is going to be a long, excruciating session. At least today's my day off work and I can relax with a book after training. I let my mind wander, and my thoughts return briefly to yesterday's meeting with Dragomira and this whole "destroy Lilith" business. As tired as I am, I stiffen my backbone and carry on without complaint. Well, without too many complaints.

CHAPTER 04

SWEET, OBLIGING WOMAN

BLUEBELL KILDARE

JULY 8, 2022, RED AGES

The sun shines through the windshield of my car, making me narrow my eyes against the glare. Since I've finished my book and there's nothing else on my agenda until my meeting with Dragomira, I'm cruising over to Maud's place.

I'd say that Maud is like a mother to me, but since she acts so young, I call her one of my closest friends. I met her in the orphanage where I grew up. She used to visit and read to all the children, and that hour was among the only happy memories I have of that place. When I was younger, I wanted her to adopt me, but her husband William wouldn't allow it. He felt his job was too dangerous to allow him to be a parent. Still, Maud and I remained close and became even closer after William died. She's my touchstone, and I need one desperately right now.

On the right side of the road, a sight outside of Paco's Loco Tacos has me chuckling uncontrollably. Paco must be trying to drum up business because he's twirling around on the sidewalk wearing colorful Mexican festival attire. But the best part is his sombrero. It's made with every color in the rainbow and the brim is about five feet wide. He could fit his entire staff under there with him. I can't help it, that get-up deserves a reward. I swing over and grab some tacos for Maud.

As I pull up to the curb in front of her house, Varg exudes an unhappy rumbling sound. It isn't his usual ferocious growl announcing danger, but he's clearly displeased. Worried about Maud, I throw open Varg's door and rush to the house. By the time I hit the porch, I can tell there's nothing to fear as Maud's stressed voice carries at a high pitch from the backyard.

"When I'm ready to deal with this garden, I will, and it will be in my own sweet time. If you don't like it, put up a higher fence!"

"But sweetie, I'd be happy to help you with it." Harry's placating voice is much quieter than Maud's.

She cuts in. "Yes, so you keep saying. I'll think about it, but not now when I have a pounding headache. I'll see you tomorrow."

I hear the sliding door open and slam shut, obviously leaving Harry on the other side.

Maud opens the front door a few seconds later, two red spots on her cheeks. "Blue! Come on in."

I hand her the bag. "Here's some tacos for you for later. I'm not hungry myself."

"Oh, thank you, dear." She spins around with the bag and huffs off to the kitchen, mumbling, "Of all the insufferable . . . "

The rest of her thought is drowned out by the blender, and I chuckle as I let myself in.

She raises her voice, "I'm making Alexanders, and you're joining me, hungry or not."

"Yes, ma'am!"

I sit down at the table and watch as Harry hops over the fence to his house.

Maud, with her glowing orange hair and a white-on-green polka dot dress, stomps around the kitchen. She pulls some frosty glasses out of the freezer, and with an artful grace that even her anger can't diminish, she fills them with a flourish. She sets them on the table and sinks into her chair, clearly extremely annoyed.

"Thank you. You were a little light on the cognac today, I noticed."

Maud blushes. "I'm watching my waist."

"All twenty inches of it?"

She rolls her eyes.

"And you were a little heavy on the cream today."

She throws up her hands. "Well, that man drives me crazy. I have to do something!"

I burst out laughing. "What? Did he cheat on you? Beat you? Break your crystal stemware?"

She scowls. "He wants to fix the back garden!"

"And . . . is that so bad?"

Maud quiets and traces the dew on the side of her glass as confusion spills out of her. "I'm just not ready for it." She sighs. "Did you know that William and I had a big fight about the garden the last morning he left for work?"

I sober up quickly, at that little jewel of information. "No, I didn't. What was the fight about?"

"The day before, I'd had a dizzy spell in the garden. I got overheated, that's all. The sun made me dehydrated, but I was fine by the next morning. I wanted to work on it that day, to weed it. But he insisted I wait for him. I told him I'd take it easy, but he wouldn't even hear of it. He was so overbearing sometimes. Anyway, I was so mad, that I went out and weeded the garden to spite him."

Her eyes brim with moisture. "I was probably weeding the damn garden while he was taking his last breath." With that, a stream of tears spill down her cheeks.

I wrap my arms around her from behind her chair and murmur into her shoulder, "He isn't mad, Maud. He loved how spunky you are. If you had listened to him, he wouldn't have known what to do."

"Really?"

"Truly. When you guys fought around me, and you pretended to concede, William would roll his eyes while your back was turned."

The corner of Maud's mouth lifts as she blots her face with a napkin. "Really?"

"I promise. He'd expect nothing less than you weeding the garden. Do you think he would have stayed with you all those years if he really wanted a sweet, obliging woman?"

"Hey, now!" Maud laughs as she squeezes my hands tight.

I smile down at her and take my seat again.

"I think weeding the garden is fine. William wouldn't be mad."

Maud purses her lips in consideration. "Maybe you're right."

It would be so wonderful if she got over this garden issue. She's been a prisoner to it for years.

"If you were to work in the garden, what would you plant?" I prod.

Maud's eyes start to shine as she turns to the window, contemplating the wild jungle that makes up the back yard. "I've been in a mood for peonies, maybe some hydrangeas—and you don't think it's too late for petunias, do you?"

I can picture the finished garden in my mind. "It's never too late for petunias in the South. They'd be lovely around the swing, wouldn't they?"

"Yes, they would. Maybe Harry will help me till that area tomorrow."

"I think he's dying to be asked."

CHAPTER 05

FOREBODING NEWS

JACK TANNER

JULY 9, 2022, RED AGES

As I pull in front of Blue's apartment, she comes rounding the corner, her hair flowing behind her. The lean silhouette of her softly rounded body arrests my attention. Varg walks on the street side of the walkway with his nostrils and ears on high alert, protective as always. The neighborhood is quiet, and the firefly lampposts gleam softly on the street pavers, but still I'm glad she has him, especially after dark.

Blue lets Varg in the back seat, then slides gracefully into the front where I'm immediately assaulted by her scent: clean notes of mint and tea tree oil overlapping her earthy, womanly essence. Varg smells equally strong but far less enticing. He sniffs me a few times; then settles down for the ride, apparently no more enthralled with my scent than I am with his.

As she sets her bag on the floor and pulls the buckle closed with one hand, the other hand, absently fingers the Belladonna necklace. It peeks out from beneath her white ruffled collar shirt, an unusual departure from the casual knit tops she typically wears under her vest. "Does the necklace bother you?"

Her lovely face twists into a grimace, and her stunning blue eyes spark with annoyance. "It bothers me in the sense that it's sitting on my neck and I have nothing to wear with it."

I glance down at the subtle but delectable curve of her breasts at the collar opening. "What you have on seems fine to me."

Blue's grimace deepens and she pulls her fingers away from the necklace, tucking her hair behind her ear. Her mark, the streak of blue tinted hair, stands out in vivid contrast to her long, dark chocolate tresses. She asks, "Do you think she'll be able to get this thing off me?"

"If she can't, I'll be surprised."

As I put the car in gear and head over to the Dragomir Magical Artifact Shop, she reaches over and turns the radio to soft jazz. When the track ends, a broadcaster comes on. "The dramatic and frightening increase in Dark Vampire turnings continues to plague the city of Crimson Hollow. Seven deaths were reported yesterday, and the numbers continue to climb. Be sure to stay inside when the sun goes down, and don't forget to pick up your holy water. The city's churches have banded together to donate up to five vials per family. Just stop by your local church for a supply."

Blue turns to me. "Jack, you should let me help with those cases. I've got time now."

The idea of her chasing after Dark Vampires turns my insides cold. Rarely do Norms or even the Gifted take on the job of exterminator, and usually it means an early grave. That job is best left to Daylight Vampires who can compete on an equal playing field. "We aren't there yet," I assure her. "I'm bringing in some new exterminators to help with the problem."

"When? Because the death toll is rising, and we're bordering on all-out panic. Plus the Dilectus Deo are using this to strengthen their platform. We can't afford for this to continue, or all the supernatural breeds will be at risk."

"Well, the Dilectus Deo is upset about it, no doubt. But for some reason they're fixated on the magical community."

Blue scrunches her eyebrows. "Maybe they're worried about retaliation from the Vampires and think the Gifted are an easier target."

"Perhaps."

Blue chews her lip as she ponders the situation. "It is odd, though . . . Is this issue still limited to Crimson Hollow?"

"So far, though the Dilectus Deo are riling folks up across the continent."

"Hmm."

She continues to chew her lip, and erotic thoughts slip into my mind. Oh, how I would love to pull over right now and take that lip into my mouth, biting it gently until a drop of blood forms, then soothing it with my tongue. Don't think of her that way, I scold myself.

Her damn lucky teeth . . .

Don't think of her that way, for Christ's sake!

"How's your training coming?"

Blue's entire countenance brightens, a stunning smile appearing on her face. Damn it.

"Well, besides the fact that Wang and Yao are evil incarnate, and I'm utterly exhausted from the workouts, I love it. But, seriously, four hours a day?"

"We've got to get you in shape quickly. What should I have them omit? Speed? Strength? Weapon use? Hand-to-hand combat?" I shake my head. "It has to be done, all of it."

She sighs in resignation. "So where did you find Wang and Yao? I knew you were getting me a trainer, but I never expected the two great warrior lovers of the Cathay."

I smile at that. "Who's more suited to train the future savior of the world?"

Blue smacks my shoulder. "Shut up! I don't believe that myself, and even if it were true, you better not go advertising it like that. Besides, if I do somehow manage to fulfill the prophecy, love is supposed to be my weapon, and I doubt that Wang and Yao will help me there."

I chuckle at that. "No, I don't suppose they will." But then I sober up. "You're too important to the future of all breeds and too vulnerable to attack from anyone who might wish to harm you. For your own safety, you have to be able to defend yourself."

Blue frowns and starts to fidget. "Light is my palisade, so that's my defense. Justice is my design, so that's my motive. And love is my instrument, so that is what I should use to destroy her. But how do you destroy with love? It doesn't even seem right. Love isn't destructive. It builds a person up."

"It will come to you when it's time."

Blue glares at me. "I guess I need to find someone to love, and since you aren't up for the job, I should probably start dating."

A deep pain strikes me in the depths of my chest at that thought, but thankfully at that moment we arrive at the Dragomir Magical Artifact Shop. Not a moment too soon, by my estimation. I don't care to get into that conversation.

CHAPTER 06

AN AWAKENED SOUL

BLUEBELL KILDARE

JULY 9, 2022, RED AGES

 stomp into the Dragomir Magical Artifact Shop, releasing some of my irritation at the darn prophecy and Jack.

Dragomira spots my flashing eyes. "Hah!" she barks. "So the lovers quarrel."

"We aren't lovers," I protest vehemently. Unfortunately.

Jack grimaces, and Varg releases a short puff of air through his nostrils that sounds suspiciously like a snort. Whose side is he on, anyway?

Dragomira throws me a patronizing glance. "So you say. Bolt the door behind you and follow me."

We make our way to the back room. Situated in the middle of the only open floor space, surrounded by rows of shelves containing all manner of magical goodies, is a high wooden stool. I toss my bag on the floor and take the seat, nervous about what's about to transpire.

"What are you going to do?"

Dragomira gives me a magnificent smile, clearly happily anticipating this task. "First I'll examine it with my eyes, my fingers, and then my other senses. Now, I haven't all day. Unbuckle your vest and unbutton your blouse a bit so I can examine it."

I give Jack a hard glare over her shoulder as though he arranged this just for his pleasure. His lips quirk the barest hint of a smile in response, and he can't control the telltale signs of amusement in the crinkling corners of his eyes. I glare harder.

Once I've arranged my collar to afford as much modesty as possible while still giving Dragomira a view of my shoulders and the tops of my breasts, she starts circling me.

Her penetrating gaze takes in every minute detail of the necklace as her excitement and determination fill the room. She's a woman who enjoys a challenge. She fingers the interlocking links and counts the dangling strands. She even counts the number of links per strand.

After several minutes of agonizing silence, she murmurs, "This was made around the beginning of the Red Ages. It most likely originated somewhere in the Fertile Crescent, and it's clearly very powerful."

"How can it be when it doesn't work on me at all? My gift has actually been more powerful since I've had it on."

"Hmm." She sounds disbelieving.

"I'll prove it," I insist. "Think of an emotional event in your past."

Dragomira steps back and tightens her face into an indiscernible mask, but a distinct wave of rage billows from her body.

"Rage," I say. "Give me something else." After a second, I sense tremendous loss. "You're grieving. Do I need to continue?"

Dragomira shakes her head.

I shift in my seat, and my shirt falls slightly.

Dragomira's sharp intake of breath draws my eyes to her face. She's staring at my birthmark, a dot twice encircled, the outer circle is wavy like a sun sign. She mutters, "So this is the birthmark. Well, that makes sense now."

"What?"

Still gazing at my blemish, she speaks, almost as though to herself. "You don't have a magic gift at all. Well, you do have the blue streak of hair, so you may indeed have a gift—but it certainly isn't the power you've displayed while wearing this necklace. Your birthmark signifies many things, but what it most represents is that of the eternal soul."

She peers at me intently now. "What you have, my dear Illustrissima is an awakened soul."

My eyes lock with Jack's from across the room as I ponder what that means, and a profound silence fills the air.

Dragomira sits down in one of the wingback chairs. I move to get down from the stool, but she stops me with a wave of her hand. "This will just take a moment. The Gifted have the ability to use magic, which is nothing more than the transferring or unlocking of energy. As I'm sure you know, the energy is always borrowed from one object and transferred to another in the magical act. The energy isn't retained in the body, nor does it touch the soul.

"But Blue, you're different. You don't have to use the energy of any object. You *are* the energy. It's more than that. Normally a soul is confined within the skin, and only a small amount of light escapes."

Dragomira glances at Jack. "You can clearly see that her light fills the room," she says. "It's free, so to speak."

She turns to me again. "Of course, if you allowed your soul to separate completely from your body, you would lose touch with your humanity and have a difficult time returning, so your soul must stay in residence. But you can shape it and use it at your will; it has no boundaries."

I protest, "But my soul does have boundaries. I had to push so hard to get it out at first when I was in the crypt, and I was so tired that I had to pull energy from some source in the sky. I'm not sure, but it might have been from the Plane of Light."

Dragomira purses her lips. "Perhaps you use your body as a reservoir or you don't know how to fully access your power, but either way, you can perform your 'magic,' so to speak, with your own soul. Nevertheless, this necklace must come off. It's pointless to speculate further until it does and we see what happens to your power." She jumps off the chair to examine it again.

I suspect she has some interesting theories that I wish I were privy to. Even if my soul has no boundaries, my patience certainly does. I clasp my hands together, and Dragomira begins to probe the necklace with her mind. I'm surprised I can feel her energy pushing against my skin, sometimes forceful, sometimes as light as a summer breeze.

After a few minutes, she stands back, emanating a feeling of satisfaction.

"Did you unlock it?" I ask.

"Not yet, but I believe I know the way. Patience."

Dragomira starts chanting in the same ancient language she used when I was first in her shop. Someone, whom we now assume to have been Blackwater, tried to penetrate her wards, which are the protective spells cast around her building. Just like then, her rich voice in its multitude of tones strikes a deep chord within me. She starts moving her arms in a silent language of their own in harmony with the rhythm of the chant. Her eyes seem to flicker with a golden light, and the room fills with the thrum of power, a gentle electrifying sensation. It seems as though the power is seeping through the walls and the floor. She's pulling it into her.

The necklace grows hot on my skin, and the pressure in the room intensifies. I focus on Jack and Varg to distract myself.

Jack leans back in his chair, his eyes half closed, utterly transfixed by the situation. I like to call this his panther stare; he appears relaxed, but like silk over steel, he's disguising his strength, lulling his victim into relaxation. And like the panther, he hides as he stalks, but is ever ready to pounce.

Varg grumbles low in his chest and bares his teeth menacingly at an unseen threat. The power of Dragomira's ritual continues to weigh heavy in the air, but the room is still—except that strangely, Varg's fur waves like he's in the eye of a storm, as though unfelt wind blows on him alone. His eyes are intent on me and low rumbling noises continually emit from his throat.

Dragomira peers appraisingly at Varg, then dismisses him as she circles me, the cadence of her song quickening. She moves her hands in brief, rapid strokes, alternating between cutting sharply through the air and waving gracefully, sinuously. The crushing force of the power, the weight of the air, the electrifying tingles become almost unbearable, and Dragomira's face breaks into a sheen of sweat as she whirls around me.

Abruptly, the air lightens and seems to evaporate from the room. A cracking sound snaps loudly from several directions at once as her cabinet doors shatter. The glass crashes to the floor, making a tinkling noise as the shards hit each other on the way down. The necklace latch bursts open and the chain slides off my neck and into my lap.

Jack and Varg rush toward us, and Dragomira collapses in the chair. I stand shakily with the Belladonna necklace grasped loosely in my hand. A strange sense of isolation strikes me, a colorless depression that I can't name. I wave aside Jack's unspoken offer of assistance and walk on unsteady legs to the comfort of the upholstery. I tuck the necklace into my bag, and with a deep breath, I sink into the chair.

"I feel so peculiar."

"How so?" Dragomira prods.

"I feel somehow less, like everything is coming at me through a long tunnel," I explain. "I think the necklace heightened my senses, and I'm back to normal now, but it doesn't feel like normal anymore. It feels restrictive." I sweep the three of them with my senses. "Yes, you're all duller now."

Jack glances at Dragomira with a question in his face, and she nods in return. I watch the exchange in frustration. "What?"

He eyes me with concern. "Your light is shining less brightly now. In fact, your aura is back to what it was before the necklace."

Dragomira frowns. "The necklace was subduing magic that is currently at work on you. I think someone has spelled you and it's constrained your soul. Do you know anything about this?"

I lean forward, shocked. "Constrained my soul? When would someone have done that? Blackwater wasn't Gifted in that way."

Jack asks, "Have you felt any unusual shifts in your senses? Was there a time when your senses were more powerful before the necklace?"

I puzzle at this and sift through my memories. "Maybe they were stronger when I was very young, at the orphanage."

He runs his hands through his hair, enraged. "For Christ's sake! I should have thought of that. The housemother, Anna Marie. For some reason she must have locked down your soul. Maybe that's how she got the children to stop fearing you so much."

My mind grapples with that, and the pieces click together. "Yes! She took me to the woods for a special picnic. She said we were going to sing songs so the kids would like me better. That's exactly it!"

Dragomira seems skeptical. "Pull your chair over here. Let me examine this work."

I drag the chair across the rough wooden planks until I'm directly across from her. She leans forward and applies a gentle pressure against my head. I feel a kind of light shifting feeling, like she's sifting through some airy force-field on the surface of my skin that I never felt before. It makes me shiver.

Dragomira settles back in her chair. "This isn't the work of a housemother. This is the work of a powerful sorceress. A finer weaving I've never seen from a human. She's woven gossamer, gray magic around your soul to lock it in place."

"Gray magic! But she wasn't an evil sort of woman, I would swear it. She was the kindest housemother there."

"Gray magic is not evil," Dragomira scoffs. "That's ridiculous superstition. It simply utilizes lower life forms that have already died of natural causes. It's a mix of residual energy from life and the entropy that occurs with death. Gray magic is perfect for neutralizing life-force, which you have in abundance."

"Can you undo it?"

She purses her lips. "Yes, I can undo it. It will be delicate work. But think on this. You say she had no bad intentions, yet she wove it around you. What do you think will happen to your light and your senses when we completely release your soul?"

Jack wears a contemplative expression that matches my mood. Holding his gaze steadily, I reply, "I think my light will become brighter and my senses stronger. It'll be difficult, maybe even overwhelming at first. I'll know more about people than I even know now, and it'll make them uneasy. But I'm not a child who will accidently slip and tell people what I know. I won't cause them to fear me like I did when I was young. And I'll acclimatize over time to the stronger senses. That's my best guess."

Jack nods in agreement.

I turn to Dragomira. "Please do it."

"Then come kneel in front of me."

I do as she asks, and she lays her hands on the top of my head. I relax my mind to feel her work. This time there are no hand gestures, only a soft murmuring from the back of her throat. It sounds almost guttural but is so vibrant in tone that it reminds me of the scent of rich, dark soil just after a fresh rain.

Unexpectedly, I feel Varg's warm, fluffy fur as he leans his head on my lap. I smile and stroke him as Dragomira combs through the surface of my mind and just under the skin of my body. It feels almost ticklish, like a feather brushing against my thoughts. She delves in and out with the lightest touch, and I can almost imagine her pulling threads loose as her low, rhythmic chanting progresses.

With Varg warm against me and Dragomira's psychic massage, I grow sleepy after a time. With great will, I prop my eyes open to see

Jack. He sits, watching closely with a tight expression on his face. He catches my gaze and smiles.

Suddenly, his pupils constrict and his eyes widen in alarm. At the same moment I feel a rush of, well, everything. Everything becomes larger, louder, and stronger. I can feel Jack's worry with precision, and underneath I sense his affection, desire, and even reverence. I frown at the reverence part. That needs to stop.

My face must give me away because the next thing I know, Jack has controlled his emotions, and my attention shifts to Dragomira. She feels hopeful, good, and strong, but she seethes with an unquenchable, bitter rage underneath. I reel back from her, and noticing, she smiles a bitter smile.

"Don't worry, Blue. That anger is not for anyone of this world."

I'm tempted to open up my senses to examine her soul, but out of respect for her privacy, I refrain.

Instead, I turn to Varg. He issues a feeling of watchful concern, steadfast loyalty, and a wild, predatory magic that lies just beneath the surface.

I return to Jack. "What are you so worried about?"

He whispers, "Your soul light. It brightens this room like the sun glistening on a snow-covered landscape. It's almost hard to see you through it."

Dragomira scoffs. "You will survive, Jack. You'll get accustomed to it like she will. If not, get sunglasses."

She turns to me. "Apparently the housemother Anna Marie locked your soul light down with the gray magic to make it weaker. Whether she had good or bad intentions, we can only speculate. Then when Tobias Blackwater put the Belladonna necklace on you, he assumed it would restrain your gift—But because your gift isn't a normal gift, but rather an awakened soul, all it did was counteract the spell that Anna Marie put on you. That's why the Belladonna necklace served to make your senses stronger."

The whole thing makes sense now. That explains why Blackwater thought the necklace would make it impossible to use my gift. "So the Belladonna necklace actually works?"

"Yes, it counteracted the magic that was suppressing your soul light." She clears her throat. "One last thing, and then I'll ask you two to leave so I can rest."

Now I sense weariness billowing off her in gusts, as the euphoria from her accomplishment wanes.

She throws her hand up, frustrated. "Illustrissima. I gave you a knife and gave you its name. Yet when you needed it most, you didn't call it."

I'm perplexed. "Call the knife?"

"Yes!" she hisses. "You just need to call the knife, and it will come."

"Are you serious?"

Her lips press firmly together and her frustration pours out of her like she's dealing with the slow kid in class, and maybe she is. "Yes! When things have names they should be used. Call it. Now."

Feeling silly, I do as she requests. "Guardian," I call out. Nothing happens. I regard her curiously.

A smile plays over her lips. "Where is the knife at present?"

Jack answers, "It's at my house. I forgot to bring it back to her. It was found at the crypt among Blackwater's possessions."

As he speaks, I see a flash out of the corner of my eye. Then thunk! The knife stabs the wood floor just next to my right hand. My eyes rest in amazement on my beautiful weapon with its sapphire-encrusted hilt still vibrating to and fro from the force of its landing.

A mischievous smile flits across Dragomira's face. "Remember this, Illustrissima. Names have power."

CHAPTER 07

CIRCLE OF FIRE

BLUEBELL KILDARE

JULY 9, 2022, RED AGES

s Jack drives us home, I reflect on all I've learned over the past two days. I feel a fool for not calling my knife while struggling with Blackwater, but I had no idea it would come.

I lean against the window, and the cool glass presses against my forehead as I watch downtown Crimson Hollow pass us by. There are no protests to be seen, thank goodness. The Dilectus Deo are a religious hate group who believe that Norms are the true Beloved of God and are known for protesting anything to do with Gifted people or Vampires. In fact, it's become far too commonplace to see them waving their hate signs every day of the week.

The dark streets are alight with firefly lamp posts, and glow stones illuminate the scattered benches. Banners hang across intersections, announcing the upcoming Sun Flare Celebration. A balloon vendor situated outside Comet Park packs up his truck. They've been handing them out to children to build excitement for the festival, I suppose.

It's become so commercial now. When I was younger, artists, street performers, and the Gifted filled the area with mischievous tricks, dazzling spectacles, and exuberant laughter, but I don't recall this level of build-up. It seems they're trying to draw a large crowd to make as much money as possible.

It used to be a more relaxed affair, put on solely for the enjoyment of the residents and most of the talent was volunteered by the residents themselves. I remember street mimes, jugglers, acrobats, fire performers, and even stilt walkers. My favorite was an artist who used his gift to fashion colored smoke into the shape of different animals, making children squeal with delight. The dragon was the best; it even breathed fire. Now the whole event seems to be a money-making scheme with everything designed to make a profit for the city businesses. I must remember to check with the Internal Investigations Officer for city corruption.

My memories are interrupted by the sound of Jack's phone ringing. He answers it quickly, never hesitating in his driving.

I hear some mumbling on the other side, but I can't quite make it out. It seems my heightened senses don't extend to the original five everyone is born with. The voice sounds like Ernesto, but I can't be sure. I wish I could hear the conversation because Jack exudes so much tension and worry that my heart starts to race.

"I'll be right there." He clicks his phone shut, curt as always.

"Is there a problem?"

He frowns, "That was Ernesto. He's tracking four Dark Vampires in a dense residential area, and the other exterminators are otherwise occupied. His oak stake fell down a sewer grate, and he can't retrieve it without tearing apart the sidewalk. Do you have holy water on you?"

"Of course. Three vials."

His frown deepens. "From now on, carry no less than ten vials, but three will have to do for today. I'm going to assist him, and you're going to stay in the car."

"I can certainly help, and don't you think you should just commission a Hallowed Hazer for me if you think I need that much holy water?"

A Hallowed Hazer is gun that shoots a mist of holy water. I cringe at the thought of carrying one around, though I know I can't depend on the other Holy elements to kill Dark Vampires. The sun's destructive rays are on their own schedule, and Holy ground isn't always in close proximity—and I'm certainly not fast enough to kill them with an oak stake. Holy water is the only reliable way I have to ensure their death.

Jack tightens his jaw and commands through tight lips, "You are in no way a match for Dark Vampires. Your only defense is holy water, and it should be used as just that: defense. If you have any issues with following this order—and make no mistake, it is an order—then I won't bring you to the scene, and Ernesto will be fighting four Dark Vampires on his own without an oak stake. So what will it be?"

Livid, both at him and the truth of my limitations, I respond through clenched teeth. "I'll stay in the car."

His anxiety eases, which mollifies me slightly, and I do mean slightly.

I soften a little more as he explains himself further. "There's a reason that Ernesto is our exterminator at the Supernatural Investigation Bureau. If you recall, Norms and the Gifted were near extinction before the Great Pact was made, and Daylight Vampires agreed to exterminate Dark Vampires. Only Daylight Vampires can match a Dark Vampire's speed and strength. If I allow you to hunt them, it would be like signing your death warrant."

His concern is touching, but never one to let an opportunity go, I prompt, "And the Hallowed Hazer? It would be far more accurate than throwing a vial of holy water on them. If I were in a defensive situation, I mean."

Jack's jaw clenches. "I'll see about getting one for you, but only if you promise to use it just as a defense weapon." With that said, he takes a hard and fast turn. The next few blocks speed past, and then we pull over to the side of the road. We're in a residential area adjacent to the city center, crowded by apartment buildings.

Jack's phone rings again. "Yes," he answers.

Relief and a sense of perplexity coils off him as he listens intently. "They just gave up the hunt and took off?"

He listens for a second. "We're at the corner of Boss Hardy and Hog Mountain Road. Which direction did they go?"

Jack stays on the phone this time and pulls back onto the street. He turns his attention to me and explains, "They're moving away from us. We'll swing around west and try to intercept them from the north."

He takes a hard left, drives a few blocks, then makes a quick right. He moves as fast as is safe in such a populated area, quickly maneuvering through downtown.

Ernesto says something again, and Jack mutters, "Shit."

He speaks over the phone to me. "Now that we're heading east, they're heading east too, at a dead run."

This puzzles me. Dark Vampires are more than a bit crazy, what with being soulless and, well, dead. For them to operate in such an organized manner is unheard of.

He speaks into his phone as he takes a hard left again. "We'll head a few blocks, go east until we pass them, and then try to cut them off by heading south."

He makes a quick right, turning so hard that I have to put my hand down to keep my balance. Jack's jaw tenses and the steering wheel groans at the force of his grip. Oh! I realize I'm holding onto his thigh. I pull my arm back like I've been burned. But it's a good burn.

After a minute he says to the phone, "We've reached Soul View Drive. Have we passed you yet?"

A pause, then he spits, "By how much?"

He jerks the wheel in frustration. "Okay, we just turned right. For Christ's sake!"

He speaks to me again. "They just turned south."

"Jack," I say, "That's three times they've turned when we turned. Twice might be chance, but three times? They know where we are, and they're trying to get away from us. If you want to catch them, you have to trap them."

Jack scowls but must agree with me as he shares my theory with Ernesto, and a string of curses sounds through the phone.

Jack says, "I'll corral them toward Eagles Point and try to trap them at the cliff. Stick with them until the junction of Heavenly Heights and Demon's Pass. Then take Demon's Pass and situate yourself at the bottom of the cliff."

A feeling of savagery grows behind me. I check Varg in the back seat. He's sitting erect, his nostrils and ears working feverishly.

Jack whips us left again, and we move into the suburbs at an astounding speed. The odometer climbs past eighty when I finally turn away from it to save my sanity. I hold on to the safety strap so I don't end up in Jack's lap on the next turn. Soon the suburbs become small farms, and still we race on. While it's entirely possible for Vampires to go this fast, they can usually only do so for short periods of time. Ernesto will be starving when he's done.

Both Varg's and Jack's excitement increases. It seems Jack's anticipation of the hunt has eclipsed his tension, but he's keeping it under tight rein. His jaw is clenched, and his brows furrow in concentration. He keeps up an occasional monosyllabic conversation with Ernesto. I imagine it must be difficult for Ernesto to talk at this pace.

I suggest, "Slow down before we get to the cliff to give Ernesto a chance to recover a bit."

I settle back in my seat and try to relax until he says to Ernesto, "I've just passed the fork of Heavenly Heights and Demon's Pass. Why don't we disconnect. There's nowhere for them to go now but up." A pause, and then he snaps his phone shut.

Jack says, "Get your vials ready. I'm driving to the lookout now."

Good thinking, considering it's going to be Jack against four. That's worrying, but I know Ernesto has to stay at the bottom to finish them off. I unsnap the cover of the vial case I keep on my holster.

The road has turned to dirt, a sign that we've almost arrived at our destination. Suddenly I can see only what is in the path of his headlights since this road has no street lamps. Jack takes a jog in the road at top speed and the car fishtails slightly. When he gets it under control, it's a straight shot up to the top.

I make out four Vampires, barely discernible in the darkness, heading toward the cliff. Jack slows the car and shines the headlights on the figures. I suck my breath in, they're near the edge. Three of the Vampires stop in time, but the fourth one jumps right over.

I hope Ernesto finishes him at the bottom. Even a drop that far won't kill a Vampire, but it may crush its bones. Vampires can regenerate limbs and even survive decapitation if they manage to find their head and place it back on their neck. They're virtually immortal until they turn Dark. Even then it takes one of the Holy elements to destroy them.

Jack pulls the car to a stop, leaving it running, and hops out in a flash. I unroll the window so I can hear what's happening. A wave of ferocious anger comes from the back seat, followed shortly by a fierce howl. Varg's not at all happy with Dark Vampires being this close.

Jack takes off and I watch, breathless, as he rushes toward the edge. My fear that he's going to fly right over the cliff drives deep into my gut. I lean forward, my knuckles turning white as I grip the dash. At the last second, Jack jumps up and dropkicks one of the Dark Vampires off the cliff. An unearthly scream shatters the peace of the mountains as the creature tumbles three hundred feet to the ground.

With a roll and a jump, Jack is on his feet again in an instant. The two remaining vile creatures come at him, one from each side, but curiously, they keep glancing back at the car and snarling. Varg snarls right back.

While one of them is fixated on the car, Jack gives it a roundhouse kick off the cliff. The Night-Crawler moans as it flies through the air, but the sounds stop abruptly as soon as it's out of view.

The last Dark Vampire jumps on Jack's back and sinks its fangs into Jack's neck. Jack reaches behind his head and grabs the Night-Crawler's chin. He squeezes it in his hand, crushing the beast's jaw beneath his grasp and mangling its face into a bloody pulp. A shrill scream cuts the night. The creature releases its teeth, and a spout of blood shoots out of Jack's neck.

Jack grabs the monster's head, and with a quick jerk and a sharp crunch, he breaks its neck. Relentless, it clings to Jack like a tick on a hound. He rolls with the creature, getting dangerously close to the cliff's edge.

"Please don't go over. Please don't go over," I whisper.

They spin round and round to the very brink of the drop-off. My heart thunders in my breast. Just inches away, they come to a stop. Jack grabs its hands and pulverizes the fingers that grasp him.

The windshield fogs from my heavy breath. I wipe frantically at it to clear the view.

The head of the soulless beast lolls uselessly, but it manages to hang on to Jack with one arm and both legs. Jack clutches one of its legs and throws himself flat on the ground, slamming the beast's knee into a rock. Jack's soft grunt of exertion is eclipsed by the creature's shrill whine. It now hangs by just one hand like a limp marionette. Jack twists around and releases the final hand.

The Dark Vampire, scrabbling in the dirt, still reaches for Jack, but it can't get leverage with its broken knee and hand. Planting his foot against the Night-Crawler's side, Jack shoves it over the brink. He turns around and starts heading back to the car, a bloody mess.

Tension leaves my body, and I collapse back in my seat. Jack pauses on the way to the car to rip off his destroyed shirt and use it to put pressure on his neck wound. The blood has already slowed. I'm entranced by the broad expanse of Jack's chest, golden muscles rippling in rays of moonlight. It's such a gorgeous display, and my breath catches for a different reason this time.

Then something catches my attention from beyond my hunky

muscle-bound warrior, and Varg growls savagely yet again. Behind Jack, the silhouette of an arm and head appear over the edge of the cliff. Then a leg, and the Vampire that Jack had drop-kicked, stands. It starts limping toward Jack.

I jump out of the car. "Behind you!"

Jack spins around and promptly closes the distance between himself and the last Dark Vampire. With a great leap, he latches his legs around the vile creature's waist. The Night-Crawler grasps Jack's head as though to twist it. My heart stops in horror and I instinctively step forward.

Jack's neck strains with the effort of keeping the Dark Vampire from twisting his head off. At the same time, he tightens his leg hold on the Night-Crawler and pushes its head backwards with one hand. The monster bends back at the waist under the force of Jack's strength. It flails wildly, trying to keep hold of Jack's head as Jack pushes it out of reach. The Night-Crawler's hands eventually release their grasp. A whoosh of relief escapes my lips.

Jack grasps the creature's head firmly. He pushes down on it with his thighs and simultaneously pulls up and twists the Dark Vampire's head. A sickening crunch fills the air as skin and sinew shred. Jack leaps back from the Vampire with its head still in his hands. Blood gushes. He drops the head, and it lands with a soft thud and a small roll. The body teeters over on its side, squirming and reaching. The earth is drenched with scarlet.

Jack turns to me, and I stumble back, startled. I've never seen him like this before, fangs extended and face twisted in a murderous rage. Fear, no matter how irrational, churns in my gut. Jack must see it in my eyes because he flinches and turns his head away from me.

I smash the fear down. This is Jack, I remind myself. I won't let myself be afraid of him.

With that, I rush forward to hand him my vial of holy water, but the Dark Vampire's body has already started smoking. Then its flesh blisters. It blackens.

Jack steps back. He looks at me strangely and positions himself between me and the creature. "Come here, slowly."

I creep up to Jack, and with every step forward, the Vampire's loathsome body chars even more. Suddenly it catches fire and poofs into ash.

Jack and I stand, stunned. "You really can kill Vampires with your light."

I shake my head. "No, the other one didn't die in Shroud Valley until I threw holy water on it. Something else must have caused this."

"But the spell wasn't lifted then." He grabs my hand and pulls me to the car. "Let's go see if any are alive at the bottom."

Jack floors it down to the fork, then takes a hairpin left. A few minutes later we're at the foot of the cliff, and Jack parks the car with the headlights shining directly on Ernesto Ramos-Delgado. He sits on a boulder surrounded by three headless Vampire bodies and three small piles of ash that I can only assume are the heads.

Ernesto stands as soon as we arrive, ever the gentleman. He was turned in his fifties several hundred years ago, and he holds fast to traditional etiquette. He wears his typical hunting outfit, a loose black linen pant-suit that looks dashing with his sweeping mustache. The sprinkling of grey in his dark brown hair frames his face, accenting his light brown skin

The beheaded bodies thrash around weakly as the blood drains from their necks. I rush out of the car to hand Ernesto my vials of holy water. As I near him, these bodies also start to smoke and burn. Ernesto studies the Vampire carnage as it smolders, then catches fire. He looks at Jack, who is looking at me. I cover my mouth in dismay. The flames surge, blasting the night air with their heat. Then one after the other, the Dark Vampire bodies puff into piles of ash.

Ernesto dusts off his pants and grins, appearing quite amused by the exploding Vampires. Then with a formal bow, he says "Señor and Señorita. So good of you to come and help me clean up this mess." His eyes drop hungrily to my neck for a brief moment, and I give a little shudder. He's never done that before, but then again, I've never been near him after such an exertion.

Jack immediately places himself between Ernesto and I, remaining calm but deliberate about his intentions. His bare back in front of me ripples with tension.

Ernesto turns away, embarrassed, then says, "Perhaps you can fill me in on the way back."

Jack replies smoothly, "Of course, my friend. But first, let me share some of the blood from the cooler in my trunk."

Ernesto smiles gratefully and precedes Jack to the back of the car. Meanwhile, I stand awkwardly in the beam of the headlights, between the car and the Vampire dust, waiting until they've slaked their thirst.

A few minutes later we're headed back to town, and Jack is trying to explain the unexplainable. "It appears Blue had a spell cast on her when she was young that subdued the effect of her light. Dragomira unraveled the enchantment today, and we seem to have found another of her gifts. Her light shines so strongly that it repels Dark Vampires, and that's how they knew to run from us. Somehow her light acts like one of the Holy elements that will burn them."

Ernesto is silent for a moment, then says simply, "So the circle of light that surrounds her is also a circle of fire."

CHAPTER 08

SPECULATIVE CASE

BLUEBELL KILDARE

JULY 10, 2022, RED AGES

Rubalia Devonshire raises one rigid finger at me, asking me to wait a moment while she finishes chewing out the maintenance department for not fixing the vent issue in Xavier's office. As Special Assistant, Rubalia fills the role of research assistant, office manager, and magnificent reception commander. She rules the department with an iron fist, or a rigid finger, depending on the day. Right now, her gold-tipped, wavy brown hair bounces as her head moves in accord with her agitation.

Rubalia sits behind a reception counter in our lobby. It's a warm space, decorated with beige carpet and flooded with natural light from the same floor to ceiling windows that line our offices. I let my eyes rove the space and they snag over the brown leather furniture in the seating area. I notice Rubalia's brought in another bright piece of artwork, making the space even cheerier. As always, her taste is impeccable.

When she snaps the phone down, she lifts her glittering ruby cat-eyed specs off her deep brown eyes and flicks through her organizer. She finds my tab and hands me a stack of memos.

"Thank you, Rubalia."

I'm inspired by her decorating, and when I reach my office, I give it a critical eye. It's sparsely furnished with my comfortable office chair, two guest chairs, a sturdy oak desk, and two matching file cabinets. Besides that, there's only the brown leather bed Rubalia made for Varg that sits by the wall of windows and my lush fern in the corner. The space really could use some personal touches and color, but that will have to wait for another day.

I sit down and rifle through my messages. One slips out of my hand and falls in the crack between my desk and my filing cabinet.

With a shove, I push the file cabinet to the side and see the message lying on the carpet next to another slip of paper. I wonder what that is. I grab both memos and move the filing cabinet back in place.

The second piece of paper is a note in Rubalia's elegant handwriting where she's listed the name and number of the Internal Investigations Officer with the City of Crimson Hollow. I'd asked her for this contact during the Blackwater case, so the note must have slipped into that spot some time ago. It would never take Rubalia months to finish a piece of research like this. Her entire deportment screams perfectionist, which anyone can see from her sleek skirt suits and the deathly stilettos on her tiny feet, but it's most obvious in her running of the office.

I drum my fingers on my desk as I read the name: Rita Hardgrave. Well, Rita, let's have a chat.

Someone picks up after half a ring. "Hello, may I please speak with Rita Hardgrave?"

An assertive, professional voice answers, "This is she."

"Rita, this is Inspector Bluebell Kildare from the Supernatural Investigation Bureau, Homicide Unit. I understand you're in charge of Internal Investigations with the city. Is that correct?"

She says, "That's correct. How can I help you?"

"I'd like to stop by your office tomorrow. I don't have anything to report. I just have some questions."

"Sure, stop on by," she says. "I'm pretty open tomorrow."

"Thanks, Rita. I'll speak with you soon."

I flip through the rest of the messages and find one that I was hoping never to see. The young man I tried to rescue outside of the Glenwood mansion had made it through surgery, but had some bleeding in his brain from a concussion. When I visited him, he was in a coma. His name was Matthew Pruit, and he was only twenty-three years old. The message says he passed away early this morning.

I lean my head on my hands and fight the tears prickling my eyes. It's so senseless. Why are we fighting amongst ourselves? My mind drifts back to the prophecy. "When man wrongs man . . . "

A tap on my door interrupts my grieving. Jack stands in the doorway with furrowed eyebrows. "Are you okay?"

I shake the memo at him. "Matthew Pruit. It sucks."

Jack scans the memo briefly; then his eyes soften slightly at the corners. "It does suck. Do you need a minute?"

"No, come on in."

Jack remains where he is, and frowns. "Actually, we have a woman here reporting her husband's gone missing. He's a Gifted forest ranger. I'd like you to sit in on the interview."

The thrill of a new case rushes through me. Great, a chance to be useful! "Okay, let's do this."

Varg follows us into the interview room and lounges in the corner, taking up far too much of the small space, while I settle down in a chrome-wheeled chair and await our next mystery. The door pushes open and Jack is preceded by a petite brunette woman sporting a sleek angled bob. An infant clings to her hip, and a young girl clutches her skirt. Even so burdened, she stands with rigid determination.

After Jack introduces Brigid to me, he holds out a chair for her. Instead of taking it, Brigid pats it, "Becky, You sit here, right by Mama."

Becky is all of five years old, a shy girl with long, dark hair pinned in pink plastic barrettes. With a lot of effort and wiggling, she manages to climb in the chair and sits on her knees with her elbows on the table. When she's settled, she notices Varg in the corner. With a little squeak of surprise, she says, "That's a big doggy!"

I answer, "Yes, he's a protector. He protects people, so he has to be big."

Her adorable mouth makes an O-shape in wonder.

When Brigid is seated, she shows her resourcefulness by pulling a pad of paper and crayons out of her bag. Becky starts drawing immediately with an endearingly tilted head and tiny eyebrows scrunched in concentration.

"Brigid," Jack starts, "why don't you tell us what happened."

Brigid shakes her hair out of her face and bounces her baby boy on her knee gently as she starts her story. "My husband is missing. He was supposed to be home by six o'clock this morning and he never arrived. He worked third shift last night, and it isn't like him to be late. By the time he gets home, he's exhausted and falls asleep right away. Now it's past four o'clock in the afternoon, and I know something must have happened to him." Her sharp energy saturates the air; she's tired, worried, and more than a little scared, but her resolve wins.

I ask gently, "What does your husband do for a living?"

A gleam of pride shines from her eyes. "He's a forest ranger for the Western Blue Ridge District. He fights forest fires. I called his work and spoke to his boss, and he left work at five in the morning as usual."

"Who did you speak with?"

"Randy. He's the Station Supervisor."

I jot some quick notes down as I go through my questions. "What's your husband's name and date of birth?"

"Joe Powers. He was born January 20th, 1992"

I puzzle a moment, bouncing the eraser off of my notepad. "That name sounds familiar. Was your husband a prominent political person?"

Brigid scowls. "No, he always kept a low profile, until yesterday that is."

"What happened yesterday?"

I feel her irritation and fear spike. "He did an interview for the local jazz station. He's a fire control expert." She pinches her lips. "I told him not to do it, but he insisted it was an important public awareness piece."

That's where I heard the name. They must have announced his interview on the radio when Jack and I were listening to the news yesterday. "Why didn't you want him doing the interview?"

Brigid indicates Becky. "I think my daughter may be Gifted, and with so much craziness about the Gifted lately, I don't think it's smart to advertise gifts in the family."

Becky is clearly Gifted. I can feel the vibration of her magic humming far louder than I'd expect from a child her age. If it were a bit more developed, I might even be able to tell what the gift is. However, her mother seems to still be struggling with the fact that her daughter is Gifted, so I keep my curiosity to myself.

"What is your husband's gift?"

She hesitates a moment, her reticence obvious. "He controls fires. He's in charge of all the controlled burns in the region."

"Exactly how does he control the fires?"

An expression of pride and admiration gleams from Brigid's eyes. "He can start fires and regulate their consumption of energy to stop them. That's why the Western Division of the Blue Ridge Forest Service hasn't had any deaths in the last five years. Joe supervises all the controlled burnings and can stop any forest fire. He recently won an award at the station for saving a local family, so his department has been pressuring him to do some publicity."

Brigid's feelings of pride quickly transform into resentment.

"You're angry with him about it. Did you two fight?"

Brigid stiffens in her chair as she clarifies, "We argued. We disagreed. We did not *fight*."

Her baby takes this moment to pat her cheek and slip his fingers into her mouth, tugging at her lip. She takes his hand out of her mouth and gives his palm a quick kiss before turning back to me.

My heart softens at her touching display of maternal love. "Brigid, is there any chance he's mad, and just staying at a family member or friend's house?"

Brigid's lips tighten. "He would never do that. I told him how I felt about it and my reasons why. He's free to make his own decisions. I'm not a shrew."

I sympathize, but these questions are necessary. "I have to follow every angle. I mean no offense. Is there anything else important that has happened in the last week?"

She thinks for a moment and shakes her head.

"Was anyone angry with him? Does he have any enemies? Work competitors, perhaps?"

She shakes her head vigorously this time. "No, his work buddies are practically extended family. They're all worried about him too. This isn't like him at all. He isn't answering his chimerator or work phone either." The baby starts to fuss, wiggling anxiously, obviously bored with this interview.

I give her a reassuring smile. "I believe you. But I have to ask a few other questions that are going to be uncomfortable. They're just standard procedure, though."

"Okay," she consents.

Then little Becky asks in a timid voice, "Mama, can I have a red crayon?"

Brigid fishes a red one out of the bag for her, then entertains the little one by playing itsy-bitsy spider on his back as I go through my list of questions. I ask about substance abuse, mental or physical illness, financial stress, extramarital affairs, and recent insurance policies, the whole nine yards. She answers negatively to them all.

When I'm done, Jack clears his throat. "Brigid. As far as we can see there's no clear sign of foul play. Sometimes adults just decide to leave, and by law, it's their right. I'm not saying that's the case with your husband. However, our laws are designed to balance an individual's right to leave with the concern of the people who notice them missing.

"There are things we can do, like check credit card usage, cell phone records, and his phone's GPS. But we can't do any of those things until we can officially list him as missing. When there's no clear sign of foul play, the law requires we wait forty-eight hours before we officially declare him missing and start invading his privacy. You'll need to bring in your marriage certificate, financial records, and credit card numbers and sign some forms at that time."

Panic fills Brigid's eyes. "But he could be stranded on the side of the road somewhere, dying!"

Jack's face fills with empathy. "If you know his regular route, we can send a car to scout it out, just to make sure there wasn't an accident. That's something we can do now."

Some small measure of relief fills Brigid.

Jack straightens his papers. "Aside from that, I think you should head home and be there in case he comes back. If he doesn't, then come here in about thirty-six hours and we'll finish the paperwork."

Jack turns to me. "Have Ernesto run that route ASAP."

He turns to her again. "Ernesto is a Vampire, so he can track scent and see further than a regular agent. He's my best man for this."

Brigid sits stiffly, and Jack leaves me to gather the route information from her. When I'm done and she starts gathering her things together, Becky pushes her drawing across the table toward me, staring at me with worried eyes.

I pull it close and am astounded at the extraordinary detail for a five-year-old. It's a picture of a burning church with fire shooting from the windows.

Becky asks in a small voice, "Do you like it? I made it for you."

I smile at her. "Yes Becky. I love it. In fact, I'm going to hang it in my office."

Becky's face breaks into a smile, revealing one charming gap from a missing front tooth. Oh, I just want to squeeze her up. "You really are quite talented, and I hope you keep practicing."

Becky scoots down from her chair. "I will." Then her expression grows serious. "You're a nice lady. Please find my daddy. He needs help."

Oh how my heart breaks at her grave, little face. I glance at Brigid as a thick cloud of worry crowds the office.

She squeezes her daughter's hand. "Come along, Becky. They'll do everything they can, I'm sure."

CHAPTER 09

A DISEASED TREE

JACK TANNER

July 10, 2022, Red Ages

Determined to solve the mystery of the housemother who spelled Blue, I approach the Green Tree Orphanage, ready to use my influence here for the first time in many years. The orphanage is a sprawling three-story mansion, freshly painted in a soft green and accented with white trim. A large covered porch stretches the length of the front, and the backyard is fenced in and filled with shiny new playground equipment. Everything has been well maintained. I'm glad to see my donations are being put to good use, but that doesn't quite pacify me. I should have been informed about the spell.

I tap the brass knocker and let the sounds of small feet pattering through the home calm my anger. A sharp click of heels precedes the opening of the door, and a tall, matronly woman with steel gray hair tied tightly in a bun assesses me.

"Jack," she says brusquely as recognition shows in the pinched corners of her eyes.

"Good evening, Matilda. May we speak for a moment in private?"

She swings the door wide. "Of course. I'm always pleased to meet with a benefactor."

I close the door behind me and follow her into her tidy office. She gestures toward the chair. "Have a seat, please. What can I do for you?"

I sit uncomfortably on the edge of a rose velvet armchair meant for daintier frames. "When Blue was in your charge, you caught one of the mothers performing a spell on her in the forest."

Matilda's eyes widen in remembrance, and then she grows cautious. I scent fear.

"Matilda, why was this not in my reports?"

She pinches her thin lips together. "I was asked to provide you with reports on anything that might affect her welfare, and in this instance it didn't appear to be affected."

My rage grows, but I hold it in tight control. "Regardless, I need to contact this housemother. I assume you still have her employee file?"

Matilda straightens her back. "Of course." She stands stiffly and marches over to a wooden cabinet. Using a key that hangs around her neck, she opens the drawer and hands me the folder.

I open it and read the first page. It's Anna Marie's termination sheet. The reason for termination simply reads "Gifted." It doesn't say "cast unknown spell on Bluebell Kildare," which would actually be a decent reason for termination. But what bothers me the most is that the word Gifted is underlined three times, heavily. The page is actually indented and torn along one of those lines, as though it was written with deep hatred.

I examine the signature and see it's Matilda's. My intuition tells me I'm dealing with a breedist, and more specifically, a breedist who was in charge of Blue for fifteen years.

As casually as I can, I say, "While you're at it, Matilda, I'd like to see Blue's file as well. Her complete file."

Matilda's mouth pinches again, and her lined face creases tightly. "Well, that's confidential."

My control slips, and my fangs descend. My senses sharpen, and the smell of this hateful woman's blood calls to me like a vengeful dream. I breathe evenly for a few moments to curb my fury and allow her to think she's won as she sits back down. When she taps her fingers on the desk impatiently, I slowly say, "Matilda, I expect the file to be in my hands within two minutes, or I'll disassemble your file cabinet and take it myself."

She huffs and quickly stands to retrieve the file.

Once I have both files in my hand, I order her, "Go tend to the children or something. I have some reading to do. I won't touch any other files, and I'll leave a copy of these neatly on your desk when I'm done."

She's obviously frightened and begins to protest.

I release a fraction of my rage in a low-pitched command. "Now!"

Matilda squeaks as she runs from the room, slamming the door behind her.

After copying the material, I start reading and easily find what I wanted in Anna Marie's file. Her real name is Maev Dermot, but it's her emergency contact that shocks me.

I move quickly on to Blue's file.

After a minute, my fangs start throbbing again with the desire to sink into Matilda's flesh. The edge of the solid oak desk crumbles to sawdust beneath my fingers as I restrain myself from hunting her. Damn it! I should have known Blue wouldn't tell me the worst of it. After fifteen minutes of reading, I carefully place the copies on the desk, taking the originals. With a quick tug, I open the window and slip out. Right now, avoiding Matilda is the only way she'll live.

I drive down the road until my bloodlust cools, and call Mrs. Glenwood. When her butler puts her on the phone, I say, "Valerie, I just reviewed Blue's file at the Green Tree Orphanage. Our esteemed head housemother appears to have a hatred for the Gifted. Can you please meet with the board of directors and let them know that I'm willing to quadruple my annual donation this year? In exchange, I require Matilda's immediate termination and a complete psychological review of every staff member currently in position and forevermore in the future. I'll pay for the reviews by a doctor of my choosing. And I want a copy of the results."

"Are you serious? Quadruple? Do you know how that would help us expand and improve the orphanage?"

"Yes, of course I'm serious. But I want her out of the orphanage by midnight tonight. I won't have another Gifted child being punished the way Blue was. Call an emergency meeting and give me a call to confirm their approval."

"I've no doubt they'll approve. I've never cared for Matilda myself, but she's kept things in excellent order."

I cut in. "She's a breedist, and a rather ill one. Whenever Blue showed signs of her gift and Matilda was the only mother there, she was punished in sickening ways: locked in closets, tied to her bed, starved, humiliated in front of the other children. She outlined the punishments in detail, as if she was trying to exorcise a demon. She's out. If it weren't past the statute of limitations, I'd be arresting her."

Valerie gasps.

"And any other Gifted children who are still housed there need a psychological examination and their files reviewed as well. In fact, review all the files."

"I understand. I'll make sure it happens. I'll call an emergency meeting now."

I hang up the phone and proceed to the second, equally challenging task of the evening.

CHAPTER 10

DIFFICULT EXPLANATIONS

BLUEBELL KILDARE

JULY 10, 2022, RED AGES

We trot up the zinnia-lined walk and smile a greeting to Maud and Harry who sit on the covered front porch, beverages in hand. Thank goodness the zinnias are back. The marigolds were hideous.

Maud's hair is a beautiful frosted lilac today, pinned away from her face in sparkly gray barrettes that complement her light green eyes. Her purple and gray color scheme continues to the paisley maxi dress she wears. As I approach, she gathers her skirt and stands.

"Blue! How wonderful of you to stop by. I was hoping to see you soon. Let me introduce you to my neighbor Harry. Harry, this is my dear friend Blue."

All six foot three of Harry unfolds from the rocking chair as he stands to greet me. He smiles widely and pumps my hand. "Good to finally meet you. I've heard plenty about you."

I grin in return, taking in his multicolored striped shorts and pink polo shirt. He's as colorful as Maud is.

"The pleasure is mine."

"Hold on now," Maud says, "I'll grab you a beverage." She slips into the house before I have a chance to protest, so I take a seat while Varg lounges in the cool grass, keeping an eye on the road.

I lean toward Harry and say in a low tone, "She made you replace the marigolds with zinnias?"

Harry chuckles. "Yes, I'm afraid so."

I sigh, "Yeah, I don't think she can handle all that monotone for an extended period of time."

Harry seems to contemplate that seriously. "I hadn't thought of that, but I suppose you're right."

"I recommend to go bright and varied when it comes to colors."

He smiles in return. "A good tip. I'll keep it in mind."

I lean back and relax, satisfied in my Cupid machinations.

Maud comes out holding a cold, orange drink. "It's shoo-fly punch, and it has a bit of a kick, so be careful."

I take a taste, and it hits me hard. After sputtering and gasping, I manage to ask, "What's in here?"

She winks and starts listing the ingredients. "Bitters, mint, orange, lemon, sugar, plus a dash of ginger liquor, ginger beer, and bourbon."

"Ohh!"

"Small sips, dear," she advises wisely. "It's a beverage to be savored."

"I see."

I relax in the wicker rocker and as I'm about to take another sip, Jack's car pulls up to the house.

I stand, holding onto the banister, and call out as he approaches, "Is there a work issue?"

Jack shakes his head.

I sit back down, relieved but confused.

"Good evening Maud," he says.

Then he says apologetically. "Harry, I'm sorry to interrupt your evening, but I have something personal to discuss with Maud and Blue. Would you mind excusing us?"

How does he know Harry? Oh, right. Maud and Harry were helping search for me when I was abducted by Blackwater.

Maud seems troubled. Harry declares, "Well, Maud, then I'll just head home and stop in to say hello in the morning. If you need me, give me a ring."

She stands and kisses him on the cheek. "Thank you for being so understanding." She pats his arm. "I'll be fine." Then she regally walks into the house before us.

What in the world could Jack have to talk to Maud about? Is he going to tell her about the prophecy? I haven't yet, but I was going to bring it up tonight.

We settle in the living room, which seems a strangely formal place because I'm used to sitting in the kitchen.

Jack's eyes soften toward me, his obvious compassion only deepening my concern, and then he directs his attention to Maud. "What is your maiden name?"

A huge wave of sadness flows out of Maud as she answers softly, "It's Dermot."

"Is Maud your real name?"

"Of course!" With that statement I feel a small strain of surprise coming from her.

"And you're related to Maev?"

Her lips lift in a sad smile. "Yes, I am."

I ask, "Who's Maev?"

Maud turns and pats my hand. "She's my sister, deary. You may remember her from the Green Tree Orphanage by the name of Anna Marie."

I suck in my breath.

Jack asks, "Where's Maev right now?"

Maud shakes her head. "I haven't seen her for fifteen years. I haven't a clue."

She turns to me. "Maev came to me before she left and asked me to watch out for your welfare. So I started going to the orphanage and reading to the children. I couldn't think of any other way to stay close to you."

Confusion and pain clutches my heart. "So all this time, our relationship . . . Has it just been about you doing your sister's bidding?"

Tears glisten in Maud's eyes. "No, Blue! Of course not. I came to love you exactly as I would a daughter. Never doubt that."

The relief that rushes through me is tremendous. I can tell she's speaking the truth.

"But why didn't you ever tell me?"

Her tears overflow, and her hands clench into small white fists. "At first you were too young. You might have given me away to the other housemothers. When you became old enough, the original request my sister made didn't amount to a hill of beans compared to how much I care about you. It didn't seem important." A massive rush of fear and sadness surge from her as she speaks.

I grasp her hand. "I believe you, Maud. I wish you'd told me sooner, but I do believe you."

When I tell her that, her fear fades away. I pull some tissues from the side table so she can mop her eyes. Meanwhile, I glare at Jack for making her cry. Unfortunately, he isn't done yet.

"Maud, Maev put a spell on Blue, a powerful enchantment that kept her light in check. The other mothers caught her, and that's why she was cast out. Can you tell me why she did that?"

She turns toward me, genuine concern in her still-teary eyes, "No, I didn't know anything about that."

Jack appears a bit skeptical. "What was Maev's gift?"

"She was Gifted in the use of magic. She was a first-level sorceress."

A small gasp slips out from between my lips. Very few have the gift of general magic, the heightened ability to do any spell or charm. First level is as high as you can get.

Jack asks softly, "What was such a powerful sorceress doing watching over Blue?"

I must admit that's a good question.

Maud looks back at Jack with her chin quivering slightly. But her crisp voice carries sharply through the room. "Back at the beginning of the Red Ages, one of Blue's ancestors gave her baby to one of my ancestors for safekeeping."

"Mor," I breathe.

Maud's surprise is crystal clear on her face. "You know this story?"

"Yes, I was going to tell you about it today. There's a prophecy . . ."

Her eyes widen. "You know about that too?"

"Yes, Dragomira told me about it two days ago." I scrutinize her. "But why didn't you tell me?"

Maud shakes her head. "Try to understand; it's been two thousand years, and we didn't tell any of the children because they would have thought we were nuts."

With a twinkling laugh, she covers her mouth. "Maybe we are crazy, but we believe the Bright One will emerge from your line, and

Maev was sure that it was you because of your light."

Jack looks as taken aback as I feel.

She continues, "We're called the Watchers. Maev is, anyway; I'm not really important. In each generation, one of us is strongly Gifted, and that person takes on the task of watching over Shaina's scion. Maev was the strongest yet. It was unheard of for her to leave you, but she said she had other urgent business she had to attend to back in our homeland."

"Where is your homeland?" I ask.

Maud's eyes grow wistful. "We come from the same place your ancestors do, the Isle of Erin. I wish I could visit there someday."

"Are you Gifted too, like Maev?"

"I have a very small gift, but it seems rather more like a curse. It's my hair," she admits sheepishly. As she says this she absently fluffs her hair. "I really do go to the beauty parlor to get it styled, but they don't color it. Every morning when I wake up, my hair is simply a different color."

"How come I don't sense your magic?"

Maud looks at me fondly. "Remember when you were a teenager and you tried to dye your blue streak brown to hide your gift? I knew it wouldn't work, but I bought you the dye so you could see for yourself. When I was young, I tried the same thing. In the end I decided to pretend I dyed it on purpose and asked my sister to hide my gift. She did, sort of. She performed a spell so others wouldn't guess it was my mark. I think it was a sort of diversion spell so people wouldn't be curious about it."

Jack interjects, "So what are the Watchers supposed to do?"

Maud turns to him. "Why, help the lineage anyway they can. It's their job to protect the family line while we wait for the Bright One."

Then she turns to me and squeezes my hand. "Maev nearly flipped when your parents died, and we came so close to losing you. You're the last of the line, and you're the first one with the gift of light, so she was sure you were the one."

I lean forward eagerly. "You knew my parents?"

She rubs my hand. "No, dear. Maev was the Watcher, but even she didn't really know them. She just kept an eye on them, made sure they were okay, left food by their door when they were struggling, things like that. In the old days, the Watcher could befriend the family, but it's pretty hard in modern times. It would be weird if your good friend followed you from town to town as you moved to different places throughout your life. So she had to stay on the outskirts of your life, observing from afar. But when your parents died, she joined up with the orphanage right quick."

Maud turns to Jack. "Did you have any more questions?"

"Yes, what do you think Maev's been doing all this time when she was supposed to be watching Blue? You haven't heard from her at all?"

She shakes her head sadly. "You know the wilderness Christendom has been since the Deconstruction Era. We kept in touch for a few years via chimerator, but then I stopped hearing from her. The last I heard she was preparing for the coming of the Bright One. And that was it."

Jack stands up. "Thank you for being so forthright."

Maud stands shakily and absently smoothes her dress. "Well, if you two would excuse me, I need to call Harry to put him at ease and get my beauty rest."

With a tentative and frail hope in her eyes, she asks, "You'll visit me again soon, won't you chicky?"

I give her a hug, "Of course I will."

Then we take our cue to leave.

Jack and I step onto the veranda of her pretty house to see the sun's gone down. Fireflies flit merrily through the lawn, and the whip-poor-wills have begun their evening song. Jack walks me to my car and catches my arm before I slip inside. He steps in close, his body heat searing compared to the cool evening air.

His face, hidden to me in the dusky light except for the faint edges of his features, frowns deeply. He reaches out a hand and tucks a stray strand of my hair behind my ear. His voice cracks as he says, "I'm so sorry, Blue."

He must be talking about Maud, but somehow his voice seems far more serious than the situation warrants. "It's all right, Jack."

Jack leans into me, and I think he's going to kiss me. Just as I feel his breath on my lips, he curses and turns away.

CHAPTER 11

IMMIGRATION ISSUES

JACK TANNER

JULY 11, 2022, RED AGES

As the sun peeks over Thunderhead Mountain, throwing the first red glints of dawn between the massive crests, I observe a Daylight Vampire standing in a pool of light at the corner of Mangrove Road and Shadestone Way. I approach with apprehension, not for fear of the Vampire leaning casually against a streetlamp, but out of concern for his news.

"Oliver."

"Jack."

Oliver is almost as old as I am, a man of average height with a slim, wiry frame. Though he's not as strong as I, he's faster than any Vampire I've ever seen. He's lethal. The rumors say he was abandoned as a Norm child and grew up in the forest, hunting his food with a knife. He won't confirm or deny this.

Outside the official law enforcement of the SIB office, which is specifically focused on interbreed issues, Vampires are ruled by a council of nine: the Red Council. Each member is responsible for his or her region, which is then divided into sectors. Sector Lords are usually the oldest and strongest Vampires in their respective sector. They're responsible for doling out punishment when the laws are broken. Oliver is the Sector Lord covering Blue's neighborhood.

I ask, "How's your sector?"

Oliver gazes off at the sunrise, scenting the air before responding. "Not well, Jack. But not much worse than the other sectors of the city."

"What's happening?"

His serious eyes turn my way again. "We've had an unusual amount of immigration over the past twenty-four hours. In my sector alone we've had twenty-one new Daylight Vampires. In Franco's section there are eight. Ralph's section has five. I've faxed the details to your office."

I scowl and thrust my hands deep in my cloak pockets. Damn it. I knew something was happening when I scented three new Daylight Vampires on my way in this morning. That's why I called this impromptu meeting.

"Why have they come?"

Oliver mirrors my unhappy expression. "They don't give a specific reason. Each and every one of them said they just felt like it. They had an urge to be here, more or less."

"Do they appear to be a threat?"

He shrugs. "Not that I can tell."

A few cars have passed since we started this conversation, so I gesture for him to walk with me. "Do you suspect enchantment?"

"There's no evidence of it."

"Any Dark Vampires?"

"In my sector, none have turned, but Franco's had five turnings last night. None of them were new immigrants, though."

Franco's sector is where most of the turnings have been happening. It's good that the influx isn't accelerating our already multiplying Dark Vampire population—yet. But more Daylight Vampires mean more Dark Vampires down the road.

"Can you follow a few to see what they're up to?" I ask.

"Already on it."

We cross the street and pause at an intersection a few blocks down. "What have you found?"

Oliver rubs his jaw thoughtfully. "You're not going to like it."

"Tell me anyway."

A worried expression overtakes his face. "They seem to be attracted to her neighborhood."

"Shit," I mutter.

We pause under the streetlamp at the next corner, and Oliver says, "There's more. It isn't just them." He turns aside, a bit guiltily. "We're all attracted to her neighborhood." Then he gives me a piercing stare. "Haven't you felt it?"

"Fuck no, I haven't felt it. I'm always attracted to her neighborhood." I pause, then ask, "When did this start?"

"Yesterday morning."

"Shit! That's bad news. Can they be trusted? Can *you* be trusted? What's the pull like?"

He scowls and gently pounds on the streetlamp, making the steel post jitter and the light jump. "It feels like something good, like something that lightens the dark. It feels like hope, and I don't like it at all. I haven't felt hope in a long time, and I don't care to feel it now."

"There's reason to hope, Oliver. But we have to keep her alive. I ask again, can you and they be trusted?"

He grimaces. "I can be trusted. The pull doesn't make me want to do anything to her, to hurt her or to have her. I just yearn to be closer. It's like the nearer I get to her place, the more an itch is scratched. Most of them don't know what draws them to her neighborhood. But we have all sorts of personalities here, Jack. Some of them I wouldn't trust alone with any woman. So no, they can't all be trusted."

"Shit. With that much attention, something bad is bound to happen. Do you have Vampires you trust?"

He nods. "I do."

"Then use them to enforce a three-mile boundary, and don't let any Vampires pass except for me and Ernesto."

He scowls. "She goes on walks with that damn wolf."

"That damn wolf has saved her life twice already. Have someone shadow her if she passes the boundary, but keep the boundary in place." I stare intensely in his eyes. "You know the stakes Oliver. Whatever it takes, we must keep her alive."

He bows his head in acknowledgement, and I return to my car.

Just as I'm pulling up into the office, my chimerator tightens and loosens in a distinct pattern: Blue's emergency pattern. Christ! I pull up my GPS and see her location is just outside her apartment. I chime Oliver.

"Miss me already, do you?" he smirks.

I ignore his smart-ass remark. "Blue's experiencing an emergency. She's outside of her apartment. You'll get there faster than I can."

The mockery in his eyes fades to concern. He says, "I'm on it," and his image fades out of the chimerator.

    I chime Blue, but she doesn't answer.

    Shit! Shit! *Shit!*

CHAPTER 12

THE FIRST MORTAL WOUND

BLUEBELL KILDARE

JULY 11, 2022, RED AGES

fter I shower, I pour my tired body into some clothes and I strap on my holster. Gun, check. Knife, check. Muscle strength, sadly missing. Must go on.

Varg and I exit the apartment and head down the block toward my car. Who decided that training at the break of dawn was a bright idea? My wicked tormentors Yao and Wang, that's who.

In the middle of my mental cursing of the demonic duo, Varg steps in front of me and bares his teeth, gnashing and growling dangerously at the corner of the building we're in front of. The hair on the ridge of his back stands straight up. That is *soooo* not a good sign. I liberate Guardian from its sheath. My body fills with tension.

Just as I pick up the sense of two souls, two Daylight Vampires step out from either side of the building, effectively blocking my path. One is a large male with cropped blond hair, and the other is a female with a long, brown braid.

"Hey, baby," the male calls as they continue to get closer.

I lift up my chin to brave it out. "Do we know each other?" It's difficult to tell if I have criminals on my hands or simply a pair of creepy Vampires.

"Nothing would make me happier." The male smiles arrogantly.

I barely refrain from rolling my eyes. "I'm sorry; I'm on my way to work at the Supernatural Investigation Bureau. I don't have time." I hope that my place of employment has some impact. It doesn't.

I try to step around Varg to move past him, but he refuses to let me move forward. I glance down at him again, and he's at least a foot taller at the withers than he was a moment ago. Okay, so these Vampires are a real threat. I grip my knife more firmly.

The male snickers. "We just want to chat with you, sugar."

Does he think I have the intellect of a third-grader? I speak firmly. "I'm going to ask you to move out of the way and let us pass." Remembering Jack's warning that I must use the emergency alert button on my chimerator as soon as I'm in trouble, I move my thumb and push the alert button, hoping Jack is nearby.

The female Vampire moves closer, as though trying to pen me in. Varg, larger than even the moment before, backs me toward the building. He viciously snaps at the dark-haired Vampiress, but she jumps back just in time. Then they both move in on Varg at once.

At that moment I sense a soul above me. Looking up, I see a third Daylight Vampire on the roof leering down at me with a sadistic expression. This one carries Lilith's mark on the center of his soul.

Shoot! If he jumps me, I have to attack him in mid-leap when his Vampire speed won't help him. Vampire or not, they all fall at the same rate. Just then, I feel my chimerator tighten. That's got to be Jack, but I can't answer it now. Instead, I grip my knife and widen my stance, ready for action.

The male on the roof laughs, undoubtedly seeing the fear in my eyes. He jumps.

Varg's vicious growls fill the space behind me, followed shortly by the unmistakable sound of bone crunching. Screams slice through the peace of the morning, but I can't look.

I watch the Vampire falling toward me as though in slow motion. My heart stutters in fear, but I stand strong. When he's almost on me, I jerk my knife upward, and an unseen force seems to guide it directly toward the center of the Vampire's stomach. It slides into his gut like butter, slicing upwards through his belly.

His enraged bellow fills the street. As he lands, his knees collapse from beneath him. His pain pummels my mind, joining the pain of the Vampire who had screamed. I turn my attention to Varg to see how he's faring.

Just then, a fourth Vampire steps out from across the street. "Albert! Zanna! Step down now!" Turning to me, he shouts, "Please call off your wolf."

"Not if you begged."

The blond Vampire is sitting on his butt, crying in pain as he tries to reattach his arm, which is covered in bite marks. The female Vampire lies prone while Varg enjoys the feel of her neck between his teeth.

The new Vampire announces in an oddly conversational tone, "I'm Oliver, a friend of Jack's. I'll take care of these two idiots. Just call off the wolf."

I pull out my phone and dial Jack while still clutching the blood-soaked knife in my hand.

He answers with a strained voice. "What's happening?"

"Jack, it's Blue. Three Daylight Vampires just came at me, but Varg and I handled it. I gutted one with Guardian. Varg tore the arm off one, and he's holding the last one by the neck. And a fourth Vampire, Oliver, just came on the scene. He says he's your friend and wants me to have Varg let her go. Should I?"

Jack shouts, "No! Don't have Varg let go until I get there. Everyone stays in place. I'm almost to your block now. Stay on the phone with me."

While holding the receiver away from my mouth, I say to Oliver, "He says nobody moves. He'll be here in a minute."

The Vampire I gutted, who I expect to be healing, is not. Blood still pours out from his stomach while he clutches his tattered skin together in vain. He sits in a pool of blood, and his skin is deathly white. The guy with the disconnected arm, on the other hand, seems to be making some headway with reattaching it.

I glare at Oliver, who only smiles benignly and shrugs. He acts as relaxed as if he's just stepped into a tea party. There's nothing like a little gutting and dismemberment to spice up the day.

Tires squeal and Jack pulls the car to a hard stop a few feet away. He's standing in front of me faster than I can blink. He stares at the Vampire I disemboweled. "You did that?"

"Yep."

He points to the blond. "And that?"

"No, that was Varg."

We peer at Varg, who's breathing heavily through his nostrils; what with his mouth blocked by the Vampire's neck and all that exertion . . . Right now his withers reach to the middle of my torso.

Jack and I both look behind us again at the gutted male. He's slumped over, and his whole body is shaking.

Jack says, "He isn't healing. Oliver, get him out of here, and take the others with you."

I take that as my cue and command Varg to release the female. He drops her neck and turns his imploring eyes toward me.

"Sorry, Varg. Another day."

Oliver steps forward and hoists the gutted Vampire in his arms. My assailant is passed out now, his skin tinged with gray. The female who was under Varg's mouth, stands in one piece next to the blond, who is still holding his arm onto his shoulder, crying softly. Oliver nods pointedly down the street, and the party takes off at a run under Jack's watchful eye.

Jack raises questioning eyebrows, so I tell him all that transpired. When I'm done, he asks, "You used Guardian on the gutted one?"

"Yes, and it seemed to guide my hand."

Jack's eyes light up. He does love his weapons. "That's excellent," he says. "It's the only weapon I've ever seen that can cause a mortal wound to a Vampire. I'll check in with Oliver to see if he recovers. Meanwhile, don't cut anyone you don't intend to kill with that knife. It knows its job."

"You can say that again."

Then he asks gruffly, "Why didn't you answer your chimerator?"

His concerned eyes rove over me, checking to make sure I'm okay.

"The guy I gutted was attacking me at that moment."

Jack runs his fingers through his hair. "Well, I'll walk you to your car."

"You don't have to," I protest.

He glares at me. "I damn well do."

CHAPTER 13

INTERESTING QUESTIONS

BLUEBELL KILDARE

JULY 11, 2022, RED AGES

'm here to speak with Rita Hardgrave," I say to the City Hall clerk, who peers at me from beneath over-plucked eyebrows. "She's expecting me."

The woman narrows her eyes and bobs her round face. "Yes, Ma'am. Rita Hardgrave." She scans her directory. "Rita, Rita, Rita," she mumbles. Suddenly, her emotions take a sharp turn from light to troubled. "Yes, Ma'am," she says anxiously. "May I see your ID?"

Hmm, why would her mood change upon finding Rita's name? And how interesting that she only asked for my ID after finding Rita in her listing . . .

When I show her my badge, she makes a note in a little black book on the other side of the counter. I lean over to see what she's writing, but she snaps it shut. Then she stares at me again and points across the hall. "Take those stairs down to level B and follow the hall all the way to the end. Then take two rights. You'll see the signs."

I smile brightly and thank her, trying to hide my curiosity about her sudden change of emotions. I step to the side and start digging around in my backpack, pretending to search for something. Through my veil of hair, I watch the next man in line. The Clerk directs him to his destination without asking for an ID. Very interesting.

She snaps her eyes back to me, emanating suspicion now. "Did you need some help?"

"Oh, I was just trying to find my business cards. I like to have them ready."

Another squint and a little double-chin bob, and she's on to helping the next customer. A security guard eyes me from the corner, so I give up the pretense, straighten up, and take the stairs with Varg.

He scouts ahead of me, ever the protector—and it's a good thing because level B means basement, and it's dark down here. Painted cement blocks and dim lights do not create an appealing office ambience. I'm beginning to have a heightened respect for Rita Hardgrave, even before meeting her.

We turn a corner into another hallway, darker still, and take the final right. Outside a scratched-up, white metal door, a small sign reads, "Rita Hardgrave, Internal Investigations." A sticky note next to the doorframe says "Press bell."

I comply, and a moment later, a voice yells louder than necessary, "Come in!"

I push the door open slowly to reveal an office decorated in stunning contrast to the hallway. Far from dreary, it's an explosion of color. Bright pop posters litter the walls in shades of fuchsia, lime green, and orange. Plastic plants overflow the shelves. Cute little stuffed animals decorate the top of the computer monitor.

A young woman with short, brown hair cut in a feminine pixie style pulls out her earbuds and stands to greet me. In contrast to her space, she's dressed in a sleek, modern skirt suit, with black tights and wears a high quality watch. Everything about her personal appearance speaks of conservative professionalism.

My mouth must be agape at her flamboyant decor because Rita takes my hand in a firm grip and gives me a wry smile. "The office is a defense against the dreariness of the basement."

I grin back. "You really must have rolled a bad die."

She shrugs. "It's part of the job. Everyone's afraid of the Internal Investigations Officer."

"Well, the isolation does make for private conversations."

"I hope so." she says warily. "Please have a seat."

I fish through my bag for my privacy charm. When I find it, I place it in the middle of her desk. "Well, now our privacy is assured. By the way, you can buy these at Herbal Enchantments." I never miss a chance to plug my dear friend Alexis' shop.

Rita sits back and folds her hands calmly in her lap. "What can I help you with, Inspector Kildare?"

"You can start by calling me Blue." I smile, and turn to the matter at hand. "I was working a case a few months ago involving Tobias

Blackwater. I'm sure you heard of it."

She grimaces. "Yes, nasty business, that." Then she studies me sharply. "I'm glad you've recovered fully."

I nod. "I'm doing fine, thank you. But over the course of the investigation, I happened to speak with the Vice President of the Rotary Club. I understand they're in charge of organizing the Sun Flare Celebration each year. And this includes hiring vendors."

Rita tilts her head at this. "Hmm. Is that so?"

"Yes, public knowledge, as far as I know. Anyway, as a concerned citizen, I was wondering what sort of controls were in place to protect the public interest. I only ask this because I've grown up in this town, and it's obvious the celebration has become much more commercial over the years. In the past, most entertainment was volunteered. Not so now."

Rita purses her lips. "These are interesting questions, Inspector Kildare."

"Well, as I said, I didn't have anything specific to report. I just noticed a rather large temptation at the hands of our esteemed businessmen and wanted to make sure it was being watched. They organize the event and select the vendors. They could be selecting their own businesses or selecting the businesses of others for kick-backs. They clearly have conflicting interests."

I can see the calculations turning in Rita's brain. Her sparkly eyes might as well shout, "This woman enjoys a mystery."

"Yes," she says. "These are all very interesting questions, and I'd like to get some answers."

I smile at her. "It seems I've come to the right person." I hesitate for a moment. "Out of curiosity, when I asked to see you, the clerk required my ID. But she didn't ask for the ID of the guy behind me. Do they ID everyone or just your visitors?"

Rita's eyes go cold, and anger swells in the room. "Really? I'm not sure. That may be the most interesting question of all."

I stand to leave, as I wasn't here for answers anyway.

Rita's eyes warm again. "Thanks so much for stopping by, Blue."

"Thanks for seeing me on such short notice. By the way, with your earbuds in, how did you hear me ring your bell?"

She laughs, and all traces of anger are replaced with a brilliant smile. "Oh, it isn't a bell. It's a flashing light." She picks up a remote control and presses a button, indicating the wall behind me, where a red, fluorescent neon sign flashes, "Your next victim has arrived."

CHAPTER 14

ADRIFT

BLUEBELL KILDARE

JULY 11, 2022, RED AGES

ubalia glares at me over the reception counter with her fingers still flying across the keyboard. "Can I help you?"

"Do you have any messages for me?"

"None whatsoever."

I cock my head. "Are you sure a woman named Brigid didn't call?"

Rubalia frowns and stops typing. "What does the word 'none' mean to you? There's a dictionary on the bookshelf if you need it."

Snap! She's feisty today. "Well, she could have called for Jack."

Her fingers fly again. "Unless Brigid has his private line, she didn't call this office at all."

"Did we get anything from the missing person's BOLO?"

"Nope." Her fingers are still cruising.

I sigh and walk down the hall to Ernesto's office. As I enter, he relaxes back in his chair and greets me. "Good afternoon, Señorita Blue. What can I help you with today?"

"Are you sure you didn't see anything suspicious on the route between Ranger Station #9 and the Powers' home? Did you check over every hill and downslope? What if he rolled off the side of the mountain?"

Ernesto frowns. "You are very worried about this case, aren't you? Has the wife come by yet? Has it been forty-eight hours?"

I plop down in the chair across from him. "I'm just really concerned, but I don't know why. I just have a feeling."

"I assure you that if a car had rolled over the side of the road, I would have seen a broken blade of grass at least. Several, in fact. More likely than not, I would have seen mutilated shrubs and some saplings flattened. There was no sign of any car going off the side of the road for the entire route."

"Hmm."

Ernesto frowns in sympathy for my worries, then heartlessly changes the topic. "So, have you been practicing with your gun?"

I glare darts at Ernesto and defend myself. "I'm a fair shot. My issue was that Blackwater grabbed my right arm, so I had to reach around my back and try to grab my gun on my right hip with my left hand while being dragged. You can understand how that might be a bit tricky for a human, can't you?"

"And your knife?"

I slam my hand down on the desk. "No one told me it would come if I called it, until yesterday. That little tidbit would have been nice to know. How was I supposed to guess? How often do you call your knives?"

"My apologies, Bluebell, I just meant you should carry it with you always. Please understand mi amiga; we were very worried about you. We came *this close*"—he pinches his fingers together in demonstration—"to losing you."

I stand up in a huff. "Well, Yao and Wang are training me for four hours a day, so that should satisfy you for a while."

"I would prefer eight hours a day."

"Then I couldn't work!"

Ernesto smiles sadly at me. "But working doesn't seem very important compared to your other task, does it?"

I gape at him. "You know about the prophecy?"

"Jack held a council with me and the Section Lords of the city when you were released from the hospital. We were briefed."

I sputter in fury. "He didn't tell me until yesterday."

Ernesto rubs his hands across his brow. "I think he wanted to wait for Dragomira, so she could answer your questions."

I throw up my hands and leave his office, slamming the door behind me.

When I storm back into my office, I glare at Varg, who's sitting by the window with his snout in his paws, feigning sleep. I know because he gives me one long, slow blink before closing his lids again.

Oh my God! I *so* need a case to distract me. This prophecy business is getting out of hand. Quit work. Train for eight hours. What do they think I am?

It's not exactly that I hope Brigid's husband is missing, but something had better happen to someone fast or I might lose my mind. I tap my fingers on my desk in frustration.

I know what I can do. I can visit Joe's workplace and talk to his coworkers.

Just as I'm about to buzz Jack to let him know what I'm doing, he appears in my doorway obviously worried. He steps in, closing the door behind him, and sits down—uninvited, I might add. Looking all sexy, I also might add, with his long legs stretched out, fabric pulling tight on his thighs, and the bulge of his biceps showing through his suit.

But I'm too mad to pay that any mind.

He asks, "Are you okay?"

I take a deep breath and lean forward over my desk as menacingly as I possibly can. "I am most decidedly not okay. I can't believe Ernesto and the Section Lords knew about the prophecy before I did."

He winces at that, but I'm not done. "And if you all don't stop treating me like a paper doll, I'm going to scream. Better yet, if you don't get me a case, a real case, something to do, I'm going to pack about fifty vials of holy water and go Dark Vampire hunting on my own."

Jack leans back and blinks. I look over at Varg, and Varg blinks. I blink and behind my eyelids I can already see the SIB psychiatrist coming to lay an opioid charm on me.

I take a deep breath. "Jack, I know Brigid's forty-eight hours aren't up so it's premature, but I'm going to the ranger station to question Joe Powers' coworkers. Do you have any issue with that?"

His shoulders drop in relief. "No, but I'm coming with you."

The urge to scream threatens again. But I stand up anyway and beat Jack out the door.

CHAPTER 15

A CONSISTENT FACE

BLUEBELL KILDARE

JULY 11, 2022, RED AGES

ack pulls us up to Station #9 in his Grundel Scout, and I can barely resist kissing the ground when I emerge, thankful for every single wheel of that all-wheel drive vehicle.

Station #9 is almost at the top of Thunderhead Mountain. To say the roads are both curvy and steep is an understatement. Treacherous is the word I'd use. The situation is not helped by the fact that Jack seems to feel the solid yellow lines are mere guidelines instead of laws. Perhaps his senses tell him a car isn't coming around the curve, but as we hang in the middle of the road, I can't possibly know that death isn't hurtling my way.

With a backwards glare at Jack, I slam through the station entrance doors, ahead of Varg for once.

Station #9 is not just a ranger station; it's also a visiting center for Thunderhead Park, which features three picturesque lookouts that allow you to see the whole of beautiful Crimson Hollow Valley from every angle. When I enter, I'm greeted by a welcome desk and a gift shop. After flashing our badges and asking for the Station Supervisor, we're ushered through some employee doors and into the heart of the operation.

A lanky man with defiant sprouts of red hair poking in all directions exits an office separated from the main room by a large glass window. I wonder if his hair does that naturally, or if he's been pulling it in frustration.

He greets us with a kind face and flat smile. "Hi, I'm Randy," he says. "Why don't you come on back and we can talk in private."

We follow him into his office, and Randy seats us across from him with our backs to the window.

Jack starts out. "Randy, Joe Powers' wife reported him missing yesterday."

Randy rubs his forehead as if easing the tension of a headache, then fingers his hair. I guess that answers the hair question. His emotions tell a similar story. He exudes anxiety in abundance, so much so that he seems almost sick from it.

"Brigid called me yesterday asking if Joe had left on time because she was worried."

"What time did she call?" I ask.

"She called at about seven o'clock in the morning."

"Did he leave work on time?"

Randy slams his hand down. "Yes, damn it! He left on time. Nothing was unusual. She called me again last night to see if he'd shown up, but he hadn't. He didn't call in sick either."

"Has this ever happened before?"

Randy shakes his head. "No, Joe . . . he's a dependable guy. He's been working as a ranger for ten years, and he's been our lead fire controller for the past five. He's never even been five minutes late without calling in."

His gaze sweeps through his window, to the desks on the other side. "I know exactly which of my rangers might go on a bender on occasion, and Joe isn't one of them."

I turn to Randy. "I have a list of standard questions we have to ask in the case of a missing person. Let me know if any of these situations apply to Joe. Does he have a drinking problem that you're aware of?"

After getting negative responses to every question in my regular litany, I decide that Joe Powers seems like a pretty stand-up guy as his wife's portrayal matches Randy's. At least Joe presented a consistent face to the world.

Jack leans forward. "Randy, he hasn't been missing for forty-eight hours yet, so, we're early asking these questions. In most cases when adult men disappear, it's nothing more than a midlife crisis or a desire to be missing. Perhaps an affair . . . "

Randy interrupts. "Joe loves his wife and those kids. He's crazy about them. He didn't just decide to ditch them. Come with me; I'll show you."

He stands and takes us out to the main office area where he points at a bookcase behind a vacant desk. There are at least thirty pictures of Brigid, Becky, and the baby in a variety of frames. His computer screensaver is on, and it flashes even more shots of the family. One particular picture catches my eye. In the photo, Joe holds a younger Becky as she giggles. Becky's little fingers are gripping a chocolate ice cream cone, but most of the ice cream is smeared all over her face and hands, and a tiny chocolate hand print is stamped on Joe's cheek. Joe's laughing heartily, clearly unfazed by the chocolate attack.

I throw Jack a worried look, and he returns it. Then he turns to Randy. "Thanks for showing this to us. Still, we need to give him the full forty-eight hours. Brigid is supposed to fill out the rest of the missing person's paperwork if he hasn't shown up by then."

Randy sighs his disappointment saying, "I understand. If there's anything else I can help with, just let me know. My guys and I are all sick over this."

I reach out and clasp Randy's hand. "We will. In the meantime, stay hopeful." I give his hand a little squeeze, and we head out the door.

When we're back in the Scout, I turn to Jack. "He was genuinely worried, and he has a lot of respect for Joe. That's the only thing I got from him. Mostly just worry and lots of it."

Jack shakes his head. "It isn't sounding good, but I guess we'll find out tomorrow."

CHAPTER 16

ALPHA FEMALE

JACK TANNER

JULY 11, 2022, RED AGES

I stride through the front doors of St. Michael's Church and make a B-line to the nave where I smell Father O'Brennen. I slip in quietly and find him deep in thought, staring at the crucifix hanging front and center. With a soft clearing of my throat, I break through his reflection.

He smiles up at me. "Oh, hello Jack. How good to see you."

"Likewise, Father. Do you have time to speak with me privately?"

Father scoots over and pats the bench. "No one comes in at this hour. I think we'll be undisturbed."

I sit next to him and chuckle. "Clever way to get me in a pew again."

His smile broadens. "Sometimes a little practice helps. So, what's on your mind, son?"

"I noticed you have an empty apartment across the way from Blue's and I'd like to rent it. I'm willing to take it as is, and I'll take on the expense of modernizing it. I'll be happy to pay whatever you consider reasonable."

Father O'Brennen asks me sharply. "Can I ask what's driving this decision?"

"Blue was attacked again. She's fine, but she needs to be watched over."

"Who would be doing the watching?"

"I would. Only me."

He raises one eyebrow delicately. "And what sort of watching would you be doing? The kind of watching a dog does over a bone?"

My head snaps up and my fangs descend in anger, but a quick

look at Father O'Brennen assures me he's testing me out of concern for Blue. "I would be watching over her like a lowly pack member watches over the alpha female, as though she were the most valuable member of the pack, because she is."

His eyes soften. "Okay then, you may rent the place. The cost of rent for the next year is modernizing it. No rent will be due until the year is up. However, if Blue brings reasonable objections to me, I reserve the right to change my mind, and the renovations stay at no charge to the church."

"You drive a hard bargain, Father, but I think I can swing it." I stand up to leave, but his voice catches me before I hit the doorway.

"Jack. Does this mean we'll see you in church more often since you'll be just next door?"

I chuckle. Ever the opportunist, he is. I turn around with a smile. "If I can convince Blue to accompany me, I'll most certainly be here."

Father O'Brennen's face brightens with an amused grin. "Well played, Jack, but I'm not giving up yet."

CHAPTER 17

EMOTIONALLY MANIPULATED

BLUEBELL KILDARE

JULY 12, 2022, RED AGES

"Ugh." I slowly drag the covers off my eyes, blinking and cursing my new charmed alarm clock. It's a floating orb that hovers over my face, glowing as bright as daylight. I reach up to grab it and, I don't know, throw it against the wall, perhaps? But it lifts out of the way, avoiding my lethargic reach.

Oh, forget it. I'm awake now.

With aches pummeling me with every movement, I get out of bed and glare at the dark windows. What kind of insane people expect me to train when the sun isn't even up? As I think of all the terrible things I would do to Yao and Wang if they weren't such wonderful people, I gingerly and painfully pull my jeans over my stiff legs. This is the way it is every morning. I thought I'd be over the soreness already, but they keep pushing me to new limits.

I grab my knife, gun, phone, and chimerator, and Varg and I rush out the door . . . where I come to an immediate, complete, and absolute stop.

The apartment door across the hall is propped open. I've lived here for five years, and never has that blue door been open. Not only that, but workmen are pulling up the carpet and painting the walls.

I knock on the frame of the suspicious door and hear . . . . No, it can't be. It had better not be.

Oh, but it is. Jack's voice calls out, "Coming."

My reality tilts just a little more when the tall length of his sexy body fills the doorway. He's wearing worn blue jeans slung low on his hips and a button-down shirt that's unbuttoned All. The. Way. Down. A sprinkling of dark golden hair covers his chest, fades then picks up in a V-shape that goes . . . Well, never mind where it goes. There's enough to admire with his six-pack abs and well-defined chest. My gaze seems stuck as I enjoy what I am seeing.

He places his hand on the doorframe and leans in, so close to me that I can smell his skin. He says, "Good morning, Blue."

"Is it a good morning?"

"It is for me." Jack smiles, but it's not his office smile. Oh, no. That would be too easy. This is the devastating, disarming, makes-me-want-to-eat-him-for-breakfast smile with crinkling eyes and a glint of humor.

I manage to wrest my eyes from his provocative expanse of manly flesh and cock my head. "What exactly brings you to my neighborhood?"

"I've decided you've had too many attempted abductions when I'm not around, and I'm tired of the roof."

"Did you think, perhaps, that it might be reasonable to discuss this with me first?"

Jack's voice drops into a low, seductive tone filled with imploring undertones. "Blue, it won't be so bad," he cajoles. "I'm a quiet neighbor. I mind my own business. Plus, I'm renovating the space for Father O'Brennen. It might have been a decade before he could afford to do that without me. Think how nice it'll be for the church."

My cheeks flare as I realize my eyes are riveted on his washboard abs again and I'm tracing the line of hair from his abs to his waistband.

I snap my gaze back to his face, and he smiles knowingly.

"Jack, you did not just try to emotionally manipulate me with your sexy, unclothed body and your substantial donation to the church in the form of renovation expenses, did you?"

Jack's smile widens. "Why, I believe I did, Blue."

"Well, I . . . I . . . Oh, come on Varg. Let's go!"

Oh my God! That man drives me insane! Retreat seems to be the only option, so I stomp down the stairs. Yao and Wang had better give me something to punch today.

CHAPTER 18

NEW MATRICULATIONS

JACK TANNER

JULY 12, 2022, RED AGES

Satisfied with this morning's encounter with Blue, I kick back in my office chair. It actually went better than expected. She has no great love for religion, but she does have a heart for charity, so I'm relieved that angle played out.

I spread the maps out on my desk, section by section. Little yellow dots indicate Daylight Vampire sightings, and black dots mark Dark Vampire sightings. The Dark Vampire activity is centered in the southwest section of town, but the Daylight Vampire activity, the new matriculations, are centered in the northeast and alarmingly concentrated in Blue's neighborhood.

I slam my fist on the desk so hard that one of the legs breaks and my phone starts to slide down the slope. I deftly catch it and buzz Rubalia.

"Rubalia, I'm afraid I broke one of the legs off the desk again. Can you bring the brick in so I can prop it up?"

"I left it outside your door, Jack."

"Thank you."

"You're welcome. I'll put in a maintenance request."

I release the buzzer and consider the issue with Blue's neighborhood. Thankfully I'm in her building now. All these Daylight Vampires around her worries me as who knows what sorts of characters are mixed in with the bunch. The thin veil of civilization is more translucent on some people than others.

I get up to retrieve the brick, thinking that with the way things are going, maybe I should just keep a stack of bricks under the desk.

CHAPTER 19

AN EGO THING

BLUEBELL KILDARE

JULY 12, 2022, RED AGES

One more!" Yao commands.

My breath, rough and gasping, sounds loud in my ears despite the hum of the huge metal fans blowing from the top of the warehouse. My arms strain and my whole body shakes at the force of my muscle tremors. I must get my chin over the bar.

"Pull!"

I pull with all my might, stretching my neck, extending my chin, until finally it inches above the bar. Then I drop to the mat below in an exhausted heap. My arms and back throb from the effort.

Yao smiles with pleasure as I shake out my arms.

I peer curiously at him. "Why are you happy about this? I've been working for two months, and I can still only make it to fifteen pull-ups. That's pathetic."

He puts his finger under my chin and raises it until my eyes meet his. "How many pull-ups could you do when you started?"

"Um . . . none."

His easy smile spreads his beard wide across his face. "Success is about doing better than yesterday. A consecutive string of doing better than yesterday will bring you far. And as a woman, you have less upper body muscle mass and a higher body fat content. You'll have to train harder and longer in this area than a man would. Accept it. If you must feed your ego, consider how you can wrestle a man in the dark."

A shock rolls through me. My ego? Is this an ego thing with me? I've never considered myself to have much of an ego, but perhaps I do. I hate to fail, and in the arena of physical strength, I fail a lot.

Maybe he's right. I should just accept my skill level and stop judging myself so harshly. Instead, I need to focus on improving. I square my shoulders and decide to do just that.

Wang calls from across the warehouse, "Blue, I want you shooting for twenty minutes, and then we'll move to something new."

With a deep breath, I step over to the shooting range. One side of the warehouse is piled with sacks of sand from floor to ceiling, a few layers deep. Several cardboard men run on a pulley system from left to right in front of the sand barrier. About thirty paces away is the obstacle course, or as I like to think of it, the impossible journey.

Wang sets the cardboard dummies moving at a fast pace. My goal is to hit the moving targets from every segment of the obstacle course—a feat I've yet to accomplish.

I run up a twelve-foot slippery slide, stopping halfway up to push my feet apart so each foot is wedged against the short guard rail. From this position, I throw a few shots, but one foot slips out from under me. I grasp desperately at the edge of the slide with one arm while trying to holster my Glock with the other. When my gun is secure, I grab the rail with both arms and keep climbing. At the top, I scrabble into standing position.

Next is the horizontal rope challenge. A single thick rope spans about twenty feet of space between platforms, taunting me with its length. I have to cross it and kill my cardboard enemy at the same time. Thankfully I can use my legs on this one.

I grab the rope, then wrap one foot around it and let my body swing upside down until I'm horizontal with the floor. My feet help hold my weight, but arm over arm, I have to drag myself across the rope. My biceps protest vehemently, still tired from their earlier abuse. But determination swells within me. Images of all the victims I've seen over the years flash through my mind. If Lilith wins, she'll do far worse than anything I've seen yet. I can do this. I grit my teeth and go on.

Midway across the rope, I release one arm. Suspended upside down in the air, I pull my Glock out and fire at my targets. The recoil rocks me a bit, but I hold on tight. My hands burn. My arms ache. But still I go on. At the end of the rope, I drop to a platform and reload my clip.

On the opposite side of the platform, I descend a rope net, firing more shots as my cardboard nemeses roll by. Now for the staggered tires.

Cripes! Wang has changed the tire spacing, and I'd just gotten used to the old layout. I widen my stance and take the first few tires slowly until my legs memorize the new pattern. Then I lift my gun and shoot three more times at the enemy as I run through the rest. The sharp retort of the gun echoes off the walls of the warehouse, the reverberations filling my ears. Yes! I hit one for sure, but I don't have time to see if I hit any others.

Next up is a balance beam, only ten inches off the ground. Hey, this one is narrower than the one I've been using. The beam is only about five inches wide now. I grit my teeth and start walking across.

When I reach the center, I squat with one foot in front and my butt almost resting on the heel of my back foot. I pull out my Glock and aim with both arms, then lean forward and let her rip. I try to use my forward position against the force of the discharge to balance my body, but the impact is greater than I anticipate. The shock rips through my upper body, pushing me backwards. I grip my toes into the beam for support, but no luck. I throw up my arm, trying to stop the fall, but I swing too wildly and tilt off the beam. I catch myself on the mat with my forearm and tuck into a roll as Wang taught me, then land on my feet and holster my Glock.

From the side of the obstacle course, he says, "You killed four men this time. You're improving. Now practice that balance beam for the next twenty minutes."

This is always how it is. Wherever I fail, Wang makes me stop and repeat until the session is complete. By the time his stopwatch goes off, I've fallen countless times, but I've also made it across the beam three times without falling. I'm learning. There are a bunch of segments I still haven't reached, but eventually I'm sure I will.

When we're done, I stand at attention at the beginning of the course and give Wang a short bow.

He bows back and flashes me a lopsided smile. "Come here, Blue. I have some new tools for you."

"Tools?"

"Yes." With a secretive grin, Wang hands me a small parquetry safe box covered in interlocking blonde wood geometric shapes.

Ooh, it's beautiful. It resembles the safe boxes I admired in Dragomira's store. I hold it in my hands, examining all sides for an opening. Finding none, as expected, I ask, "What's the keyword?"

He hands me a slip of paper with two words written on it. "This box is special. Both the box and the tools inside use the same keywords."

With budding anticipation, I whisper, "Liberum."

The spell activates, and the geometric shapes come alive under my hand. They move gracefully, shifting around in a mesmerizing way. Entranced, I watch them glide into different positions until they finally come to a stop, and a clear outline of a lid appears. Carefully, I open the box.

Inside, lying on a lush, blue velvet interior is a set of many thin, sparkly silver bangles.

"They're lovely," I say, "but they don't look like tools. They seem to be jewelry."

"Take one out and focus on it while you think the keyword again," he prods. "Don't say it out loud this time. Just think it."

I do as he says and whisper in my mind, "Liberum." It springs open in my hand into a straight band of metal about six inches long. I jump back in surprise.

Wang's full-on grinning now, his dimples adorably highlighting his amusement. "Now place it on your arm and think of the second keyword."

I place it over my wrist.

"No, not there. Put it higher, over your bicep."

"But it's too small to fit there."

Wang's eyes sparkle as he urges, "Trust me."

I place it over my bicep and whisper, "Carcere." The metal quickly snakes out and expands over my muscle, locking into place. It seems like a small silver bangle that I've pushed up my bicep. "Wow!"

His smile just won't quit. "Now try to pull it off. It's just a thin piece of metal, after all."

I try to slip two fingers under the band to pull it off, but every time I dimple my flesh to get my fingers underneath, the metal conforms to the dimple, always staying flush against my arm.

"Holy cow! That's wicked."

He laughs. "Yes, it's wicked. These are handcuffs, Blue. There are twenty, and they're all magically charmed to conform to any shape, making them inescapable. No one can slip out unless they cut off their appendage."

I'm truly captivated by these narrow, glistening bands that serve such a useful purpose. "That's amazing. I can easily wear them without anyone guessing what they're for."

"Yes." Then he warns, "But don't forget to say the word only in your mind. You don't want your captive hearing it."

"Do I have to wear them on my bicep?"

"You can wear them wherever you want, but make sure they're easy to get to when you're in combat."

I eagerly place them all on my left forearm while Wang watches with approval. "Now, as with all tools, they require practice. For the rest of our session today I want you to practice cuffing both my hands and my feet. Yao's going to time you, and I'll struggle. Our goal is to get it down to one minute per cuff."

"Why, Wang," I tease, "I didn't know you liked such things."

Yao, who has been watching our conversation with interest, bursts out with his deep, bellowing laugh.

Wang winks at me. "You don't know me very well, then, do you?"

This is going to be so much fun.

CHAPTER 20

SHIFTING LEADERS

BLUEBELL KILDARE

JULY 12, 2022, RED AGES

 slip into a chair in the conference room where Jack asked us all to meet and scan the note that Rubalia gave me just moments ago.

Message from Brigid Powers
I've heard from Joe. Please cancel the report.

It's an odd message. Usually we would get an explanation and an apology of some sort.

Next to me, Xavier, Gifted locksmith and expert finder of all hidden things, rolls his chair back and forth restlessly. He's always moving.

Ernesto is the exact opposite. To my left, he lounges back gracefully in his chair, totally relaxed. I lean toward him. "Do you know what this meeting is about?"

He cocks his head toward me. "No, Señorita. But don't worry."

I clench my jaw in protest. This is highly unusual. We typically have our Monday meetings in here, but never has Jack called an impromptu meeting—and without an agenda.

Just then, Jack walks in followed closely by a man I've never seen before. He's probably in his mid-forties, his eyes gleam intelligently beneath his furrowed brow, as if he's in deep thought. For some reason, his suit stands out to me. It's a basic suit, the kind I'd expect a man could afford on an SIB salary. I compare him to Jack, whose quality of cloth and expertise of cut is so pronounced next to the stock suit. I wonder at how unobservant I've been to not notice that Jack dresses better than his salary should allow. Yao and Wang are right. My senses are closed to some things.

The stranger sits next to Jack at the end of the table, and Jack takes us all in with a sweep of his eyes.

"I imagine you're wondering why I called this meeting," he says. "I'd like to go over the current situation in Crimson Hollow and discuss how we'll handle it. Additionally, I have an important announcement to make."

Jack places his hands on the table, and with a serious expression, he continues. "We have two different phenomena taking place. First, as you all know, we've had an alarming increase in Daylight-to-Dark Vampire turnings over the past several weeks, and that means an increase in Norm and Gifted deaths."

He points a remote control at the overhead projector in the corner of the room and clicks a button. A map appears on the screen showing a circle of red dots in the northeast corner of Crimson Hollow.

"This was day one."

He starts flipping slides, and we see the mass of black dots move around throughout the northeast corner. "You'll notice the circle is getting larger. So whatever is causing this change, it's growing stronger."

I gulp silently. The circles are concentrated in my neighborhood.

Jack flips to the next slide. "This is the map as of two days ago,"—he clicks again—"and this is today. You can see a drastic change. The hotspot has moved to the southwest corner of Crimson Hollow, exactly opposite where it started."

A little of my tension drains. The idea of being surrounded by Dark Vampires is never welcome. But still, I vow to double my stock of holy water.

The next slide shows a mass of yellow dots in the northeast corner. "This is also from two days ago," Jack explains. "On the same day that the Dark Vampire activity moved out of the northeast quadrant, we had a massive influx of new Daylight Vampires to the city, and they centered in this quadrant. Whatever repelled the Dark Vampires is attracting the Daylight Vampires."

Cripes. I think I know where this is going, and it's so not good. A sense of anticipation fills the room. Clearly I'm not the only one starting to connect the dots.

"As you know, Blue had the Belladonna necklace put on by Blackwater. We removed it two days ago. What you don't know is that we also removed a spell that had been put on her many years ago. The spell blocked her aura. Now her aura is brighter than I've ever seen. For those of us who see these things, it's almost blinding at times."

All eyes turn to me. My face burns, and I just know my cheeks are splotchy red.

I speak up. "So you're saying that the Dark Vampires were surrounding me until two days ago when the spell was lifted. Now the Dark Vampires are repelled by my light, but the Daylight Vampires are attracted to me?"

"Exactly. That is the pattern I believe is playing out."

"Are you sure?"

"I'm not a hundred percent sure. But my gut instinct says yes. Plus, we've confirmed that Daylight Vampires are, for reasons unknown even to them, attracted to your neighborhood. They're just drawn there. We've already experienced how the Dark Vampires are repelled by you. So this is not all guesswork. We're not making any big leaps in logic here."

Ernesto leans forward. "But why, mi amigo? Why are the Vampires giving into bloodlust? Now they're turning away from Blue, so we know she isn't triggering their turning."

"I don't know yet. But my guess is that whoever's instigating this is a threat to Blue and wants the Dark Vampires near her. Because of her aura, they fortunately haven't been able to get close enough. You all know of the prophecy now, and I've asked you to keep it confidential. The more people who know, the more danger she's in."

Ernesto covers my hand with his and gives it a comforting squeeze.

Jack's eyes fly to Ernesto's hand on mine, but he presses his lips together and looks away.

"I believe dark forces are coming into play, and it's all centered on Crimson Hollow. Surely the pendant Blue found has a part to play as well, but we don't know exactly how. I told you there were two phenomena occurring, and there they are: the conversion of Daylight Vampires to Dark and the Daylight Vampires' attraction to Blue.

"But we have other issues at hand. As you know, with each Dark Vampire turning comes a death. Tension is building among the breeds, and violence is escalating. If this continues, we could have an increase in breedist homicides. We still have regular cases to manage, and right now our load is heavy.

"Additionally, the threat to Blue is significant. Even though it's Daylight Vampires and not Dark Vampires that surround her, any one of them could give into bloodlust and turn Dark. With their obsession with Blue for whatever reason, this elevates the danger to her."

Jack takes a quick pause and turns to the stranger, who I'd almost forgotten about. "Everyone, I'd like to introduce Mike Kramer. I've asked him to come on to help manage the office for the time being. I'll still be the director in title, but I'll be working closely with Blue and searching for the vector of the Dark Vampire escalation. Mike will be acting director and handle the office. He'll take care of reviewing reports, submitting requisitions, as well as managing correspondence with our regional management. Basically, he's taking over all administrative and liaison duties. He's worked as a region director for the past ten years, and I've known him even longer. I know he'll do good work for us, so I hope you'll join me in welcoming him."

The room settles into a heavy silence as varying degrees of shock shift over my co-workers' faces.

Rubalia cracks the ice by saying, "Welcome, Mike. Perhaps we can speak after this meeting, so I can learn what your needs are. I'm the office's special assistant."

Mike replies, "I'll be glad to, Rubalia. Your services are legendary in the region. I'm thrilled to have the opportunity to work with you."

Rubalia manages a stiff smile.

Ernesto takes his turn. "Welcome, Señor. It's been a long time since we've worked together. I'm glad to have you aboard." Mike smiles at this vote of confidence.

Jack clears his throat. "We also have three new exterminators coming on board who'll be taking on the Dark Vampire cases in the hotspot. Ernesto will work our regular Dark Vampire cases. Meanwhile, Xavier, Blue, and I will keep our normal caseload. Does anyone have any questions?"

An awkward silence fills the room. I sweep my senses around the room. Ernesto is pleased. He probably wants a guard on me twenty-four hours a day. Xavier is puzzled, but not overly concerned. Rubalia, on the other hand, is not happy, but she puts on a brave face.

When no one raises a question, Jack says, "Then this meeting is adjourned."

CHAPTER 21

FORTIFICATION

BLUEBELL KILDARE

July 12, 2022, Red Ages

Weary to the bone from my daily training on top of work, I trudge up to my best friend Alexis' shop seeking relief. Curiously, two men are placing a large glass pane in Herbal Enchantments' front window while Alexis Demetriou hovers nearby. The firefly lanterns hanging from the eaves of her shop shine off her dark brown curls and her perfect chocolate skin, giving her a satin glow. She's wearing a beige shift dress, which is the epitome of elegance and professionalism as always. But today her usual indomitable attitude is missing. Instead she feels sad and beaten down.

"What happened?"

Varg rubs his body against Alexis' leg in greeting, and she absently strokes his fur as she scowls. "A breedist threw a huge rock through my window. It shattered into a million pieces and even cut up one of my patrons."

I freeze. "Someone vandalized you while the place was full? How do you know it was a breedist? How's the customer?"

Alexis shoos us inside and points to a large black stone the size of a grapefruit that she's placed on the counter. The word "Witch" is scrawled on it in stark black letters.

"Holy smokes. Did you report it?"

Alexis nods, and her eyes fill with an unnatural shine. "I called the ambulance for Ms. Wimbly and offered to pay the costs. She had glass sticking out of her arm and her cheek. It was awful."

I give her a big squeeze.

"Are you installing glass or plastic?"

"Glass, but one of the installers is putting a ward on all the glass."

"Excellent. If you have any more trouble like this, please let me know."

She gives me a wry smile. "Well, no one was dead."

"But they would have been if I'd caught them."

Alexis laughs and reaches down to scratch Varg's head. "Come on, boy, I've got a treat for you." She smiles up at me. "I'm so glad you stopped by. I'm pretty sure the installers were about to leave with the way I was pestering them."

"You didn't let your control issues get the better of you, did you?" I joke.

"Always." She laughs as we walk through the door to her back kitchen.

It's a comfortable space, eclectic in its mix of commercial stainless steel and country ambiance. I grab a stool at the butcher block island while Alexis pulls an oxtail bone out of the freezer. "Leftovers," she says as she unwraps it and hands it to Varg. He doesn't seem to mind frozen one bit. An oxtail popsicle is just the thing, apparently.

She turns to me. "So, what has you so dragged out?"

"That's why I'm here, actually. Jack's super training program is beating me to the ground. They have me running seven miles now, half of it uphill, and I'm not used to that. Plus hours of training after that. I'm physically exhausted. Not a muscle in my body feels good, and the training gets worse every day."

Alexis checks me over closely. "Are you feeling sluggish, or just sore?"

"Sluggish and sore. I have no energy."

With a sharp tug she opens a cabinet and pulls out a large blue bottle. "Fill a wine glass with this every evening before bed. It'll rejuvenate you while you sleep."

She hands me a familiar salve in a glass mason jar. "Put this on your sore muscles before bed."

And finally she pulls out a small red bottle. "Take one teaspoon of this before your workout sessions. It'll give you strength and endurance."

"Wow. I came to the right place. Thank you." I lean over and give her a gentle hug. "So, did you see who threw the rock?"

Her face immediately sours again. "Yes, he walks by every day and sometimes stops to peer through the window, but he never comes in. Some young man, I'd guess twenty-two to twenty-fiveish. Sometimes his mother is with him, and she gives us the evil eye through the window too. She's clearly trained him up to be a nice, young, breedist gentleman."

"Ugh. I hate that."

"I hate it too. I'm installing a camera so the next time he walks by I'll get him on film."

"Great idea. I hope you catch him soon."

Alexis' hopeful face falls. "The police officer said this sort of thing was happening a lot lately and they were pretty backed up. Trudy's Séances was vandalized two days ago. Melinda's Magical Juice Bar has been getting threatening letters. And then there are all the Dark Vampire killings. What's all this about?"

"Alexis, I have a lot to tell you."

Alexis pulls out a wooden stool opposite me at the island. "Well, it just so happens that I have a lot of time."

I heave a large sigh, take a seat, and tell her the whole sordid tale. I start with the spell Maev put on me all those years ago, the Belladonna necklace, the knife, the prophecy, the Vampire attack, the influx of Dark and Daylight Vampires, the whole shebang.

Two plates of pasta, a donut, and some ice cream later, and Alexis is sitting there with rapt attention as I finish up. Her mouth forms a large O. "Holy shit."

"Yes, you've got that right. This is some messed up holy shit. You should really get this entire building warded. I have a feeling things are going to get a whole lot worse before they get better."

CHAPTER 22

ROOFTOP FLAMES

BLUEBELL KILDARE

JULY 12, 2022, RED AGES

With my folding lounge chair, a beach bag, and a beer bottle in hand, I try to negotiate my apartment door. The bottle begins to slip out of my grasp, but after some wild flailing, I manage to regain my grip and close the door. Argh. I'm glad Yao and Wang aren't here to see this.

Varg gives me the what's-taking-you-so-long! stare, impatient as always. We're just going to the roof for some early evening rays. It's not that exciting.

I manage to navigate the two doors and stairs to the roof without further issue. My terrace is shaded at this time of day, but the half wall surrounding the roof provides enough privacy and sunshine. This is really the perfect spot for evening sun.

After wrestling the lounge chair into its proper position and laying the towel on top, I'm ready to relax. I slip off my robe and stretch out.

The sky is a brilliant azure with a smattering of fluffy clouds floating about. The sun blinks at me from just above the wall. I estimate I have about an hour of good rays before the sun dips too low.

This is a great time to think, and I've got a lot to think about—the most important being that supposedly I'm destined to destroy Lilith.

Do I really believe that? I don't know. And what does a prophecy really mean? Does it mean *for sure* that stuff is going to happen? Even the prophecy said the ending was uncertain.

If the prophecy is really supposed to happen, what if it isn't supposed to happen to me? Maybe a different girl was destined to save the world, but she fell off a cliff. Yeah, something like that could happen. Then, naturally, they assume I'm the one. Maybe every Watcher is predisposed to believe the person they're watching is destined to be the one.

As an investigator, I have to say there are a lot of uncertainties and no real proof. All that said, though, if I happen to have the chance to destroy Lilith, I'll gladly do it.

With that settled in my mind, I pick up my book and start reading.

About fifteen pages in, I hear the roof door swing open. I crane my neck toward the door and see Jack staring at me.

I feel no small amount of pride that he's looking at me, but still, I'm not letting him get away with it. "Take a picture, Jack. Then move on."

His voice rasps, "What are you doing up here half-naked?"

I assess my body and grin at him. "Actually, I'm pretty sure I'm nearer to seven-eighths naked. And this is called sunbathing, which is safest done in the early morning and late evening hours. I'd appreciate it if you didn't stare."

With that, I reopen my book and pretend to read, but I'm far too aware of Jack's presence to do anything even close to that.

He approaches on silent feet, but I know he's there when his shadow falls over me. "Don't you think it would be wise to wear something a little more modest?"

"Jack, you're in my sun, and this is supposed to be an all-girls dormitory, if you recall. What are you doing up here anyway? Planning to barbeque? I thought Vampires liked their blood raw." I can't help but laugh at my own joke.

He squats down by my face, and his gaze sears a heated path down my neck. He whispers, "We like our blood wrapped up in pretty packages."

My throat goes dry. This is not professional Jack. Nor is it smiling, gorgeous Jack. This is sexy and dangerous Jack. There's nothing I'd like more at that moment than to have his lips on my neck, but I've been stung by his rejection too many times. I'm not putting myself out there anymore.

His eyes, a wild deep green, bore into mine as I try to wrench my gaze away from him.

But what kind of nerve does he have anyway, coming to my apartment building, standing in the hallway half-naked, teasing me this morning? Then coming up here this evening, in my private space, and being upset that I'm wearing a bikini when I didn't even expect him to be up here!

At that thought I get even more annoyed and flip over to my stomach to plan some revenge. "Jack, in my bag is some sunscreen. As long as you're up here, would you mind rubbing it on my back? I have about forty-five minutes of sun left, and I might get burned."

Jack's breath comes out in a hissing rush.

Good. Serves him right.

He grits out, "That wouldn't be wise."

I fling my hair over to the side so I can observe him. His lips are pressed and his shoulders strained. As casually as I can, I say, "It's the neighborly thing to do, Jack."

Then I rest my forehead on my arms and let him struggle with my request. I never hear him, so instead I feel for his shadow. It's still in the same spot, shading across the small of my back. The seconds tick by, then surely a few minutes go by, and finally victory.

I hear the bag rustling and the cap popping off the sunscreen, and then shockingly, torturously, I feel a slow tug at the bikini bow at my back. That's more than I expected. My whole body tenses for his touch, but I lie perfectly still, afraid to move an inch. This has got to be all him.

After another pause, his large, rough hand glides up my back in one long stroke, spreading the slippery lotion over my skin. My victorious smile fades, replaced by a rush of desire. His hand smoothes down my back again, going all the way to the waistline of my bikini bottoms.

Jack doesn't rush. Oh, no. Each stroke of his hand is deliciously slow, moving up my skin as though he owns my flesh. The rough calluses of his hands only add to the sensual experience. I keep my face buried in my arms, afraid to look. Afraid to speak. My lungs tighten and my breath quickens. Desperately, I try to slow it down because I know he knows what that means.

When his hands wrap around my sides and glide slowly to the underside of my breasts, I have to clench my teeth to keep from moaning. Finally, I feel him retie the strings of my bikini.

But when he's done, he's not done. His hand covers one calf, smoothing the lotion over it, then stroking softly at the flesh behind my knees. He gives my other calf the same loving treatment and then slides up to my thigh. He starts with my right thigh, rubbing the lotion in with small, narrow strokes so he has to go up and down many more times than necessary. By now, my breathing is out of control, and desire pools low in my belly. I know he can smell it. I keep my eyes hidden for a different reason now. I don't want to acknowledge my desire for him.

He moves to my left thigh, laving the lotion onto me, going so slowly up toward my bottom that I fear I may die of anticipation. He takes this leg slowest of all, like he's as loath to end this as I am. And when no one in their right mind could possibly imagine that my thigh needs any more lotion, he runs both hands up the insides of my thighs to the crotch of my bikini bottoms. My silken core clenches, and moisture soaks through the thin fabric. His fingers slip just inside the seam and trace a path outward to my hips.

Then his hands disappear, and I feel their loss acutely. My breathing is coming like a race horse now and I can't calm it. I prop myself up on my elbows and flip my hair over so I can see him.

Jack squats down and leans in close. So close that I can feel his breath hovering over my lips. Desire rages in his eyes, but they also blaze knowingly. The crinkles in the corners of his eyes speak of amusement and declare his own victory. He whispers, "Don't play with fire, Blue. You're likely to get scorched."

"Why did you come up here?" I demand.

Jack stands up, and a mask of coolness slips over his face. "I'm doing a perimeter check as I do periodically throughout the night."

He proceeds to walk around the half wall, gazing out over the neighborhood, and when he completes his circle, he throws one more steamy glance my way, and says, "Remember, don't get burned."

He disappears down the stairs.

I take a large swig of my now tepid beer. I'm burnt, all right. I'm a hot mess.

CHAPTER 23

OVER MY DEAD BODY

BLUEBELL KILDARE

JULY 13, 2022, RED AGES

he cold, sharp drizzle of rain pitter-patters against my umbrella as Varg and I take our morning walk. Dawn hasn't yet arrived, but the birds chirp in merry anticipation. Earthworms, evidence of the long overnight soak, litter the sidewalk and struggle to find their earthen homes before the sun rises. The porch lights and shimmering firefly lanterns cast a soft glow through which to observe the world.

Varg stops for a moment, eyeing an odd toad trilling his song from inside a garden birdbath. The house the birdbath belongs to is set back a bit on a small lot, and the entire front yard is lush with flowerbeds and vegetable patches. I contemplate the obvious lack of lawn and after a moment, I decide I approve. Why not use your yard to grow food?

As I stand there, my sixth sense alerts me to a presence approaching from behind. I turn quickly, only to see Yao peek from behind a tree. I call out, "I see you."

Yao steps out. "Very good, Blue. You're learning." He catches up, remarkably agile for his size, and Varg, tired of his toad inspection, moves on.

"So, how are you feeling this morning?" Yao asks.

"Oh, I'm okay. My friend Alexis . . ."

Just then, a force barrels into me from behind, knocking me off balance. My umbrella flies. I hold my hand out to break my fall, and my palm scrapes along the walkway, tearing my skin. My assailant lands on top of me, knocking me toward the yard. I find myself face down in the mud with the rich scent of earth filling my nostrils. Cripes!

Before I know it, an arm is tightening around my neck. Desperate to escape this man's hold, I tuck my arms under my breasts and plant my right leg on the ground. Then in one smooth pivot, I curl in and push off with my arm to get into a position on my side. At that point, I can see my attacker.

"Cripes, Wang!" I yell, shoving him off me.

Wang's cheeks dimple. "You must stay aware even when you have distractions."

I give him a sour grimace as I stand up, covered in mud. But I do understand his message. I'm more peeved at myself actually for falling for their trap. My clothes are a mess, and my palm is bleeding.

Yao acts like nothing happened. "So, you were saying about your friend Alexis?"

Still scowling, I reply, "My friend Alexis gave me some herbal remedies for sore muscles and fatigue."

Yao frowns. "Nothing charmed, I hope. You must work with your natural abilities."

I shake my head and try to straighten out one of the bent metal stretchers on my umbrella. "They're just herbal. I'm using them while I build my strength, and later I'll probably only use them if I have an injury or a particularly bad workout."

Yao grins in approval. "That should be fine, then. I know we're pushing you to ramp up quickly."

The darn umbrella won't straighten, and my palm is bleeding from my fall. I can't hold the umbrella, Varg's leash, and fix my hand all at the same time. With a huff, I give up and close the umbrella. A little rain won't kill me.

"I'm going to head home and get changed for training," I tell them.

Wang graciously takes my defunct umbrella. "We'll walk with you." He walks beside me, but Yao is so large he has to trail behind to fit on the sidewalk.

In silent companionship, we trudge through the cold drizzle. The sky is still black, and the road is quiet, but the occasional window glows with light. One early riser sits on her covered porch with a steaming beverage warming her hands. Oh, how I wish I were her right now.

By the time we arrive home, rain is dripping through my hair and my clothes are soaked, but the sight that meets my eyes makes me wish

I'd kept walking. Parked outside my door, blaring brilliant white under the corner lamppost, is a large truck emblazoned with the words "Dog Pound."

I hope against hope the truck isn't there for Varg, but as I turn to walk up my stoop, a portly, balding man steps out. Wang and Yao quickly flank me, and Varg stands in front of us.

The man steps forward. "Ma'am, is this your animal?"

I arch my brow at him. "Why do you ask?"

He ducks his head, evading my eyes, "I've got an order to pick him up. Says he's dangerous. A complaint's been filed."

Varg utters a low, slow growl. Not the best timing.

With a tug, I pull on the leash. "Varg, get behind me."

Varg grumbles again but acquiesces.

I say, "I'd like to see a copy of the order."

The man pulls a folded square of paper out of his pocket. I take it from him and read it swiftly, cursing under my breath. The complaint was filed by none other than Dean Schmidt.

I stare directly into his beady eyes. "I'm not inclined to hand him over. So what happens now?"

The man shrugs and steps forward. "I take him anyway."

Yao and Wang step in front of me, blocking the man.

The man scowls, clearly threatened by the size of my two warriors. "You can't stop me. If you try, I'll file charges."

Yao speaks softly and calmly. "This animal is a weapon of defense. This young lady's life is in danger. I won't touch you, but in turn you won't touch me, or I'll file assault charges."

The man steps back. "See here lady. You don't want to do this. If you don't hand me the animal, you'll have additional charges brought against you for obstructing the seizure."

I examine the order briefly. It seems I have a court date. With a hard stare at the dog catcher from between Yao and Wang's shoulders, I say, "I'll be happy to deal with that in court with my counselor present. But for now, I refuse to give him to you. Feel free to mark that in your report."

With that, Varg and I turn and walk up the stoop, letting Wang and Yao block the man from entering.

"We'll wait and escort you to training," Wang says as I head inside.

I nod briefly to indicate I heard him, but the only thing really going on in my mind is that they'll take Varg over my dead body.

CHAPTER 24

HOT CIRCUMSTANCES

JACK TANNER

July 13, 2022, Red Ages

When I hear Blue enter her office, I'm outside it in a snap. A light rap on the door and she calls me in. Her hair is damp from her post-workout shower, and the smell of her body oil entices me to step in a bit closer. The memory of last night on the roof washes over me, unbidden but not altogether unwanted. I shouldn't have done what I did, but her challenge was too provocative. I'm sure my last image of her before I left the roof is permanently emblazoned into my mind.

She was raised up on her elbows with the round globes of her breasts resting on the lounge chair. The curve of her firm ass was outlined against the backdrop of the half wall. And all that gorgeous skin, right there in the open air, begging to be tasted.

But it was her face that was most arresting. Her hair was thrown behind her, wrapped like a silk veil around her head, exposing her sinuous neck where her pulse throbbed rapidly, tempting me. Her mouth was slightly parted, lips pink and flush, and her blue eyes blazed with desire. While I might have seemed the victor, a full night of aching for her proved otherwise.

I wrestle the vision out of my mind, though I'm sure I'll visit it time and time again. Now, I attempt to adopt a professional demeanor. If we are ever to get through this, I must regain control of myself.

When I study Blue more closely, I immediately notice her grim expression. Usually she's bright and chipper first thing in the morning. I greet her. "Good morning, Blue. How was your training?"

Blue unfolds a piece of paper with shaking fingers and hands it to me. "My training was fine. But a dog catcher tried to take Varg this morning, and I refused."

Is it my imagination, or did her gaze linger on my lips for a passing moment?

I glance over at Varg, who's lying by the window with his snout on his front paws. "It's good you didn't let them take him."

I skim the paper and my fangs throb when I see Dean Schmidt's name as the complainant. I catch Blue's eyes and hold them. "Dean's with the Dilectus Deo now, so this must be an attempt to make you vulnerable. We'll get you a counselor, but you'll have to go to court."

"Of course. There's no way I'm handing him over. They'll have to lock me up first. But you didn't come to my office about this, so what's up?"

I nod and hand the order back to her. "Have Rubalia copy that for me. I have some contacts I'll put you in touch with."

What I really want to do is rip Dean Schmidt into pieces. But now there's a court date, so I have to be careful.

Back to the subject at hand. "Blue, Chief Mack called. There was a suspicious fire yesterday, and he wants our take on it. He's doing his inspection now. There were five deaths, and the fire doesn't seem natural."

Blue stands up. "Well, let's go."

CHAPTER 25

SYNCHRONOUS BURNING

BLUEBELL KILDARE

JULY 13, 2022, RED AGES

We pull up to the site of the fire and park behind a white car with the red Crimson Hollow Chief of Fire Department logo on the side. I'm thankful the sun has risen and dried up the rain because my umbrella is out of commission. Jack, Varg, and I walk past the car, through the caution tape, and up to the house, though it's hardly a house any longer.

Approaching Chief Gerald Mack is like wading through a thick fog of frustration, bewilderment, and sadness. When he sees us, he pulls off a pair of unusual bronze framed glassicals and wipes the sweat from his forehead. Then he steps through a window frame and onto the grass beside us.

"Good afternoon, Blue, Jack."

He stomps his feet, and wet, slushy ash falls in clumps off of his uniform's pant legs.

Jack says, "Good morning, Chief," and I smile into Chief Mack's troubled eyes.

Chief Mack gestures to two small piles of firewood sitting next to a butane canister. "I need you to see something," he says. He sprays the butane on one of the woodpiles and starts its center on fire. "Now we wait five minutes."

As we wait, we watch the fire burn, and Chief Mack points out how the flame spreads from the center out. When the time has passed, he lights the other pile of wood on fire and repeats the process.

He hands Jack his glassicals which seem to have three sets of lenses on a lever so they can be flipped down into position or out to the side. It appears each set of lenses can be used separately or at the same time. "Look through these," he commands.

When Jack complies, Mack says, "Do you see how the wood I first lit is the palest yellow in the center, but the second pile of wood is white?"

"Yes."

"Why don't you pass the glassicals to Blue so she can see?"

I pull them over my head and have to adjust the strap a little so they'll stay on. When I give it a look, I see exactly what Chief Mack described.

While yanking the glassicals off, I ask, "What does it mean?"

"Each set of lenses is charmed to show something different: the time the fire started, the time it ended, and the highest heat level. Right now I'm only using the lenses charmed for the time the fires started. In just a matter of minutes, the color changes from white to the palest yellow. The color values pass through white, yellow, gold, orange, red, maroon, and then finally black, depending on how long ago the fire was. After about forty-eight hours, everything shows up black."

"So in two days the wood that's yellow now will turn black, and the outer edge will be just behind it as a dark maroon?"

"Yes, Ma'am. It would be a very dark maroon, almost indistinguishable from black, but there would be a difference. With these lenses, the darkest part is always the part that started on fire first."

Jack's eyebrows are furrowed. I can see he's caught something I haven't. He asks, "Chief, may I look at the house with those glassicals?"

Chief Mack says, "Yes, I think you both should. I have some spare gear you'll need to wear. Some areas are still hot."

He pulls the attire out of his trunk, and in a few minute we're both suited up in heavy tan firefighter uniforms. Mine is so large that I have to cuff the pant legs to keep from tripping.

"Follow me and walk where I walk," the chief says.

This time he takes us through what used to be the front doorway. The acrid odor sticks to my nostrils, and I cough as the ashy air assails my lungs. We wade into what was probably the living room, and I slip the glassicals on.

"Oh my God," I whisper. I spin around to make sure I'm not missing anything, but it appears I'm not.

The frown on Jack's face deepens. I pull off the glassicals, hand them to him and turn to Chief Mack incredulously. "Every bit of this room is the same shade of maroon. That means everything caught fire at the same time."

Chief Mack agrees. "Every room of the house is the same. The entire house caught fire all at once." He pauses and drops his head. "Two adults and three children. No one had a chance."

Jack runs his fingers through his hair. "But there's more, isn't there, Chief?"

Chief Mack frowns again. "Yes, everything stopped burning at the same time too, within a matter of seconds."

I feel Chief Mack's anger well up and ask, "Chief, could anything in the natural world burn like that?"

He closes his eyes for a minute, then opens them to peer at me. "No, Ma'am."

"Where are the bodies now?"

"At the city morgue."

"Please call us as soon as you can if you have any more suspicious fires. I want to check the scene for magic while it's still fresh."

I move to go, but the chief halts me, and I feel his anger swell into a huge wave of rage. "One more thing you should know, Blue: this fire happened around midnight. The neighbors heard what sounded like an explosion, which is how a fire sounds when it flashes over. A flashover is when an entire room catches fire at the same time. It's usually caused by hot smoke from the origin of fire heating the material in the room to its flashover point. But as you can see, there was no origin of fire that started before the rest."

"By the time the neighbors noticed it, the fire was already out and all the occupants were dead. When we got here just a few minutes later, there was nothing for us to do except cool it down. Usually when a fire happens in the middle of the night, the occupants die of asphyxiation from the smoke. Not this time. The occupants caught fire. They literally burned to death."

The vision of the family on fire causes my mind to reel in horror and my stomach to revolt.

Fortunately Jack has the stomach to respond. "Thanks, Chief Mack," he says. "Keep us informed of any new information you get."

I offer the chief what I hope is a reassuring smile. "We'll definitely be in touch with you. I'll visit the morgue soon."

With that, Chief Mack leads us out of the cinder graveyard.

CHAPTER 26

BARBEQUE

BLUEBELL KILDARE

JULY 13, 2022, RED AGES

We stand in front of the clerk in the slick new steel and cement city morgue. Good old Sally takes her time examining my SIB ID. She knows who I am but delights in aggravating me.

"Dr. Perlman is very busy right now," she says.

"He's expecting us."

She flips through her calendar pages. "I'll just call him to see if it's okay."

At the end of my patience with her breedist attitude, I lean over her counter and hit the "Open Door" button myself, then sashay through the metal doors with Varg and a chuckling Jack trailing behind.

Sally screeches, "You can't do that!"

"I just did."

We've gained entrance and Sally's right behind in the doorway, sputtering.

The smell of charred flesh fills my nostrils. I hack and cough to no avail as the scent continues to assault me. Varg whines softly in complaint and lies down in the far corner of the cavernous space. Jack holds his hand over his nose and screws his face up in disgust. I can't imagine what this must smell like with Vampire senses.

Dr. Nathan Perlman, large and jovial, smiles from behind his mask. "Hello, Blue. Jack, it's been a while." He hands us each a mask, but poor Varg has to suffer.

Sally pinches her nose and complains, "She busted in."

Nathan frowns at her. "Sally, that's enough. You knew I was expecting her. We'll talk about this later."

Sally slams the door, and the sound reverberates around the room, bouncing off the cement walls.

When I put the mask on, my nose is immediately relieved of the smell. "Are these charmed?"

"Yes, Ma'am. I dip them in a solution from Herbal Enchantments."

"Oh, very nice," I say. "That's my friend's shop."

Nathan's eyes crinkle in a smile again. "They make for a much more pleasant work experience. They aren't cheap but they're worth every bit."

"Alexis is a smart businesswoman."

Nathan agrees as he pulls the sheet off the first body.

"Lady of Light!" I exclaim.

The skin of the body is entirely blackened on the outside with deep blisters and bubbles marring the surface. The top layer of skin is cracked and splitting in a coarse, shattered pattern, showing red flesh beneath. I've never seen anything so awful.

I turn my face away and walk to the opposite side of the room. Breathe. In. Out. In. Out. In. Out.

When the shock wears off, I turn around again and notice Jack's holding himself rigid, his entire face like granite.

Nathan stands there with a patient expression. "Why don't we make this easier on you? I'll give you a quick summary while you examine the body. Then you can read the detailed preliminary report."

"Sounds great," Jack says quickly, and I agree, willing to take my blessings where I can find them.

Nathan goes on with a voice slightly muffled by his mask. "All five family members are burned in a similar manner. The fire didn't burn for long, but it burned hot and did the job. Their bodies are evenly charred from the skin inward, each to the same depth. The fire hit all of them at the same time and stopped at the same time."

I take a step closer to the body. "So this was murder?"

"I have no plausible natural explanation for this."

"Okay, you can put the sheet back on. I need all five of them out here so I can feel for magic or Gifts."

Nathan rolls out the other four carts. The little shapes under three of the sheets break my heart. My gut clenches at the smallest; it must be just a toddler. I imagine a fat, toothless, smiling baby, waving a toy in his arm.

"Can you uncover the baby?" I ask.

Nathan's eyebrows furrow in concern. "Are you sure?"

Jack looks at me skeptically, but I remain firm. "Absolutely."

Nathan uncovers the body. It's a black, charred mess with bloody flesh peeking through his cracked skin. I race to the garbage can, ripping my mask off, and the contents of my stomach hurl their way into the plastic liner. I wave my arm back at Nathan. "Thanks. Cover him back up."

"Her," Nathan corrects.

I hurl one more time, imagining the chubby face of a little girl now, a beautiful child with curly hair and bright eyes.

Once my stomach settles, I put my mask back on and tie up the trash bag for Nathan. "Sorry. I had to see the worst of it."

Nathan covers the body up. We've already gone over why I insist on seeing even the most mutilated bodies. The images from the morgue seared into my mind keep me going on a case even if I feel like giving up.

After rinsing my mouth with cool water from Nathan's sink, I walk back toward the bodies. Five carts with five sheets. Five people who went through untold horror.

My sixth sense is so heightened now; my attention is immediately drawn to the tallest of the children. I can feel a tingling of residual magic swathing her body. "Who's this?"

Nathan reads the paperwork attached to the cart. "That's Hannah Rose. She was eight years old."

Thank goodness I can feel Gifts because no one would recognize a mark on any of their bodies. "Hannah was Gifted," I tell Jack and Nathan. "No one else in the family was. But one thing is clear. Whoever did this is a monster."

CHAPTER 27

GOOD NEIGHBORS

BLUEBELL KILDARE

July 13, 2022, Red Ages

When Jack and I are back in the privacy of his car outside the morgue, I turn to him. "Jack, this is too coincidental. Joe was a fire controller who went missing, and now we have some unexplainable deaths cause by fire . . . "

Jack throws his arm over the back of my seat and turns to me. "We have no clear indication that this crime was committed with the intent to do harm to the Gifted specifically. But it is clear the arson wasn't conducted by ordinary means. We should still pursue the case, in conjunction with the normal arson investigation."

He turns back and throws the car into gear, but he doesn't point it back to the office.

"Where are we going?"

He smiles. "To see Brigid, of course. This is a welfare visit to check on Joe."

"Good thinking."

About twenty minutes later, we're standing in front of Joe and Brigid's home. It's a small, white, wooden plank farmhouse on about an acre of land, bordered by small farms in all directions. I knock on the freshly painted barn red door and check out the covered porch. A bin of toys sits next to a child-sized table. Next to the door, a wooden rocking chair, softened with plaid cushions, creaks as it sways back and forth gently in the wind. A storm's rolling in. Strong gusts of wind blow the leaves of the houseplants hanging from the porch eaves, and their vines rustle in a low murmur.

After a moment of silence, I knock louder, hoping against hope that someone comes to the door.

Jack leans toward me. "I don't hear anyone inside." He flares his nostrils, checking for a scent shaking his head. "Let's do a perimeter check."

We slowly walk around the house, skirting a pink bike with training wheels that's been knocked over on its side. Pastel streamers on the handlebars ruffle in the breeze. In the backyard, I notice a doghouse with an empty tie out. There's no food or water to be seen.

Jack's inspection confirms what I'm thinking. "The entire area smells like dog, but the scent is lingering from at least twenty-four hours ago. The dog is gone. I'm not smelling any fresh human scent either."

"So Joe came home and the entire family left and hasn't been back? That's strange."

Jack shakes his head. "I haven't smelled anything fresher than a few days old for the male. Let me check the bedroom."

He pulls his arms back and with a mighty leap, he jumps onto the back porch roof. I can't help but sigh a little at the way his trousers pull against his solid thigh muscles when he jumps. It's been more difficult than usual to keep him off my mind today, but the case has been helpful.

Jack walks the perimeter of the first floor roof until he reaches a set of windows facing the road. He tests their strength. "These are old painted windows. The only way I'd open them is to break them, but they do leak a lot, and I'm still not getting any fresh male scent. Brigid's scent is more recent, but even that isn't from today."

Jack jumps down in front of me. "What do you want to do?"

"Well, we obviously can't break in, but something's strange. I'll give Brigid a call."

As soon as I hear the first ring, Jack says, "Hang up. It's the house phone. I hear it inside."

I snap my phone closed. "Should we leave a note?"

"I'd rather not. If something fishy is going on, I'd rather keep the element of surprise."

"Well, let me see what I can find out."

I step up to the porch again and expand my sixth sense into the house. I'm immediately slammed with the feelings of grief and terror. I pull my sense back and grab onto Jack's arm for support, whispering, "Something very bad happened in this house."

Jack places his warm hand over mine, and I'm grateful for the comfort. I push my senses deeper into the house and focus. The feelings all mix together at the door, so I push farther inside.

"I feel terror and panic upstairs, but no pain. The trail of emotions leads all the way down the stairs where it turns to desperation and fury. The trail is followed by another signature, another person. Their feelings were more twisted, a mix of hate, resolve, and regret. Down at the bottom of the stairs I feel rage, an incredible fury, fear, grief, and loss, all from the same person." This feeling is so pronounced it beats at my mind and rips at my heart.

I must stumble back because I feel Jack's chest behind me and his arms wrapping around me. But all I can focus on is the desperation and loss. It screams at me to do something.

I wrestle my sixth sense from that spot and continue through the house. "There's another feeling from the same person. It's a more controlled desperation and panic that's spread throughout the house. That's the most recent feeling I can sense." With relief I say, "But there's no pain anywhere. No sense of true violence."

Jack stiffens, then murmurs, "Someone's coming from across the lane."

I rein in my sixth sense and quickly pull away from Jack. "That's fine. That's all I can sense anyway. There was no magic used."

We walk down the porch steps and watch a short, stout older woman wearing a faded paisley dress approach. Her mousy brown hair catches in the breeze and blows over her sun-aged face. She walks with a bit of a limp but appears strong and hardy. Wisps of anxiety escape from her air of determination. With her arms crossed defiantly, she stops a good ways away. "What are y'all doing sniffing and poking around the Powers' place?"

I step forward, badge in hand. "We're investigators for the SIB, and we're following up on a report Brigid gave us a few days ago. Do you know where she is?"

The woman sniffs suspiciously at us, apparently not too comforted by my badge. "They've gone. Had to head out of town, and Brigid asked me to keep an eye on the place. How do I know she didn't want me to keep an eye out for your snooping?"

"We just want to talk with her," Jack responds.

I add, "We're very worried. Did she say where she was going or when she'd be back?"

The woman leans back on her heels and assesses me, clearly not sure if she should say anything. "Can't say that she did. She asked me to check the mail and take her dog for a spell. Said she had a family emergency, and that was it." She stares into my eyes with her chin jutting out. "Brigid's always been a good neighbor, and around these parts that's all the explanation I need from a good neighbor."

I nod at her wisdom, and with disappointment nipping close at our heels we turn to leave. I can't help but wonder what happened in that house and if we have more missing people.

CHAPTER 28

A WARNING TO OTHERS

JACK TANNER

JULY 13, 2022, RED AGES

The sharp clip of Dragomira's heels lends a rhythmic staccato to the soft chirping song of the crickets filling the night air. She rounds the corner with her scarf flying behind her in the wind and a scowl on her face.

"Jack," she demands, "why am I here to save the life of a Vampire who attacked the Illustrissima?"

"Good evening, Dragomira." I reply smoothly.

Not to be deterred, she scowls more deeply. "Answer me, Jack."

I dip my head and oblige her, knowing she won't like the answer. "How do you think Blue would like being the first person ever to kill a Vampire who hadn't yet turned Dark?"

Dragomira's eyes flare bright yellow, and her lips tighten. "Very well. Take me to him."

I open the door to Oliver's building and walk her through the scuffed hallways and up the worn, red staircase. The whole building appears rundown from the street, but it's mostly a façade to deter visitors, part real age and neglect and part illusion. At the top of the stairs, we open the door to a hallway of gleaming black stained wood floor, cream walls, and intricate ceiling moldings. Oliver's personal apartments are refined, the crystal inside the rock.

At the end of the hall I push into a bedroom suite where Oliver reclines in a studded leather chair next to the fireplace, facing the patient. He stands up, wearing an unusually somber expression.

"Thank you for coming, Dragomira." He gestures toward the patient. "Can you do anything with him?"

The patient, Ranulf, lies sickly white and unconscious with the gruesome gash in his belly still open. A young nurse replaces the bloody cloth on his stomach with a fresh towel. A gavage tube hooked to an IV bag of fresh blood drips steadily into his stomach.

Dragomira assesses the nurse and commands, "Leave us now. You may return when I'm done here."

The nurse startles and defers to Oliver, who says, "Just wait in your quarters until I call you, please."

Bobbing her head, the nurse exits quickly.

Dragomira spares Oliver a brief glance, before whipping her scarf onto a nearby chair. She leans over the bed and assesses the injured Vampire. Then she closes her eyes and performs a closer inspection with her mind.

Her eyes fly open and drill into Oliver. "This is not a being I'd choose to save."

Oliver nods. "We have our punishments. He'll be served adequate consequences."

"For threatening the only hope your breed has? What consequence is adequate for that? Tearing off his limbs and requiring they regenerate in a barrel of saltwater?" Dragomira scoffs at that idea.

Oliver leans back. "It will be the gravest of punishments, I assure you."

Dragomira huffs but acquiesces. She leans over Ranulf and starts chanting in a low voice, singing the song of her tribe in her native tongue, a song so old and ancient, the very air in the room seems to still and await her command. Oliver watches, fixated as she melds the deep rhythmic sounds with sharp hand movements, coaxing the magic into obedience.

Minutes pass—or perhaps hours, it's impossible to tell—as her voice fills the room with softened whispers and guttural commands, mesmerizing, beautiful, and wild. A force of wind blows through the open window, rippling the curtains in an undulating movement matching her hand movements, beat to beat. Still Dragomira works, with sweat beading her brow and her eyelids closed, but unerringly she moves her hands over the wound in their age-old dance.

Finally she raises two clenched fists and then releases them, bringing about an unnatural silence and stilling the wind at once. She lifts her gleaming eyes and pronounces, "It is done."

Oliver sits forward. "Is he to live then?"

Dragomira shrugs, ambivalent. "He may; he may not. I neutralized the magic as much as possible, and now we'll see if he heals before you run out of blood."

Oliver slumps in relief, but Dragomira isn't done. "I've exacted my own punishment as well."

Both our gazes fly to her face where the light in her eyes dances like a windblown flame. She lifts her chin proudly. "If he survives, for one hour each day for the rest of his life, he will feel the pain of his injury as though it were new. Perhaps that will teach him a bit of empathy and consideration."

Oliver scowls, "And if it makes him a raving lunatic?"

Dragomira smiles wickedly. "I assure you, he wasn't that far off to begin with. Lilith's mark pulls him stronger than most, and the Plane of Fire awaits him eagerly. This will either save him or hurry his eventuality."

Oliver stands abruptly and protests, "But we would have . . . "

Dragomira's power grows, and a searing heat fills the room as she slices the air with her hand. "Enough! It is done. His life has no value except to be used as a warning to others who might interfere with the Illustrissima's purpose. Every time he doubles over in pain, it will remind your kind to keep their hands off her. If you wanted kindness, perhaps you should have turned to the Illustrissima for help, and not I. Perhaps she would have forgiven him on his way to the Plane of Fire. I am no Goddess of Mercy. I exact retribution as my price."

With that, she grabs her scarf and leaves the room with a slam of the door that echoes the finality of her decision.

Oliver stares at the door speculatively. "She isn't a Goddess of Mercy, but she's no human either, is she Jack?" He turns his intelligent eyes on me. "What exactly is she?"

Taking that as my cue to leave too, I turn on my heel and throw over my shoulder, "You don't want to know. Just don't get on her bad side."

CHAPTER 29

THE COUNSELOR

BLUEBELL KILDARE

JULY 14, 2022, RED AGES

 thumb through a vanity magazine in the small waiting room, trying to quell my anxiety. Yeah, right, that mascara *really* makes lashes appear that thick and long. What they need is one of Alexis' enchanted oils to dab on so the lashes would be truly thicker and longer.

Does Jack like long lashes?

And this A-line dress with no waist . . . exactly who do they think that would look good on? Okay, the model looks stunning in it, but if I were as tiny as she, I could wear a burlap sack and still look good. So that isn't saying much for the dress.

"Inspector Kildare?" a warm voice calls out from the doorway.

An unexpectedly rumpled man with hair that's overgrown its cut by about twelve months stands in the doorway. The eyes behind his heavy, black-framed specs are gentle, expressive, and intelligent, so I have some hope. Varg and I follow him into a large office dominated by a massive scarred wooden desk and old school black file cabinets.

I sit in the chair opposite him, taking in his name plate: "Johnathan Michael Redblood, Esq." How refined.

"Thank you for seeing me so quickly."

"My pleasure. I owe Jack quite a bit, and I'm happy to repay the favor," Redblood says as he rests his elbows on his desk. He rubs his two-day shadow of a beard with a large, meaty hand. "I've seen the order for seizure and reviewed the documents on file, so why don't you tell me what happened on the day Varg attacked Mr. Schmidt?"

I take a deep gulp. This is the part I was dreading, but I know it's necessary. So, as quickly and unemotionally as possible, I recount the story of the attempted rape. Counselor Redblood turns his attention to what lies outside the window as I tell my story. I don't know if he does it to give me a feeling of privacy, but his eyes alternate between tightening at the corners when his anger swells and softening when he's feeling empathy.

"So he attacked you unprovoked in the alley, and your wolf escaped a locked apartment to rescue you."

Hmm. That doesn't sound plausible even to my ears. "Yes, Varg has some magical capabilities."

Counselor Redblood's eyes shift to Varg. "It would probably be best not to mention his magical capabilities, or the fact that the apartment was locked. And I understand Mr. Schmidt was a law enforcement official at the time, but he no longer is?"

"Yes, that's true. But I'm not sure what reason he gave the precinct for quitting."

"Do you know why he quit?"

"I'd rather not say."

He gives me a soft smile. "Surprises on the day of court are not a good thing, Inspector Kildare."

I remain firm. "You'll have to talk to Jack if you want an answer. That's his story to tell."

He seems satisfied with that for now.

"So Jack found you, and he can bear witness to your condition?"

"Yes, and Jack is a Vampire, as you know." I blush thoroughly at the next part. "He can testify to my battered appearance and that he scented Dean Schmidt all over my clothes."

Counselor Redblood captures my eyes. "And you chose not to report this?"

I examine my hands. "It would have been difficult to prove an attempted rape, and Dean Schmidt ended up the worse for wear, so battery charges probably wouldn't have gone my way," I explain. "I was also afraid of Varg getting threatened with a case like this, and I'd hoped if I didn't press charges, which seemed futile anyway, that Schmidt might just go away."

He nods in understanding. "I agree that proving an attempted rape would have been difficult. But luckily, proving the need of a defensive weapon—in this case, your wolf—shouldn't be hard at all.

Has he ever harmed anyone before?"

I wince at this. "He killed a man. But it was just after the man killed me, or almost killed me. My heart had stopped, and Jack gave me blood and somehow got my body working again."

Redblood stares keenly at me, then at Varg. "He sounds like a good defensive weapon indeed, but that could complicate things. Let's hope that doesn't come up in court."

"Counselor, what should I do when the dog catcher comes back around?"

He seems thoughtful. "Can he escape any locked area?"

"I think so. I don't really know."

"Well, if it were me, I'd let him take the wolf and see if he gets away. But I have a feeling you aren't likely to do that."

"No, sir," I say emphatically.

The Counselor frowns. "Then do as you must, but know it could subject you to fines. I'll do what I can in court for you."

I stand up. "Thank you so much."

"One more thing," Counselor Redblood says before I exit. "Once you get this cleared up, you need to get the dog . . . er, wolf . . . registered as an official defensive weapon with the city. I can help you submit the correct paperwork."

A great load of relief slips from my shoulders. "I'd be very grateful for that."

CHAPTER 30

MAD MOLLY

BLUEBELL KILDARE

JULY 14, 2022, RED AGES

Jack and I slide into one of the red, leather-upholstered booths lining the front window of the Hag and Harpy. Normally I prefer the wooden tables on the side of the diner, but I can keep an eye on Varg from this position. Right now his nose sticks out the back window of my car as he sniffs the air in all directions. Poor Varg has a constant job keeping me safe.

"I need a truck," I muse. "If it weren't for the elevation, it would be too warm already for Varg to stay in the car. I could tie him to the truck bed with a thin leash to give people the illusion he's secured. What do you think?"

"I think it's a smart idea. If you backed into this space, he could wait in the truck bed and see right into the restaurant."

Thoughtfully, I add, "I'd need some sort of cover so he wouldn't be stuck in the sun and rain. But with all that fur, I doubt he cares about the cold."

Just then Gambino slides into the booth opposite us, throwing his arm over the back of the seat and stretching out.

"Jack." He acknowledges before turning to me, smiling broadly. "Well, I never thought I'd see you working a case again, but here you are."

I haven't seen Gambino since I got out of the hospital after the Blackwater case. As the primary precinct detective working the case, we were practically inseparable for a while. He's still dashing in his almost comically elegant suit and shoes polished to a high shine.

"Yeah," I laugh sardonically, "I'm like a bad penny that keeps showing up."

Gambino mumbles, "Not so bad as a bad penny." And then,

shockingly, his face turns pink as if he hadn't meant to say that aloud.

I reach across the table and pat the top of his hand. "Don't worry; I'm here to stay if I have anything to say about it."

Jack frowns, and his thigh is suddenly touching mine under the table, branding my skin through my jeans with his heat.

Gambino, lips twisting in self-mockery, pulls his hand away and fake coughs into it. "So," he changes the subject, "you two are on the Rose arson case?"

Oh, Gambino. It seems one moment of emotion is all you can take.

Jack breaks the tension. "Yes, we went to the site and spoke with Chief Mack. I assume he gave you the rundown?"

Gambino leans forward and tightens his fists. "He did. About that, though. Chief Mack doesn't know of any natural fuel that would burn everything all to the same degree and all at the same time, except gas. But a gas fire would have caught everything in the house on fire, and we would have a regular house fire. This fire started and ended at the same time, though, all over the building. So it may have been gas, but there's more to it."

Just then Mad Molly meanders over. I grin as I take in her purple hair, which is done up in an incomprehensible swirl atop her head and stuck together by sparkling pins that are rumored to be dangerously sharp weapons. She pulls a notepad out of her black apron and a pencil from behind her ear, then puckers her bright red lips and says, "What can I get y'all?"

Jack orders a warm Bloodvine, a combination of blood and wine served in an amber bottle. Bloodvines are the favorite social drink of Vampires when in mixed company. I order the Hissing Hummus plate and some elderberry tea.

Molly turns to Gambino and gives him a broad smile. "How about you, big boy? The Murderous Meatloaf is on special."

Gambino turns bright pink again, this time all the way to the tips of his ears. "I'll have that and a coffee, please."

"Coming right up!" Molly says, lifting her arm toward the ceiling for emphasis and straining her blouse buttons in the process.

I turn to Gambino and wait patiently for his attention to move from Molly's taut blouse back to us. When it does, I turn the conversation back to the fire.

"The fire was a day old when I got there, so I couldn't catch any residual magic, and we've visited the morgue and found that only one of the family members was Gifted."

"Yep, Hannah," Gambino confirms. "We've spoken with the families of the parents. No animosity among the family, no enemies that I can see. I've got the notes from the interview here."

Gambino hands me a file, which I spread out on the table so Jack can view it with me. We flip through the notes and the information sheets on each of the family members. "What about their activities on that day? Financial information? Work situation?"

"We got it all, but I'm still writing it up. I'll fax it to you later today along with their cell phone records."

Jack raps the wall under the window with his knuckles and leans forward. "We have another situation. A woman came to report her husband missing a few days ago. He was the fire controller for the Western Blue Ridge District up at Station #9. The wife called in to say he'd turned up, but when we went to the house yesterday, I didn't smell any recent male presence, and the house had been vacant for at least twenty-four hours."

I interject, "I've left a message for his boss, Randy, to see if he's heard anything, but Randy isn't expected back in the office until tomorrow. Meanwhile, Rubalia is tracking down family contact information."

Gambino grunts. "Sounds pretty suspicious to me. First he's missing, then he's not, but he hasn't gone back home yet."

Molly interrupts us by sliding our drinks onto the table.

As I take a sip of my hot tea, I stare out the window and see Varg is still deceptively relaxed. I can tell he's on the job, though, because his nostrils are flared and his ears flick to and fro.

I turn back to my dining companions. "The thing is, his wife was worried about him, and she wasn't lying when she made the first report," I explain. "We do think it's suspicious that a fire controller goes missing, and then a mysterious fire happens right after. I can't quite connect the two things yet, but still we're following up. That's all we have for now."

"Umm," Molly says pointedly.

I move the files off the table so she can set down our food. I chuckle softly when she puts Gambino's meatloaf in front of him. It looks like two full pounds of meat in the shape of a loaf, but what's most amusing is the heart-shaped ketchup dollop decorating the top.

Gambino turns a distinct shade of scarlet and says to Molly. "Thank you, Ma'am."

Molly winks at him and sashays away, hips swinging widely.

"Gambino, I think she's sweet on you," I tease. "Do you and Molly have something going on?"

I swear Gambino's ears are about to start bleeding, they're so red. "No, she's just a nice lady." He delicately cuts a slice off the meatloaf in a very gentlemanly fashion, then in a deliberate ploy to change the subject, he says, "I've got one more thing to say."

"What?"

"Molly's going to kill you when she sees that mutt inside." He nods to the front door. Sure enough, Varg is walking as calm as you please into the restaurant—no sign of how he opened the restaurant doors.

I wave my arm to get Molly's attention. "Molly, we'll take the check and some to-go containers."

A few minutes later, Varg is safely tucked in the backseat again. I slide into the car with Jack and say, "I've always been curious: why is Mad Molly called Mad Molly?"

A slow smile spreads across his face. "She had a fight with a lover about ten years ago and he left her in an embarrassing situation. She was found in the restaurant one morning, unhurt but handcuffed to the counter, wearing nothing but high heels and a mask. When the morning crowd found her, she was so mad she busted up every plate in the restaurant. Then, when everyone laughed, and started calling her Mad Molly, she got even madder."

Jack runs his fingers through his hair. "Well, she took note of everyone who laughed at her, and for a month straight she added hot peppers to their orders until she got an apology from each individual. She then changed all the menu items to the ridiculous names they have now: Murderous Meatloaf, Hissing Hummus. After that, she simmered down. She says the menu names are her way of making a fool out of the customers to even the score. Some of the customers really liked the hot peppers she added, though. That's why your hummus plate is so spicy."

I raise my eyebrows. "So how does Bloodvine taste with hot pepper in it?"

Jack chuckles. "Not good. I apologized straight away."

CHAPTER 31

GATHERING STORM

BLUEBELL KILDARE

JULY 14, 2022, RED AGES

'm sitting at my desk, poring over the documents Gambino gave me earlier when Rubalia buzzes. "Randy McKnight is on line one."

Eagerly, I open the line and say, "Hello, Inspector Kildare speaking."

"Inspector, I'm glad I caught you. I just got your message. Sorry, I've been in the forest managing a burn. How's Joe's case going?"

"Randy, has Joe been back to work at all?"

"No . . . " Randy sounds concerned. "Why? Is he back?"

"I'm not sure I can answer that. Have you spoken with Brigid at all?"

"Yes, I spoke with her two days ago. She said that Joe was still gone and that she'd opened a missing person's case. What's going on?"

"Randy, this is going to sound very strange, but if Brigid calls you again, or if you hear from Joe, I want you to call me without informing either of them. Did Brigid say anything else to you about it?"

"No, she didn't. What's going on?"

"I'm afraid I can't say for sure. But I'll certainly be investigating it. Again, please call the minute you hear from either of them. No one is in any trouble, but I'm not sure everyone's okay. I can't give you any more details than that."

Randy agrees in a weary voice, "Okay, Inspector Blue. I'm sure you're acting in their best interests."

"Thank you, Randy."

No sooner does Randy's line click than I buzz Rubalia. "Rubalia, do you have that research I asked for?"

"I'll bring it right over."

Next I buzz Jack and ask him to come to my office.

Rubalia opens my door first, but Jack is right behind her. "Here are your documents," Rubalia says, handing me a stack of papers. "And Gambino just faxed these over." She hands me another stack.

"Thank you, Rubalia."

When Rubalia leaves, Jack closes the door behind her and drapes himself over the chair. His shirt cuffs are undone and rolled up, pushing his suit jacket sleeves up just below his elbows. The sun shining through the window glints off the golden hairs on his forearm, showing every ripple of muscle. His deep voice fills the room. "What's going on?"

I rip my eyes away from his skin to peer steadily at his face. "Before we get into the case, what happened to that Daylight Vampire who attacked me? Did he live?"

Jack's eyes soften. "Blue, Oliver told me he jumped off the roof practically on top of you in an obvious attack."

I steel my emotions and pin him with my eyes. "That's not what I asked, Jack. Did he survive?"

Jack sighs. "We called Dragomira out and she did the best she could to neutralize the magic in the knife. He's still fighting for his life, and we aren't sure which way it'll go. Volunteers are giving him blood for the time being."

A small cry of dismay threatens to escape my lips, but I swallow it down. "Keep me posted, please. If I'm responsible for a death, I need to know."

Jack leans forward and covers my hand with his. The heat of his palm burns into me, and I'm tempted to turn my hand over to caress his, but I don't want pity affection from him.

I pull my hand back to my lap and switch topics to our investigation. "Randy, Joe's boss, just called asking about the case. Apparently Brigid told him she'd filed the missing person's report. He hasn't seen or heard from Joe or Brigid since."

Jack hits the desk with his palm. "Shit. If these two cases are linked, then there are only a few possible reasons and none of them are good."

"I know. Let's think positive and hope she's just covering for Joe.

Maybe he left her for another woman and she's too embarrassed to say."

"It's possible. But I'm not liking it."

Thinking back to all those photos and the chubby chocolate handprint, I'm not liking it either.

I flip to Rubalia's notes, which include the contact information for all of Brigid and Joe's family members.

Jack leans forward. "What do you want to do?"

Grateful he's letting me take the lead, I stand up. "Let's go visit Brigid's mom. If I were in big trouble, I would go straight home to my parents. If I had any, that is."

Jack winces at that statement.

CHAPTER 32

A FAMILY AFFAIR

JACK TANNER

JULY 14, 2022, RED AGES

We pull down the last winding road, which is flanked by a steep drop-off on one side and rows of crops on the other, arranged in a pleasing checker pattern along hills and vales. The blue skies and sweet country air tempt me into relaxation. But when I pull up the drive to Beth and Matt Richardson's home, my tension quickly returns.

A man who I hope is Matt Richardson sits on the porch, rocking back and forth in an old, wooden rocking chair with a large shotgun in his lap. I pull the car to a stop just outside shooting range.

Blue turns to me. "Why are you stopping?"

With her normal eyesight, she wouldn't be able to see the gun from here. "Mr. Richardson appears to be expecting some trouble. He's sitting on the porch with a shotgun. We're out of range right now, so you need to stay in the car while I go talk to him. If he means no harm, I'll call you."

Blue's eyes crinkle with worry as she gazes toward the porch. Her hand lands on my arm. "Be careful."

On impulse, I lean over and kiss her temple. "I will. Remember, I'm faster than his trigger finger. Just sit tight."

With that, I climb out of the car and raise both arms high to show I'm unarmed. Mr. Richardson picks up the gun and aims it at me with a steady hand. I keep walking forward slowly as I yell out, "Mr. Richardson, I'm Jack Tanner with the Supernatural Investigation Bureau. I just want to talk."

Mr. Richardson pulls the trigger, aiming low and short. The gun goes off with a bang, and buckshot sprays the ground in front of me.

He keeps his sights on me and yells back, "That's a warning! Now stop right there. How do I know you're really with the SIB?"

"I've got a badge. I'll toss it to you."

The car door slams. Shit. "Blue, stay by the car."

"I am," she replies.

I yell, "I'm reaching into my jacket slowly, just to get the badge."

With my eye on Mr. Richardson's trigger finger, I slowly pull out the badge out, giving him time to see what it is. Then with an easy throw, the badge lands on the porch by the man's feet.

He keeps the gun in his hand as he leans over to pick it up. After a slow perusal, he yells, "Well, come on up here, then. Let's have a look at ya."

Blue and Varg follow me up to the house while I keep a studious eye on the gun.

Mr. Richardson, who appears to be in his mid-fifties is clad in blue farmer overalls. This is a small hobby farm from what I can see: a few small crops, a garden patch, some cows and chickens. I turn my attention to the house, where I can hear two adults and one baby. But where's Becky?

When we reach the porch, Mr. Richardson peers skeptically at us. Blue steps forward and offers her hand and an introduction. "I'm Inspector Bluebell Kildare, and this Inspector Jack Tanner. We're both with the SIB, and we're concerned about Brigid."

I'm amused that Blue just demoted me from Director of Homicide to Inspector. She probably thought my real title was too threatening.

Mr. Richardson leans back in his chair and spits a long line of chew juice off the porch. "I don't know that she's gonna talk to ya."

Blue asks, "So she's here then?"

"Yes, Ma'am."

"Can you tell her that Inspectors Blue and Jack are here to talk to her about Joe?"

He yells out through the house without getting up from his chair or releasing his gun, "Beth, some inspectors here want to talk to Brigid about Joe. One's a Sunwalker. I seen 'is badge and it's gen-u-ine, near as I can tell."

Mrs. Richardson, I presume, opens the door a crack. Her pale, drawn face is framed by shoulder-length dark hair with threads of gray running through it. "What do you need?" she demands.

Blue steps forward and shows her badge. "Please, Mrs. Richardson. We're worried about Brigid, and we'd like to help her. May we speak with her?"

Mrs. Richardson glances up at me; then searches Blue's eyes. She must see something she likes because she slowly opens the door. "Well, come on in then. She's in the living room."

Blue makes a beeline for Brigid, who sits in a chair with her hands clutched tightly in her lap, gently tapping a baby bouncer with her toe. Her little boy sleepily rubs his eyes with his tiny fists. Brigid's eyes are cold, almost blank, and her face taut.

Blue immediately kneels at Brigid's feet and takes her hand, speaking softly. "Brigid, what happened?"

Brigid averts her face from Blue's searching eyes and tightens up even more. But what captures my attention the most is the stench of fear and pain seeping out of her pores. My throat thickens as I repress my predatory instinct. Brigid smells like a small animal with a great wound.

Brigid whispers in a cold, hollow voice, "I'm not supposed to tell you or I could lose everything."

The baby gives a small cry. Brigid had stopped bouncing him as she spoke, so she starts tapping her toe again.

Mrs. Richardson puts her hands on Brigid's shoulders. "Honey, maybe they can help."

Brigid looks at Blue again, then me, then the baby. At last she unclenches her hands. Between them lays a photo of Becky. Her eyes lock on Blue again, a fierce, driving stare. "If I tell you, you have to swear to keep baby Joey safe."

Blue squeezes her hand, and I step forward as this is a vow I can easily make. "Brigid, we will keep baby Joey safe with our very lives. We have safe houses if necessary."

Brigid's eyes slide to me again, then back to Blue. It's to Blue who she speaks. "The night after I came to you, the doorbell rang. I thought it was Joe, so I unlocked the deadbolt to let him in. Three men pushed their way inside. Two of them grabbed me and covered my mouth so I couldn't scream. One of them went upstairs and grabbed Becky. They told me they were taking Becky to Joe and that if I told anyone, they would come back for baby Joey."

"Brigid," Blue says, "this is really important. What were their exact words?"

Brigid closes her eyes tightly and speaks with a thin voice. "The middle guy—not the tall guy, not the small guy—he did the talking. He said to the tall guy, 'We need the girl for leverage. Get her. Check the bedrooms upstairs. Cover her mouth so she doesn't scream.'"

She opens her eyes now, her gaze darting between me and Blue. "I struggled and kicked, but I couldn't get free. I couldn't stop them." Tears stream silently down her face now, running in rivulets down her cheeks and onto her neck.

"Then they brought Becky downstairs. She was terrified. She was crying, but the tall guy had her mouth covered. She was reaching for me, but I couldn't get to her. She wanted her mama, but I couldn't keep her safe."

Brigid gasps for air through her tears and lifts her clenched hands to her heart in apparent agony, but her voice, still hollow, thin, and cold, continues. "The man turned and whispered in my ear, 'If you ever want to see her alive again, you won't tell anyone. We'll know, and we'll come back for the baby too.'"

Now Brigid turns to Blue again with deep, dark eyes, no longer cold, but filled with great pain. "So you see, I may have just killed Becky."

Tears stream down Blue's face too. "No, Brigid. You're doing the only thing you can. This situation is bigger than you can handle, than any one person can handle. You need help, and we'll help you as much as we can."

I decide it's time to chime Ernesto. "We have a hostage situation. I need you to come watch a family for us until nightfall, and then we'll move them to our safe house." I turn to Brigid. "I assume that's okay? You and Joey will come to our safe apartment? It's right in our headquarters, and no one will know you're there. Your parents can come too."

Brigid nods.

I turn back to Ernesto and give him the address, then snap the chimerator closed.

"You should try to rest," I tell Brigid. "Our colleague Ernesto will move you out at night, and when you arrive at headquarters, we'll have a sketch artist get a full description of each of the three men. But for now, we'll wait for Ernesto."

Brigid wipes the back of her hand against her eyes. Her posture is still stiff and tight. She gazes down at the photo of Becky, thumbs it lovingly, and whispers, "Becky, I'm afraid I did the wrong thing. I'm scared they won't bring you back to me and it will be all my fault."

Blue leans in and holds Brigid's hand. "No, Brigid. We must stay hopeful."

CHAPTER 33

ATTEMPTED SEIZURE

BLUEBELL KILDARE

JULY 15, 2022, RED AGES

s the morning sun peeks through the trees, Varg and I finish our daily walk at an energized clip. Suddenly, I spot something that causes me to come to a complete stop and jerk on Varg's leash. There, parked in front of my apartment door, is the dogcatcher again.

I pivot and start walking in the opposite direction, hoping against hope that he didn't see us. My plan is to go around the back way. A glance over my shoulder proves it won't be so easy. The bald man is huffing his way toward us with a catch pole in his hand. No way is he putting that thing around Varg. It looks way too much like a noose.

"Run!" I command.

Varg and I take off at top speed. Admittedly, it's my top speed, as Varg easily glides along next to me without a single pant for his effort.

At the end of the block, I take a swift left and peer over my shoulder. The dogcatcher is pumping his arms around his portly belly, carrying himself faster than I'd have guessed him capable of.

We keep running, and I consider my options. I've got to get to the opposite side of the block with enough of a lead to get us in the car.

We run past a house with kids playing ball in the small front yard. They stop and stare at us, then watch as the catcher passes them by. I keep pumping my arms, thankful for all the training Yao and Wang have been forcing me to do.

At the corner, I risk a glance back. He's about a quarter of a block behind us now. Drat! I won't have enough lead by the time we hit the final stretch.

I turn to Varg. "This is the plan. You can outrun him easier than I can. So when we get to the car, I'm going to jump in, but you keep running. Run your fastest straight down the street. I'll follow you in the car, and when you're a few blocks ahead of him, I'll pick you up. Got it?"

Varg gives a low growl, which I take as a yes.

We take the final left turn, and I curse under my breath. I forgot my car was pointed in the wrong direction. Sticking to the plan, I stop at the car, and Varg stops with me.

"Run, Varg!" I wave my hands wildly at him. He yips, then turns around and starts running toward the dog catcher in the same direction my car is pointed.

Ohh no. This is sooo not the plan. I stand there, frozen in place with my heart in my throat.

Just as he's about to close in on the dogcatcher, Varg vaults himself into the air, then manages to turn sideways in mid-flight. His powerful hind legs kick off the side of the brick building we just ran past, then he sails over the man's head and the catchpole by a solid six feet. He lands gracefully on the other side and keeps at a full run. Holy cow!

The dogcatcher's face is beet red. He turns around and starts pumping toward Varg again, his belly shaking with each step, but despite his impressive effort, Varg is out of there like a shot. I can hardly see him anymore.

I hop in the car and pass the catcher. In a few minutes, I catch up with Varg who's easily loping along, glancing back at my car as though he doesn't have a care in the world.

This wolf is going to be the death of me.

CHAPTER 34

SAFE HOUSE

BLUEBELL KILDARE

JULY 15, 2022, RED AGES

Warg pushes ahead of me on the stairs leading to the rooftop safe house apartment. We like to call it the penthouse suite, though no one who stays there has the enjoyment one would normally associate with a penthouse. It's really a transient space, meant for keeping the occasional family safe while an investigation is in progress.

A strong buzz surrounds me as I hit a thick, invisible wall sheilding the first door. When I say the password, the ward dissolves to let us through. The second door requires my handprint on a keypad, which gets me through to the third and final door. Here, I knock.

"Who's there?" Mr. Richardson calls.

"It's Inspector Kildare."

He opens a small wooden shutter that covers a window at head height and promptly sticks his rifle on the warded glass. I dip my head down, slightly nervous because I'm staring down the barrel of a very large gun held by a very capable man, even though the entire door is warded against bullets.

Mr. Richardson peers at me, then drops the gun. The door swings open to a modern and comfortable living room awash in sunshine.

One entire wall of the living room is warded glass with doors to the terrace. Unfortunately because of the security features, the terrace feels more like a prison. It's sixteen feet wide and borders the entire length of the apartment, but it's surrounded by a ten-foot cement block wall and covered by an electric chain-link fence. The shadows from the diamond-shaped fencing that covers the terrace fall onto the terracotta terrace floor, giving it a distinctly prisonlike appearance.

Still, at least the occupants have access to sunshine and fresh air.

Brigid sits out there now with the baby sleeping in a spot of shade. She seems no better than yesterday, sitting stiffly with dark circles under her eyes. She appears brittle, as though she's trying too hard to be strong.

Mrs. Richardson says, "Please have a seat and let me get Brigid for you. I'll watch the baby while you talk."

I take a seat on the living room sofa, and Varg curls at my feet. Mrs. Richardson takes over care of the baby, and Brigid slips inside a moment later. I indicate the sofa next to me and ask, "Are you finding the place comfortable enough? Did we provide everything you needed?"

Brigid takes the seat at the far end of the sofa, leaving an empty cushion between us. Meanwhile, Mr. Richardson joins his wife on the terrace to give us some privacy, I imagine.

Brigid's lips twist in a bitter smile. "You provided me with everything I need from the grocery store." Her unspoken message is that she needs her husband and her daughter, and we haven't provided that yet. Then her cheeks redden with shame. "I'm sorry I didn't mention that they wore masks. So the whole artist thing was futile."

I grimace at her unnecessary apology. "I should have realized that myself when you described the men based on their height and size rather than hair and facial features."

Brigid relaxes a little. She asks hopefully, "Did you find anything on his GPS?"

I shake my head sadly. "No, it must be turned off."

Her face falls, and threads of despair wrap around her like a dark cloak.

"Brigid, when the man said he needed to take Becky for leverage, what did you think that meant?"

Now Brigid's mind turns troubled. She says, "I don't know." But she's not being honest.

"Brigid, if you have any guess, you have to tell me. We need an idea of where to start."

Pain crosses Brigid's face, and her hands tighten into fists. "I'm guessing they wanted to use Joe's gift, and he wasn't cooperating. So they took Becky to make him do something for them." Brigid fidgets with her fingers. "If he does something bad with his gift to keep Becky safe, will he be in trouble?"

Oh, I feel so bad for her, but she needs the truth. "If Joe does something that hurts other people, unless it's in self-defense, he'll have to answer to that. But if he's truly abducted and the abductors are using Becky as leverage, he has a good chance of getting leniency on any crimes he commits. But let's not worry about that now. Our main concern is getting them home safe. So you think that someone would use him for his power?"

Her shoulders drop, as though in defeat, and she says, "He's always known his gift is extremely powerful. That's part of why I was mad he did the interview. He made himself—made all of us— vulnerable." She looks at me with imploring eyes, "You must believe he's not the sort of man to do bad things. He's dedicated his life to saving others. The only reason he did that interview was as a public service piece."

I reach over the sofa and squeeze Brigid's hand briefly. "I understand. Now, is there anything else you remember about that night or about the three men that might give us a clue?"

Brigid's eyes go dark. "I did remember one thing, but it probably won't help. I remember one man had a scar on his neck that extended below his mask. It was on the left side, and it was pretty pink, like it happened recently. It wasn't the leader; it was the tall one."

My heart brightens. "That's great news. Everything helps. How big was it? What did it look like?"

Brigid shudders and makes a clawing motion down the side of her neck. "It was the whole side of his neck. It resembled claw marks."

Varg growls low in his throat.

CHAPTER 35

THE TRIO

BLUEBELL KILDARE

JULY 15, 2022, RED AGES

y sixth sense alerts me to the presence of four people in the hallway outside my door. Jack's leaning against my office doorway, filling the space with his broad shoulders.

"Blue, do you have a minute? I'd like to introduce you to our new exterminators."

"Oh, sure. Come on in."

Jack enters, followed by three other Daylight Vampires. Jack gestures to a tall, dark, and delicious man and an equally beautiful woman. "This is Lazare Beaumont and Gia Winters. Both have been working in the eighth district and are on indefinite loan."

Lazare is simply exquisite, his features so perfectly symmetrical it seems almost impossible. He lays on the charm by winking at me and flashing a dimpled smile with million dollar fangs. But compared to Jack's raw sexiness, he's nothing but a doily.

Gia is of average height, amazingly fit, and dressed in leather pants and a tight military vest. Her short hair and angular face only accentuate her large eyes and phenomenal bone structure. I feel woefully inadequate next to her.

Next, Jack indicates the tall, swarthy, and scary Vampire to the woman's left. "This is Ammon Zaro. He's new to the region. He has extensive experience with personal security."

Ammon's lips press together in a tight line that must pass as his smile. Physically, he reminds me of a boar, but I sense an honorable soul.

I stand and shake everyone's hand. "Hi, I'm Bluebell Kildare. I'm a Gifted Empath and primarily responsible for non-Vampire homicide cases. Welcome aboard."

Once the niceties are observed, Lazare, Gia, and Ammon take their leave, but Jack lingers. He braces his arms on the steel support of a window panel as he watches the trio walk into the parking lot and drive away. Only then does he turn to me.

"Ammon is someone I've known for many years. I trust him. But I'd rather Lazare and Gia not know that Ammon and I have a connection because that might cause them to close themselves off from him. What were your impressions?"

Pleased that Jack is consulting me on their character, I reply, "I get a good vibe from Ammon. I didn't sense bad intentions from either Lazare or Gia, but Lazare could be a wildcard. My guess is he mostly serves himself. Gia feels fierce and strong. Her loyalty definitely runs deep, and I get the impression she would fight to the death for those she's loyal to. But I don't know where her loyalties lie."

Jack blinks his eyes lazily. "As I said, I trust Ammon. So out of the three, if you need an extra hand, Ammon would be it."

"Duly noted. So how do you know him?"

Jack lowers himself into my chair. "I met Ammon when I first came to the New World about two hundred years ago."

"Oh? Did you meet him here?"

A small wisp of fury escapes He-who-is-so-controlled and something dark passes over his face when he replies, "Yes, he was in the Blue Ridge Mountains when I first arrived."

"You are being very mysterious, but you don't have to tell me, if you don't want to."

Jack smiles wryly, "It's okay. Ammon was newly turned and his maker was the cruel sort. When I came upon him, Ammon was pinned beneath a large boulder on purpose and left to starve. I let him out then had some words with his maker, and Ammon has been out of his grasp ever since."

"But enough with dark tales." He lets his eyelids droop in his lazy, catlike way. "So, I've been meaning to ask, how is your training coming along?"

Hah! I'll bet Jack had more than a few words with Ammon's maker, but I let him change the topic if he wants. I reply, "Awful, terrible, grueling, and much-needed."

Jack's eyes soften. "Sounds like you're enjoying it."

"Huh?"

His eyes get mischievous. "I'd love to see how your skill is coming along."

Without waiting for an answer, he stands up again. "Well, I have to run a short errand. I'll be back soon." And with that, he leaves my office, flashing me a little smile.

As soon as he leaves, Rubalia announces through the phone, "Chief Mack on line one."

"Put him through, please."

When I hear the line click over, I answer, "Inspector Blue speaking."

Chief Mack's smooth as silk voice comes over the phone. "Blue, we've got another fire I think you should examine."

I take a deep breath. "Give me the address. I'll be right there."

CHAPTER 36

A MAN UNACCOUNTED

BLUEBELL KILDARE

JULY 15, 2022, RED AGES

Ugh," I say to Varg as we wind toward downtown. "The only way to the site of the fire is through the city center, but the protests suck. It'd be nice if they'd give it a rest. Don't you think?"

Varg huffs a little snort, and I take this as agreement.

As we pass the protesters, we come to the downtown area, strewn with banners and park displays pumping up the upcoming Sun Flare Celebration. On the edge of Memorial Park where the celebration is going to take place, a balloon vendor hawks his wares, but he seems to be short on red balloons as mostly blue remains. Red must be very popular for the kiddies.

We turn onto Murky Meadow Road and arrive at our destination. This whole area used to be a meadow before the recent construction. It's called Murky Meadow because the mountain peaks surrounding it cast deep shadows on the land. Now, this entire subdivision is nothing but stick framed row homes with shared walls.

The gaping hole in the otherwise pristine pattern of two-story homes sidled up snuggly tight is as conspicuous as a smile with two missing front teeth. But the charred frame gives it a sinister appearance.

We walk past two fire trucks and men rolling up their hoses. I don't see Chief Mack, so I call out, "Chief Mack? I'm here."

I sense a sad and troubled soul come up behind me at the same time a sonorous voice responds, "I'm here."

I pivot and take in Mack's mournful eyes. He's wearing blue jeans and a light brown plaid shirt today. At mid-summer his golden brown skin sports more freckles than ever. It's difficult to smile on such an occasion but I manage a slim one. "What have you got for me?"

"A single mom and her five-year-old daughter died in the fire: Yana and Kalina Bacheva. It's still too hot to enter, but I thought you'd want to see the building fresh."

"Are the bodies still in there?"

"No, we managed to get them out. But too late." He pauses, and I feel his deep regret as if it were my own. "On the outside looking in, it seems the same as the last fire. Everything is the same color through the glassicals. Luckily the joining walls are double brick and the roof had fire prevention measures, or else the whole row might have gone up."

I glance up and down the street and see home after home, at least thirty of them stretching as far as I can see until the road bends. The enormity of what could have happened sinks in.

Neighbors gather on their front lawns. A few have dragged lawn chairs into their yards, aimed toward the fire scene. There's nothing like a little death and destruction to liven up an otherwise boring evening. Firefighters mill around, stringing up tape and plastic barriers.

"I need to get close and have some silence for a few minutes. I'm sure I'll be giving the neighbors a bit of a show. Can you keep them away from me?"

Mack nods.

"How close can I get?"

"You can stand on the cement stoop, but don't step inside, not even one foot. The whole first floor is burnt through, and it drops to a garage basement. Don't touch the frame. It should be stable, but if you hear any grumbling noise, come back out fast."

I step toward the house. Most of the front of the house is burned up. The stoop does appear to be the best place to stand. At least through the front doorway I can get some perspective.

I climb the stairs and peer in, or rather down, as there isn't anything inside but a gaping, cavernous space. The heat emanating from the home assaults my face, and the acrid scent turns my stomach. My skin breaks out in sweat, and as I take a step backwards, my hand brushes against the brick. "Ouch!" I pull my hand back from the still-hot surface.

I close my eyes and shut off my other senses, then reach out with my sixth sense to probe the space. A feeling of intense agony swells up, invading my mind. Pain like I've never felt assaults me, invades my very soul. Fear. Agony. Helplessness.

A scream rips out of my throat, and I fall back, desperate to get away from it. My foot lands on open air from the steps behind me, and I grasp wildly for the handrail. Just as I'm sure I'm about to crack my head open on the cement stairs, a strong arm catches me. I shut down my sixth sense, but still I crouch down and huddle into a ball, heaving deep breaths as the memory of that pain ricochets through my mind. Eventually a voice breaks through my head.

"Are you okay, Miss? Miss? Are you okay? What happened?"

Warm brown eyes stare at me in concern. When I realize I'm balled up on the stoop with this man's arms around me, I uncurl shakily and stand up.

"I'm sorry. I wasn't expecting the pain."

"What pain? Are you hurt?"

Mack speaks up from behind him. "Finn, she's an Empath and a Sensitive."

The brown eyes crinkle, but the concern lessens. "Oh. I see."

He doesn't really see, but at least he's trying.

Mack suggests, "Maybe you should try tomorrow after it's settled a while."

I shake my head. "No, I should have prepared myself better. I just wasn't thinking. I'd prefer to do this now while everything is fresh."

Mack nods at Finn. "Stay with her. I don't want her falling in."

Okay. This is an arrangement I can live with. "Come on, Finn. You can hold my arm this time."

He moves forward with me until I'm again standing at the doorway. This time I shut down my five senses gradually and even more slowly open up my sixth sense. I hold my mind in an iron grip and fill it with the litany, "This is not my pain. This is not my pain." With deep, even breaths, I let the scarlet pain roll over me.

One signature tells of pain and desperation, and another of pain and confusion. Both are laden with shock. I push past this, trying to overcome the massive wall of pain to find other feelings, earlier feelings.

And I do find them. Sensations of happiness ripple through every corner of this house in soft waves. Contentment is deeply embedded in the very pores of the home. There was undoubtedly much love here. I search for anything unusual or turbulent in recent times. With concentration, I'm able to decipher a sliver of emotion from a third person, but not pain. Instead, I feel passion and sexual excitement. Anger and hate seem to be entirely missing from this home. At least their lives were carefree and joyful while they had them.

I sense sexual excitement again, much stronger this time, and it's coming from right next to me of all things. Nice to know Finn finds me attractive, but ugh, this is a murder scene for goodness' sake!

Somehow I manage to shut out his lust and project my senses through the house to feel for magic. And it's there. Soft and subtle, like a fine mist, it's sprinkled evenly throughout the upstairs. Traveling down with my sixth sense to the first floor and the basement, I feel the same even, light dusting of magic. It feels like energy, like the breath of life. But mixed with it is another vibration, thick like a humidity you can cut. It feels almost like a ward.

When I pull back my sixth sense, the rush of my five senses takes over. Finn's arm is around my back now, gripping me tightly, and sweat is pouring down my face and drenching my top. My hair is a wet sticky mess.

In a gravelly voice, Finn says, "Are you okay?"

I give him a sharp glare. "You heard that I'm an empath, right?"

Finn agrees warily.

"Then you should probably not indulge in fantasies on the job when I'm around."

Shock rolls over Finn's face, and then amusement. He bursts out laughing. "You haven't had many boyfriends, have you?"

"What?" I sputter.

Laughing even louder now, not that I care, Finn tugs me down the stairs. He lets go of me once I'm safely on solid ground and asks, "Do you need me to hose you down to cool you off?"

I glance down and notice my armpits are stained and my shirt collar is soaked through. I give him the evil eye and turn my attention to Mack.

"This was a happy family," I tell him. "The home was filled with love. They suffered a short but horrifically painful death. Magic was used in the fire; it was evenly spread throughout the whole home. And a third person was here recently, but I didn't get much from their signature. One thing I can tell you is there was no anger or hate at this house."

Finn is staring at me seriously now, and Mack's eyes brighten as he absorbs my information. "Hmm. The way you describe the magic sounds like gas to me, but these homes are all electric. You're sure you were sensing magic and not gas?"

"I can't sense gas, Chief. I sense emotions, souls, and magic. That's it. Of course, it's possible for magic to be tied to any substance, including gas. Let me know what you come up with. Oh, and one more thing. It feels like a ward accompanied the magic, maybe to control it. When did this fire happen, and how long did it last?"

Mack rubs his hand across his forehead. "It happened at about midnight again. It didn't last long, but this one burned much hotter. We had to hose it down just to cool it off."

"You know, Chief, I bet if you were to throw a burning stick into that house, it would go out immediately."

Mack purses his lips. Then he ambles over to his car and takes out a massive weapon of some kind.

"What is that?" I ask.

Mack hefts it to his shoulder and walks to the doorway. "It's a flame thrower. Sometimes we fight fire with fire."

Mack gives the lever a quick pull. Flames burst through the air, arcing forward, but they billow out at the doorway as though hitting an invisible wall.

Mack mutters, "Well, I'll be."

Finn's eyes widen and he glances from me to the fire and back to me again. This is when the guys get freaked out, and this is why I don't have a lot of experience with men. I glare at him one more time and stalk off with Varg.

CHAPTER 37

COIL OF ROPE

BLUEBELL KILDARE

July 15, 2022, Red Ages

I peer down the street at the fire engines, feeling simultaneously mad, frustrated, and embarrassed about the scene with Finn. He didn't really do anything wrong except remind me of the freakiness of my freak and why I can't be with normal guys. It isn't that Gifted people can't be with Norms. It's that normal guys don't want to be with a woman who can tell every time he gets excited when another woman walks in the room, or when he's lying if he says she's beautiful. Not that Gifted guys handle it better, but at least they can understand somewhat. It just sucks.

We walk around the corner and are almost to the car when Varg steps in front of me and lets out a vicious growl. Now, I may be pissed at Finn for no reason, but I'm no fool. I listen to my wolf, pull out my gun, and quickly scan for threats.

Three men step out from the side of a house. My senses warn me that two more men stand not far behind me, blocking my only potential escape route. Jack's threat about consequences if I don't use my alert button is ever present in my mind, so I discretely press it as soon as I notice the guy wearing the red tee and the guy with the spectacles are holding handguns. The third holds a dart gun. Aimed right at Varg.

The back door of a large white van parked against the curb opens, and yet another man steps out, this one wearing a jacket. So that's the game. They want me in that van, and the odds are six against two.

"Keep back!" I shout. "One step closer and he's going to attack."

Varg growls so viciously, drool drips from his jaws. His entire body is tense for the pounce.

When he sees Varg's size, Dart Man's eyes bulge, and his face blanches. Varg's up to my shoulders, the largest I've ever seen him.

Dart Man seems to be the leader, so I aim my gun straight at him.

I taunt brazenly. "Didn't you load that gun with enough to kill an elephant? What are the chances you'll bring him down before he rips off your head?"

The man sneers, and then several things happen at once, so quickly I'm not sure I believe my eyes. Dart Man pulls the trigger, and Varg jumps toward him. The dart flies right toward Varg. Dead on. My heart stops. Just as it should hit Varg—flash, he vanishes in midair.

The dart travels beyond the space where Varg had been and hits one of the men who came up behind me in the thigh, causing him to shout and curse. Then Varg reappears with his jaw wrapped around Dart Man's shooting hand. Thank the Lady of Light. The Dart Victim collapses.

While I was watching Varg, Jacket Man managed to sneak up behind me, and as soon as Varg is safe, my senses warn me of his presence. But it's too late. His jacket covered arm wraps around my neck from behind. He grabs my gun arm.

Oh no. This can't be happening. Visions of being captured by Blackwater flash through my mind. My head starts to pound with the force of adrenaline. I tuck in my chin to protect my windpipe. He's choking me. I gasp for breath, but it eludes me.

I consider gutting him with my knife, but as appealing as that is, I know I don't need to. Instead, I let my training kick in. I shift my gun to my left hand and move my legs to the left so I can get to his groin area. Then I punch backwards, hitting him right in the nuts. Hard. With no small amount of satisfaction. He bends over, groaning in anguish, but still holding my neck. He drags me down with him. My vision grays, and I'm desperate for air. Still fiercely determined, I pull to the side and elbow him in the face. Thankfully he releases his hold, and through blurry vision, I peer between my legs and manage to shoot him in the foot.

I drag in deep, greedy gulps of air and straighten out while Jacket Man cries out, collapsing to the ground behind me. Now that my own crisis is averted, his pain whips me like a lash. It brings me to my knees at the force of his agony. He grasps for his foot and tries to move away by scooting on his butt

As I gather my wits, the sound of crunching metal and bone comes from behind me, and then a horrendous ear shattering scream.

Again, agony invades my brain, so sharp, it feels as though it's mine. I manage to stand on shaky knees and turn, making sure Varg is okay. He's incapacitated Dart Man, thank goodness, and now he's circling me, trying to keep me safe.

Both the remaining armed men move toward Varg with vile intent. Varg sets his sights on Red Tee Man and launches, at the same time both Gunmen shoot at him. I feel frozen in time as I watch with horror. Varg disappears in midair again. A pain sears my thigh and stuns me to action. I shoot at the other armed guy, Spectacle Man, but he moves too quickly and I only get his hand. Varg appears again with the forearm of Red Tee Man trapped in his mouth like a gruesome trophy.

The pain of my leg, the pain of the man's arm being torn off beneath Varg's teeth, and the pain of the man with the hole in his hand all hit me at once. I stagger under the weight of anguish, white hot, ricocheting through my mind. The last man, the guy who had initially come up behind me, takes advantage of my emotional state and tries to pull my gun out of my hand. I get my first good look at him just as burning and numbness rip through me. Somehow I push through the feelings invading my mind to defend myself by leaning toward him, twisting, and pulling out of the man's grasp while cries of agony storm me from all sides.

Suddenly a blurred figure appears on the scene, and the last man attacking me disappears from my view. In the time it takes me to blink, he's passed out on the ground. Who did this? A Vampire? Jack? No, it's Oliver who flashes into view.

Holy crap. I quickly tally up the wounded to make sure we got all the guys. Dart Man with his crushed arm lays close to Dart Victim who's still passed out. Red Tee Man is deathly white and by the way he's shivering I guess he's in shock from losing his forearm to Varg's teeth. Varg really got him good. Jacket Man is trying to take his shoe off, I imagine to stop the blood from flowing out of the hole in his foot while Spectacle Man presses his wounded hand between his knees. Finally, there's the Last Man who's passed out from goodness knows what Oliver did to him.

Yes, that's all six of them. Red Tee Man is in the worst shape with his arm severed at the elbow. His gun lies by his side, forgotten in his agony. I snatch it away, and then take a moment to examine my wound.

The bullet grazed my thigh pretty badly, but it's just a flesh wound. I pull out Guardian and cut a strip from the hem of my shirt to tie around my thigh.

Oliver leans lazily against a tree, flashing his quirky smile. I ignore his flippant attitude and open the chimerator.

Jack's eyes, two green, glass orbs, peer at me. "You okay?"

"I'm fine, but I'm still securing the scene. Please send six ambulances with you. Send Ernesto. These are Dilectus Deo. Gotta run."

Amazingly, the emotions and pain coming from the wounded men cut me far worse than my own injury. And now, as the men's initial shock wears off, undulating waves of hate hit me with the force of an ocean at high tide. I begin to repeat my mantra: "These feelings are not mine. These feelings are not mine."

I decide to take a peek inside the men's van. Sure enough, there's a coil of rope there. It doesn't take a genius to guess what they were planning on doing with this. It didn't escape my notice that neither of the gunmen were trying to shoot me, so their orders must have been to capture me alive.

Oliver watches me go through the van from his relaxed position.

I yell at him, "Would you help already?"

"I thought I did."

I wave my arms furiously toward the injured men. "Search them for more weapons."

He sighs and reluctantly steps away from the tree to do my bidding.

Slicing a length of the rope with my knife, I fashion a tourniquet of sorts and wrap it tightly above the elbow of Red Tee Man, hoping to keep him alive until the ambulances arrive. He's passed out cold now and his chances aren't great. Next, I tie a tourniquet around the ankle of Jacket Man, whose foot I shot after he tried to strangle me. I don't feel even slightly guilty that the whole time I'm tying the tourniquet, I'm wishing I wasn't an Empath and could just let him bleed out. While clenching my jaw, I tie off the arms of Spectacle Man with his shot hand and Dart Man with his shattered arm.

I use my new bracelets to make sure all the men are immobilized, thanking Wang silently for the gift. Though they can't hurt me anymore, their feelings assault me still.

The emotions and the sound of their crying bombard my brain. As soon as the scene is secure and everyone is searched, I shout out to Oliver, "Keep an eye on them." The pain is too much for me so I walk down the block.

"Hey, where you going?" he yells back.

"I'm just stepping away. I can't stand the noise. I'll be right over here."

With my hands over my ears to block out their cries, I position myself near the corner of the block and watch two fire trucks light up and head toward me. Cripes! Did they have to send Mack and Finn down here?

Before I know it, men are pouring out of the trucks, shouting. Bandages come out. The ambulances arrive. Lights flash and sirens blare, further invading my brain. Stretchers are brought out. Then Jack and Ernesto arrive.

By now, I'm sitting on the ground with my back to a tree and my hands still over my ears, as though that makes a difference. It may muffle the noise, but it doesn't stop the feelings of anger, hate, and pain from invading my being.

Jack sits down next to me. "Are you okay?" Then his nostrils flare. "You've been injured." He peers at the blood-soaked rag tied around my thigh.

I lift up my head with my hands still on my ears and whisper, "I'll be okay as soon as they leave. It's just a flesh wound on my thigh, and their caterwauling bothers me much more than any physical pain."

As the last man is loaded onto a stretcher, Finn steps away from the crowd with his arms folded against his chest and looks my way. His brow is furrowed.

Yep. Get a good look at freak girl.

Jack watches my gaze and stares hard back at Finn. Finn turns without a word and jumps back on the fire truck.

I feel Jack's hands on my thigh as he pulls my bandage down and calls the medics over. They cover the wound with gauze and try to convince me to go to the hospital, but I refuse. It's nothing Alexis can't help with, and the last place I want to be is in a hospital right now. I need mental peace more than anything.

When all the ambulances and fire trucks leave, it's just Jack, Varg, and me sitting under the tree. The emotions dissipate from my head, and only my own pain remains. I slowly lower my hands from my ears and wrap them through Varg's thick fur.

I tell Jack what happened, including the part about Varg disappearing in mid-air.

As I recount the events, he shudders and wraps his arm around my back. I lean my head on his shoulder and just soak in his warmth for a bit.

"I'm sorry I freaked out," I whisper. "I had a bad time at the fire scene, and then all this pain and anger was inside my head from everyone's injuries. Everything hits me so much stronger now, and I'm just not used to it. I didn't open my sixth sense, and I could still feel everything so clearly."

Jack strokes my back and I suddenly feel uncomfortable. He keeps giving me pity affection and I don't want it. I pull away from him and struggle to stand up. My injured leg shakes a little, but I make my voice strong and clear. "Well, we knew something like this was going to happen, and it's fine now. I better get home to take care of this wound."

"Blue," Jack croaks.

I refuse to look at him; that will just break me down again. Instead, I brush off my pants and limp toward my car. "It's my left thigh, so I'm fine to drive. I'm going home for the day. I'll write up a report in the morning."

When I reach the car, I glance back at Jack. He's still sitting by the tree with one knee bent and his forehead in his hand.

I call out, "Thanks for having Oliver tail me and help out. We might have been okay, but then again, we might not have."

Jack lifts his head and a small smile crosses his face.

I sit down, gingerly arrange my legs in front of me, and drive off.

CHAPTER 38

ALWAYS AND NEVER

BLUEBELL KILDARE

JULY 15, 2022, RED AGES

B lue, you don't look your best," says the concerned voice from my chimerator.

That's Alexis: always frank. "I know. I was shot, but not badly."

Her eyes grow soft and worried, like when she's taking care of stray animals. "Where? How long and deep? How much blood?"

"On the edge of my thigh. It's about five inches long and very shallow. Like half the width of a bullet. But the skin is missing from there."

Alexis winces. "And how much did it bleed?"

"Well, it didn't gush, really, and I'm not faint or weak or anything. But it did bleed through three bandages. It's stopped now."

Her eyebrows draw together. "I'll close up shop and come take care of it."

"No! You'll do no such thing. If you could just bring home whatever I need, that'll be fine. This bandage will hold."

"You already have everything you need. The salve I gave you for Varg works just as well on humans. It's an antibiotic that's charmed to speed up healing. What you need to do is clean the wound out with plenty of sterile water. That means boil it for fifteen minutes—no regular tap water! Wash your hands well before you touch the wound. After it's clean, let it dry. Then apply the salve. You'll need butterfly bandages to bring the edges of the skin together. You'll want to apply a bandage over the whole thing to keep it clean."

"Okay, I think I can manage that."

Her eyes crinkle in concern. "Are you sure you don't want to get it stitched up? It's gonna leave an awful scar."

"I'm so tired, Alexis. It's been a terrible day and I just can't take one more thing. I'm going to clean this up and then crash. How about I stop by your place tomorrow morning, and you can tell me if it needs stitches?"

Her expression softens. "Okay." Then her eyes become fierce again. "Sterile!" she reminds me. "Everything must be sterile!"

With that, I flip my chimerator closed and limp to my bedroom. I grab a clean pair of little black workout shorts and a tank top, then hobble to the bathroom and undress.

Clearly shower water isn't sterile, and Alexis' command echoes in my mind, so I guess it's a sponge bath for me tonight.

In front of the sink I complete my ablutions, cautious not to drip any non-sterile water onto the wound. I may forever see tap water as non-sterile. Curse her.

When I'm reasonably clean, I slip on my clothes and limp to the kitchen to heat a big kettle of water. Varg comes in and sniffs at the wound, but I shoo him away. Last thing I need is for him to lick it. That certainly isn't sterile.

Eventually when the water's cooled to a reasonable temperature, I gather my supplies and take them back into the bathroom.

The searing pain is gone, but the throbbing, pulsing feeling is getting worse, not better. I wash my hands thoroughly, then stand in the bathtub with my leg up on the side, and pour the water over my wound. I suck in my breath; it hurts so bad. I spread the skin out and keep pouring. I can't help the moan of pain that escapes.

Someone knocks on my door. I gnash my teeth when I hear Jack's voice. "Blue, are you okay?"

"Not a good time, Jack," I yell across my apartment.

He curses under his breath, then demands, "Let me in. I can help."

I yell again, "I'm in the bathroom cleaning my wound. You'll have to let yourself in."

Before I have a chance to blink, he's standing in the bathroom doorway.

I take a deep breath and start pouring the water into the wound again, stretching it out, trying to clean every nook and cranny.

He visibly winces. "That needs stitches."

"I'm not going to the hospital. I can't handle feeling any more pain today, and that place is loaded with it. I'm tired and I'm going to bed."

"It'll scar."

"I'm not vain."

"It could get infected."

"I have antibiotic salve."

"I could give you some of my blood," he offers in a strained voice.

That gets my attention. My entire leg is shaking from the pain coursing through it and all the wonderful ways he could give me that blood start swirling around in my thoughts. But I remain firm.

"This isn't serious enough to warrant that," I say. "It'll heal just fine."

Jack steps into the bathroom. "It wouldn't take much, and you would be healed right away, so your training wouldn't be interrupted."

Now, that does warrant some consideration. Especially after today, it's clear how important my training is.

His voice, deep and soft, entices me. "It won't hurt a bit."

I protest, trying to talk myself out of it. "But that seems an excessive waste of the total lifetime allotment of Vampire blood I can have before turning, don't you think?"

Jack leans casually against the wall, but I can see the tension underlying his move. It sits just under the surface, wild and restrained. "That has to be your choice. But I offer it gladly."

I feel the weight of the kettle in my hand. It's still half full of the torturous sterile water. Jack, is all gorgeous and hunky, leaning against my wall in his shirtsleeves with the cuffs rolled up. His concerned eyes bore into mine.

Pain on the one hand, sexy Vampire on the other. Knowing myself a fool, I whisper, "Okay."

Jack takes the kettle from my hand and scoops me up in his arms.

"I can walk." I protest.

"Shh," he breathes into my hair. "Let me help you." He effortlessly carries me into the living room, where he sits on the sofa and sets me on his lap with my injured thigh facing out. His hard body underneath me feels so delicious.

His voice husky, he asks, "Where do you want it? My wrist? My finger?" He pauses. "My lip?"

All those delicious possibilities. It's almost enough to make me forget the throbbing in my thigh. But I know my answer. "Your lip."

Jack's pupils dilate at my response. His eyelids drop lazily, roving over my face. He runs a hand down the side of my neck, soft as a feather. "Are you ready?"

"I think I am."

"Let's be sure," he whispers. Then he lowers his head and gently nibbles at my lips, running his tongue across the seam, begging them to part.

And they do. Willingly. Gladly. He takes full advantage. His arm tightens around me, and his other arm strokes my breasts through my tank top, brushing against my nipple. He teases it with the lightest touch until it strains for more.

Jack deepens his kiss, and I intertwine my fingers with his hair, trying to pull myself closer to him. Slowly, he disengages his mouth, but still he strokes my breast. Hot strains of desire shoot to my core, burning me. Enflaming me.

He pulls back and captures my eyes. Then his fangs descend, and he bites his lower lip. I move in. I take his lip between mine and suckle it, accepting what he offers. A tingling heat begins to build all over my body. Jack pulls back and bites again as the first piercing is already healed. And again I take from him, bringing his lip between mine. This time, my sensation is so heightened that every nerve ending sings with desire.

Jack deepens the kiss, delving into my mouth with his tongue, taking command. He leaves me breathless, wanting. I reach out and run my hands up and down his chest, desperate to feel him. Jack rips his mouth way from mine and tracks hot, hungry kisses across my jaw. Then he suckles my neck right over my jugular, smelling my skin and laving it with his tongue.

"Jack," I ask, "do you want to . . . " I don't know the right thing to say. Bite me? Feed from me?

Jack pulls back, his eyes half closed, hot with desire. His hands on either side of my face capture me. Hold me. He groans, "Yes, I want to taste you. Always. But I won't. Never."

Then he kisses me gently. Small, soft kisses on my forehead, my cheeks. Kisses that speak of affection, not lust, and cools our ardor.

"Soon," he says, "you'll be very sleepy like last time. Just rest, and your body will heal."

"Are you leaving?" I ask.

Jack takes my hand and turns it palm up. He brushes his lips against the center of it. "No, I'll wait till you wake up."

I can already feel myself getting tired. I snuggle into his chest as he caresses my fingers, one by one.

I don't remember falling asleep, but when I wake up, the sun is gone and the apartment is pitch black save for two sets of glowing eyes. I roll over, and Jack's arms tighten around me.

"How long did I sleep?" I ask in the dark.

Jack's voice whispers into my hair, "It's about two o'clock in the morning."

"Jack, you didn't have to stay here the whole time. I thought I'd only sleep for a few minutes like last time."

I can hear the smile in his voice. "You must have been tired. Your thigh is completely healed, by the way."

Then some of the happiness bleeds from his voice as he says, "I should go now."

I scramble to get off of him, but he lifts me up in his arms and carries me to the door. Only then does he let me go. He slides me down his body so every inch of my flesh is pressed against his; leaving no doubt about how much he enjoyed holding me.

"Lock the door behind me," he commands.

And he leaves me alone in the darkness.

Chapter 39

Mistaken Intentions

Jack Tanner

July 16, 2022, Red Ages

I relax in my easy chair, reading a volume of poetry and letting the sounds of the building wash over me. My home library is extensive, but obviously this little apartment can't hold all that, so a few treasured books came with me. It will do for now.

The city birds have started their chorus, and dawn gently approaches. The muffled sounds of Blue padding through her apartment fill me with contentment. My heart thrills to be even this near her.

This is the most peaceful time of the day for me. I can almost forget that a serial arsonist still runs free, Dark Vampire activity is ever-increasing, and tension is running so high in the city it feels like it's about to implode. Almost, but not quite.

I push those thoughts aside as Blue's door opens and her soft footfalls sound down the stairs, following behind the whisper of Varg's pads.

I flip my page back, realizing I was so wrapped up in listening to her that I missed several stanzas. Suddenly, I hear a thud outside the building followed by the soft thumping sound of flesh meeting flesh. Fear strikes my heart. I throw open my window and see a dark form on top of Blue pinning her face down to the sidewalk. The man has his knee in her back, holding her as she wrestles to get away. My vision burns red.

I jump out the window, land on the sidewalk, and launch myself at the body. I grab him from behind and roll him off of Blue. He curls under me and maneuvers to get away. Shockingly, he almost does. I use Vampire speed to flip my position around to his front. I pull back my fist and slam into his gut. The sting of a blade sears my arm at the same time I make impact. A great whoosh escapes his lips as he doubles over in pain at my punch. Ignoring the knife completely, I reach for his throat.

Blue grabs my shoulders and yells, "No! That's Wang! He's training me."

Somehow, through the haze of my violent need to end this male, her voice stays my hands. Sanity returns and I release his neck. My vision focuses, and it is indeed Wang His bloodshot eyes are filled with relief as he catches his breath. With a grunt, I pull the knife out of my arm and rip off my shirt to apply pressure to the wound.

I stand up and offer Wang a hand. No wonder Varg had been sitting idly by.

"Is this a common practice?" I ask Wang.

Wang bends over, still trying to catch his breath, and his voice rasps out, "She is ill-prepared for a sudden attack. So we attack when she least expects it."

"Sorry about that. I didn't see it was you. I should have realized it when you almost got free from my hold. But now that I've got you here, I've been meaning to check on how training is coming. Do you mind if I stop by soon to observe?"

Wang, still short of breath but managing to stand now, says, "Yes, that's a good idea."

Blue stamps her boot in outrage. "That's it? You almost kill a man and get stabbed, and all you do is ask to watch me train?"

"It was just a mistake. If you were faced with a real attacker, Wang would be glad I stepped in. His windpipe isn't crushed. Both Wang and I will survive. I'll stop in and check on your training tomorrow."

She shoots me a deathly glare. "Is that necessary?"

I tilt my head toward Blue. "I won't be critical. I'm just interested."

She stares at the ground and bites her lip in that delicious way. "I didn't think you'd be critical. I just have a long way to go, that's all."

"All learning starts somewhere. I just want to take a peek." Then I turn and walk back inside, holding my shirt to the wound.

I slide into my chair with a grunt, my bare back sticky against the leather. The wound is deep but narrow, and I'm well fed, so it should take but a few minutes to heal.

This time of morning is the worst, after Blue has left and I still have hours to wait to see her again in the office. I relax in my easy chair and pick up my volume of poetry, but for some reason the lyrical words now seem as flavorless as sawdust.

CHAPTER 40

AN UGLY FUTURE

BLUEBELL KILDARE

JULY 16, 2022, RED AGES

As I sift through my pile of report paperwork on the attack yesterday, Jack appears in my doorway, tense, eyes glittering with introspection. All in all though, he's none the worse for his morning stabbing. If it weren't for that whole bloodlust and Plane of Fire thing, being a Vampire wouldn't be too bad.

"Yes?"

"As you know, out of the six attackers from last night, only one was released from the hospital: Fred Moore. We've been interrogating him, and we're coming up empty. I was hoping you'd give him a shot."

I stand up. "I'd love to." I grab Fred's file off my desk, reading his profile sheet as I follow Jack out of my office.

The interrogation rooms are below ground, across the hall from the magically reinforced holding cells. On the way downstairs, Jack explains what they've learned so far. "He's admitting his part, but when we try to find out who directed him or why they wanted you, he says he can't say."

We reach the stairwell and Jack presses his hand on the hand pad. When the magical scanner recognizes his essence, the door opens. We push through the heavy wards into the cement stairwell itself. "And have you offered him any bargains?"

Jack rubs the back of his neck with his hand and grimaces. "Yes, we've offered him all kinds of bargains, but he still says he can't say anything."

"Is he in his right mind? That doesn't sound rational in his situation."

We reach the bottom floor and when Jack is properly identified by the scanner, we enter a wide, cinder block hallway, stretching deep into the earth. Jack passes the Daylight Vampire on guard and takes a quick right toward the interrogation rooms.

In the dimly lit viewing room, I see Fred Moore through the one-way mirror. He's the man Oliver took out. "How did Oliver knock him out?" I ask Jack.

"He punched him in the jaw. A quick jab will rattle the brain against the skull and cause a knockout."

I frown at that. "Do you think that may be why he's not talking?"

Jack shakes his head. "He's perfectly cognizant of everything else."

Fred Moore, wearing a bright green prison robe, is slumped over the interview table with his head resting on his cuffed hands. Ernesto sits opposite him, leaning back in his graceful manner as he contemplates Fred. I slip into the room, leaving Varg in the viewing area, and Ernesto stands to give me his chair.

Fred utters a long snore, and from this angle, I can see drool coming out the side of his mouth. Ernesto moves behind him and shakes him gently. I say, "Fred, wake up. It's time to wake up."

Fred's head jerks up, and his eyes widen when he sees me. I'm sure he wasn't expecting a female, and definitely not me. He turns away and wipes his chin with his cuff.

"I'm sorry," he says. "I didn't get any sleep last night."

"Well, normally I'd feel for you, but you and your armed buddies were trying to load me into a van yesterday, so I don't have a lot of sympathy."

His brain must be functioning now because here comes the hate, spilling out of him. "You're an Aberrant," he spits.

"And what has a Gifted person ever done to you to inspire such hate?"

He scowls. "Plenty. They take our jobs. They commit crimes against us. They defile the House of God."

Well, that reply was honest. He actually thinks our existence hurts him in those ways. "So in other words, they've done nothing to hurt you personally that Norms have not also done?"

Fred wrinkles his nose, his dislike of the Gifted still abundantly clear.

"Well, Fred, luckily I'm not here for a debate on breedism. I understand you already admitted you attacked me and tried to get me into the van. Was the rope in there to tie me up?"

Fred glares at me hatefully. "Yes."

Truth.

"And you were anticipating that I'd have my wolf with me? That's why one guy had the dart gun?"

"Yes, we knew you'd have the unnatural beast."

Another truth.

"If I'd gotten in that van, where would you have taken me?"

Fred's eyebrows draw together, and his throat works like he wants to speak. Then he spits out, "I can't say"

Truth. He really can't say.

"You know, you've been offered some very lenient deals if you cooperate. So tell me: who asked you to put me in the van, Fred?"

Again Fred tries to work his throat to speak, his eyebrows lower and his eyes narrow in his frustration. But all that comes out is, "I can't say."

Truth, accompanied by a lot of confusion.

I lean back in my chair and think about this for a moment. "Fred, I understand you have a wife and daughter."

A wave of fierce protectiveness fills the room. Good. I can work with that. "How will they support themselves while you're rotting away in jail?"

Now worry pours out of him.

"How long do you think your wife will wait before she asks for a divorce?"

Now, fear and jealousy take the lead. But his face is disdainful. "She'd never do that."

"Well, she can't let your daughter starve just because you're being loyal to someone who asked you to harm me. You'd want her to find someone to help support your daughter, wouldn't you?"

The jealousy transforms into unadulterated rage.

"Oh, I'm sure your wife supports your hatred of Aberrants. But now that you're caught, it's a different story. Food has to be put on the table. Hopefully, whoever she finds won't mistreat your daughter. Not all men like caring for children who aren't theirs. How long before your savings run out, Fred? Six months? A year? And how long are you going to be incarcerated if you don't cooperate? Five to ten years?"

Fred glares at me with spiteful eyes, but all the while, his mind is spinning as I show him the potential future.

"But maybe you're right. Some women aren't very practical. Some are flaky and don't manage their households well. They hardly notice their kids and wouldn't care much if they missed meals."

I lean forward and ask with exquisite deliberateness, enunciating every syllable, "So Fred, tell me: is your wife . . . the practical sort?"

He snarls and stands up. And I've got him. His wife is very much the practical sort. Women are usually practical creatures, especially when it comes to feeding their children. He obviously underestimates a woman's resourcefulness though, but that's fine with me at this moment.

Ernesto calmly places his hands on Fred's shoulder and pushes him back into his seat.

Now I lace my voice with empathy. "Actually, I believe you Fred. I believe you can't tell me who ordered the capture, why they did it, or where they wanted to take me. I believe that when you say you can't, you really can't."

I know that Fred hates magic, so I use that to my advantage as I chip away at his loyalty to whoever's bidding he's doing. "Whoever it was put some sort of *magic* spell on you. But why would someone put a spell on you? Clearly it wasn't for your benefit; it was for theirs."

Now Fred's eyebrows furrow, and his emotions bleed confusion. He vacillates between feelings of loyalty and betrayal.

I let disappointment drip with every word. "But still, you can't tell us anything. So, I guess we'll have to give the plea deal to one of the other five guys when they get out of the hospital later today. At least we'll save one marriage."

I stand up to leave.

"Wait! I want to tell you. I just can't."

I frown in pity. "I'm sorry one of your Holy brothers has spelled you to protect themselves. You physically can't tell us who it was. What can we do?" Then I hesitate, letting the fear and desperation coming out of him culminate to their highest point. When the time is just right, I offer the alternative. "Unless . . . maybe the spell doesn't keep you from telling us details about this person."

His eyes brighten.

"Let's test this. What color is their hair?"

Fred sits there a minute, then says, "Blond."

"Very good, Fred. Ernesto is going to sit down with you now and get all the details you're able to give in exchange for a bargain. The more details you can give, the better your deal. Think about how long your savings will last."

Then I start to walk out of the room. But at the last minute I turn around. "Fred, one more thing. You tried to hurt me yesterday. You committed a crime against me. And I, this awful, horrible, evil person who you hate, just had mercy on you. Your religious fanatic brother who spelled you, though? He tried to get you canned up in here for five to ten to save his own hide. Remember that."

I know that fell on deaf ears, but I feel better anyway. Jack is grinning from ear to ear when I enter the viewing room, and I can't help but smile a bit too.

"He was under a compulsion spell, so he couldn't share any of the big details—who, why, where. But Ernesto should be able to get a lot out of him."

"Excellent work, Blue."

"Now the question that I have is, what bigwig at the Dilectus Deo is buying spell-caster services? Or maybe he's Gifted himself?"

CHAPTER 41

TASK FORCE

BLUEBELL KILDARE

JULY 16, 2022, RED AGES

As I walk past Rubalia's desk after lunch, I notice two strangers wearing SIB IDs sitting in the lounge area. When I ask for messages, Rubalia hands me some faxes and says, "Jack will be with you in a moment."

As soon as I sit down and start reviewing the documents, Jack and Mike enter my office. Their expediency does not bode well. Nor does their coming in force. Nor do their sour expressions. I brace myself.

Jack, always fast with the facts, says, "There were two arson attacks last night. A family of four and a family of three."

"Cripes!"

He says, "It's happening too fast for us to investigate, so we're pulling together a task force, borrowing from other districts. We need to analyze every detail of the lives of these families. I want to know everything about them and everything they were doing in the week before the fires."

"Who's on the team?"

Mike says, "I gave my list of candidates to Rubalia early this morning. She's already called a few in, and they're waiting for you. You and Jack will screen them and make the final decisions."

That must be who was sitting in the waiting room. "Okay, then. Let's get started."

Jack and I spend the rest of the day interviewing fifteen candidates and familiarizing our final four selections with the case. Yepa Estrada is the youngest of our crew, having just come on the force a year ago. She's our tech guru. Sidney Prichett is our analytics expert. Oscar Wiley and Marian Walter are in general investigations.

Both have some psychology education, so they'll assist with the extensive interviews.

Gambino arrives at six o'clock and joins our team in a makeshift war room so Jack can lay out the facts of the cases. When he finishes, I hand out the initial assignments.

"Yepa, we need each family's phone records, plus anything you can get off of their Internet accounts. We want the who, where, and when. You'll feed that data to Sidney."

I turn to Sidney. "First we need you to track the movements of the victims on the day of the fire and as far back as a week to see if you find any similarities among them. You'll use their phone records, credit card receipts, and any info we get from the interviews."

"Oscar and Marian, you'll help me with the interviews. We'll want details on anyone they might have been with that day, how they were feeling, any major life problems they might have had. You'll feed relevant information to Sidney as well. If anything sounds even remotely suspicious or important, I want to be brought into the interview. You can interrupt me at any time."

I survey the room and everyone seems fired up and ready to roll.

"One more thing, at yesterday's fire, I sensed a third person had been in the home on the day of the fire. We need to find that person as quickly as possible so I can interview them."

Jack suggests, "It would be best if we met daily for updates and to exchange information. How's noon?"

"Sounds like a plan."

CHAPTER 42

BLINDFOLDED

JACK TANNER

July 17, 2022, Red Ages

I can't take my eyes off Blue. Her tight black pants and sports bra leave nothing to the imagination. The sight of her damp hair and the sheen of perspiration covering her naked skin is nothing short of arresting, but the blindfold is puzzling.

I'm intrigued. I move closer.

Wang calls out, "Greetings, Jack. Right now we're working on Blue's ability to use her sixth sense to detect an opponent and anticipate the direction of an attack. I'll be attacking her, and she'll have to put me on the defensive."

Blue tenses up when she hears Wang call my name. Then she visibly shakes herself loose and widens her stance.

Wang throws a punch at her face. My fangs descend. But she anticipates the move, bringing her left arm up in a block. My panic subsides. She hooks his arm with her arm, pushing it away. I'm amazed. She throws a sharp jab at his middle, all the while blindfolded. Then they break.

Wang moves in again, grabbing her left shoulder with his right arm. Blue braces herself, knows it's coming. Sweeps her arm in, blocking. Hooks his arm. Twists it to the side. She puts her hand below his chin and pushes up, tilting his head backwards. Control the head, control the man. She steps back into position.

Wang circles around her. She spins, following his movement. He reverses direction. She mirrors him. He sweeps her with a roundhouse kick toward her stomach. I clench my fists, but she scoops his leg up with her arm and plows into his stomach with her other fist.

Time after time Wang circles her and attacks her, but she's able to anticipate the move and tag or block him almost every time. Wang is fast, and Blue drips sweat in exertion, but she manages to keep up.

I'm astounded she's working blindfolded. Naturally, I didn't come here thinking she'd defeat a seasoned warrior, but the fact that she's able to handle his moves at all is amazing, especially without sight. A Vampire's night vision gives them a great advantage over Norms and Gifted and she's just annihilated that advantage.

After a few more runs of this, Wang indicates she can take the blindfold off for the next set of rounds.

They face off again, and it's apparent that Blue's performance is about the same with or without the blindfold. Fascinating. That means she can see her attacker as well with her sixth sense as she can with her eyes open. She's already advanced to a point where she'd likely defeat the average male Gifted or Norm. All this improvement pleases me immensely.

When they finish, Wang and Blue bow to each other and he releases her from training for the moment. She runs over to me with lithe grace, her eyes shining with a mixture of pride and humility. "I'm not that good yet, but I know I could have beat Blackwater if I knew then what I know now."

I can't help but smile back at her timid boast. "I bet you could have. How are you enjoying it?"

She beams even wider. "It's hard work, and I hate the conditioning, but I love the fighting. Yao and Wang are starting to teach me knife moves too." She pulls her knife out and flips it. It spins up three times before descending, and she catches it deftly.

Wang joins us. "We're teaching her a variety of long-range and close-up techniques. We've sacrificed concentration on form perfection to pack in as many forms and techniques as possible."

"What's her training schedule?"

"She starts with a run, then completes an hour of strength training. We work forty-five minutes on Jiu-Jitsu and forty-five minutes on Taekwando. She has to practice at home every evening as well. The rest of the time is divided between shooting practice, knife throwing, knife fighting techniques, and a variety of other weapons. We've also covered a segment on survival techniques, including Morse code and navigation. Down the road we'll add strategic battle planning."

This all sounds good, but it still isn't enough. "Right now Blue's at risk from Norms, Gifted, Daylight Vampires, and Dark Vampires. The Jiu-Jitsu and the Taekwondo are good arts to use against the Gifted and Norms. Her knife provides mortal wounds to Daylight Vampires. But she has nothing against Dark Vampires besides her light and holy water. I don't think we should depend on that. I'd feel better if she were trained with an oak staff and stakes. I also have a Hallowed Hazer on order for her."

Blue interjects, "I'm right here, guys. You don't need to speak about me as though I'm not." She turns to me. "Why should I be concerned about Daylight Vampires specifically?"

I gentle my eyes. "There are too many Daylight Vampires surrounding you, and too many are turning Dark. I'm sure you don't need me to remind you how they turn. They seem drawn to you."

"I see. I hadn't thought of that."

I'm glad she's taking the threat seriously. "Well, I'm headed to the office. I'll see you in a few hours."

Before I turn to go, I capture her eyes for a moment and smile. "You're progressing well, Blue. You should be proud."

Her eyes shine as she absorbs my words.

CHAPTER 43

BEPPE'S BAKERY

BLUEBELL KILDARE

JULY 17, 2022, RED AGES

till whirling from the feelings of pride and affection I felt from Jack earlier, I settle in the car to head for the office. He really was proud of me despite how weak I must seem compared to him. As I hit downtown, traffic starts to congest and my foot itches to push the gas. Suddenly the line of cars in front of me comes to a full and complete stop. My tires squeal as I slam on my breaks.

Impatiently, I unroll the windows for fresh air and tap my irritation on the dash.

From the back seat, Varg lets out a vicious growl, and he isn't playing. He bares his teeth and drool drips from his jaw. While I crane my neck to see what's going on around the line of cars, he leaps out of the window and plants himself by my door. What the . . . ?

I manage to pull the car into the parking lane and get out. I step over the curb and follow the sidewalk forward, trying to see what's got him so riled up. But Varg keeps shouldering past me, making this task more difficult than it should be. His behavior is unnerving, so I keep my hand hovering close to my Glock. I glimpse a truck with flashing lights surrounded by construction horses a few blocks up. Someone lays on the horn.

Small storefronts line the street, most with residential apartments in the stories above them. Three display windows are boarded up on this street alone, and breedist grafitti prominently decorates each one. A group of five men stroll down the street toward us, dressed in nice business suits. One man seems to be doing all the talking while the rest wear dour expressions. While they don't appear to be interested in me, Varg growls all the louder.

I put my hand on my Glock and slip into a shop's entry alcove to let them pass. As they get closer, I catch feelings of tense excitement, like they're thrill seekers, which in my experience is a very dangerous feeling. It's often accompanied by erratic or risky behavior. Unfortunately, they don't pass. Instead, they pivot at the entryway and move to block me in. Two men block the sides of the alcove and two men step toward me pulling out guns.

I pull my gun just as fast. Cripes. I must be the most wanted woman in town.

The man who I thought was talking stands in the middle. It turns out he isn't talking at all. He's muttering a continual, low chant. I press my alert button and set my sights on him.

One of the men holding a gun speaks politely. "Miss Kildare, we'd like you to come with us."

I swing my gun toward him while Varg growls, getting ready for the attack.

Irritated at this stranger's nerve, I sass back, "That's Inspector Kildare to you, and I'd like your men to step aside."

In an overly congenial voice, he replies, "I'm afraid I can't do that. I have orders to bring you with us."

I grit my teeth. "Orders by whom and to bring me where?"

One of the men on the side starts to work another spell. His high-pitched chanting echoes through the alcove. Cripes. There is no way I'm going with them willingly, but I'm afraid whatever he's chanting for won't give me the option. I'm not fast enough to take out both gunmen before they can attack me.

My sixth sense catches the soul of another person behind me, on the other side of the business. Shit. The door creaks as it swings open.

I spin toward the person, and my jaw drops as a giant of a man steps out next to me. He's wearing an apron covered in flour and holding an impressively thick twelve gauge, double barrel, sawed-off shotgun aimed toward the center of the group.

His face red with fury, he snaps, "Get behind me."

Since his gun is aimed at them, I oblige, but I swing my aim at the second chanter from slightly to the side of my giant.

My flour-covered titan threatens in a low rumble, "Magic guys, you chant one more thing, and I'll blow you all to smithereens. This gun will get you all in one shot."

The chanters' faces pale, and they grow silent. I can't help smiling in satisfaction.

"Hoonnkk." The traffic noise filters through and I realize it's continued unabated all along, but the chanter was blocking it. I glare at him but my ears are all for my champion.

My giant's blood vessels pop out from his forehead, and his temple pulses with his rage. He bellows, "Now, I'm sick and tired of these breedist fights. This lady—"

I interject softly, "SIB Officer."

"This SIB Officer was minding her own business when you guys pulled guns on her. I saw the whole thing. I've had three businesses in my row close up because of you idiots, fighting over breeds. And I'll tell you, I'm not having it."

He's a man full of righteous indignation. Not someone I'd want to mess around with.

His temple throbs violently now, and his lips curl. "With one shot, I'll get every one of you and be glad to do it. Now I'm counting to three, and you'd better drop your guns and be out of here, or I'll blast you out of here. You got me?"

"One." The guns are dropped.

"Two." The men turn and run.

"Three." The men disappear completely into thin air.

I flip open my chimerator, and Jack's worried visage appears. "Jack, The crisis is over. I'm at . . . "

I look behind me for the business' sign. "Beppe's Bakery. But an escort out of here would be nice. It was a group of Gifted men. They used a diversion spell to disappear, so they could still be around."

Jack curses, then says, "I'll be there in a few minutes."

Beppe, hearing me, steps out onto the sidewalk, searching right and left, up and down. He points his weapon everywhere he turns.

Jeez, he's going to shoot someone with the way he's swinging that thing around. I should get him inside.

"Are you Beppe?"

His face is still red with rage, but he seems less likely to have a stroke now. "Yes, Ma'am."

"Thanks so much for your help. My boss is coming to escort me to work. Do you mind if my animal and I wait inside?"

Some of his tension drains. "Sure, sure. Come on in."

Beppe swings the door open for us so that Varg and I can precede him.

Hopeful, I ask, "Do you happen to have a surveillance camera?"

Beppe presses his lips together. "Had it installed last month when my neighbors started getting harassed. The place is warded too."

"Great. Can I get a copy of that recording?"

"Sure thing." He strides behind the counter and through a doorway.

While Varg and I wait, I survey the place. Delicate white curtains hang open from the front windows. A table sits in each window alcove, decorated with red gingham tablecloths. The walls are butter yellow and the floor is tiled in terracotta. But it's his glass-front countertop that snags my attention.

It's sin under glass. Orange Italian cream cakes, sweet ricotta pies, and, glory of glories, a six-layer cassata. An entire case is filled with lavish Italian desserts, and next to it is the pastry case: napoleons, lemon and pistachio biscotti, cannoli, fig cookies, and so much more.

Beppe comes back into the restaurant area, ushering in a waft of fresh-baked lemon something. I can't help it; my stomach gurgles. He hands me the quartz recording. I slip the gem into my vest pocket and continue to drool.

"Thank you so much, Beppe. You've been so much help already, but could I trouble you for one of those cannoli? I'm happy to pay whatever you ask. My first born child?" I ask hopefully.

Beppe leans back and gives a great, booming laugh, then leans forward again clutching his stomach. I'm astounded. I didn't know that amount of mass could be that flexible. When he straightens, he says, "It's on the house."

He places his shotgun on top of the glass counter and serves up a cannoli on a white porcelain dish. He finishes it with a triple shot of espresso with a strong nutty aroma.

Thanking him profusely, I carry my luscious dessert to one of the tables while he tucks the shotgun under his arm again. Between bites of the delicious, creamy, sweet ricotta and perfectly crunchy shell, I say, "I have to be honest, I'm Gifted and so were those guys. It wasn't really a breedist situation.

Beppe's cheeks tinge pink. "I couldn't see your mark through the door." Then he mumbles softly, "Still that's no way to treat a lady."

"So what happened to your neighbors?"

Beppe's jaw starts ticking in anger again. "The Irish Hound, the local pub, was the first to go. Breedist bar fights every night. Conor couldn't keep up with the expense. Then Kristina closed up her resale shop. She said if one more person asked her if the original owner of the dress was a Norm, she was throwing in the towel. And just two days ago the Kountry Kitchen closed its doors. Pamela had two Gifted cooks, and she was getting pressure from her customers to fire them. But Pamela isn't the sort to do that, so she took her business to the suburbs where she hopes things will be different."

Beppe scowls. "Pamela is a fine woman, and the Kountry Kitchen was the best diner around here. I used to eat there every night for dinner. After baking all day, I don't care to cook for myself."

Based on Beppe's emotions, I think he liked more than Pamela's cooking. He feels lonely and sad.

I must blink, because in the next instant, Jack is sitting in the chair opposite me. Beppe picks up his shotgun and aims it at Jack. I try to dive in front of him, while yelling, "No, that's my boss!"

But Jack is too quick for me. He grabs me and pushes me up against the wall with his body between me and Beppe.

Beppe lowers his shotgun, rather abashed.

"Jack, that's Beppe. He helped me out."

Jack looks down at my face, his heated eyes roving over every square inch. I can't help but enjoy the feel of his hard body pressed against mine. Each drag of breath brings in his deep, spicy scent. His thighs are firm against mine, and my breasts ache as they press against his chest. For a moment, I'm lost in the feel of him. Somehow I manage to wrestle my mind back to reality. I'd prefer this happen when we didn't have an audience.

"Jack. You're squishing me."

He steps back. Then he listens to my quickly recited blow-by-blow of what happened, and several grunts later, he's shaking Beppe's hand.

After they perform their gruff, manly introductions, he turns to me. "Are you ready to go? We're headed to Dragomira's."

"Yeah." I shove the last of my cannoli into my mouth. "Hold on."

I walk over to Beppe, who's absently dusting flour off his apron. I stand on my tip-toes to give him a quick kiss on the side of his jaw, as that's as high as I can reach. I ignore the low rumble issuing from Jack's throat and instead say, "Thank you so much, Beppe. You might have saved my life today. I wish there were more people like you who would stand up to this nonsense."

CHAPTER 44

CONFERRING

BLUEBELL KILDARE

JULY 17, 2022, RED AGES

When we're settled in the car, Jack turns to me and puts his hand on my right cheek. "Hold still," he says in a low voice as he slowly turns my head toward him. He licks his thumb and glides it over my lower lip, then sweeps it up to the corner of my mouth and off my face. He smiles as he presents me with a plop of cannoli filling on his thumb before slowly sucking it off.

My face heats in embarrassment. To cover my tracks, I say, "Hey, that's food. You aren't supposed to eat that, are you?"

He ignores my question and puts the car in gear. "The number of factions after you is ever-increasing. I don't care for you to be out of my eyesight at this point."

I give him a sharp glare, not liking where this is going. But I'm also not liking being attacked at every turn. "So what's our business with Dragomira?"

Jack twists his lips as though he tastes something sour. "We need to confer with her on the Vampire population explosion."

Good. I have a few questions for Dragomira of my own.

When we stride through her door, Dragomira looks up from the counter with a gaze just for me. "I was wondering when you would arrive, Blue." Her eyes flick to Jack. "You are a surprise, though."

Jack states boldly. "I'd like to discuss the Vampire activity with you."

Dragomira locks the door behind us and waves us into the back room. "Fine, fine. But let's get to Blue's questions first. She's late."

Does this woman read minds? How did she know I have a load of burning questions for her? I huff into the seat by the fireplace, barely sparing the beautiful books a loving glance before spearing her with my eyes.

Jack seems curious as he tucks his large, graceful frame into the chair besides me.

While still studying Dragomira, I ask. "How old are you?"

Dragomira blinks. "I'm two thousand and thirty-seven years old."

It's my turn to blink. "That's very old."

Dragomira chuckles. "Indeed."

Jack's eyes flit between us, showing more surprise at my question than her answer. I'm not surprised at his lack of surprise, but I'm also not even warmed up yet. "What are you?"

"You couldn't pronounce the name of my kind with your throat." She leans back. "Suffice it to say, I'm a being of very old, wild magic, and I am a Shifter of sorts."

A Shifter? I've heard about them in fairy tales, but I didn't know they really existed. "What do you shift into?"

She smiles gently. "I shift into a human."

I sit back at that. "So what are you originally?"

Dragomira stares back at me, long and hard now. "Is my original form so very important to you? What will it tell you? That isn't really what you need to know, is it?"

"No, It's not. I need to know how you fit into this story."

Dragomira's deep eyes spark with a ruby red fire, and her expression turns grave. "At the time of the birth of Vampires, my people lived in the Sea Caves on the Isle of Erin. I was but fifteen years old. We were called the Dragon tribe.

"Lilith was angry after her transaction with Patersuco because she wanted the power that was held in the Grimoire. My people's magic is such that we can easily traverse the planes while Lilith is stuck in what you know of as the Plane of Fire, so we were not concerned about her. The Vampires are no threat to us, so we didn't worry about her machinations. But we underestimated her."

I can see that Jack's as wrapped up in this tale as I am. At least some of this must be news to him. His hooded eyes are calculating, and I imagine him reviewing the facts against what he already knows, fitting the pieces together.

"Once it was discovered by the Sorcerer Council that Patersuco used the Grimoire to call Lilith, a meeting was called to discuss how to handle the situation. In those days, the Sorcerer Council was the self-appointed governing body of the Gifted, though no formalized structure was in place. They more or less acted when they felt damage control or punishment was required. In this case, they located the Grimoire and called on the Dragon tribe to guard it while the key was fashioned. A young, powerful Sorcerer by the name of Magi presented the Grimoire to my people for safekeeping. About six months later, Magi came to take the Grimoire back. She was earlier than anticipated, but we didn't find that unusual.

"But once she breeched our safe-hold, she called Lilith."

Dragomira's eyes swirl a deadly black now and a massive storm of rage blasts through the room. "I recall that day well. I was on guard at the entrance of the safe-hold, and my intended, Favnir, was inside. When Favnir broke the silence of the cliffs with his mighty bellow, I left my post to aid him. He stood between Lilith and the Grimoire, and behind that lay the archway to our nursery. Magi had already fallen to Favnir's flame, and Lilith stood opposing him. I tried to get by, but Favnir would have nothing of it. Lilith demanded the Grimoire, and he refused. Then she threw a curse at me, and I quickly evaded it. Without realizing, without thinking . . . "

Dragomira goes still a moment, but her magic flares up and the room physically trembles from the force of her silent fury. Her voice continues, ice cold. "The curse traveled beyond where I was standing and instead of damaging me, it entered the nursery and killed all the young in one blow. Favnir attacked Lilith and bound her so she could not escape him. But that was only his undoing. By then my people started pouring into the hall. Lilith knew she wouldn't get past them all, so she used Favnir's binding against him to bring him with her to the Plane of Fire."

My hands are shaking. "She killed all the babies? She took your fiancé?"

Dragomira blinks, and for a moment the slit pupils of a serpent show in the depth of her eyes. "She killed all our young. Nine in total. Our young are not like yours. It takes over a century for them to come into being." Her voice breaks now, her anguish rising up like a black tide on a moonless night. "She devastated my people."

She clears her throat and with the darkest eyes imaginable, she says, "All my people have gone on to other planes since that Day of Death. I have remained here, though, and traveled to the Plane of Fire countless times to try to free Favnir. His physical binding is no more, but she's bound him in other ways, inconceivable ways, in order to use his power. To release him would mean his death unless Lilith's demise undoes his bindings."

The musty smell of the store invades my consciousness when a knock at the front door breaks through the silence. I move to stand, but Dragomira's hand stays me. She dismisses the sound, and settling down again, I sweep my eyes around the place.

"And so you study to find a way to kill Lilith?"

Dragomira barks a laugh that holds not a hint of amusement. "I began studying for that purpose, but man hasn't written of such things. The only book on this plane that holds that sort of knowledge is the Grimoire, and that book can't be read by such as I." Her eyes pin me. "Mostly I studied to fill my time while waiting for you to be born."

Holy smokes.

"What happened to the Grimoire?"

Her voice lowers in a regretful tone. "When the counsel arrived hot on Magi's heels, and when my elders ascertained they were not in Lilith's grip, it was released into their hands. I was searching for Favnir in the Plane of Fire at the time, or I wouldn't have let it go."

"So were you there when Mor came to the Dragon tribe with baby Sorcha?"

"Yes, Mor came just after my first attempt at releasing Favnir."

It's all clicking into place now. "So you and Lilith are mortal enemies."

Dragomira's eyes flare. "There's nothing mortal about it. Except that I won't divert until she's ended. However, even as our battles coincide, your battle with Lilith is quite different. Lilith wanted the Grimoire to begin with, and now you hold part of the key. Further, you were prophesied to destroy her. I'm sure in her mind the only way you'll destroy her is with the knowledge in the Grimoire, and that may be the case."

Jack sits up now. "And what of all the Dark Vampire activity lately? Is that her doing?"

Dragomira sits back and lowers her eyelids. "To what extent she's driving events, I'm unsure, but Dark Vampires are tied to her. She is certainly pulling those strings in some way."

Jack curls his lips. "They can't even get close to Blue without exploding when her light shines on them."

Dragomira huffs in amusement and her eyes twinkle. "Is that so? I'm sure that has Lilith in a fine mood." Then she captures my eyes and leans forward, her fingers gripping her chair. "Don't rest easy, Blue. Lilith will be sending them after you one way or another. They're her minions, and you're her enemy."

My throat feels thick as I swallow.

Jack cuts in, "Enough. We'll be watching her."

Dragomira leans back, apparently satisfied she's scared me enough.

Jack clears his throat. "Several parties are after Blue. The Dark Vampires and the Dilectus Deo, as we'd expect, but a group of Gifted men accosted her today. I'd put them in the same camp as Blackwater. Out of all of these parties, who do you think has the Grimoire?"

With her hand dragging across her brow, Dragomira considers this. At long last she answers, "Blackwater's group was after the key, so it could be they already hold the Grimoire. A group of Gifted individuals would be most likely to have the skills to have found it. However, it's highly unlikely they've volunteered this knowledge to the Dilectus Deo. So one wonders why the Dilectus Deo are after Blue at all. Perhaps they have one of the three pieces."

She shakes her head. "It's impossible to tell."

I sigh in frustration. "We need more information."

A small smile plays about Dragomira's lips. "There are a few magical artifacts that could help us."

My hope surges.

Dragomira's eyes dance in amusement now. "Oh, don't get too excited. I don't have them on hand."

I refuse to be daunted. "What are they?"

With relish, she describes them. "One is the Rod of Elias. It's a finding tool. Rather like a compass that points north, but instead it points toward what you seek. It would be particularly useful right now. Then there's the Eternal Specula. Specula means 'many mirrors' and it reflects images from times gone by. It can show you where something existed in the past, but never where it is at the moment, nor does it necessarily show you where it was last, so, it's a bit of a treasure hunt. Finally, there's the Pipe of Ogden, Keeper of Wraiths. Those who smoke from it will be shown the item they seek in a dream, but those who seek must have a pure heart or the Wraiths will make sure the seeker never leaves the dream."

Jack, who's been leaning forward in rapt attention, says, "The Rod of Elias sounds most effective. Any idea where any of these artifacts are?"

Dragomira's eyes glaze over as she thinks. "I haven't heard a peep about the Rod of Elias since 400 R.A. The last time I saw the Eternal Specula, it was briefly in the hands of the King of Belantine around the fifteenth century. I'm afraid that isn't helpful either. But the Pipe of Ogden was rumored to be in this area just two centuries ago."

The Pipe of Ogden, Keeper of Wraiths sounds ominous and gives me a chill.

Jack, seeing my shiver, stands. "Well, we need to get to some present day concerns now. We still have a serial arsonist to locate."

CHAPTER 45

POTENTIAL MOTIVE

JACK TANNER

JULY 17, 2022, RED AGES

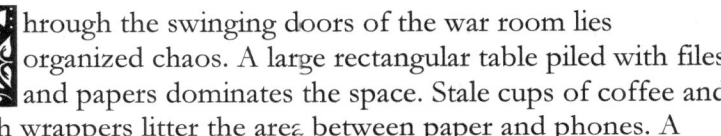hrough the swinging doors of the war room lies organized chaos. A large rectangular table piled with files and papers dominates the space. Stale cups of coffee and leftover lunch wrappers litter the area between paper and phones. A regional map is tacked to the wall, dotted with red indicating deaths: fourteen and counting. It makes me sick.

Blue pores over files while typing busily into a computer. I lean over her shoulder. "How's it going?"

She lifts a hand to still me. "One minute." She finishes a few more keystrokes and turns to Marian, one of the four new recruits.

"Marian, are you done with your piece?"

"Almost," she replies.

I pull out the chair next to Blue. A phone rings, and Yeppa picks it up. Blue sweeps her hair behind her ear and swivels toward me. "We still haven't found any shared relationships between the victims. We've ruled out any purchases at a common place by a thorough analysis of bank statements and receipts. We can't find a common service that might have a connection to them all, beyond utilities, of course. In no instance was there any indication of a break-in or any alarm. All victims seemed to be in bed at the time of the fires."

Blue takes a deep breath, and her eyes hold the first excitement I've seen in days. "But we have found two things. Despite what we thought earlier, the Beck family did have Gifted children, so all families had at least one Gifted child."

Jack slams his hand down on the table, making coffee slosh over the side of Styrofoam cups. "Damn it! I was afraid of that."

"I know."

She looks over at Marian, who gives a nod. Blue stands up, walks to the map, and sets her laptop on a stand nearby. She sticks orange thumbtacks into a few streets and ties string to them.

"We're tracking their movements on the day of the fire," she explains. "Some of the information is uncertain because it's speculation from friends, but other information comes from financial records. The orange tacks are financial records, and the yellow tacks we're less sure of. I'm just showing you orange tacks now."

I watch as Blue lays out the tacks for the four families and then steps back. She taps the board. "Are you seeing what we're seeing?"

"Yes, all but one of those families traveled in the vicinity of downtown Crimson Hollow the day they died. And you're unsure about the fourth. Do they all pass a certain location?"

Blue huffs and sits down. "No, we can't find a common location. But they definitely all cross through Downtown at some point on the day of their respective fires. Further, we've confirmed that for three of the families, passing through downtown wasn't an everyday occurrence." Then she turns to me with bleak eyes. "The Sun Flare Celebration is in four days, and it's right in the middle of Downtown."

The phone in front of Blue rings and she grimaces an apology before picking it up. "Inspector Blue speaking."

I hear the voice on the other end of the line saying, "This is Janice. You called?"

Blue smiles. "Yes, Janice. I had some questions for you, but can you hold on just one minute?"

Blue puts the call on hold. "I have to take this. It's going to be a few minutes."

"Sure. Meanwhile, I'll call the mayor and ask if there's any way he can postpone the festival."

Blue smiles her thanks and switches back to her waiting call.

CHAPTER 46

THE HAG AND HARPY

BLUEBELL KILDARE

JULY 17, 2022, RED AGES

I slide into the booth at The Hag and Harpy and do a visual check on Varg through the window. We had a little talk about coming into establishments when danger wasn't present, and I hope he abides by his side of the agreement.

Mad Molly, looking gorgeous this evening with her purple hair and retro sunflower dress, asks, "What'll it be?"

"Hi, Molly. Tea please, and a basket of your Charming Cheddar Cheese Fries."

Molly chews on the end of her pencil. "You want a pickle with that?"

"Yeah, that would be nice." I hand her my menu and turn to my window vigilance, watching Varg.

Varg sits in the front seat, watching me through the window. Ammon, one of the new Vampire exterminators, steps out of my car and makes himself scarce as soon as Jack, Ernesto, and Xavier arrive. Yep, Ammon is enjoying this little guard detail as much as I am, poor guy. He was brought on to kill Dark Vampires, but instead he's babysitting an Empath.

My co-workers sit down at my table. "Oliver is coming," Jack says.

Oh, this is a surprise. "Has he still been helping us out?"

Jack nods. "Primarily I want him watching the Daylight Vampires who've been tracking you." A twinkle lights his eyes. "He's been helping them keep their distance."

"And today?"

His shoulders shrug. "He has men on the ground who can help with this search."

Goodness knows we have a lot of ground to cover.

Molly saunters over and asks, "What can I get you big boys?"

Xavier orders the Swanky Swiss Burger and passes her his menu. Molly winks at him and says, "I'll make that meat extra thick."

I choke on my coffee and grab for napkins, narrowly avoiding squirting the beverage out my nose. Jack wears an enormous smile, and Ernesto is trying to uphold his dignity with difficulty. After everyone has given their order, Molly crosses the restaurant whistling, the picture of innocence.

I turn to Xavier. "And here I thought she had a thing for Gambino. Are you and Molly personally acquainted, perchance?"

Xavier's eyes play hide and seek with mine as he sits up straighter. "Almost. Not quite, though. Let's discuss the search."

Jack breaks in. "By all means."

Just then, Oliver slips in and takes the end seat. Serious discussion proceeds.

By the time Xavier and I finish our food, and Jack, Ernesto, and Oliver finish their third Bloodvines, sections of Downtown Crimson Hollow have been distributed as we slice up the city in our search— though what we're searching for, we don't know.

Then without warning, the clatter of metal objects crashing together echoes from the kitchen, accompanied by a large crack, like a tree splitting in half. A terrified squeal peals through the air. Everyone in the restaurant, like one united force, turns toward the kitchen.

The next thing I know, I hear a snarling growl from that direction. Holy cow, that sounds like Varg! Jack is already through the kitchen door. I glance through the window, and my stomach drops at the obvious lack of wolf in my front seat.

I push my way through the kitchen doors, following Jack, to find utter chaos. Kitchen equipment is scattered about the room, the sprinklers are on, and a small fire is petering out on the grill. Most conspicuous is Mad Molly with her hair tumbling down her back in wild disarray, standing on a chair with a hairpin in each fist and panting heavily. The alley door is split in half, and Varg unhappily inspects a pile of smoking ash not far from it.

My eye catches on Molly's hairpins. Both are wooden with silver caps on the ends, so they appear purely decorative when enmeshed in her coiffeur. Very clever. "Was it a Dark Vampire?"

Molly's nostrils flare wide. "Normally I can smell them a mile away, but this one didn't have a smell. He was cloaked."

Jack rubs his face with his hand. "That's not good. How'd you kill him?"

Molly pants. "He started smoking, and the sprinkler system has holy water mixed in as a precaution. Then that . . . that"—she points to Varg—"beast came bursting through the door. I thought he was going to eat me."

I move over to Varg and pat him. "He's my wolf. He's as harmless as a dog unless you get on his bad side. He was probably going to try to eat the Dark Vampire. He does that, you know. He doesn't like the way mortals taste."

Molly is slightly mollified, and she takes a tentative step down off the ladder. Then she yells, "Caleb, you coward, come out of the broom closet before I pin you!"

The closet door opens a crack, and a burly man wearing a chef's apron slowly appears.

I pull out my business card. "Molly, I'm so sorry about your door. I assure you Varg was only coming to your rescue. Please call me when you get it repaired and I'll take care of the bill."

"Oh, he didn't break the door. The Dark Vampire did."

Xavier steps up beside Molly and lays his hand on her shoulder. She gives him a glare and shrugs him off. "A little too late for that, Cowboy." She sniffs.

After helping Molly straighten up a bit, we have to get started on our search. As we leave the kitchen, I shiver at the busted door. I guess Dragomira was right. Lilith would find a way to get them close to me.

CHAPTER 47

RIPPING AT THE SEAMS

BLUEBELL KILDARE

JULY 17, 2022, RED AGES

ack and I head for the northeast quarter of downtown, walking past all the advertisements for the Sun Flare Celebration. We pass Memorial Park, the site of the celebration, where a bunch of kids crowd around a vendor cart waiting to get balloons with the Sun Flare logo on them. I sure hope the mayor considers pushing the date back.

I imagine that without me cramping his style, Jack could have this search done in no time. But this really isn't about finding anything in particular because we don't know what we're looking for. It's more about seeing something that we haven't noticed before.

We pass the train station and cross over the tracks. "You know, Jack, most of those families were just enjoying their day, doing family things: visiting the library, going shopping, eating out at a restaurant. All normal things."

"They didn't stop to eat lunch at the same spot or anything?" he inquires.

"No, of course it's not that simple. They weren't even all on the same street."

We cross over Scagglethorpe Street, and I'm arrested by the number of boarded up buildings on this road alone. Graffiti is everywhere. "Is all this vandalism recent?"

His deep voice responds sorrowfully. "Most of it, yes."

"Who's handling all these cases? Does the SIB have enough help in the regular Crimes Division?"

"They're working closely with the precinct, and they've brought help in from other cities."

I notice the porch of the boarded-up house I'm passing is filled with children's toys. A red wagon lies overturned near the sidewalk with a doll caught underneath, like the victim of a vehicular accident. I pause to turn the wagon right-side up and gently place the doll on the porch, where at least it can stay out of the rain.

Jack waits patiently for me on the sidewalk. With a backwards glance, I wonder if the homeowners will ever be back.

The moonlight dapples the sidewalk through the cover of old oaks and maples. A few lush magnolias grace some lucky yards. Summer is in full swing, and the breeze is hot and sticky tonight. The soft murmur of Varg's padded paws follows the silent footfalls of my new rubber-soled boots. Yao had a fit about my boots a few weeks back and insisted I replace them. It's a welcome change. I glare at Jack's shoes, but I suspect that with the way his muscles perfectly support his body, he would be completely silent even in wooden clogs.

My training with Yao and Wang is paying off because I notice every bird, cat, and mouse in hearing distance. I watch Varg's ears and nostrils flare. He certainly senses more physically than I can, but we're in accord far more than we used to be.

We pass Crooked Creek Road and Willow Avenue. My eyes dart to and fro searching for anything unusual. All I see are front yards, many neglected but some still tended. Even the manicured yards have a closed-up feel to them, as if everyone is hunkered down waiting for a storm. Normally on a fine summer evening I'd expect to see families on their porches with late-night beverages, watching over children catching fireflies. Sadness fills my heart.

Next to me, Jack tenses and Varg jumps forward to block my way. Immediately more alert, I listen carefully, but whatever they heard must be far beyond my senses.

Jack murmurs, "This way," and leads me through an alley. We quickly cover about six blocks when I hear the first of the shouting.

"You piece of shit Norm! Come closer and say that to my face."

"Freak!"

Then a mix of young voices rise at once, obscenities flying. Jack and I round a bend, and Varg dashes into the middle of an impending street fight. On one side, a boy whirls a heavy chain threateningly in the air. Three boys are spread out behind him with wide stances and pain infliction on their minds. On the opposite side, a single boy, loosely dangling a baseball bat from his muscular grip, curls his lip.

Jack becomes a blur before my eyes, and in a flash he's holding both baseball bat and chain. "What's going on here, boys?" He says to me, "Chime Ammon."

When I've got Ammon's visage reflecting off my chimerator, I give him our coordinates. Varg has his paws full shepherding the extra boys to make sure they don't get away while Jack holds the two leaders in place by their ears.

"What's going on, Jack?" I ask.

"Looks like a little gang fight. These boys take exception to each other's heritage."

I switch my scrutiny from one boy to the next. They seem about high-school age and should be busy with sports and homework, not rough-housing on the street. "Have you guys always fought, or has this just started?"

Chain Boy averts his gaze. Baseball Boy spits on the ground and says, "Ain't talking to no Aberrant bitch."

I'm not sure who growls first, Jack or Varg, but luckily they're both too occupied to beat the crap out of the idiot. The amount of fear and anger emanating from both boys is enormous.

From Baseball Boy, the bigger of the two, I sense a little guilt, but not much. So I switch to him. "Well, when did you begin to hate each other?"

He sneers at the boy across from him. "I never liked him much, but since he beat the shit out of my friend who wasn't doing anything, I made it my personal mission to kick his ass the hell out of my town."

That small waft of guilt is completely gone now. There's nothing like vengeance to wipe empathy totally out of existence.

Chain Boy, who's skinnier and older, stares back with defiance and little guilt. "No freak is going to push me out of my town."

I hold up my hand. "Enough boys. I get it. You both own this town, and the other person is a piece of garbage while you're a specimen of deserving humanity. I've heard the same song a million times."

Just then two cars pull up, and Ammon and Gambino join us in the street. They secure Chain Boy's cronies first, then take the leaders off Jack's hands and load them into the cars. After a briefing they drive off.

I kick a rock on the sidewalk. "Jack, this town is falling apart at the seams. We'll never stem this rage. A few months ago that would have likely been harmless name calling, and now they bring bats and chains into it."

Jack runs his hands through his hair. "I know, but we can only do so much. For now, our top priority is this search." I see the lines of sorrow around Jack's eyes and the worry tightening his mouth.

"You're right. Let's go."

Unfortunately, all the enthusiasm in the world doesn't guarantee results. Hours later, we head back home for the night with nothing new learned, except how quickly the hatred in Crimson Hollow is spreading.

CHAPTER 48

A PROMISE MADE

BLUEBELL KILDARE

JULY 18, 2022, RED AGES

he midmorning sun shines full and bright as I run my morning errands. It's in stark contrast to my depressed mood from our failure to find any clues last night. Our arsonist continues to elude us. Vampires continue to turn at a rapid pace, and as long as they do, the city will remain on edge and interbreed relations will keep falling apart. So this morning's task is important. It's perhaps one step closer to resolving the Vampire issues.

Robert LaRoche's mansion stands strong and dignified in front of me; its large stone exterior speaks of permanence and fortitude. Robert gave me some great information on the Grimoire during the Blackwater case and seemed amazingly well connected with the magical artifact market. I'm hoping his knowledge as a collector will aid me now.

Ammon is in the vehicle behind mine and a scowl sticks to my face. Jeez, having a watchdog is so demeaning. Well, having a real watchdog like Varg isn't demeaning, but having a Vampire guard is.

I move to grab the heavy knocker, but Robert's butler beats me to it and opens the door, causing me to fall halfway inside. I straighten myself with as much dignity as possible and lift my eyes to the staunch view of the butler, who sniffs elegantly. "This way. Robert is expecting you, and your, er, companion."

He walks us to a private conservatory where Robert relaxes among the greenery. I peer around at the lush foliage and wonder what it might be like to live like this.

"Do you grow your own vegetables?" I ask.

Robert smiles at me, as handsome as I remember him. Today he's sporting tan pants and a soft cream shirt. His hair is still in need of cutting and that, combined with his spectacles gives him that adorable scholarly appearance. He unfolds his long, elegant form to greet me. "I've never met anyone with more engaging questions." He takes my hand and brushes his lips softly against my skin before reluctantly releasing it.

I take the chair opposite him, and he gestures for tea to be poured. Once we're settled in, he turns his warm brown eyes to me. "So, to what do I owe the pleasure of your visit?"

"I'm shopping for some magical artifacts."

Robert quirks an eye as his face grows serious. "Indeed. Then I'm glad you came to me."

By the look of it, Robert just switched gears from pleasure to business.

"Are you seeking particular pieces, or is there a feat you're trying to achieve?"

I say, "I won't discuss my goals, but I assure you they are one hundred percent for the good of all."

I list the names of the three magical artifacts Dragomira told Jack and me about. Robert listens patiently, then carefully takes a sip of tea when I've finished. The sharp clink of his cup in the saucer is the only sound disturbing the silence. I notice the butler has made himself scarce.

Robert clears his throat, and I note concern on his face. He tilts his head, pondering his teacup. "Well, Blue, you are ever full of surprises."

I give him an inquiring glance.

"The artifacts you've mentioned are quite old, and many believe they're only the stuff of legends. But I disagree. Some believe Patersuco used the Rod of Elias to find the Grimoire, but after that it seems to disappear from historical documents. I imagine it's buried as deeply as the Grimoire and key. Perhaps it was even destroyed."

"The Eternal Specula has popped up from time to time, as has the Pipe of Ogden, but I'd counsel against going with the latter as it often leads to insanity."

I perch forward in my chair. "Do you think you can find them? Any of them?"

Robert furrows his eyebrows. "Are you sure you want me to enquire? The Eternal Specula can be a labyrinth of misleading clues, and the Pipe, as I've said, is quite dangerous. Could I interest you in a scrying mirror?"

All my excitement dissipates.

"Come, Blue, don't be so disappointed. I haven't said that I wouldn't look. It is just that I'd rather not. But if it's that important . . . "

With my hands clasped so firmly together I'm gouging dents in them with my fingernails, I answer gravely, "It's of the utmost importance. It's imperative."

Robert sighs. "I'll endeavor to find them." Then a mischievous glint enters his eyes. "Under two conditions . . ."

Dubious, I arch one brow.

"Don't be so worried. The first is that the article will become part of my personal collection, though I'll let you use it as long as you need. The second is only that I request the pleasure of your company for dinner tomorrow evening."

My whole body relaxes as relief washes over me. "Done, done, and triple done."

Thankfully, one thing is checked off my list. Now on to the next. I want to check in with Rita Hardgrave to see how her investigation is going before getting back to the dreaded war room.

CHAPTER 49

SOMETHING FISHY

BLUEBELL KILDARE

JULY 18, 2022, RED AGES

he City Hall clerk is struggling to locate Rita in her directory, as evidenced by the way she pinches her nose and furrows her brow as she searches. "What did you say her name was again?"

Oh, for crying out loud. "Rita Hardgrave."

She scans down her page. "Hmm, Halbert, Hanson, Harrington. Nope, no Hardgrave."

I glare at her. "Hardgrave. Don't you have a Hardgrave here? I met with her a few weeks ago."

The clerk eyes me doubtfully, and declares, "I don't know a Rita Hardgrave. Don't you think I'd know someone who works in my own building?"

What the . . . ? She might not know Rita because she's tucked away in some abysmal corner of the basement. Unfortunately, I can sense that the clerk is telling the truth.

I lean over and whisper, "She works in Internal Investigations."

She says, "What was that? I couldn't hear you."

I raise my voice a little. "She works in Internal Investigations."

The clerk practically bellows, "Ah, Internal Investigations. That spot has been filled temporarily by the mayor's assistant."

I step back, shocked. "What happened to Rita?"

"She was transferred."

"Transferred where exactly?"

She peruses her directory. "I'm sorry, it doesn't say."

"For Pete's sake." I throw up my hands and stamp out, more than a little worried about Rita.

As Varg and I rush down the City Hall steps, I ask him, "Do you think something fishy is going on?"

Varg's eyelids flutter wisely.

I'm glad he agrees. I've never heard of someone from the Mayor's office taking over internal investigations. Talk about a conflict of interest!

Well, for now, we need to get to the office.

CHAPTER 50

A MAN IDENTIFIED

BLUEBELL KILDARE

JULY 18, 2022, RED AGES

Blue," Marian calls "Rubalia is on line three for you."

I pick up line three. "Blue speaking."

"Blue, Mack confirmed there were no new fires yesterday, and I've got Yana's mother, Melina Bacheva waiting for you."

"Oh! Great news, and thank you, Rubalia. Please send her into the interview room and offer her a beverage. Be sure the tissues are stocked."

I click down the phone. "Okay, Marian, can you give me Yana and Kalina's file?"

Marian hands it to me, and I scan it quickly as I head to meet Melina.

Outside the interview room door, I steel myself against the emotions I already feel pouring from Melina. Then, as calmly as I can, I open the door.

Melina is a portly woman with round, reddish cheeks and brown flyaway hair. She's dressed professionally in a gray skirt and a feminine mauve blouse. I smile gently at her. "Thank you for coming, Melina. I know this is a hard time for you."

"Marian?" she asks timidly.

I present my hand and answer, "No, I'm Inspector Bluebell Kildare. Marian set up the interview for us."

Melina shakes my hand with an unsure grasp, and I slide into the seat across from her.

"So, Melina, the funeral was yesterday?"

She nods and dabs her eyes with a tissue as a gray shroud of sadness and grief wraps around her.

"I asked you here to learn a little about Yana's life. As you know, we believe the fire was arson, and we're committed to finding the person who did this."

Melina folds her hands gently on the table.

"Did Yana have many close friends?"

Melina nods again. "She had two good girl friends: Raya Victorov and Kim Bayer." Melina hesitates a moment, then says, "She also had a fiancé, Milan Ivanov. They were to be married in the fall." She raises her eyes to me. "He seems like a good boy, respectful and kind. He seemed to love little Kalina too."

"Do you know what Yana was doing the day of the fire?"

She hesitates and tightens her mouth.

I reach over and pat her hand. "No one's in trouble. Right now we're just trying to get an idea of how she spent her time."

Melina relaxes a little. "Kalina needed new shoes, and Milan was going to pick them up and take them shopping."

"Do you know where she was shopping for shoes?"

"She usually goes to Skippers downtown."

"Do you know what time she was going?"

Melina thinks a little. "Well, Milan works until five o'clock, so it would have to be in the early evening. She wouldn't want Kalina to stay up too late."

"And how did she spend the week prior? Any special outings?"

Melina smiles tremulously and grabs a fresh tissue. "On Saturday she attended a baking contest and won first prize for her biskvitena torta. I watched Kalina while she set up at the church. Besides that, she worked at the college. She is—I mean, she was an art professor, you know." Melina covers her face with her tissue, and her shoulders gently shake.

I cover her hand with mine, offering what little comfort I can. It's heartbreaking the way she has to learn how to be proud of a child who just died. I say, "I didn't know. You must have been so proud of her."

After a moment, Melina pulls herself together and furiously dabs her eyes, but she offers me a smile. "Yes, I was very proud. She was the first to graduate college in our family. We immigrated here when I was just young."

"I'm sure she worked hard to earn her degree. What about Kalina's father? Was it Milan?"

Melina scoffs. "No, he was a man she met in college, Bruce Wagner. He was not a nice man. He dropped out of college and disappeared as soon as he found out about the baby."

"Oh, I'm so sorry she had to deal with that. It must have been hard for her."

"Yes, but she was a good mom and took excellent care of Kalina."

"Do you know what Kalina's gift was, by chance?"

Melina says sharply. "We weren't sure if she was Gifted. None of us are Gifted, but Kalina had a strange pink strawberry mark on her knee. We were hoping it was just a birthmark."

"Perhaps it was," I say to soothe her. "Was there anyone that was upset with Yana that you know of? An ex-boyfriend or a work colleague?"

She shakes her head and I can see she's still disturbed by the Gifted question.

"Well, if you can't think of anything else unusual about Yana's week, then I'll just ask you for the contact details of everyone you mentioned, though I might have to call you with additional questions."

Melina seems relieved the questioning is over for now, and she obediently retrieves her mobile phone from her purse to produce the numbers.

As soon as she's left, I give Rubalia Milan's number and ask her to have him come in for questioning as soon as possible. This interview is essential. He's our first witness who spent the day with any of the families and survived the night.

CHAPTER 51

LOOSE ENDS

JACK TANNER

JULY 18, 2022, RED AGES

 lean out of my office door and call out to Blue as she heads back to the war room. "Blue, do you have a minute?"

She turns sharply toward me, and I lead her into my office. When I take a seat, she stands there awkwardly, chewing her lip again like an errant child waiting for punishment. Thoughts of the orphanage come up. Is that why she's always nervous when I call her into my office? Does she feel like she felt when she got in trouble there? Curse Matilda to the Plane of Fire for eternity

To make her more comfortable, I offer my guest chair.

She sits and asks, "What's up?"

I procrastinate. "Where's Varg?"

"Oh, he's milling about. He's taken to roaming the entire department since all the new people have come. Rubalia isn't too happy about it. So, what's up?"

"I bet she isn't." I lean forward, my forearms on the desk. "Remember when you interviewed Fred Moore and got him to agree to give us all the details he could?"

She sits forward now, eager for news. "Yes?"

I wish it were good news. "Well, he was able to give us a physical description, but he wasn't able to give us any details about the organization or why they attacked you beyond the fact that you're Gifted."

Her lips turn down and she stares out my window in concentration for a minute. "He could have been compelled with phrases like, 'You may not speak of this organization or tell anyone who I am or why we want her.' If those had been his orders, that would explain why he could describe the man, but give no other important facts. Are the other guys out of the hospital yet?"

This whole mess is so damn irritating. I pace in front of the window and try to rein in my frustration. "We have three more of the men here now, and we're having the same problem with all of them. We even had an artist do a sketch, and ran it through our facial recognition software."

I slam my fist on the steel window supports. "Whoever this guy is, he's not in our database. We even checked drivers' license photos."

A moment of silence, then she says, "So you're saying we've got nothing. He must be an out-of-towner then, here visiting. What you need is someone to undo the compulsion. Why don't you ask Dragomira?"

I stand at the window gazing out at the darkening sky while tension courses through me. This should be so simple, but we're being blocked in every possible way. "We tried already. She said the compulsion is embedded too deeply, and it would unravel his mind if she were to undo it. It isn't a container like your spell was. It's enmeshed with his mind."

Blue suggests, "Then you need someone Gifted as a Memory Sifter."

I turn to her. "Yes! That's exactly what we need. I'll have Rubalia find someone."

She cautions, "Of course they'll have to give you consent, and depending on how many illegal deeds they've done in the past, you may or may not get it."

Damn it. She's right. "Well, we have four of them now, so hopefully one of them will give."

"So which three are out of the hospital?"

Shit. That's exactly why I didn't want to have this conversation with her. She always feels responsible for anyone she hurts, even when it's necessary. How can I avoid this discussion?

She leans forward as though she knows what I'm thinking and pierces me with her brilliant blue eyes. "Don't you dare sugarcoat it for me, Jack. Tell me exactly how the men are."

There's no way out of it now, so I give her a rough brush of the situation. "We've got the guy who took the tranquilizer and one that

Varg attacked. We've also got the guy you shot in the hand. After one surgery each and some bone-knit charms, they're healing nicely and have been transferred to our medical ward."

She gives me a penetrating glare. "And the guy whose foot I shot and the one with the missing forearm?"

I lean forward and hold her eyes with mine. "One had his foot amputated, and the other had surgery to clean up the end of his arm. They're still in the hospital, but they're both expected to make a full recovery."

Blue clutches her stomach as if she feels sick.

"Blue, look at me."

She turns back and I capture her eyes again because this is so important. "You can't blame yourself. I can't have an investigator who's afraid of defending herself. I couldn't let you out on the street!" I slam the flat of my hand down on my desk in emphasis.

"I know, Jack. But I don't have to be happy about it. I'm an Empath; of course I'm going to feel bad."

I'm relieved she sees it that way. As long as she can deal with it, then we're okay.

But she's not done. She hits me with another question. "So did the Vampire I gutted survive?"

At last a question I like because I can give her the answer she wants to hear. "Yes, he did. His name is Ranulf Windmere, and he turned the corner yesterday. He's healing quickly now."

Her whole countenance, including her aura (and by way of it, my entire office) lightens with that news. It's so great to see her smile.

CHAPTER 52

STICKY BUSINESS

BLUEBELL KILDARE

JULY 18, 2022, RED AGES

Despair nips at my heels as I duck into Sticky's, otherwise known as the Sticky Dough Pizza Place. We've made no new discoveries in the last twenty-four hours on the case, and my heart aches at the thought of more deaths. The only hope I have is the interview scheduled for tomorrow with Milan Ivanov, Yana's boyfriend. With any luck, he'll give us a clue as to who's starting these fires.

I am so occupied in the morose depths of my thoughts, it takes a moment for the fetid and stale scent of tension at Sticky's to penetrate my consciousness. My eyes fly immediately to Alexis, who rises from the waiting room bench with a pinched expression and nervous stance. I cast a worried glance her way as I step up to the hostess to be seated. Alexis stands slightly behind me and touches my arm.

The hostess, Susan, her nametag tells me, gives me an unpleasant glare as these unbelievable words spill out from the twist of her mouth: "I'm sorry. We don't serve your kind."

My jaw drops. I snap, "What do you mean you don't serve my kind?" But I already know what she means. I can feel the hate wafting off her, noxious as the stench of burning plastic.

She points at the blue streak in my hair that marks me as Gifted. My face flames hot from anger.

Then Sticky himself steps out from behind the counter and wipes his brow, avoiding my eyes. "I'm sorry," he says nervously. "We've had fights in here three nights this week. We had to do something about it, so we're only letting Norms in now."

Well, now, I almost sympathize with Sticky. Almost.

I brace my legs and fold my arms. "Sticky, I've been coming to this pizza parlor since I got my first paycheck. You know exactly how I like my pizzas: thin and crispy with lots of veggies. Where am I going to get that kind of service elsewhere?"

Sticky seems embarrassed, but widens his stance. "I had to replace seven chairs today from last night's fight, and two days before that someone threw a table through the front window. Either I stop letting one of you in or I'm not going to have a pizza parlor left. And since I'm a Norm, I guess that's the side I've gotta pick."

"Sticky, there's got to be another way."

Sticky shakes his head. "You got money to get me a bodyguard? If not, this is the only way I've got."

I pierce Sticky with my eyes. "You know what? I'd feel bad for you, but you've got breedists among your employees. How's that helping? And don't you think turning people away is going to incite even worse violence?"

Sticky pulls a rag out of his pocket and wipes the sweat from his brow again, refusing eye contact.

Alexis tugs my hand, trying to get me to leave with her, but I've got one more thing to say to Sticky. "You know, you do have to pick a side. You either pick the side of people trying to get along or the side of people who are part of the problem. And it's clear what side you're picking. I hope you're ready for the consequences."

I follow Alexis out and shout to nobody in particular, "Lady of Light! I can't believe that just happened."

Alexis shakes her head. "As soon as I walked in, that girl gave me dirty looks like she was suspicious even though she couldn't see my mark. I had a feeling . . . "

"He knows I'm going to report him, too. Of all the stupid, idiotic—"

Alexis pulls me down the street. "Let's go to Moonlight's. I don't care what I eat as long as food hits my stomach fast."

Fog covers the street in a thin, white haze. Glittering streetlights reflect off the damp roads and cast long shadows across our path. The blinking sign of Moonlight's Diner shines blue through the translucent white, guiding us into friendlier circumstances if not more succulent fare. At the entrance, a chalkboard sign announces meatloaf as the special of the day, and that is about as special as it gets. But at least we aren't insulted or persecuted here. It's amazing how wonderful a little human decency makes you feel.

As we eat, Alexis starts filling me in on her shop news. "I've decided to push my veterinary line, and now I have regular orders set up with half the vets in town!" she tells me.

I smile. "That's so exciting, Alexis! You'll have a monopoly before you know it. And Dr. Perlman was raving about the solution you gave him to block scent during his autopsies."

She grins proudly at that.

"So how's Penelope doing? Is she still seeing that boy . . . was it Blake?"

"Yes," Alexis chuckles. "He came by yesterday looking so sweet, dressed up all nice in a sweater, but he was sweating like a pig from the heat. He brought her a rose, though, so I'm sure she didn't even notice."

"Aw, that is really sweet. Any dates for you?"

Alexis averts her gaze. "No one since I stopped seeing Brady. I've been so busy trying to get ahead with the business."

My heart saddens for Alexis. She and Brady had been together for a long time. Too long. Brady was a go nowhere, do nothing kind of guy, and Alexis is the complete opposite. She finally got tired of picking up after him, cooking for him, and doing a million things he never even noticed needed to be done, let alone by him. I believe they really loved each other. They just weren't compatible.

Alexis' eyes sharpen on me in an obvious ploy to change topics. "So, how's Jack doing?"

"Jack is Jack. He's keeping his distance but hovering at the same time. His eyes say he wants me, his mouth says it's just professional. I can't make headway with him, and it just so happens I have a date with another man."

"Ooh. Who, may I ask?"

A woman walks by our table, petite and weathered, wrapped in a light gray cloak, unusual for midsummer. Her eyes catch mine for a brief moment, and the steely gray pierces me as though she is delving into my soul. She passes the table, and I turn to watch her take a booth at the back.

"Do you know her?" Alexis quietly asks, but I'm too preoccupied by this puzzle of a woman to respond. I check my sixth sense and oddly find that she doesn't register. I'm getting nothing from her at all.

I start to turn off my regular senses to open up my sixth sense more when Alexis' voice distracts me. "Blue? Is everything okay?"

I remember where I am and turn to my friend, who deserves my attention right now.

"I'm sorry. That woman seems strangely familiar, but I can't place her. What were we talking about again?"

Alexis casts the woman an inquisitive glance, then turns my way again. "Who do you have a date with?"

"Remember when I asked if I could borrow an outfit and you lent me the cream silk pantsuit?"

Alexis, attention fully on the subject at hand now, practically purrs. "Yesssss."

A huge grin breaks over my face. "It's Robert, Magical Artifact Collector Extraordinaire."

Alexis' eyes sparkle with delight. "Dish!" she demands.

I drop my eyes because the story isn't as exciting as it might be. "Well, I enlisted his help in finding some magical artifacts, and he insisted on the date as part of his finder's fee."

Alexis has her smile firmly in place. "He must really want to date you then."

"I guess he does. I don't know how I feel about him, though. I mean, I really like him. But I don't feel for him what I feel with Jack."

Alexis covers my hand. "Just plan on having a nice time. That's enough."

I agree. I can't put my life on hold for someone who's clearly shown they don't want to be involved in that way. There's no harm in enjoying the evening with a nice man.

Tired of the subject, I lay enough money on the table to cover us and look for the strange woman. Curiously, the booth is now empty, and I didn't feel her pass us. "Come on. Let's go. What do you want to bet Varg is sitting by the front door of the restaurant already?"

We step out into the evening air, and sure enough Varg is waiting for us. He leads the way as we begin the short walk back to the car. The sun has set, and the moon hangs low in the sky, casting the area in a dim glow.

As we approach the car, Varg lets out a low warning growl and jumps into some hedgerows lining Sticky's property. He crashes through the branches and the shrubs shudder in response. A moment after he disappears, a shriek sounds from that direction. Since I doubt the bushes are screaming, I quickly surmise I'm in the middle of another ambush. I yell, "Alexis, get behind me!"

Someone emerges from the side of the building, barreling toward us at full speed. I position myself solidly in front of Alexis to protect her. I brace my legs and prepare for impact. Varg exits the bushes and intercepts our attacker with a lunge, knocking him over and causing him to face plant onto the sidewalk.

I sense someone behind me just as Alexis' scream of pain has me whipping around. She's fallen on the sidewalk, and a young man is pulling her arm, trying to drag her away. He mutters, "Come on, freak."

That's all I need to hear before I leap toward him and give him a roundhouse kick in the gut as hard as I can. He grabs his stomach and lifts his head in shock. He's too late. I'm already flying at him again, furious that anyone would dare touch Alexis. I sweep his feet with mine, and down he goes. With a twist of his wrist, I have him on his belly and his arm behind his back. After slapping my cuffs on him, I finally have a moment to press the emergency button on my chimerator.

With my knee pinning him to the sidewalk, I glance over at Alexis, who's huddled in a ball on the sidewalk. Waves of agony roll off her, making my heart ache. "Are you all right?"

Alexis looks up with tear filled eyes and says in a pained voice, "My arm. I think it's broken."

"Cripes!" I flip open my phone and call an ambulance. Just then, Ammon surprises me by stepping out of the bushes with the first man Varg attacked in his grip. The man is unconscious but unscathed. Ammon, however, is clearly irritated. "Must I collect a new batch of miscreants every night for you?"

"Breedists," I spit out while glaring at Sticky's.

Ammon just shakes his head and frowns. "You're like a Goddamn magnet for trouble."

Eventually we get all three guys loaded into Ammon's car and on their way for questioning.

The ambulance arrives and loads Alexis on the gurney. "I don't need a hospital," she protests. "I'm a healer."

I shake my head. "Alexis, you need an X-ray. You can knit bone back together, but you can't realign it with herbs and charms. And you can't fix your own arm. You need two hands for that. You're going to the hospital, and I'm going with you."

Alexis glares at me until one of the ambulance drivers steps in front of me to strap her in.

Unbelievably pissed that those breedists hurt Alexis, I kick a nearby tree so hard my foot goes numb. This needs to stop. Now!

CHAPTER 53

RECONNAISSANCE

JACK TANNER

JULY 18, 2022, RED AGES

Xavier Ramsey's rich sable skin and black clothes camouflage him in the deep shadows of the old oaks. Even without the benefit of dark skin, and despite his barrel chested build, Xavier can be practically invisible when he wants to be. Now, he steps out from behind a stout tree trunk behind the Center of Enlightenment, the Dilectus Deo Headquarters.

At my three o'clock and six o'clock two guards lie unconscious, fully trussed and divested of weapons. Like a shadow in the mist, Xavier slips through the greenery until he reaches my side. As instructed, he jumps on my back, and I leap onto the second story veranda where a third guard joins his colleagues in a less-than-gentle slumber.

While I'd love to just muscle the rest of the way in, Xavier is Gifted at disabling electronic security systems, and covert is the name of the game tonight. This mission is pure reconnaissance.

As Xavier works his magic, I restlessly scan the massive parking lot. Only fifty-four cars line the lot. Based on our intel, the Dilectus Deo higher-ups are holding a big meeting here tonight, though about what, I don't know.

By the time I pivot around toward Xavier, he's managed to deftly open a window toward the back of the veranda. Based on the map we reviewed earlier, this puts us in the guest wing of the residence end of the fortress, which is unfortunate because we need to be on the other side of the building. Instead of making a beeline for our destination, we head to the housekeeping stairwell in the opposite direction. Xavier slips an ID card out of his pocket and swipes the reader.

We exit into a dimly lit basement and head toward the far wing. Though muffled by solid concrete and steel beam construction, the patter of feet overhead tells me we're nearing our destination. We pass beneath the main hall and keep going until we reach a twin stairwell on this wing. With another swipe of the card, we head up to the third floor.

Through the narrow pane of the service door the path seems clear. I ease the door open just as a guard enters the hallway at the opposite end. I sneak up behind him, put one hand over his mouth, and apply a sharp blow to his vagus nerve. He crumples. In an instant I've got him tied, blindfolded, gagged, and safely stashed in a supply closet.

Across the corridor, we slip through the door on the empty third floor of the main auditorium. While keeping close to the far wall, Xavier moves into deep shadow. I grip onto a support beam and shimmy up to the rafters where I can watch the proceedings.

The Patriarch of the Dilectus Deo, Hayden Balor, stands at the pulpit, his sharp eyes scanning the assembly. The attendees are all wearing their golden robes with cowls up, so I can't see their faces, but the air is thick with the stench of human sweat and oil trapped beneath cheap polyester. Incense burning on an altar does a poor job of masking the aroma of their fervor.

Hayden begins by discussing regular business, covering membership growth, conversion rates, and new programs of indoctrination, all mixed with heart-stirring righteousness about how they're taking their rightful place as the true Beloved of God. Of course. This must be just a regular meeting of region leaders. I gnash my teeth in frustration. Did we come here for nothing?

Next, a line of twelve men forms at the altar, and Hayden announces that the blessing of the new Apostles will commence. Familiar with their system, I know Apostles are the lowest ranked members, just above the general congregation. Apostles undergo intensive training and serve underneath the region Chosen, or sometimes they serve under special programs at headquarters. Each man steps up in turn and kneels before Hayden. He cleanses them by wafting the incense smoke around their head, then anoints them with holy water. Finally he calls their name, assigns them to a Chosen, and welcomes them as a True Believer and Beloved of God.

Nothing Hayden has done here tonight is illegal or even morally wrong, but the sound of his voice holds too much power, and it makes me uneasy. He entrances his audience, lulling them into belief with tone and tenor.

Frustrated that all I've gained is a list of new Apostles to research, I start down the support beam as Hayden welcomes his last Apostle. "I welcome you, Apostle Schmidt." My head snaps to the man in front of Hayden. "You'll be assigned to the Divine Conference of the Center of Enlightenment under Otto Cromwell with the Spiritual Cleansing program."

Spiritual Cleansing program? That does not sound good.

His head is bowed as Hayden dips his thumb in holy water and anoints his forehead. "May you walk as a True Believer, secure in the knowledge that you are a Beloved of God."

The man rises and for a brief moment, I get a glimpse of a terribly scarred face in the shadows of the cowl. I inhale deeply, and the unmistakable scent of Dean Schmidt fills my nostrils. A powerful urge to kill rips through me, and I find myself starting down the beam again. The thought of his neck snapping beneath my hands holds an allure too rich to ignore.

A sound in the corridor snares my attention and breaks through my rage. A quick glance at Xavier tells me he's still well-hidden and reminds me I'm responsible for getting him out safely. In a flash, I'm back in the rafters.

A security guard with a flashlight steps onto the auditorium balcony. One of the men we took out must have been found. The beam of the guard's flashlight sweeps slowly through the seats, working its way toward the corner where Xavier hides. He aims it directly at the corner where Xavier was just a moment ago and I grip the pole, ready to pounce. But when the light hits the corner it's empty.

I scan my eyes across the space and smile when I notice a deeper shade of black amongst the shadows beneath a row of auditorium seating.

Shit! My security ring for Blue pulls tight on my finger. My muscles bunch as every fiber of my being desires to leave immediately. I glare at the security guard, who sweeps the auditorium again, excruciatingly slowly. My body relaxes in relief when he turns around and starts to leave.

Wait . . . He pauses at the door and turns around once more, this time glancing up toward the ceiling. I press myself flat against the ceiling joist, masking myself in the dark. The seconds tick by, and my mind screams to just expose myself and run to Blue. But I must think of Xavier.

At last the security guard turns and exits the balcony level.

Xavier slips out from under the seats, and I quickly join him. A glance through the sidelights tells me the corridor is empty. I whisper to Xavier, "Blue's emergency alert went off. We're making a quick exit."

Xavier follows me through the corridor to the first window. I slam my foot through it and tell Xavier to grab onto my neck. Then in one powerful leap, we sail through the night sky and land on the ground. In a flash we disappear into the mist.

CHAPTER 54

UNCIVILIZED

BLUEBELL KILDARE

JULY 19, 2022, RED AGES

I've been sitting in the packed reception area of the Civil Division at SIB Headquarters for over an hour, bored out of my mind. Unfortunately, this downtime has given me plenty of time to go over the events of last night—in particular, the Jack fiasco.

I failed to call off my emergency after our attack. He drove like a bat out of hell to respond to my alert, arriving at the scene just as I was starting to follow the ambulance. Big oops.

I grimace. My preference would be not to use the alert at all unless I'm in truly dire straits, but even as he scolded and stormed, he told me I had to use it. He kept reminding me that I'm an investigator, not a street cop. It's true, but it burns.

"Ms. Kildare?"

Thank goodness, they are finally calling my name.

"Coming!" I say almost too eagerly. Varg and I stand up and follow the receptionist to an interview room, where hopefully we won't have to wait another hour. She ushers us in, but I note she doesn't offer a beverage. Rubalia would be horrified at this gauche lack of manners.

The room is decorated much like our interview rooms: beige linoleum tile, taupe colored walls, a little side table with office supplies. The center of the room is dominated by a round, wooden table and stiff-backed chairs.

Just as my butt is about an inch from the chair seat, the door opens again, so I stand up. I turn and find a young man about my age with dark circles under his eyes and long bangs flopped over his right eye.

He holds out his hand. "Hi, I'm Agent Robinson. And you're Ms. Kildare?"

I shake his hand firmly. "Inspector Kildare, actually. But I'm here to lodge a personal civil complaint."

His eyes widen a little at the fact I'm an inspector, which is above his rank, but he quickly masks his emotions. We sit, and he says, "What seems to be the issue?"

"Last night I went to a restaurant I frequent, the Sticky Dough Pizza Place, and I was refused service on account of my breed."

His eyes flick with annoyance, and his feelings shout as bright as day that he's bored. "Really?" he asks.

"Really. I'd like a report filed, and I want it investigated."

He rubs his chin with his hand. "Couldn't you just go somewhere else for dinner?"

I think my mouth drops. I can't believe he just said that. Then my rage-o-meter reaches the top level. "No, I can't just go somewhere else. According to Amendment 16 of the Great Pact, Section 20.14, 'No one shall be denied services based on breed.'"

"Well, I know that," he says, "but you're an inspector. That rule is to protect civilians. Surely you can handle a little discrimination."

My mouth works in several shapes, trying to get words out, but my brain is temporarily in shock. Finally, I lean forward and burst out with, "What in the Plane of Fire is wrong with you? File the darn report or I'll report you to your superior."

He shrugs his shoulders. "Fine. Not that it will do you any good."

"Why wouldn't it do me any good? The business should be investigated, and if you find what I say is true, you should revoke his business license. That's standard procedure."

"Look, Lady—"

I snap. "Don't 'Lady' me. That's Inspector Kildare, thank you."

His nostrils flare and his lips thin. "Look, Inspector Kildare, my office has one hundred and seventy-three business complaints to investigate before yours. It'll take us months to get through them as it is."

"Well, now you have one hundred seventy-four. Hire more men if you need to, but write the blasted report!"

CHAPTER 55

Elusive Clue

BLUEBELL KILDARE

July 19, 2022, Red Ages

The mood in the war room has been somber and desperate ever since Oscar came back from an interview with Mrs. Sorenson's parents. They hadn't spoken to her in two weeks before her death, so they had no idea what the family had been doing that day. It seems all our leads are drying up fast.

Marian is absent at present. She's consulting with some criminal psychologists on the case, getting a few opinions. Yepa and Sidney are holed up together in the corner, hovering over some logistical data and Yepa's fingers are flying on the computer. A few new tacks have been added to the map in the last twenty-four hours, but not many. Yepa told me earlier that she may or may not use her hacking skills today, so it's probably best not to ask what she's doing.

Frankly, I couldn't care less as long as we get a lead.

Line one buzzes, and I pick up. "Hello?"

"Milan Ivanov is here to see you," Rubalia says.

I'm filled with a surge of hope. This is the interview I've been waiting for. "Please send him into the interview room with a beverage and I'll be right there."

Yepa, Sidney, and Oscar all turn toward me with questioning faces. I answer, "Yes, it's Milan."

Smiles break on everyone's faces, and I hope their relief is well merited.

When I enter the interview room, I temper my desire to smile broadly at Milan out of respect for the heartache and misery that embraces him. When I offer my hand, he takes it in a warm grip. He's mid-thirtyish with a slight receding hairline and a touch of gray. His nose speaks of a brawl in his past with its slightly off-center slant, but if it weren't for his bloodshot eyes and the dark circles beneath them, I'd call him handsome.

I settle into the seat across from him. "Thank you for coming, Milan. I know this is a difficult time for you, and I apologize for having to interrupt your grieving."

Milan clasps his hands nervously, and asks, "Why did you want to question me?"

"I'm sure you heard that there have been other fires."

When he acknowledges that, I attempt to alleviate his concern. "Well, we believe we have a serial arsonist on our hands, and we're trying to find out how all the cases are connected. We think that somehow all the victims ran into the same person at some point. To try to connect all the dots, we need to know how Yana and Kalina spent their last day. I understand from Melina that you spent part of the day with them."

Milan nods cautiously.

"So I was hoping you would tell me everything you did together, who you saw, where you went. Does that sound all right?"

I can feel his worry ease which is exactly what I wanted. His shoulders relax and he nods again.

"So, when did you see them?"

Milan says, "The day before the fire, like Melina said. I went to their house and hung out with Kalina for about an hour while Yana finished grading some school projects. Then I took them shopping and out to dinner."

"So that was on July 15th?"

Milan agrees.

"What time did you leave their house?"

He furrows his eyebrows, thinking back. "Kalina and I had just finished watching one of her favorite programs on TV when Yana finished her work, so I think we left about five or ten minutes after six." He says all of this calmly, but his eyes get redder and redder as he speaks, and he pushes his fist against his mouth when he's done, obviously reliving a memory.

I smile sympathetically and push the box of tissues to him. "Milan, don't be afraid to cry. Trust me; it's nothing I haven't seen before."

His glistening eyes speak their thanks, but he stays silent, doing his utmost to remain stoic.

"Did you drive? And where did you go first?"

His voice comes out husky and broken. "Yeah, I drove. We went to The Biscuit House. Kalina is a little fussy about food."

My heart rips a little when I notice he's still talking of her in the present tense.

"Did you talk to anyone while you were there? A fellow patron perhaps? Or did you have any conversations with the staff that was beyond the usual?"

He shakes his head no. "Just the waiter when we ordered. Nothing unusual." He takes a deep breath and clasps his hands together on the table.

"When did you leave The Biscuit House?"

Milan scratches his head. "We probably left around seven."

I take a peek at my files, and he's pretty on target. I see a credit card purchase at 7:05 p.m. at The Biscuit House.

"And where did you go after The Biscuit House?"

"We went to Skippers. Kalina needed new shoes."

"If I recall, The Biscuit House isn't far from Skippers. Did you walk or take your car?"

He says, "We walked. The weather was fine, and we had a bit of time."

"So did you walk straight there, or did you stop on the way?"

"We walked straight there."

"I know this line of questioning is tedious, Milan. I'm sorry I keep asking the same thing. But while you were shopping for shoes, did you talk to anyone in particular, more than normal? Or was anyone paying an unusual amount of attention to any of you?"

Milan says, "The shoe salesman was friendly, but not unusually so. I didn't sense anything off. Kalina found a pair of shoes she liked right away, so it was pretty quick in and out. Probably less than twenty minutes."

"So what time do you think you left Skippers?"

"I'd guess at around 7:30 or 7:45."

"And did you walk straight back to the car then and drive home? Or did you make any more stops?"

He says, "Well, we did pass by Celestial Park, and Kalina spent some time on the merry-go-round and the swings. We only spent a few minutes there because it was starting to get dark. I dropped them off at home after that and left."

"Was there anyone at the park who seemed out of place? Like an adult with no kids?"

Milan's eyes get fierce. "No, I would have noticed that right away. There were a few mothers there with their kids. I think I was the only man. It's just a little kiddie park."

"So you went straight home after that?"

"Yes."

"And did you go in the house with Yana?"

Milan shakes his head. "No, Yana had more work she had to do after getting Kalina to bed, so I headed home. She did call me to say goodnight at around eleven o'clock. Yana had finished her work, and everything seemed fine. She didn't mention anything unusual beyond Kalina being a little overexcited about the coming festival and having a hard time getting to sleep."

I force a smile. "Well, thank you so much for your time. That's all the questions I have at the moment. I might call you later, though. And please do call me the minute you think of anything else that might have happened. I know sometimes it's easier to remember things later when you're more relaxed. It doesn't have to be a big thing, either. I want to know every little detail, even if it seems insignificant."

Milan stands and says gruffly, "I'll surely think about it."

Then his voice catches. "Yana and Kalina were going to be my family, and I want this person caught."

I agree wholeheartedly as I watch him walk out the door.

When I get back to the war room, I speak to Yepa and Sidney. "They walked from Skippers back to their car which they'd left outside The Biscuit House. On the way back, though, they stopped at Celestial Park."

Sidney places yet another tack on the board.

CHAPTER 56

OLD ACQUAINTANCE

BLUEBELL KILDARE

JULY 19, 2022, RED AGES

Exhaustion from a sleepless night and another fruitless day on the case strips me of all will—or so I tell myself as I give into the sweet beckoning of the sofa after work. I was up until three a.m. at the hospital with Alexis before they decided they had to do surgery to remove some fractured bone fragments. She was not happy about being admitted.

With a plop, I stretch out on my beloved sofa and swear never to leave it again. My beautiful brown sofa. My covered-in-wolf-hair sofa. Wait, what?

"Varg, have you been sleeping on the sofa?"

Varg averts his gaze, clearly not willing to testify against himself. Ugh. I get up and toss a clean throw over the hairy cushions and then sink into them again like I've just become reacquainted with the arms of a long-lost lover. I close my eyes and pretend there are no fires and I don't have to work seven days a week. Instead, I imagine I'm floating on a fluffy cloud. The wind is blowing by gently, and someone is lightly tapping at the door.

Wait. That's my door.

Shoot. This nap is never going to happen.

Just as I'm about to swing the door open, I stay my hand, and instead peek through the peephole, throwing out my sixth sense for good measure. My sixth sense hits a wall. I'm blocked, but my vision definitely enlightens me. The steel gray eyes of the mysterious woman from Moonlight's Diner pierce me through the circle of glass. Tentatively, I open the door.

The familiarity of this petite but powerful woman teases me as she stands rigidly before me in her soft, gray cloak. Fine hairline wrinkles embellish her heart-shaped face, and her gray hair is pulled back into a severe bun. The air seems to still around her as we stand in silence.

Her voice seems to lash through the air when she speaks. "Well, are you going to stand there all day, or are you going to invite an old lady in?"

Stilling my natural instinct to be polite and welcome her in, I recall the rules of my wards. Once invited in, I can't force someone out. "Usually it's customary for one to introduce themselves before they demand entrance into someone's home."

Her pinched lips break in a soft smile. "You always did have sass. It got you in a lot of trouble, but I can't say I didn't like it."

I place my hand on the doorframe and lean into it. "You speak like we know each other, and you do seem familiar . . . but I can't quite place you."

The woman's luminous eyes blink twice, and a moment of potent silence fills the hallway. I wait patiently until the stillness is broken with a soft, clear voice. "My birth name is Maev Dermot, but you may remember me as your housemother, Anna Marie."

I feel like I've been hit by a truck. "Maud's sister?"

She smiles slightly. "Correct."

With no small amount of bitterness I sweep my supposed Watcher up and down and demand, "Where have you been for the last fifteen years?"

Maev's back stiffens and her lips firm. "Perhaps we can conduct this interview in the privacy of your apartment?"

I consider this stranger, as that's what she is to me, and contemplate shutting the door in her face, but Varg shoves me aside with his considerable bulk and sticks his head under her hand, demanding attention. Taking Varg's recommendation in the face of my indecision, I let her in.

I excuse myself to make her a cup of tea. When I return with the steaming beverage, she's sitting primly on the edge of the sofa, her cloak discarded to reveal a coarse, gray woolen pantsuit, wholly unsuited for this climate. Her entire demeanor is the opposite of Maud in every way. Where Maud exudes vivacious energy, Maev whispers of concealed power.

I tap into my sixth sense again to try to get a feel for her. She seems encased in a thick force field, and my attempts bounce off the boundary. Skirting around the edges, I feel it give a little, and a soft flow of concern and wariness escapes, mingled with good intentions. Then the wall stiffens and nothing more comes out. "You're blocking me," I accuse.

"It's rude to scan me without asking permission. Be glad all I'm doing is blocking you."

I lean back. "Really? It's considered rude? I haven't been around people who can tell."

Maev smiles softly. "Yes, it's rude. Maud told me you haven't had any magical training, so I expected you weren't aware of common courtesy. That's why I was lenient."

"You've seen Maud since you came back?"

"Yes, I just came from her place."

I drape my arm across the back of the sofa. "So what brings you back after fifteen years, and what made you leave in the first place? Maud tells me you're supposed to be my Watcher, but you don't seem to have been watching very closely."

Her voice, thick with regret and sorrow, answers wearily, "I've been traveling the continents, tracking some things, searching for aids for the fight to come. But I've always watched and listened, if only from afar. It's the whispers of changes that have drawn me here now."

She folds her hands in her lap and grips her fingers tightly until her knuckles turn white. "I'm sorry I wasn't here to help you when Blackwater abducted you. I didn't learn of the events until they had passed and other signs drew my eyes back here."

I puzzle at this. "What signs?"

"The gathering of Vampires to this region amongst other things. That's hardly coincidental. It's time for you to step up as the chosen one."

The weight of this prophecy sits heavily on my shoulders. "I have no desire to be some exalted hero."

Maev smiles gently. "An egocentric hero would hardly be self-sacrificing enough to do the job, would they?"

Huh. She has a point.

"Well, how am I supposed to go about saving the Vampire race, anyway?"

Maev leans back slightly and assesses me with keen eyes. "Well, as challenges come to you, you will face them. Meanwhile, you'll start training with me in the use of your gifts. Your attempt to penetrate my shield was weak at best. How well do you wield your light?"

"Wield my light?"

"Yes, wield your light. How proficient are you in using it as an offensive or defensive tool?"

"Um, well, I use it to shine."

Maev frowns severely.

Apparently that wasn't the answer she was hoping for. "Oh, I did use it once to push off the souls of rats that were trying to gnaw my feet. But I'm not sure exactly how I did that. I can also sense souls with it."

Maev's frown deepens.

"I take it there is more that I can do with it?"

A slight nod speaks volumes.

"Well, do you care to show me?"

Maev checks out my apartment doubtfully. "We should probably wait to do this in my training room since you're so inexperienced. Have you had any training at all?"

My glare speaks louder than words, but just to be sure my message gets across, I ask, "Exactly who should I have gone to for training?"

Guilt washes over her face, and I feel a pang of remorse that I ruthlessly bury. Everyone says I'm supposed to destroy Lilith, but the only one who can teach me about my light didn't even stick around to prepare me. I prompt her, "No time like the present!"

Maev takes a deep breath. "Well, perhaps just a small lesson today."

My heart leaps with joy. This is something I know I desperately need. "I'd be grateful for even a tiny lesson."

She stands stiffly. "Why don't you face me and start out by pushing on my soul with your light. Because my soul is firmly anchored in my body, if you can move my soul back, you also push me back. You can't move my body with your light, but you can move my soul. Is that clear?"

"Yes, that makes sense." I stand and face Maev and ratchet down my normal senses.

She gives me a severe glare and demands, "What do you think you're doing?"

"I'm turning off my regular senses to engage my sixth sense."

"You're leaving yourself vulnerable. Stay in this world and bring your soul to life as you are."

I widen my stance and concentrate on Maev as I reach inside myself. My light is easier to reach now and comes to the surface faster than expected. I let it grow and dissipate until it touches the edge of Maev's soul.

"Hey," I say, "you aren't blocking me like you were before."

"Yes, well, you aren't skilled enough to get past my walls yet. We'll have to do it like this for now."

While deeply concerned over my obvious limitations, I do as she bids and push my light out again. It spreads gently from my center to fill the room and pushes softly at the edge of Maev's soul.

"Focus your light. Concentrate on one part of my soul and pinpoint it."

I pull my light in from all sides and contract it into one stream. The stream pulls together in a ribbon and pushes at Maev's soul, but it bends when it hits her.

"The force must be more concentrated. Try wrapping your ribbon of light around me and pulling me."

I gradually curl the light around Maev's body and wrap it around her. As it slips around her, I feel it resist against her soul's dense core. My ribbon feels so faint next to her powerful force.

"Tighten it," she commands. "Pull harder."

I try to harden my light, pulling it in like a tight wire. As dense as it becomes, it's still too slight to move her.

"Push even more light into your ribbon."

I reach into my soul and open up the flow of energy, letting more light pour out.

"More light!"

I try, but the light inside me seems to leak at such a slow pace. I think back to my time in the crypt and how I reached up to the sky for more light. I don't know where it came from, but I suspect the source might be the Plane of Light. Tentatively, I send a second tendril up into the sky. It speeds up, seeming to flow upward much more easily than it wants to conflict with Maev's soul. In seconds I feel it touching the warm glow of the light above the heavens, and a spark of light flows back down the ribbon, filling my core with energy. With a sharp push, I send a fresh burst through my ribbon at Maev.

Suddenly, Maev's wall goes up, and my light explodes into the room. *Crack!* The sound of glass exploding resonates through the apartment. Maev dives for the floor, and I leap back against the wall with my heart pounding.

Jack throws open my door and jumps in front of me in a protective position. "What happened?"

I place my hand on Jack's back. "It's all right," I reassure him. "It was just my light. I pushed it out too hard."

As the sound from glass falling to the floor slowly quiets, Maev uncovers her head and peers at me. "We'll need to practice control next time."

Jack snaps. "You're going to have every damn Vampire in the region headed this way. Who is that?"

Shakily, Maev stands up, brushes off her pantsuit and with a lift of her chin, faces Jack. "Hello, Jack. I'm Maev. You may remember me from the Green Tree Orphanage when Blue was quite young."

Jack glowers and practically snarls, "Just the woman I wanted to see. I have some questions for you."

Maev glares at Jack and then back at me, nonplussed. "Well, very good then. That is enough for today."

Just then, another head peeks around my doorframe. "Bluebell?"

I step from behind Jack to find Robert LaRoche standing awkwardly in the doorway, holding a shopping bag and staring over it with curious eyes, assessing my disastrous apartment. "Is this a bad time? Do we need to reschedule our dinner plans?"

Jack's head whips my way, his eyes piercing.

I step in front of Jack, and say, "No, not at all. They were just leaving."

I give Jack a hard, unrelenting stare until he pinches his mouth tight and stiffens.

Maev clears her throat. "We'll train at my quarters next time. My training room is fully warded against such accidents." She pulls out her card and hands it to me. "Meet me at ten o'clock tomorrow morning, and plan to stay for an hour or two. We have much to cover."

I survey the disaster of glass in my apartment. My beautiful jars of oil, my wine glasses . . . At least the warded windows and glass doors weren't broken.

I hook my thumb into my belt loop and tilt my head at Maev. "All right then. Better your place than mine."

CHAPTER 57

RAIN CHECK

BLUEBELL KILDARE

JULY 19, 2022, RED AGES

After slamming the door firmly on Jack's backside (which is also quite firm), I turn to Robert. Maev had so distracted me by her visit that our date had completely slipped my mind. I can't say I'm upset that Jack saw me with him, though. Serves him right.

Robert lifts the grocery bag in his arms and looks askance at the apartment. "Where shall I put this?"

I can only imagine what he must think of the place. A wry smile flits over my lips. "How about the sofa. It seems pretty safe."

He sits next to me setting the bag between us. "What happened, if I may ask?"

"I'm so sorry about the mess, and I haven't even dressed for our date yet. The long and short of it is that Maev stopped by unexpectedly and gave me a magic lesson that got out of hand." I survey the wrecked room with no small amount of dissatisfaction. "Apparently, I lack a certain amount of control."

Robert chuckles softly and his eyes sparkle. "I shouldn't laugh as this doesn't bode well for your use of this gem."

With a bounce on the sofa I turn my eye to the bag. "You found something already? How?"

Robert pulls out a brown leather bundle tied up with a leather cord. "Well, I had an artifact one of my fellow collectors has wanted for some time. He actually knew the location of this beauty, not I. Since I'd never been amenable to giving up that particular piece before, he dealt a swift bargain."

He pulls the cord and starts unwrapping it carefully. When the bundle is free, he unrolls the leather. My body practically thrums with excitement. "Is it the Rod of Elias?"

A grave expression crosses Robert's face as he pulls it out. "I'm afraid not. It's the Pipe of Ogden, Keeper of Wraiths."

I'm stunned speechless when I see it. The pipe is about a foot and a half long, made of a glistening ebony material and covered with deep carvings. It's the carvings that mesmerize. The shank of the pipe is sculpted into a long, emaciated woman, with a skeletal body, bones for arms and legs and wings that wrap around her sides. Her hideous, cadaverous face forms the bowl of the pipe, and her gaping mouth is the chamber for the smoking herbs. I tentatively reach for it and turn it over in my hands. Along the sides and back are more tiny, skeletal faces carved in terrifying detail.

"It's both horrific and fantastic," I breathe reverently.

Robert's face splits into a grin. "I know, isn't it? It's made of bog oak, which is oak wood that is preserved in peat."

I run my hands across it, feeling all the bumps and crevices with my fingertips. It feels solid and gleams like polished onyx.

"What do I smoke in it?"

Robert pulls out a small cloth parcel. "It's mugwort." His face turns serious again. "But remember what I told you. Legend says that if you use this pipe for selfish intentions, your mind will be lost to the wraiths. Only one of pure heart can find what they seek with this."

The mugwort appears innocent enough. "Is this safe?"

"I'm afraid to say, I don't know much about it."

I smile sadly at him and stand up. "My best friend happens to be an herbalist. Unfortunately she's in the hospital at the moment. I was planning on visiting her after our date, so I'll ask her about it then."

With a stretch, Robert pulls himself up too. "Blue, you seem to have a lot going on today." His hand sweeps in the room and smiles gently. "Your place is a mess, and you have a friend in the hospital. How about we postpone the date for now? I'll help you clean up a bit, then we can swing by and visit your friend."

My mouth spreads in a wide grin because as much as I like Robert, Alexis has been weighing on my mind. "Oh, Robert, would you really not mind?"

Robert smiles back. "It would be my pleasure to accompany you."

CHAPTER 58

UNEXPECTED EVIL

BLUEBELL KILDARE

July 19, 2022, Red Ages

Varg and I stand impatiently outside one of the hospital service doors. He lazily yawns and plops down on the sidewalk next to me. Well, perhaps he's patient but I'm certainly not. I tap my boot on the ground, anxious to get in.

At long last the door swings open. Robert's eyes twinkle as his long arm stretches out for us to enter. I glance one more time at the back of the parking lot where Ammon sits in his car, trying to go unnoticed. It's so embarrassing to have a guard when I'm out with a man.

Turning my attention to Robert, I note, "You're pretty good at this whole sneaking and entering thing. It must be your practice with all those hidden passageways in your house."

He leads us upstairs and lets out a soft chuckle. "Indeed, having hidden passages to navigate in my own home would certainly increase my stealth."

"Just admit it. I know it's true."

Varg runs ahead of us up the stairs and waits patiently for our arrival at each landing. When we stop at the third floor, Robert whispers covertly, "Okay, the nurses' station is at the end of the hall, and Alexis' room is just to the right. I'll go out first and move to the left to try to block Varg from view. When it's clear, I'll tap three times on the door and you two can slip in."

He's so excited; I love it. "You're enjoying this more than a date, aren't you?"

Robert chuckles. "I don't want to incriminate myself by answering that."

I snicker, then tuck myself against the wall by the door. "Okay,

I'm ready. I'll wait for the sign."

Robert slips out into the main hall. A few minutes pass, and I hear his soft tap. Varg and I bustle through the door and to Alexis' room.

When we enter, she lifts her head and glares at me. "Blue! Get me out of here. I'm bored out of my freaking mind."

The door closes softly behind Robert, and Alexis' eyes snap to him. "Alexis, this is Robert LaRoche," I say, ignoring her friendly greeting. "Remember I told you I had a date with him?"

Alexis' eyes snap right back to me. "You brought your date here?"

Robert intercedes on my behalf. "It was my idea, actually. Blue was having a rough day as it was, and it seemed better to postpone the date."

After doing the proper introductions, I flop down on the side of Alexis' bed. "So how was the surgery?"

"It was fine. They put me under, and I woke up a few hours later with stitches, great drugs, and this stupid cast." Alexis waves her arm around wildly. "They said I can go home today. They just have to wait until the stronger drugs wear off."

"So how bad was it?"

"It was basically what they thought from the X-ray. Some bone fragments were embedded in my muscle, so they removed the shards and straightened the bone. As soon as I go home, I'll use a bone knit charm, and I'll be right as rain by morning."

Robert's eyes light up at that. "You have a bone knit charm? Is it made of malachite?"

She answers, "The center stone is lavender fluorite, but it's encased in a mesh, silver wire globe made of Celtic knot links that are interspersed with malachite beads. I found it at a traveling flea market a few years ago."

I consider Alexis and Robert. They seem to be speaking a different language than I am at the moment. Just then, the door opens, and a nurse walks in.

"I'm just here to get your final labs."

Varg growls low in his throat and stands next to me. The nurse smiles brightly and proceeds to clean a patch of Alexis' arm. I feel the nurse's nervousness and wonder if she's new.

When she moves to insert the needle, I avert my gaze.

Suddenly, the nurse whispers softly and harshly, "Bluebell, I've got a needle full of sodium hypochlorite solution embedded in your friends arm."

My head snaps back to the hospital bed where the nurse is holding the needle in Alexis' arm. I can sense now that she's terrified; a thin sheen of perspiration covers her forehead, and her hand is shaking.

Alexis' eyes are as round and shocked as I've ever seen.

The nurse says in a tremulous voice, "None of you move or make a sound. If your wolf makes a move, all I have to do is flick my thumb."

Robert stands stiffly next to me, waiting for my direction. With the amount of fear pouring off the nurse, I don't want to make any mistakes or sudden movements. I slowly lift my arms up. "I'm not doing anything. What do you want?"

"There's a van backed up to the exit at the bottom of the stairwell you just snuck up. You are to go downstairs alone and get in the van. The driver will call the room. When I speak with him and know you're in the van, I'll let Alexis go."

I glare at the nurse. "So you expect me to believe you'll just pull the needle out of her arm and my friends will let you walk out of here?"

"Yes, you'll be in the van before I pull the needle out, and my friends in the van will expect me to meet them. If I don't, then things won't go well for you."

I suspect things won't go well for me anyway. In fact, they don't seem to be going very well right now. But at the moment, they're going considerably worse for Alexis, and I don't care for how the nurse is twitching with that needle.

"Okay, fine," I relent.

I speak to Robert, but really intend this message for Varg. "Varg must stay until the phone call comes in. He isn't going to want to, but he must stay."

Robert accepts my decision solemnly and Varg whines softly.

"Okay, I'm going. Stay, Varg."

I quietly exit the room. As soon as I'm in the stairwell, a shadowed form steps out from behind me. My instinct is to fight, but I resist. I press my chimerator emergency button instead as the man grabs my arm roughly. "Just do as I say, and your friend will be fine."

I can see his face now as he walks me down the stairs. He's an average man with a two-day-old shadow and a slight paunch, but he's broad, and his shoulders strong. Later, I tell myself. I can fight him later. Later never seemed so tempting.

We step outside the building, and there's that damn white van again. Beyond it, a laundry delivery truck is conveniently blocking Ammon's view. Maybe this is a different van than the one from the other day. They—whoever "they" are—probably have a whole fleet of white vans driving around town searching for me. Somehow I've got to figure out who is behind this, or it's never going to end, but at this moment, I need to worry about stepping into the van and committing to memory the two men who are pulling me inside.

As the doors close behind me and the driver takes off, I yell, "Call the nurse now!"

CHAPTER 59

HASTY EXIT

BLUEBELL KILDARE

JULY 19, 2022, RED AGES

 brace myself as the van lurches down the road. My hands are tied and I'm blindfolded, but the sun has been heating my back almost the whole way. We're headed north, out of town.

The men disarmed me and threw my chimerator and phone out the window as soon as they tied me up, so Jack can't track me. At least I was able to sound the alarm, but the loss of my knife stings deeply. Soon, I tell myself. I'll get it back soon.

The driver's phone rings, and I listen closely to his side of the conversation. "You made it?" Pause. "Good." Followed by, "We'll drop Noah off when we pick him up." Then a click.

Jeez, this guy must have gone to the same phone etiquette class as Jack. Trying to remain calm, I ask, "Is my friend in the clear?"

The guy they've been calling Burt answers, "Yeah. Now shut your trap."

I shut it, all right. I have more important things to do than chitchat with him.

Swiftly, I send a small filament of light up toward the sky, reaching for that welcome warmth. It's handy to have a gift that only a few people can see, especially one so illuminating. I am worried because it was night when Jack saw my light at the crypt, and now it's daylight. Will he even be able to see it?

Energy courses through my light and starts filling me up. I shoot another, much larger ray up to the sky, hoping it acts as a beacon as we travel on.

We seem to stay on the same road, an old highway, by the feel of it. We're driving at a fast clip based on the sound of cars rushing in the other direction, and I deduce we must be on a two-lane highway because I don't hear cars passing us in the same direction. A long two-lane highway, headed north up into the mountains pretty much narrows it down to Skull Cracker Highway or Skull Cracker Highway. Skull Cracker is a nickname for moonshine and this road is known for being an old whiskey route that conducted a lot of commerce about a hundred years ago.

The van pulls to a stop. One man gets out, and another gets in.

So far I've learned that Burt is driving and Edward sits next to me. Aaron sits across from me, but I don't know the name of the fourth guy who just came in. He's been silent. One thing is for sure, the fact that they're openly using their names doesn't bode well for me.

The van slows down and makes a right. Then after about ten minutes of winding, it goes straight again for a pass. We must be on the final stretch, heading through the wilderness. I can tell when the air changes and the faint sent of forest drifts through the ventilation.

The van slows to a stop, and the rear door opens. Edward grabs my arm and pushes me out the back. One of the men is waiting for me. He grabs me tightly and drags me forward. "Aaron, grab the rope," he says. This is a voice I haven't heard yet. He must be the fourth man. That voice, I know it from somewhere.

I purposefully trip and fall into the guy dragging me. He yanks me up, and in a derisive tone demands, "Watch it."

Holy smokes! I know that voice, all right; it's former Officer Dean Schmidt.

I'm more anxious to escape than ever now, but somehow I don't think that I can fight four men while blindfolded despite my training.

I try to keep my cool. "You know, Schmidt, it would be easier to watch it if you removed my blindfold and I could see." I punctuate that by tripping again.

Schmidt snarls and drags me up. After a moment's hesitation, he rips off my blindfold. We're standing in the doorway of a small, dilapidated church. A thick layer of dust covers the floor and rustic benches, and beer cans and fast food garbage litter the floor, speaking of teenage parties.

"So, what now?" I ask.

Schmidt's lip curls. "Now we wait for our leader to arrive, and then we get the Grimoire back from you."

"Are you insane?" I sputter. "I don't have the Grimoire!"

Schmidt smirks. "Then why did Blackwater kidnap you?"

I obviously don't want the Dilectus Deo to know about the amulet, so I lie. "He thought I had the Grimoire too. But I didn't have it then, and I don't have it now. So do you plan on torturing me? Because I've already been killed once over this damn Grimoire you all think I have, and it didn't get Blackwater anywhere."

Schmidt snickers. "Right. You were killed and brought back to life. That's rich."

"Have you ever heard of a woman surviving a hundred and fifty lashes with a horse whip before?"

Schmidt blanches, suddenly uneasy.

"I thought not."

"Shut your trap," he says as he pushes me into a small room to the right of the pulpit. "I'll be back for you later." The door locks behind me.

I inspect the room and immediately assess my options. It's a windowless square, devoid of furniture save for a rough wooden chair. No vents. But compared to the crypt, it's a five star resort.

There's exactly one option: I have to go through the wall, and not in a magical way. But first, the bindings. I use my teeth to rip furiously at the rope around my wrists, inching one end out, twisting my hands like Wang taught me. Layer by layer, I pull it through until the rope loosens and falls to the ground.

Now for the wall. I pick up the chair and rest one of its legs on the wall about two feet from the corner, close to the floor. By pushing all my weight on that chair leg, I'm able to concentrate my force onto a tiny area. Success! The leg pokes a small hole through the drywall. It's no bigger than the entrance to a birdhouse, but it's enough to reach my fingers in and grab hold of the drywall. Satisfied, I wedge the chair under the door handle.

Carefully, quietly, I start pulling at the drywall, trying to widen the hole. Damn it! It's too tough or my hands are too weak. Oh, what I wouldn't give for Vampire strength right now. This is not working as I'd hoped.

I push out my sixth sense and feel for the souls of my captors.

They're congregated around the front of the church. Good. While keeping my sixth sense on alert, I nervously take the chair out from under the doorknob again and use my weight to punch more holes into the wall with its leg. I focus on a two-foot by two-foot square near the floor. The first holes are difficult to make, but as cracks develop, the work becomes easier. In about fifteen minutes, I've got a nice patchwork of holes and a pile of drywall dust beneath it

Shoot! As I finish this task, I sense Aaron's soul coming my way. Quickly, I flip the chair in front of the wall and sit down, wrapping the rope around my wrists so I seem still tied up.

The door cracks open, and Aaron stands in the door way. I capture his eyes with mine, defiantly. I sit up straight and lift my chin in a silent challenge. Desperately, I hope that this will keep him from noticing the wall behind me. He narrows his eyes, then steps back and closes the door.

I breathe a great sigh of relief. Holy cow, that was close.

When I sense that he's moved back toward the other men, I use the chair to block the door again and start tearing at the broken drywall, pulling out chunks. There's nowhere to put it except on the floor of the room I'm in, so I know that if they come to the door again, I'll be busted.

After a few minutes pass, I've cleared the area of drywall between a pair of two-by-fours. Then I get to work on the outer planking. I can't kick the boards off because that would be far too loud. Thank goodness this is an old, decrepit clapboard building and not a brick church. The lowest two boards move easily enough. They're rotted from being so close to the damp ground in this wet region. That gives me a hole about fourteen inches wide by eighteen inches tall. I need one more board gone, and then I can fit through.

I glance anxiously at the door. The chair isn't going to hold them for long if they decide to come in. I push at the third board, but this one won't budge. The seconds tick by as my heart pounds in anticipation for the inevitable rattle of the door knob. Do I risk using the leg of the chair again? Or should I give it a mighty kick with my boot? That will surely bring the men running.

Another idea pops in my mind. I stick my hand out the hole in the wall and whisper, "Guardian," hoping fiercely that it works.

Within seconds, the solid weight of my knife fills my outstretched hand. Never have I loved a hunk of metal more. I take the blade and lever it between the wood plank and the two-by-four. The groan of wood against metal sounds alarmingly loud to my ears, but I press forward until a satisfying pop finishes the job. The board is released from one of the stubborn nails and hangs limply from the other.

I hear movement outside the door and sense Aaron just on the other side. The knob twists, and the chair shakes from the force of him trying to open the door. I throw myself headfirst through the hole just as I hear the chair crash to the side and the door slam open.

He shouts, "She's getting out!"

My arms are on the ground. I pull myself forward on my elbows, but Aaron grabs my boots. I push my weight into the ground with all my might. No way am I going back in there.

As I struggle against the force pulling me backward, I reach up, up for the light, and grab hold of it. I feel the energy shooting down into my center, so I focus it and shoot it out down my body and through my feet. I let it explode in a massive burst of energy. The instant my feet are released, I pull them through, then stand up and start running for my life toward the forest.

By the time I reach the tree line, I hear men following me. Four or five men against me; rather grim odds. I pump my arms like mad, thinking wonderful thoughts of Yao right now as I practically leap through the air with each step, but I'm not losing them.

I hear a savage snarl and my heart jumps for joy. Shooting like a bullet, Varg runs straight at me. I don't slow my pace for a second, and before we collide, he curves around me and charges at the first man.

I'm no idiot. I keep running.

My hair is flying back, snagging on branches, and my greatest fear is tripping. I use all Yao's training, high steps and loose joints, to avoid tree roots and manage uneven ground. I reach a ridge. It's steep on the other side, but I don't pause. A man's scream shatters the sounds of the forest. Varg must have gotten one.

Without hesitation, I angle myself sideways and start descending. I don't sense or hear anyone close to me now, but that means nothing. My brain screams to get as far away as possible. Keep going, keep going.

The slope is covered in a thick pad of pine needles and forest debris. My foot slides with each step until it catches on enough debris to hold. Moving as quickly as I can, I keep skidding down, doing everything I can to avoid tumbling to the ground.

Up the ridge Varg is peeking down at me. He's defending my escape route! He gets a big juicy steak if we get out of here. Forget that; he gets a whole antelope haunch if I can find one. Sure enough, as another man approaches the ridge, Varg, draws his lips back in a wicked growl and flies at the man.

Distracted by this, my footing slips, and I tip over. I cover my face with my hands and let myself roll. Branches stab me from all angles until my roll is slowed by the gentling of the slope. On shaky legs, I stand and glance back up at Varg. He's wrestling with another man now. That's three down that I know of. One or two more to go, depending on whether their leader has arrived yet. I have to keep going.

I turn around and stare straight into the barrel of a gun.

Worse yet, the face on the other side of that gun is Dean Schmidt.

My instincts and defensive training kick in. I step in closer to the gun and hold my arms up in surrender, keeping them close to my face. Sweat beads my brow as I stare directly into the gun. I soften my gaze at Schmidt and beg in the most pitiful voice I can manage, "Dean, you don't want to do this. Please don't do this."

His lips thin in irritation, but I don't give him a chance to think. As soon as the gun is inches from my head, I grab the barrel with my right arm and duck. At the same time, I grab his wrist with my left hand and push him to the right. While the gun is still in his hand, I lever it back, bending it the wrong way against the joint until the trigger slot slides back on his finger. Then I push down on his wrist and push back on the gun. With one quick jerk, I snap his finger and wrench the gun into my hands.

Schmidt howls in pain as he drops to his knees.

I step away and hold the gun on him.

His scarred face turns beet red, and his jaw clenches. His wild eyes fume at me. Then he stands up with a roar and charges me, in spite of the gun in my hand. I widen my stance and turn at an angle as he approaches like a steam engine. "Closer, come closer," I murmur to myself.

Now! I spin around on my left foot, swinging my right foot into a dropkick and knocking his head as hard as I can with my boot. His neck snaps to the side, and he lands on the ground in a roll.

And he keeps spiraling down the hill. The grade steepens and comes to an end in a berm, but after that, there's nothing but sky. I hope for his sake he slows on that tiny berm, but he's going too fast.

I scream, "Schmidt! Watch out!" But he can't stop. In horror, I watch him go over the brink.

Oh my God. I'm stunned. I never meant to kill him. I only wanted to get away.

With slow, careful sideways steps to maintain traction, I make my way down to the bottom of the ridge. Varg joins me just before I reach the precipice. His fierce growl speaks to his opinion on the matter. I tentatively peek over the ridge and suck in my breath. It's almost a straight drop, but about ten feet down, Schmidt is holding on to some shrubbery that juts out from the cliff edge. His whole face is strained with the effort of holding onto that green shrubbery, as his feet dangle below him.

His eyes are full of fear. He expects death at any moment, I can see it on his face. Still, he strains to hold on and doesn't ask for help. Why doesn't he ask for help?

I swiftly search around for what I can do to save him. My eye catches on the long kudzu that drapes off a nearby tree. I stuff the gun in my waistband and use Guardian to cut through a bunch of vines.

"Hold on, Schmidt!" I yell.

I grab another handful and cut through them. Then I gather them all up and twist them loosely together. That will have to do.

I toss the ends of the vines, still attached to the tree, over the edge at Schmidt. Confusion flashes through his eyes, but he quickly reaches his left arm out and wraps it around the makeshift rope. He releases the shrubbery and grabs on with his right hand as best as he can with a broken finger. His legs catch on the vines, and he starts scooting up.

In the distance, I hear a car door open and shouting from the ridge above. That must be the last of their party. It's my cue to get out of there. No way am I waiting for more men to arrive. I take off running, and Varg jumps in front of me, leading the way.

He takes us down the mountainside in a zigzag formation, cutting right through the forest. Branches tear at my face as we rush through the woods, so I protect myself as best as I can by holding my arms in front of me. I keep my senses on alert for any signs of pursuit. I feel and hear nothing, but every second is filled with the fear that Schmidt is going to jump out and grab me from behind.

Varg starts following a deer path that provides some relief from the sticks and brush. This new path jogs so often, it seems to take two miles to go one, but we can't run through trees.

He takes a mighty leap over a fallen tree in our path and waits patiently while I skirt around it. I'm fairly sure we aren't being chased now, but still the urgency to put more space between me and those men propels me on. We follow a dry creek bed for a while and circumnavigate an open meadow. We run and run until I can't run anymore.

Finally, I slow my pace and use the mountain to come to a stop. With my hand clutched to my side, I lean over and gasp for breath. I croak out, "Varg. I need to stop." He turns back toward me and rests by my side as I collapse on a stretch of cool grass. I lay back on the ground and notice it's twilight. Eventually my breathing eases and my heart slows down.

When my body has calmed down a bit, I push out my light again, gently, shooting it up into the darkening beyond.

Stars start to pop into the deepening sky, a brilliant display up here in the mountains. I must blink, because suddenly instead of the stars, I'm staring into Jack's worried eyes.

CHAPTER 60

Step Up or Shut Up

JACK TANNER

JULY 19, 2022, RED AGES

I track the beam of light to a small clearing in the thick of the woods, where Blue comes into view. In the first instant, my heart twists when I see her lying there on the ground. In the next instant, my whole body sighs with relief when she lifts her hand to stroke Varg's fur.

I rush to her side as she lays her head back. She smells okay. No blood. Wait, is that Schmidt I smell on her?

My eyes brush over her lovely face and pause on her lower lip, which she chews mercilessly. "What happened, Blue?"

She turns her head to meet my eyes, and I lean over, propping my elbow on the ground next to her. She's so close. I wish I could just reach out and run my hands over her sweet belly and down her thigh.

She squeezes her eyes shut. "I went to visit Alexis, and a nurse stuck a needle in her arm and threatened to shoot her up with bleach if I didn't get in a van. They blocked the van pulling a laundry truck beside it so Ammon couldn't see me." Blue opens her eyes, her sorrowful expression piercing me. "None of my friends are safe, Jack. What should I do?"

I pick up a lock of her hair and feel its silky smoothness between my rough fingertips. "Alexis called me. She's safe now, and she's been released from the hospital. Robert's going to stay with her. She's still scared, but she was mostly worried about you."

"Well, I was wondering how they knew Alexis was in the hospital. I think those guys outside of Sticky's meant to hurt her to put me in that situation. Originally I thought they were just random breedists. Are they still in holding? They must be watching me pretty closely to know she's important to me."

Her hair is so soft. I rub the strand gently across my lips and inhale her scent.

"They were released this morning, but we'll track them down and question them. Tell me what happened once you were in the van."

She opens her eyes, and her gaze catches on the lock of hair I'm brushing across my lips. A slight pucker of her brow and frown tell me she's not happy about it. I divert her. "In the van . . . "

"They tied me up and blindfolded me so I couldn't see where we were going. They tossed my chimerator and phone early on so I couldn't be tracked. I let my light shine, but I didn't know if you could see it during the day."

"I can see it, day or night. I tracked you into this region, but then your light went out." My voice catches as I say that because I can't even relive the fear I had the moment her light went out. That torment is more than should ever be borne. "What happened next?"

"They brought me to an abandoned church and stuffed me in a room while they waited for their leader to arrive. I tore through the drywall and busted out."

I raise my eyebrows at that.

Blue scoffs. "You'd probably expect a wall to be stronger than that, but that building was dilapidated. It was a piece of cake. No insulation, just clapboard."

I pick up one of her soft hands and rub the palm with my fingertips. She has some new calluses from training, but these are not the hands of a woman who can punch through walls. I peer at her skeptically.

Blue admits, "Okay, so I used a chair leg to bust through."

Still, impressive. "Did they follow you?"

"Yes, Varg held them off. I did end up in an altercation with Dean Schmidt, though."

At the mention of his name, black rage boils through me. "Dean Schmidt?"

"Yes, he may or may not be alive." She pulls a gun out of her waistband. "I took this from him."

My heart pinches anew. "He pulled a gun on you? Did you shoot him with it?"

"Yes and no. After I got the gun from him, we struggled, and he rolled off a cliff. I left him hanging, but I threw him some vines, so he might have made it up alive."

"So let me get this straight. After he abducted you and pulled a gun on you, you went out of your way to save his life?"

Blue tilts her face toward the stars. "He wasn't a threat to me at the moment. And I couldn't just let him die." Then she directs her gaze at me, and with a firm set to her chin says, "It's time to press charges, though. I'm ready for him to be arrested. I've had enough."

"I'll kill him," I mumble. The desire to snuff out his life fills me with a vicious joy, and I start contemplating the many painful ways I could end him. The vision of his face turning purple as I choke the life out of him fills me with glee.

Blue grabs my hand. "No, Jack. We'll press charges and issue an arrest warrant. And you will *not* kill him. I need you."

"Fine," I say. "We'll do it your way." Then I stand and snatch Blue up in my arms.

She pushes at my chest. "I can walk."

"I'm not walking." Then with a blast of Vampire speed, I race through the forest to the road where I left my car. In moments, I'm tucking her into the seat and fastening the seatbelt.

"Don't forget Varg."

Surprisingly, Varg is sitting by the back door, waiting to be let in. How interesting.

On the ride home, Blue hardly speaks. Her unseeing gaze is directed out the passenger window, watching the blurs of headlights pass us by. She feels unreachable to me. I reach out and grasp her hand, but she gives it a quick squeeze and pulls away.

When we arrive at the apartment building, I follow her upstairs to the hallway that separates our abodes. Reluctant to part, I call to her as she turns toward her apartment. "Blue."

I don't know what I want. I just want. I want her.

She turns to me with sad eyes. "Yes?"

I reach out my hand and gently stroke her shoulder. She flinches away, and pain knifes through me. Thinking of her date with Robert, jealousy grips my heart. "Blue, are you and Robert serious?"

Blue snaps her eyes at me. "Jack, you need to make up your damn mind. I am not a plaything for you to cuddle with when you feel like it and then force away when you have other ideas."

I pull my hand back as though burned, but she isn't done. "If you want me, you need to step up and say so. Otherwise, keep your hands to yourself and don't worry about who I date."

With a huff, she lets Varg into her apartment and slams the door behind her.

CHAPTER 61

TIES OF FRIENDSHIP

BLUEBELL KILDARE

JULY 20, 2022, RED AGES

My worry over Alexis hasn't subsided, and I know it won't until I check on her, so I swing over to her shop on my way to training with Maev. Varg and I walk through her doors and the bells merrily declare our entrance. Alexis turns from a customer and flies at me. I hold open my arms and hug her for all I'm worth.

"I'm so sorry that happened to you because of me. You don't hate me?"

Alexis leans back and says, "Please, a little wicked nurse isn't going to scare me away."

She says this, but she's wearing two amulets about her neck, which is unusual. "How's your arm?"

She holds it up. "It's right as rain, now."

From across the room, her customer stares impatiently at us and suspiciously at Varg. "Do you need to finish up with your customer?"

Alexis pulls back. "Yes, I'll just be a minute."

When she's done, she calls Penelope to mind the store and takes us into the kitchen.

She grabs two mugs and declares, "I'm making hot chocolate while you tell me what happened."

So typically bossy; I love it. As she stirs the pot and fills the cups, I tell her the story.

When I'm done, she asks, "Well, why do they want you?"

I knew this question was coming, but I say as little as possible. "They think I have a powerful magical artifact from the Blackwater case, which I don't have." The more she knows, the worse for her.

"Hmm," she says. "And is there any way to convince them you don't have it?"

I think on this. "The only thing would be if they found out who really had it, and I don't know who really has it. I don't even know if anyone has it at all."

Alexis seems about as stumped as I feel. But there are other issues to discuss. "Alexis, clearly they know we're friends. I'm worried about you."

"And I'm worried about you."

"But I carry a gun, handcuffs, and a wolf."

Alexis leans her arms on her butcher block countertop. "Well, then, I'd better get cooking up some protection charms, collecting some amulets, and preparing some spells."

"You should take every precaution, and if you ever feel like even the slightest thing is off, call me right away."

Then to lighten the mood, I ask, "So, what did Robert think of this whole mess?"

Her eyes gleam. "Now that is a fine man. He took charge after the nurse left. He called the nurses' station, who notified hospital security. The nurse had apparently been there for a long time. They were all shocked, and if Robert hadn't been there, I don't think they would have believed me. He dressed them down and called his lawyer. I suspect I'll be getting a nice settlement from them before this is over. And . . . " she trails off.

"What?"

"I actually spent the night at his mansion last night."

"Really?"

She smiles teasingly. "Well, in one of his many guest rooms. But we did have breakfast together. He didn't think I should be alone."

"I'm glad, Alexis. You know I don't have any deep feelings for him, right?"

Alexis smiles even wider. "Good to know."

CHAPTER 62

BLUE SKIES

JACK TANNER

JULY 20, 2022, RED AGES

I tuck the arrest warrant for Dean Schmidt in my pocket and whistle happily as I run down the steps of the old courthouse to my car. This bit of good news lightens my dark mood considerably. The church Blue escaped from was empty and the injured gone when I sent Lazare and Gia back there last night, but this warrant almost makes up for that. In minutes, I'm pulling into the Center of Enlightenment parking lot accompanied by five squad cars and cuffs ready to be filled by Schmidt's wrists.

Detective Tony Gambino steps out of his car and directs his men to cover the exits while he accompanies me to the front door under the watch of a benevolent blue sky and brilliant sun.

I swing open the doors, and a young man, a greeter decked out in gold robes, steps forward boldly. "You're not welcome here."

He actually makes me smile with that statement. "I know. I'm not asking to be welcome." I flash him my badge and pull out the arrest warrant. "I'm with the Supernatural Investigation Bureau and I'm here for Dean Schmidt. Will you get him for me, or would you prefer I search the premises on my own?"

The greeter turns a furious shade of red. "Hold on," he spits through gritted teeth before stalking out of the room.

Still feeling unusually joyous, I whistle another little tune in the lobby, making Gambino crack a smile. Some days my job is more enjoyable than other days This is looking to be a fine day indeed. While I'd get more enjoyment out of sucking Schmidt's blood from his body and feeling his life drain out of him, Blue's right. I can't give into bloodlust now when the stakes are so high. At least knowing he's rotting in jail will give me some sort of perverse joy.

A few minutes later, two men accompany the greeter back to the lobby. The larger one, wearing a full beard and an unhappy expression, says, "I understand you're interested in Dean Schmidt?"

"Yes, I am."

The shorter man, smaller framed and bespeckled says, "May I have a copy of the arrest warrant?"

I feel victory just around the corner. With an easy smile, I hand him a copy for his perusal. He studies it and confers with the larger man. "It appears to be real."

The larger man purses his lips. "I'm Josiah. I oversee the residential quarters. Dean Schmidt left us yesterday and hasn't been back since. I can show you to where he was staying if you'd like."

At my side, Gambino curses under his breath, and suddenly my day seems a little gray. "Please do."

We tail Josiah to a quiet residential hallway and wait while he unlocks a door. The room is sparsely furnished with a single bed, a chest that serves as both a nightstand and a dresser, and a slim desk beneath a small window. No personal affects remain, and there's no closet to peek in. Cursory examination of the chest and under the bed confirm that nothing remains of Schmidt's possessions, but the room definitely reeks of Schmidt.

I turn to Josiah. "Where did he go?"

Josiah opens his mouth to speak, but the weaselly little man steps forward. "Dean left the brotherhood, and we have no knowledge of his whereabouts. We've neither seen nor heard from him since he left. He is no longer affiliated with us, and he didn't leave a forwarding address."

With a scowl, I look to see if Gambino is ready for the next step. He nods back at me, and I tell the scrawny man, "We'll need to search the premises now."

An hour later, I step out of the Center for Enlightenment empty-handed and glare at the mocking blue sky and overly bright sun.

CHAPTER 63

OF MYTH AND LEGEND

BLUEBELL KILDARE

JULY 20, 2022, RED AGES

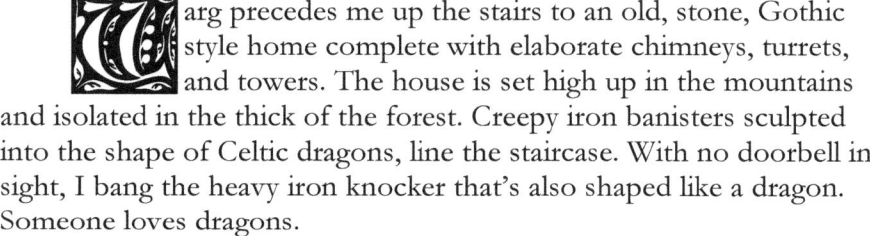arg precedes me up the stairs to an old, stone, Gothic style home complete with elaborate chimneys, turrets, and towers. The house is set high up in the mountains and isolated in the thick of the forest. Creepy iron banisters sculpted into the shape of Celtic dragons, line the staircase. With no doorbell in sight, I bang the heavy iron knocker that's also shaped like a dragon. Someone loves dragons.

The door swings open to reveal Maev, dressed all in black today. Shiny black practice shoes peek out from underneath a heavy knit skirt, and the black, ruffled chiffon collar of her blouse practically swallows her petite frame in its layered folds. Bright gray eyes glint in eagerness. "You made it."

I feel relief and excitement fill the hall, and I wonder if she expected me to stand her up. It's no less than she deserves for completely disappearing for fifteen years.

But I'm distracted from the buzz of her emotions when I notice Varg running around Maev and doing the happy dance as though he's met a long lost friend. "He acts like he knows you."

Maev smiles down at him. "That's because he does."

My eyes flick from Maev to Varg, and from Varg to Maev again while a cold, tight fist wraps around my heart. "He found me in an alley not long ago. Is he yours?"

Maev's eyes narrow. "No, he is not *mine*. He belongs to no one. Whoever got the bright idea they could own another living being, I don't know. Come with me, and I'll tell you the story."

I follow her through the house, admiring the stained glass windows and arched entryways into every room off the main hall.

"I was busy while I was away. I wasn't exactly vacationing on the beach. One of my tasks was to find a guardian to help you fulfill the prophecy."

"A guardian?"

"Yes, you require three guardians to fulfill the prophecy."

She takes me down a winding metal staircase into a wing of the home set lower than the rest. We must be toward the back of the hill. The room is enormous and completely empty aside from a bench and a few mats, but it has the most stunning view. I walk over to one of the many stone framed, arched windows where almost all of Crimson Hollow spreads out before me with distant houses sprinkling the mountainsides.

"You can see everything up here," I say in awe.

Maev smiles at my obvious enjoyment. "Yes, that's why this site was chosen when my family first followed your family to this area. Anyway, as I was saying, I was searching for a guardian for you. There aren't too many real guardians left, and they aren't easy to find. It took me years to track down Fenrir and free him so that he could come to you."

"Who's Fenrir?"

Maev's sharp eyes glint with some mysterious thrill. "Fenrir is Varg's real name. He's the son of the god Loki and the giantess Angrboda."

At that, I sit right down on the mat, completely shocked. Varg, taking that as a sign, lies down too and sticks his head in my lap. With wonder, I ask him, "Varg, are you the son of a god?" His tail thumps a few times in response.

Maev sits down with me, leaning against the window.

I inquire as I lovingly stroke Varg's fur, "So you freed him. From what?"

"I traced the path of the legends through time. He was trapped deep in the marshes of the Lapland region near what used to be the city of Oulu on the old Gulf of Bothnia. I found him, as the legends say, tied to a massive bolder with a deceptively thin, enchanted chain. He'd been stuck there for thousands of years, so naturally, the bargain I struck with him was well received."

"What exactly was the bargain?"

"Simply to manifest himself in physical form on this plane of existence and act as your guardian in trade for setting him free."

My heart breaks in two, and I rub Varg all the more. "Why was he chained for thousands of years?"

Maev reaches over and flicks one of his ears playfully. "As the son of a giantess, Fenrir grew to be massive and powerful. The gods feared him, so they made many attempts to chain him. Eventually they found a way."

"So that's it? He was too large, and they were scared of him?"

"Basically. The gods are vain and fiercely concerned with maintaining their power. They saw him as a threat."

I lean over and give Varg a big hug. "Well, I'm glad you're free now. Who knew you were a demigod? No wonder you can do so many tricks."

Maev smiles at this. "His physical form limits him, I'm sure, but he'll make a loyal and fierce protector for all of your days. He can be wounded severely in his physical form, but his essence is essentially immortal. But enough of that; we must get to training."

The phrase "all of your days" rings in my ears with a sinister note. Do I really have the right to keep him tied to me for all of my days?

"Wait!" My heart breaks at what I'm about to do, but it must be done. My conscience will have it no other way. "He isn't really free yet. He's free from the chain but not from your promise. To me, that's little more than slavery."

Maev frowns. "It was an agreement, freely made."

"By a demigod who was bound for centuries! I want you to undo the agreement. I won't have him helping me like that. He should be truly free."

She grows very worried. "Are you sure Blue? I spent the better part of fifteen years searching for him and tracking down the magic required to free him. There's no time to find a replacement."

Scared and heartbroken, I repeat myself. "He must be free. I won't have him bound to me that way."

Maev's eyes pierce me as though trying to determine how serious I am. I pierce her eyes right back.

She smiles gently, then to Varg she says, "Fenrir, you are absolved from your requirements under our contract."

Varg blinks, then wags his tail.

My heart breaks, but I know this is right. "Let him go. Let him outside so he can leave."

With heavy steps, Maev opens the sliding door, and Varg turns his head to look at me.

I kneel down and wrap my arms around him, digging my fingers deep in his fur. "I'm going to miss you so much, Varg. You've been my best friend, and you're the best wolf ever." Then I stand, and mindless of the tears tracking down my cheeks, I wave my hands to shoo him out. "Go! You're free!"

Varg walks to the door and steps halfway out. A breeze blows by, and his fur undulates under its invisible fingers. His nostrils flare as he catches the scent of the wind. His ears perk as he listens to its song. The whole valley lies before him—the whole world, really.

He starts to dissolve in the air, becoming insubstantial and transparent. He takes a step forward. Then he solidifies, but still he scents the air. His whole body trembles with excitement, and he dissolves again until he's hardly more than a shimmer in the air. I kneel down to reach my hand out toward him, to touch him one last time. He turns to me and solidifies again as he rubs his body against me and walks back into the training room. He lies down in the far corner.

I've never been so happy in my entire life. I laugh and cry, and ask through both, "Are you sure he knows he's free?"

Maev smiles. "Yes, it was only honor that kept him to the contract. He wasn't physically bound. My guess is that love keeps him with you now; a far stronger binding than an honor contract."

Well, whatever it is that keeps him here, I'm so grateful for it.

When I've calmed down and wiped my tears on my shirt sleeve, Maev announces, "Well, let's proceed, shall we?" She stands up and walks to the center of the mats, and I follow suit.

"Your light," she says in her teacher voice, bringing back memories of my time in the orphanage, "is made up of particles of energy. Unlike matter, it has no mass. However, every atom that makes up matter contains energy. You can use your light's energy to confuse the energy in solid matter, to manipulate it and even control it. You can do this by directing your light at the *energy* in matter, not the matter itself."

I think about this a moment. "So that's why when I pushed at the balls of energy in the rats, I was able to push their bodies back. I was focused on the energy coming from the rats and not the bodies of the rats."

"Exactly. Today we're going to practice suction."

I laugh. "Suction?"

"Yes, suction," she responds matter-of-factly. "Suction is when matter flows from a high-pressure area to a low-pressure area. This is how a vacuum sucks up dirt particles. The high pressure in the room pushes the dirt into the low-pressure vacuum. In much the same way, you can use your light's energy to create a low-pressure area that matter can be sucked into."

"How do I do this?"

"The concept is simple. You pull energy from the air into your light, creating an area of lower pressure around your light. Then matter will be sucked into that area. It's a bit harder to accomplish than to explain, though." She thinks for a moment. "The other day, I saw you reaching up with your light and pulling energy down. That's what you need to do, but you need to pull energy from the air this time.

"The first thing I want you to do is create a flow of light from the energy in the room. You need to find the energy in the small particles in the room and call it to you. The energy of just one particle is great, great enough to create a massive explosion, big enough to demolish this whole city. So go easy. You only need to focus on a small area of air and pull gently. We aren't here to rip particles apart. Neither of us will survive that, wards or no wards."

Now slightly scared, I focus on a small bit of air about three feet from me. I call to the energy in the air, beckoning it toward me. I feel a brief rush of air but no light apart from my own.

I let my sixth sense magnify until I clearly see Maev's soul as a firm outline. I magnify it even more until I see the energy signature of every piece of matter in the room. By sinking even further into my sixth sense, I begin to see the faint glow of energy from the very air. I focus on the energy in the area between Maev and me. I beckon the diffuse light toward one point in the air and it pulls together sharply into a bright glow.

"Excellent," Maev praises. "I can see the light you created."

She reaches into her pocket and pulls out a fluffy white ostrich plume that curves delicately on her hand. "Now I want you to create a ball of light above this feather and call the energy into that light to create a vacuum. You'll pull the energy from under the light but over the feather. This will lift the feather up. Remember, go gently. I don't want my hand to implode."

I do as she asks, creating a globe of light by concentrating the energy in the air. I feed the globe by pulling energy into it, from above the feather. The feather shifts slightly in Maev's hand. Slowly and cautiously, I increase the flow of energy from the air above the feather. The feather flutters rapidly, and my heart matches its flutters with excitement. But it still isn't lifting. Beads of perspiration pop up on my brow, and I concentrate harder, increasing the flow even more. The feather seems to struggle, dancing on Maev's palm a bit, until finally it lifts up from Maev's hand and hangs there in the air just below my light.

Maev beams at the accomplishment, and I may be doing some beaming of my own.

She walks toward a closet and reaches into it. "Now for something a bit harder." She turns around and holds a round red metal ball the size of a grapefruit.

"Holy cow! That's a lot different than a feather."

With a tip of her head, Maev encourages, "Yes, but you can do it."

I'm soooo not sure about this. Nevertheless, I'm willing to give it a shot.

This time Maev sets the ball down and stands beside me, which is still too close for a massive explosion if I make a mistake, but wise nonetheless.

I focus on my sixth sense again and concentrate the energy from the air into a loose, thrumming orb over the metal ball. Repeating my process from earlier, I pull energy from the air above the red ball into my light. The heavy ball sits there, undisturbed.

I try to grab more air from around the room and pull energy into my light.

Maev whispers softly, "You're reaching too far. Only the air right next to the ball will affect it. You don't need more air. You simply need to pull more energy from the air just over the ball. Remember, the energy in a single particle is massive. Just focus on pulling the energy in a more concentrated way, but go gently. Don't pull too much."

I focus my pull into a tight stream, and little lines of light crackle around the metal ball like tiny electric bolts feeding into my sphere of light. The red ball wavers and rolls a bit.

I grit my teeth and try again, this time pulling even harder. My orb of light starts to glow a hot white in the center and the red ball seems to lift off the ground a tiny bit. I pull even harder, and the heavy ball shoots up six inches and hovers there, just under the orb of light.

Maev claps her hands together and smiles broadly.

"Oh my God, this is telekinesis. I can't believe I'm doing telekinesis."

"You'll be able to do a lot more than that before we're done. But yes, the essential heart of this particular lesson is telekinesis. Now I want you to reshape your light into a ribbon and wrap it around the ball as it hangs there."

With effort, my light stretches out and reforms into a rod shape—not quite a ribbon, but I think it will do. I move the light so it snakes loosely around the red ball in three directions.

"Very good. Now while your light is still wrapped around the ball, I want you to move it a bit, and the ball should move with it."

With my body trembling from the force of concentration, I move my ribbon of light a few inches to the left, and wonder of wonders, I'm moving the ball!

Maev stomps her foot and shoots her hands in the air, shouting, "Yes!"

Her waving arms catch my attention, and *thunk,* the ball drops. Still, I can't help my grin. This is so much fun.

Maev turns serious now, though. "You can use this lesson to protect yourself. With practice, you'll be able to lift, push, pull, or even contain any object or person. When you surrounded the ball with your light, it had vacuum suction on all sides, so it couldn't move. There are so many degrees of expertise with this. Today was just a start. In the end, you should be able to manipulate many objects at once while you do other things, like fight assailants. So your ability to focus needs a lot of improvement."

Holy smokes! I picture wrapping my light around five perpetrators while I fight another. That would be so helpful. Jack could never complain about me going out on my own again.

Maev puts the orb back in the closet and turns to me. "That's enough for today. You should try this at home with small objects if you think you can go lightly and control it. This room is warded against damage, but your place is not. You wouldn't want to create such a great vacuum that it sucked you in. It's a dangerous art, and you should practice a healthy respect for its potential."

Fair enough. Definitely no creating great, big, sucking black holes.

CHAPTER 64

GENOCIDE

BLUEBELL KILDARE

JULY 20, 2022, RED AGES

ambino, the final addition to our war room meeting, sits wearily down next to Marian. Everyone is stressed and drained. Yepa is on her fourth cup of coffee already, having only slept a few hours, so her hands practically vibrate. Sidney sits next to her in yesterday's rumpled shirt, sifting through pictures on his handheld device. Marian, fresh and clean but with bloodshot eyes, confers in whispers with Oscar, who indicates agreement. Jack, who sits between Gambino and me, is the only one of us who seems well-rested and alert.

We have much to discuss, so I begin the meeting. "All right team, I'll start with a review, and then we'll go around the table and get updates."

When all eyes turn toward me, I say. "Joe, a master fire controller, was reported missing on Monday, July 10th. Late on Tuesday, July 11th, his daughter was abducted, presumably to use as leverage against Joe by his abductees. Wednesday, July 12th, just before midnight, we have our first fire.

"Chief Mack called us in to examine the first fire the next day. The victims were the Roses, a family of five in which the only Gifted person was the eight-year-old daughter, Hannah."

"Around midnight on Friday, July 14th, we have the Becheva family fire. This was a family of two in which five-year-old Kalina was Gifted.

"On Saturday, July 15th, we have the third and fourth fires: the Pennington family of four with a Gifted father and two Gifted sons, and the Sorenson family of three with one Gifted daughter.

"I've confirmed with Chief Mack that there have been no more fires of this nature in the last four days."

Yana and Oliver both knock on the wood table for good luck. At this point I'm willing to accept prayers, chants, good luck charms, voodoo dances, and anything else that might help.

"So right now our total stands at four families with fourteen dead. Plus we have two missing people: Joe and his daughter, Becky. Okay, let's go around and everyone can give their updates, starting with you, Oscar."

Oscar clears his throat. "I conducted seven interviews yesterday with the Penningtons' friends and family. I wasn't able to confirm that they passed through downtown, but everyone I interviewed knew that the boys were Gifted, as you mentioned, so that makes at least one Gifted child in each family. I've broken down where the family was confirmed or assumed to be on the day of their deaths and passed that to Yepa and Sidney for analysis."

Yepa leans forward, twitchy and eager to share some news. "Yepa, go ahead," I say.

Her eyes shine with excitement as she delivers her update. "I've had a big break. The last known stop for the Penningtons was at the Pit Stop gas station on the west side, based on credit card receipts. I projected how long it would take their car to pass every major street in every direction from the gas station and hacked into the appropriate camera systems—mostly banks and gas stations because they're the only ones with decent systems. Sorry, getting off track. Anyway, I was able to locate them heading north on Center toward downtown. I lost them after that. The last verified location was in front of the Crimson Hollow Credit Union at 2:46 p.m. I gave Sidney the coordinates of each location I was able to verify."

"That is the best news we've had yet! So we know all parties went through downtown. What did you find, Sidney?"

Sidney's crisp, precise voice fills us in. "Based on when Yepa last saw the car and their estimated arrival time back home according to their neighbor, we have a fifteen to twenty minute block of time that's missing, so it's clear they stopped somewhere along the way.

"I've studied the other families' timelines and found the Rose family had ten to twenty minutes unaccounted for, and the Sorensons had a very precise twenty-two minute block of time missing. I thought the Becheva family had unaccounted time as well, but then Milan said that time was spent at the park. Still, we have three blocks of ten to twenty-two minutes missing from our timelines.

"I did find one pattern I can confirm. Chief Mack sent me the data points for the times of the fires, the durations, the temperatures, and the damage. For each subsequent incident, the fire is becoming more controlled. The duration of the burn is lowering, and the temperature is remaining steady. The damage, however, is less with each fire. The first house was demolished. The second was partially burned, and in the third and fourth houses, only the interior was burned. That's a valid pattern, but it's all I have."

Marian says, "Very interesting. They're testing and getting better. Maybe that's why we haven't had more fires: because with the last set, they perfected the burn to one that has little chance of burning neighbor's houses. Now that begs the question, what were they perfecting it for? To use it in the future, obviously. Now, if we assume this is a hate crime against Gifted children, then we have to assume they were perfecting this to perform more atrocities in the future, perhaps on a grander scale."

Oscar chimes in. "If they weren't waiting for some event, then they would keep picking the children off one-by-one. We wouldn't have this lull. And I don't think any of us can ignore the fact that the Sun Flare Celebration is in two days."

I speak up. "When a group targets the children of one breed, with the intent of mass murder, then that's genocide. That's what's happening here."

The room suddenly feels like a pressure cooker with the weight of concern exploding from everyone present. Eyes widen, and teeth clench. The seriousness of this situation is crystal clear.

I turn to Jack. "What did the mayor say about putting off the celebration?"

Jack's face darkens. "He refused. He said four fires by a random arsonist had nothing to do with the celebration, and he wouldn't put it off. In fact, he informed me that they're opening the festival at ten o'clock in the morning instead of noon this year."

Fear, swirling grey and murky, flows through the room, filling my sixth sense. "That means we have one day to figure it out. I understand it seems impossible, but we must all have hope."

CHAPTER 65

UNSTOPPABLE LOYALTY

BLUEBELL KILDARE

July 21, 2022, Red Ages

The thin light of dawn filters through my window, casting a weak glow on my apartment as I assemble my weapons. The gloom of the room matches my mood since I worked until four in the morning and only caught a couple hours of sleep. With just one day to catch a genocidal arsonist, there's no time to waste. Varg and I step into the hallway, and I run smack into Jack.

"Oh, sorry," I apologize. "I was thinking about the case."

Jack is unusually grim, his eyes a deep green, his mouth strained. But most telling of all is the grief eluding the iron grip of he-who-is-so-controlled. He grabs my arm. "Wait. I have something to tell you."

This is not going to be good news, I can tell. I lean against my doorframe. "Not another fire?"

Jack shakes his head. "It's Mike Kramer. He was assassinated early this morning on his way home from the office. A small poison dart laced with a nerve agent. At least it was quick."

"Oh, Jack." I place my hand on his arm, trying to offer some comfort. "I'm so sorry. I know you two were friends."

With his voice gravely and breaking, he says, "He was a good man, and we'll find whoever did it."

"Where did it happen?"

"He left the office shortly after the war room team broke for the night, and they got him outside his home. His wife saw the car in the driveway and knew he hadn't been to bed, so she went outside and found him in the yard."

"Do you know who would do this?"

He straightens his shoulders and runs his fingers through his hair.

"No, but you must be suspicious and constantly vigilant. This isn't random."

The seriousness of the situation sinks in.

"You can trust Ernesto, Xavier, Rubalia, Ammon, Dragomira, Wang, and Yao. But that's all. Regard everyone else with suspicion."

I probe his eyes gently. "And you, Jack. I can trust you."

Jack's face twists into a hard-won smile. "Yes, in this situation, you can trust me. Come now; I'll walk you to your car."

We somberly take the stairs, and as Jack walks with us, his eyes sweep in all directions, searching for any sign of trouble. I let Varg in the backseat and then find Jack still standing there awkwardly.

"Was there something else you wanted to say?"

Jack smiles that gentle, caring smile. The smile that doesn't belong to a boss, or to a bloodthirsty Vampire, the smile I love so much. "Yes, I've been thinking about what you said the other day about making a decision about us. You were right, and I'm giving it serious thought."

Then he leans over and softly kisses my temple before walking away.

My heart tries to leap for joy, but I shove it down, far, far away. I've been through too many ups and downs with him. What will happen will happen.

I get in the car and lock my door, more cautious than usual. Then I pull out into the light traffic of early morning. While I hate waking up early, I do love this time of day. The sleepy city is just awakening as the sun starts to brighten the sky. A woman in a robe and slippers steps outside to grab a newspaper while an old man walks his dog in front of her house. A diner flips its sign to open as the street lamps slowly blink off.

A few blocks down, a huge moving van pulls in front of me and meanders along at five miles below the speed limit. Frustrated, I throw my arm over the backseat and check my blind spot to get in the left lane. No luck; a car is coming up quickly, so I relax and wait for it to pass. When I check its trajectory, the profile of the driver catches my eye.

Holy cripes! That's Schmidt! His scarred face makes him unmistakable. He glares at me as he drives by. I move to follow him, but another car blocks my path. It hangs out, side by side with the moving truck, and I can't get by. It's probably for the best. Schmidt isn't my priority today. We've got to crack the arson case. I stay behind the moving truck as we pass into the outskirts of the business district.

As I slow to a stop at a red light, my car shifts and reels to the right without warning, a loud popping sound coming from beneath me. Shoot! I can't possibly have a flat tire after getting four new ones installed just a couple months ago. More than a little nervous now, I coast into the parking lane.

Varg and I get out to inspect the damage when the back of the moving truck door pulls open. A hoard of men comes pouring out toward us, several of them carrying machine guns. Holy smokes! I push my emergency button faster than I ever have before and yell, "Run Varg!"

I try to take off too, but the air thickens around me, and no amount of force can propel me forward. It's like I'm mired in quicksand. The more I struggle, the more stuck I become. It must be some sort of force field.

The men are upon me, at least twenty of them dressed in black capes with deep cowls. One man stands to the side, holding his hands out and chanting a spell. He must be holding the force field in place.

I'm out-gunned, out-magicked, and out-manned at least twenty to one. Two of the men grab my arms and pull me toward the truck. Through the force field, I can faintly hear Varg growling and barking with malicious violence. When I turn around, Schmidt's car is parked next to mine as he watches the scene intently. I ignore him.

All my attention is on Varg, who's breaking my heart as he jumps helplessly against the unseen barrier, snarling and fighting ruthlessly to get to me. He backs up and runs full force, then disappears before reaching the wall. The next I see him, he's reappeared on his side as though he bounced off the barrier. He gets back up and tries again, growling viciously all the while. Again, he lands on his side. But still he doesn't give up. He backs up farther and makes a running leap. He disappears, and I hear a thud like he impacted the force field, but he lands on the ground yet again. Oohhhhh Varg.

"Run, Varg! Get Jack!" I yell. But Varg keeps throwing himself against the force field. As I watch him, my heart crumbles into a million pieces. He continues fruitlessly as the men keep pulling me into the truck and I can't see him anymore.

CHAPTER 66

AMPHITHEATER

BLUEBELL KILDARE

JULY 21, 2022, RED AGES

Once in the truck, the men shove me onto the dirty floor, then disarm me and toss my chimerator and phone. That is the second phone this week, and Rubalia is so not going to be happy about that.

These men are definitely not Dilectus Deo as a good many of them are Gifted. Schmidt probably got a thrill seeing them drag me into the truck, but he wasn't a part of this. Their bodies fill the small space with heat, making the summer air all the more hot and sticky. After a moment, I realize not all my captors are men. A few women are interspersed throughout the group. Yep, definitely not the Dilectus Deo, as they don't allow women to serve in the brotherhood. Women can only attend as members. My guess is this is an extension of whatever group Blackwater was in.

Their mood isn't hateful like the Dilectus Deo, either. By peeking into a few of their souls, I get a good idea what I'm dealing with: arrogance and greed. That definitely matches Blackwater's ailment, but unlike him, this group is perfectly sane and totally focused. Most of their mouths are set in grim lines and their stances rigid and determined. But the feeling I get from them is nervous excitement mixed with a bit of anxiety. They're anticipating something, and I hope I'm not the main event.

I scoot along the floor until I'm tucked into the back corner where I can lean my head back and think. I concentrate on pushing a small beam of light up through the top of the truck, knowing that Jack is probably already searching for me.

My heart twists again as I think of Varg and the arson case. What rotten luck that I'd be caught on this day of all days. Well, there's still a strong team working on the case, so hopefully they'll figure it out. But the last thing Jack needs is to spend his day chasing after me. A shiver runs through me at the thought of any more horrific, fiery deaths.

My plan is to be a docile prisoner until I can find a chance to escape. With only my light, my handcuffs, and hopefully my knife, I'll have to be choosy about the moment. We drive on for about forty-five minutes in the sweltering heat of too many bodies in too small a space, and I keep my light shining the whole time. The truck twists and turns so much that I have absolutely no sense of direction at this point— except up. We're definitely traveling up a mountain.

The truck finally comes to a stop, and a blast of fresh air rushes in as the door opens. I'm rudely dragged out of the truck, and I take in the terrain. My jaw drops. We're at some sort of gathering place with concentric semicircles of crumbling, stone slab seating facing a stone stage with a huge building behind it. The building is made of the same stone, apparently hewn out of the surrounding mountains. It's covered in vines and seems partially absorbed by the forest. The whole setting appears to be an ancient amphitheater of sorts. Before the Great Pact, many secret meeting places such as this were created where those in hiding could come together.

That isn't why my jaw dropped, though. I'm shocked because several hundred black-robed people sit about on the stone slab seating, watching with an air of curious indifference as I'm dragged into the building. What is this group? I had no idea such an organization existed at all, let alone on the outskirts of Crimson Hollow. And why is it they blithely ignore a woman being dragged across the ground? Is this a common occurrence for them, or were they expecting me? What's their purpose? And most importantly of all, why do they want me?

Only their faces and hands show from underneath their shrouding cloaks, but many are clearly marked as Gifted. A familiar feeling of anticipation emanates from the group, although some are also throwing up an ugly, dark cloud of fear.

My mind staggers at the power of all these Gifted individuals in one place. At the same time, I recognize my chances of escaping just got much slimmer.

Two men drag me into the building as armed men surround us. The inner chamber is lit only by the sun filtering through the open doors, leaving most of the chamber in degrees of shadow. Flambeaux, torches that use magic to fuel the flame, are held in place on the walls by iron rings but remain unlit.

As soon as I enter, I immediately sense old magic, a subtle, hidden magic, and my eyes fly to the middle of the room. A big, flat altar indicates the room is used for magic rituals, but what pulls my gaze is the small object that sits upon it. It's a flat, ruby-encrusted box made of yellow gold and embossed with platinum. The sun glints off the many facets of the jewels, and the reflections dance upon the walls and ceiling of the room.

Two men flank the altar. They wear the same robes as everyone else, but their waists are cinched with red braided belts where the others have none. Another man leans against the far wall, enshrouded in shadow, with only his white belt clearly distinguishable.

The man on my right steps forward. "Bluebell, I'm glad you arrived safely. We've been anticipating you."

His face is hidden within the deep cowl of his robe and the gloomy lighting, but the reflection from the jewels illuminates intelligent, soft, blue eyes and a strong jaw.

"Who are you, and why did you bring me here?"

He folds his hands together as though carefully considering my question. "You can call me Vesh, and this is Emmet." He gestures toward the other man flanking the altar, but he doesn't introduce the Shadow Man. "We are of the Order of Lily, and we want the key for the Grimorium Cantionum Spiritualium, of course." He indicates the box as he speaks.

Emmet, who stands in a streak of sunlight, is middle-aged with short, brown hair and a full beard. He steps forward and interjects, "And you proved quite stubborn while in Tobias Blackwater's care, so we've had to take this measure."

I can't help the rush of pride that washes over me, but it doesn't do much to help me now. My eye is drawn to the box again. I try to step forward to inspect it more closely, but the men holding my arms stop me. "That's the Grimoire?" I ask.

"Yes," Vesh answers, "and we know you have the key."

My mind reels from the fact that the most powerful book in the world is right here in front of me, yet the magic feels so innocuous. No wonder this book was hard to find.

Realizing the man is waiting on my response, I pull my thoughts away from the book and answer honestly, "But you're mistaken; I don't have the key. Blackwater kept saying I did, but I don't."

The man's face turns solemn. "I thought you would say that. As you know, tonight is a full moon, and at midnight we'll be calling the Great Demon Lilith to question you herself."

I startle at that. "But how can you call Lilith when you don't have the key?"

The man smiles at me as though talking to a child. "Blue, we don't require the Grimoire to call a Demon. With the correct knowledge to call her and enough power, she simply requires a sacrifice."

I never in my life wished I'd had a chance to go to magic school more than now. Of course, I should have remembered that from Dragomira's story. Only blood and the knowledge to call her are necessary. Patersuco used the knowledge in the book, but Dragomira never said that others didn't have the knowledge.

Vesh continues, "We'll have to keep you in one of the holding chambers until she arrives. I apologize that our accommodations are so poor, but I think they're a step up from Tobias' arrangements for you." He shudders slightly, then waves his hand to dismiss me.

The guards drag me through an arched doorway to a corridor lined with ancient doors made from heavy iron and thick planks of wood. The last door is secured from the outside with an enormous iron bolt. They stop here, unbar the door, and unceremoniously shove me in.

CHAPTER 67

TRACKING THE LIGHT

JACK TANNER

JULY 21, 2022, RED AGES

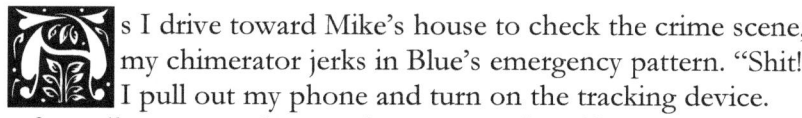s I drive toward Mike's house to check the crime scene, my chimerator jerks in Blue's emergency pattern. "Shit!" I pull out my phone and turn on the tracking device. She's a few miles away on her regular route to the office, but her green dot isn't moving. I make a quick left, and ignoring the speed limits, I race to her location, adjusting my route as the dot starts to move. Keeping one eye on the road and the other on the device, I watch the blinking green light move northeast toward Black Mountain.

Suddenly the light isn't moving anymore. I'm almost on it, but Blue is nowhere to be seen. "Damn it!"

As soon as I hit the target, I scan the area. Nothing. I pull the car over and hop out. Over by the curb is a pile of broken metal and plastic. Her phone. About ten feet up, I catch the gleam of her chimerator. Both hold the scent of Blue, but I also smell several male hands that have touched it even more recently. My heart squeezes tight as I try to decipher the clues.

She pressed the emergency button a few miles from here. Then men were touching her chimerator and phone on her way here and now they're here on the curb. She's been abducted again. As I realize this, the color seems to bleed out of the world, leaving me on a plane of dull grays, as though mourning her loss with me. I swear, this time when I get her back, I'm going to lock her up myself. I can't take it anymore.

My fangs descend and my senses sharpen. I will get her back. Flaring my nostrils, I deeply inhale to pick up additional clues or scents I can track. One scent comes through loud and clear: Varg.

I jump in the car and roll down the top. With the wind blowing in my face, I can easily track the wolf. I just hope he's got the scent of the vehicle. Varg's trail brings me northeast as I head toward city limits. His scent gets stronger as I close in on him. They must be taking Cripple Creek Road, the only road in this area that goes all the way up the mountain.

When I hit Cripple Creek Road I'm able to floor it along the first stretch. When the suburbs turn to country and the buildings clear from my path, I can see a faint beam of light shooting out from the trees. I breathe in relief. "Blue."

After another minute, I spot Varg running at incredible speeds, pushing himself forward with enormous bounds. I pull up beside him and shout, "Jump in, Varg!"

With a mighty leap, he flies through the air and lands in my backseat. Hoping he understands me and expecting he does, I instruct, "If her light goes away, I need you to jump out and guide me again, as you've got the scent."

Varg puts his paws on the back of the front seat and strains his neck forward, nostrils twitching, the wind blowing through his fur. I flatten the gas pedal. In a few minutes, a moving truck appears ahead of us in the distance, and Varg starts growling low and savagely. I can make out Blue's light coming from the top of the truck, and I know I've got her now. My instinct beats at me to pull up close, jump on the truck, and rip it apart. Blood and death. Crushing skulls and severed spines. Screams of pain and pleads for mercy. I want it all. The fantasies are relentless.

But I hold onto my sanity. Just barely.

While most of my mind screams vengeance, a small portion stays rational and calculates as I close the distance between me and the truck. When I'm close, I pull the car off the road onto a small incline, then open my trunk and pull out my sword, a semi-automatic, a sharpshooter, and a long knife.

I run into the woods and uproot some shrubs, which I use to block the car from view. Then, stepping deeper into the forest, I chime Ernesto.

"Ernesto, listen," I say as calmly as possible, "Blue's been taken. Mike was killed early this morning, I suspect as a diversionary tactic. I've followed her to the turnoff at Nightshade Lane on Cripple Creek Road. We're taking it on foot now."

Ernesto asks, "Who is we?"

"Varg's with me. Somehow they separated her from Varg, so either there are lots of them, or they used magic. I need you to gather the extermination team and Xavier. You'll also need to call in Oliver, Dragomira, and Maev. Keep the war room staffed as usual, but get the men armed and send everyone out here. Find cover, and don't go any farther than Nightshade Lane until you hear from me. I'll scope it out."

With that, I hang up. Varg paces restlessly and stares up the mountain towards Blue, his every muscle rigid with tension. I surge forward, and Varg takes off with me, straight up the mountain. We have the advantage of not needing the road, which winds back and forth to keep a safe grade. After about ten minutes, I give a soft owl hoot to call Varg to a stop. We're almost on them now, and we have to give them time to stay ahead of us. Slowing our pace, we track the truck up the curves of Black Mountain until the paved road comes to an end. The incline steepens, and still the truck moves on.

We follow it a ways farther until we lose it behind the crest of a hill. When we arrive at the top, Varg stops in a copse of young pine. I stand next to him and take in the valley below, hardly able to believe my eyes. The truck comes to a stop in front of a building on the opposite side of a small amphitheater. The grounds of the amphitheater are teeming with hundreds of Gifted dressed in black robes.

"Holy Christ."

The truck door opens, and out flow enough people to have packed it like a sardine can. Toward the end of the line, two of the men pull Blue roughly out of the truck. Bloodlust sings in my veins. The desire to bleed them dry washes through my black-tinged soul, but I can't risk fouling it up. I must move wisely.

My eyes soak in the sight of her. Every pinprick of light that reflects off of her is scorched into my mind. Every step she takes across that small span of space in this small moment of time, I drink in like a drug-starved addict as they drag her toward the building. Then she disappears inside.

My knees collapse and I bury my face in my hands. The pain. The longing. The need to protect. The need to crush, demolish, and shred. I'm doubly cursed. If I could, I'd rip this excruciating love right out of my heart.

Chapter 68

Beginnings of a Plan

Bluebell Kildare

July 21, 2022, Red Ages

The room's actually quite luxurious compared to my previous imprisonments. A small cot, complete with bed linens and pillows, is pushed against one wall. A chamber pot sits in the corner, and it amuses me how pleased I am for that small luxury. The room is finished with a wooden rocking chair and a table, upon which sits a washbowl and pitcher. Everything a girl needs for a fine toilette.

The walls themselves are made of the same rough-cut stone blocks as the rest of the building. The sole window is about a foot square and sits high on the wall over the table, secured with three thick, iron bars. I could definitely use it to escape if I knew how to shift into a bird. However, it is good for one thing. I hold my hand out and call, "Guardian." It takes a minute, but a flash of metal catches my eye, then my hand tightens around the jeweled hilt of my blade. It's entirely possible that I love this knife.

After giving the door closer scrutiny, I have no additional ideas on how to escape. It looks as solid as it did from the outside. The planks are banded together by welded iron, and the hinges are on the outside of the door. I could saw a leg off the table with my knife to use as a second weapon, but even if I hit someone over the head when they came in, I'd have to make it down the hall and outside through the guarded entrance. I have zero options for escape this time.

I sit with a huff on the bed to consider the situation. I don't want to admit what I know to be true: maybe I shouldn't try to escape. I can't keep living my life in fear of strangers attacking me all the time, and Lilith and I are due for a confrontation. I certainly can't fulfill the prophecy if I never deal with her.

A shudder runs through me at that thought, and I pull my feet up on the bed, hugging my knees tightly. I still don't know what the prophecy's "one life given" means. I hope I'm not supposed to be the sacrifice today. No, I must believe they want me alive until Lilith comes.

It's just the wrong damn day to get captured. We were so close to solving the arson case. I could feel it, teasing me like a word on the tip of my tongue.

Jack must be searching for me, but even he won't be able to get past all these Gifted people if he finds me. He'll need lots of backup. I push my light up in another pulse to give Jack a marker. Hopefully he gets some help and doesn't try to storm two hundred Gifted by himself.

Settling in for a long haul, I stretch out on the cot and hug one of the pillows close. If I can't investigate the arson case, at least I can think about it. I know we're on the edge of discovery, like there's some connection right in front of my eyes that I should be making.

So what do we know about the case? We know magic was present at the inception of each fire, so we assume that magic is used to start the fire. We know the fire spreads out similarly to the way gas does. We don't, however, know whether it's gas or magic that starts the fire. We also don't know who is starting the fires, though we assume that Joe is being forced to. We don't know how the spell or gas is getting into the homes as none of the homes have shown signs of forced entry. All of the victims had traveled through downtown on the day of their deaths, so they may be unwittingly carrying the source into their homes.

We know all the families have at least one Gifted child. We assume the Gifted children are the target because the fires have been controlled so as not to hurt any innocent neighbors. Joe and Becky's kidnapping rules out an individual vigilante. That leaves us with the Dilectus Deo. Though there are some other cults and fringe hate groups, they're small because they're disorganized, and these attacks have been highly organized.

So the families with the kids travel downtown, end up at home with the vector, the source of the fire. The vector explodes into a gas-like fire at midnight. All but one of the families have a ten to twenty-two minute window of time that we can't account for as they pass downtown.

Wait, that's not exactly true. Yana and Kalina also had a block of time missing until we spoke to Milan. He said they spent that time at the park. Is that how all the families spent their missing minutes?

I pull up the image of the map in my mind, covered in strings and push pins. Yes! All the families did pass one of the downtown parks. Did someone scope them out and follow them home? Did someone give them something at the park?

Gas-like fire, kids, parks, downtown. The images of downtown Crimson Hollow flash through my mind: the protests, the celebration banners, the balloon vendors hawking their wares.

"Great Abyss!" I snap to a sitting position. Suddenly it becomes so clear. I know exactly what the vector is and how it's getting into the homes. Milan forgot to tell me an important detail about their visit to the park; I'm sure of it.

"Holy Lady of Light!" I think about the festivities tomorrow. If I don't get out of here, every single family with a Gifted child is going to be burned to a crisp at midnight tomorrow, of that I have no doubt.

But where are they keeping Joe and Becky? The only place I can think of is the church where the Dilectus Deo dragged me. But it was so rickety and Jack said he searched it. Or rather, Jack said he had it searched. Who did the searching?

I stand up now and start pacing the room restlessly as energy burns through me. I send a beam of light up, willing Jack to see it. I flash it on and off a few times to get his attention. Wait—I can do Morse code with my light! A million thanks to Wang and Yao for making me learn it as part of the survival segment.

I sit cross-legged in the middle of the floor and force myself to concentrate. Then I think over the message. It must be short but clear. I tap my fingers on the floor, going over every letter of the message to make sure I remember the code. Once I'm confident, I close my eyes until all is quiet inside me.

Then, hoping with all my soul that Jack's watching, I use my light to flash the code over and over again until my mind is bleary with fatigue:

Vector Balloon Vendors Red Leave Me Until Midnight

CHAPTER 69

THE CODE

JACK TANNER

JULY 21, 2022, RED AGES

eething, I circle the amphitheater grounds from well inside the tree line to study the situation. The attendees gather in small clusters, talking and lounging and just being generally relaxed. They may be powerful, but they don't appear to be battle ready Gifted warriors. Rather, they appear to be businesspeople at a social gathering. I surmise that few of them have ever entered battle at all—with or without their Gifts. All the better.

The front entrance is guarded by ten men. They stand firmly between the attendees and the building as though they're keeping the people out. Surely they wouldn't plant ten armed guards just to keep Blue in. That seems excessive.

The building abuts the mountain, and it's impossible to tell how deep inside the mountain it extends. Fortunately, this gives me an advantage because the mountain provides easy access to the roof, which is only protected by four armed men.

As I consider my next move, Ernesto's warbler call rings through the trees. I heed the call and meet with the team in the thick of the forest, east of the grounds.

"This is a large outdoor amphitheater, probably dating back to about 1400 R.A. Blue's inside the building behind the stage. Some two hundred Gifted are gathered around the amphitheater like they're waiting for something, and more are still trickling in."

After giving them the details about the guards, I talk to Maev and Dragomira. "We're outnumbered two hundred to nine, and we'll need a distraction to pull her out."

Dragomira directs her gaze above my head. "Jack, speaking of distractions, the Illustrissima seems to be sending a signal."

I turn quickly and see a beam of Blue's light shoot out of the west wing of the building. "Excellent! Now we know where she is." Something is off about the way her light flickers on and off, as if in a deliberate pattern. "Wait, is that Morse code?"

I grab my phone and start typing in the pattern I see.

Oliver steps forward. "What code?"

Dragomira answers, "The Illustrissima is using her light as a beacon and flashing it in Morse code. It's visible only to those who see auras."

Keeping my eyes peeled on her light, I continue to record the signal in until Maev speaks. "She's repeated it three times now. She must be done."

I hold the device out and carefully translate it for all to hear.

"Until midnight vector balloon vendors red leave me until midnight vector balloon vendors red leave me"

Xavier is puzzled. "Shit, she wants us to leave her until midnight?"

Maev speaks up. "On the night of the full moon at a gathering of the Gifted, no less."

Dragomira whispers fiercely, "Oh, enemy of mine. Soon we will meet again."

I take them in as their expressions become grave. "What do you two know that I don't?"

Maev's eyes tighten. "It's no coincidence that so many people have assembled on a night such as this when the veil between planes becomes thin. These attendees are here to lend their power to create a portal."

"And," Dragomira adds, "there's only one being from another plane who would request the Illustrissima's presence."

"Jesus Christ! They're calling Lilith, and Blue wants me to wait? Blue wants to confront her? We have to get her out soon."

Dragomira says sharply, "Jack, you can't stop the prophecy."

At the same time, Maev speaks, "You must let Blue direct this."

My eyes move from one face to the other in disbelief. But they're serious.

I bend forward and cover my face with my hands. I'm supposed to let Blue confront the Great Demon of the Plane of Fire? A volcano of objection builds up in me, threatening to explode. Slowly, excruciatingly slowly, I tamp it down. Of course Blue would want to confront Lilith. That's who she is. That's what she's supposed to do.

Xavier breaks the tension. "What does the rest of the message mean? 'Vector Balloon Vendors Red.'"

My mind goes into overdrive. "Balloon vendors? The balloon vendors are downtown, and they have red balloons. Vector . . . " I trail off. "Holy shit!" I snap my head up.

"Ernesto, she just solved most of the case. She's saying the families are picking up balloons at the vendors downtown. She must mean the red balloons are the ones charmed to explode at midnight. They must only be given to the families with Gifted children."

Ernesto spits on the ground. "Filthy pigs."

"Ernesto, I need your help downtown. Can you track the balloon vendors back to wherever they're getting the balloons? That's most likely where Joe and Becky are being held. Don't let anyone walk away with red balloons today, but don't give yourself away until we find Joe and Becky."

Ernesto replies, "Si, Señor. It will be my pleasure."

I turn to Oliver. "Can you give him a few trusted men to help?"

"Yes," Oliver says, "you'll find Fitz and Bear at my place."

Ernesto takes off, and I'm sorry to see him go. I could have used him tonight, but the fires stink of Dilectus Deo, which is Ernesto's pet project. Obviously, I'm not moving from this mountain without Blue.

I turn to the rest of the group. "Okay, I'll give her until midnight, but not a moment more. We're out-numbered two hundred to eight now, but this is the plan. First we'll need some of those robes . . . "

CHAPTER 70

INCANTATION

BLUEBELL KILDARE

JULY 21, 2022, RED AGES

The cold mountain air seeps in through the stone of my prison, robbing the warmth from my bones. The darkness of the room envelops me, offering calm as the night wears slowly on. By the pale glow of the moon, I make out the edges of the sparse furnishings. The dark, shimmering souls of two men mark where the guards stand, outside my door. Another two are placed at the end of the corridor, just at the entrance to the main hall.

Surrounded in a pool of midnight, I consider my plan for meeting with Lilith. There's very little I know about calling and binding, but thinking back to Dragomira's story of Patersuco gives me some clues. Lilith will be bound to the person who calls her and gives the sacrifice, and it's with that person she must bargain. I assume some magical chant will be used to call her, and blood must be spilt on the altar. The stiff length of Guardian tucked safely in my waistband reassures me as the beginning of a plan slowly emerges.

I know what Lilith wants, and I won't give it to her. But what do I want? I want to know how to defeat her. To do that, I need to know more about her.

A shuffling in the corridor disturbs my deep thinking. It must be time, then. I stand tall and throw off my blanket, giving one final thought to Varg and Jack, hoping they stay well away from this place until my meeting with Lilith is finished.

I hear the scrape of the bar being lifted, and the door swings outward. The guards come in and move to grab my arms.

I lift my hands in protest. "No need to drag me. I'm not fighting."

One guard grabs my arm still, but at least he holds it more gently as he ushers me to the main hall.

Four flambeaux are afire now, casting pools of bright, flickering light across the circular stone floor with deep pockets of darkness between them. The room is vast, with soaring ceilings, lending echoes to the slightest movement. Vash and Emmet keep their post beside the altar, their cowls still drawn, but Shadow Man has his cowl thrown back. His face is covered by a gruesome, horned Demon mask.

The two guards position me on the opposite side of the altar, holding my arms tightly. I try to shake them off. "You don't have to hold me. You have a ton of armed men outside that door. I'm not going anywhere. Besides, as soon as Lilith figures out I don't know where the key is, this will all be over."

The men exchange looks that I pretend not to notice. They clearly aren't planning on letting me go, after having been witness to their secret society regardless of the outcome of the meeting with Lilith. But I need my arms free, so when Shadow Man gives a slight nod and the two guards drop back, I'm relieved.

Then Shadow Man calls out in a sonorous voice, "Let the invocation begin!"

The two great doors to the outside open and moonlight streams in, adding a thin blue hue to the golden lights of the flambeaux. The sound of two hundred chanting voices softly rises from the amphitheater grounds, filling the night air. A row of armed men darken the entrance, casting long shadows through the doorway as they separate those of us within from those without. The volume of the chorus increases until I can distinguish the words.

Lady Lilith, Great Demon of annihilation,
Maleficent Angel of final revelation,
Monarch of earth, who cracks the ground,
Mistress of fire, who burns the field,
Empress of wind, who bends the woods,
Queen of water, who floods the plains,
Lady Lilith, we command you to this location.

I glance around the room, wondering where she'll appear. The stone floor is set in a circular pattern with a white chalk line going around the edge of the circle. The circle's edge is between me and the altar, putting me inside it. Will I be trapped in the circle with Lilith?

Shadow Man calls out in accord with the chant, "Lady Lilith, Great Demon of annihilation"

I open my sixth sense and repeat each of his words softly, barely moving my lips, but with the greatest intention.

"Maleficent Angel of final revelation . . ."

A sense of heaviness fills the air, and power crackles through the room. The chanting builds up to a crescendo, in accord with our words.

"Monarch of earth, who cracks the ground . . ."

The ground of the hall starts to rumble, and stones shift beneath my feet. The building groans in complaint around us.

"Mistress of fire, who burns the field . . ."

The flambeaux roar to life, casting the chamber in a vivid red glow. Tendrils of flame lick wildly up the walls, threatening to consume the rafters. The red cast from the fire highlights the planes of Shadow Man's mask in grotesque mockery of a Demon. The vision has such a startling effect, I almost forget the chant.

"Empress of wind, who bends the woods . . ."

A cold gust of wind blows in, whipping the fire into a frenzied dance. Vash and Emmet's robes undulate wildly, but Shadow Man stands serene amidst the turmoil. Behind my back, I slip my knife out and cut my palm deeply, letting the blood flow freely and drop unseen to the chamber floor.

"Queen of water, who floods the plains . . ."

The force of the wind increases, blowing sticks and debris through the doorway. With it comes pelting rain, carried by the wind licking at our faces. Still, Shadow Man chants on, and I keep time with him in my own hushed intonation.

"Lady Lilith, we command you to this location . . ."

Lightning cracks the sky, flashing brightly in quick succession. The low rumble of thunder adds to the cacophony of the wind.

Shadow Man pulls out a knife and cuts his wrist, but before he lets it drip into the bowl on the altar, I lean my bloody palm on the altar as though I'm holding on from the force of the wind. I keep whispering the chant.

"Oh, with this blood offering, I summon the Great Demon Lilith.

I call on thee to rise from the Plane of Fire. So mote it be!"

I know the last line already because it's so standard in spell casting and I make sure to finish it before he does.

A great crack rends the air.

CHAPTER 71

INCURSION

JACK TANNER

JULY 21, 2022, RED AGES

The moon hangs large and bright in the sky, illuminating the forest far beyond my liking. But thanks to the generosity of eight of the attendees who now lay magically stunned and disrobed, we blend in with the rest of the crowd.

Everyone is in place now. Dragomira and Maev are settled in the crooks of two of the tallest poplars surrounding the amphitheater. Lazare, Gia, and Oliver are up the mountain waiting for my signal. Xavier, Ammon, and I mirror their position on the opposite side of the building. Varg is the only wildcard. The last I saw him, he stood under Maev's tree, staring predatorily at the crowd, every inch of his body tense and ready to spring. With everyone situated, it's just a matter of tracking the moon across the sky till it sits at its midnight post. Every second ticks by with agonizing slowness.

As I watch the crowd below, a man in the front row steps up to a center podium and throws out his hands. The crowd, standing now, begins a low chant.

My forehead breaks out in sweat as I will the moon to move faster. My chest feels as heavy as granite, and my muscles clench with my desire to move toward Blue. Every fiber of my being shouts, *Find! Protect!* But with a strength of will that comes from an unknown source inside me, I hold myself in check.

Blue, you had better know what you're doing.

The ground beneath my feet begins to shake, and the very forest trembles. Leaves rattle, and animals scurry for cover.

As I scan the amphitheater, a shadow slips in front of the building. A new guard at this late hour?

The chanting increases. The air thickens with power. Storm

clouds gather overhead, and I welcome their shelter from the moonlight. Shadows deepen, and the chanting reaches a fevered pitch. A wild wind blows in from the north, bitter cold and scented with magic. Trees bend at the force of the gale, and the grass flattens. Then the storm lets loose. Rain pours from the sky. Fat droplets drench the landscape, pulling topsoil off the mountains and draining in rivulets to the valley below.

Still the chanting goes on.

I hoot three times like a horned owl, signaling it's time to move in. Ammon and I advance, each with a man in our sight, while Xavier watches our back. Silently, we creep down the mountain, and just at the edge of the trees with the roof of the building below us, Ammon and I jump.

A flash streaks across the sky as Maev's translucent magic shield drops into place. Good; now the members are cut off from the building as though by an impenetrable wall. The barrier shimmers with the wild colors of the aurora borealis over the translucent shield. In their state of confusion, the guards step forward to the roof's edge. The wind catches one guard, and his comrade's quick arm is all that stops him from plummeting to his death.

I land on the roof and hear the soft thud of four other Vampires with me. Moving at top speed, I overtake the first guard before he has a chance to turn around. Gagged, bound, and divested of his weapon, he flops around on the roof, unable to regain his footing.

I whisper in his ear, "If you fling yourself off the roof that will make my job much easier."

He stills.

I check on the others' progress and all four of the guards on the roof have been incapacitated. Ten more to go. Xavier has reached the roof now and takes over watching the prisoners.

The guards below have been thrown into a panic by Maev's shield and the sudden tempest. With the dark of the storm, they can't see who created it. They wildly shoot at it to no avail. The wall flashes blue upon impact, but the bullets bounce off the barrier and drop harmlessly to the muddy earth. I hold my men on the roof, letting the guards below expend their ammunition on their useless task.

On the other side of the translucent curtain, pandemonium lives. The Gifted crowd shouts and erratically throws spells at the barrier, confused and frightened. One leader sends an arc of red light over the crowd and pours the power into the shield. It bends, but it does not break.

I hoot two more times to signal Dragomira. The massive tree she's perched on groans under her enormous weight as her body shifts into its fearsome natural shape. An immense streak of fire shoots across the entire arena and over the heads of the milling crowd. Screams of terror sound through the night, and a flow of members starts trickling toward the road. Dragomira lets loose another arc of fire. This time it hits the ground near the barrier as she herds the people to her will.

Flashes of lightning streak across the sky, lighting the valley up with an ethereal glow. When the sky darkens again, I give another signal. As one, we jump to the guards beneath us. I land squarely on one man's back and rip his weapon from his hands. I leap off him to twist the gun from his neighbor's grip. A sharp jab to the vagus nerve drops the second guard.

Pain rips through my side. I reach behind and find a knife embedded in my back. I rip it out and I turn toward the first man. His eyes widen in fear as he recognizes my otherness. I grab his shoulder, and snap his head back with a gentle uppercut to his jaw. He crumples to the ground.

I count only one guard remaining, still struggling with Gia. Lazare swipes his feet out from under him, and in no time, all the men are restrained.

A vicious, snarling growl comes from my right. Varg rushes forward and joins me at the entryway. As I breach the building and see what's happening within, rage overtakes me.

CHAPTER 72

THE BINDING

BLUEBELL KILDARE

JULY 21, 2022, RED AGES

pool of darkness fills the circle in front of me. I reach up and grab onto the light from the heavens, feeling its warmth and vibrancy. It streams down and fills me with energy. As quickly as I can, I push a ribbon of light out and wrap it around me, forming a circle to protect myself.

With my eyes glued to the pool of darkness, I let go of the altar and stand strong, ready for battle. A shadowy form begins to emerge. Pinpoints of light seem to be sucked into the shadow, absorbed into nothing, until gradually a figure appears and its features start to materialize.

In the center of the circle, a female warrior stands, seven feet tall, naked and savage. Her black skin stretches over a perfect, muscular form and glows with a reddish cast. Her black hair hangs, long and silky, surrounding the terrible beauty of her face. Yellow, slit eyes blink at me.

She bellows in rage, "You summoned me!"

Shadow Man steps back. "But we agreed . . . "

Lilith turns on him and advances but stops at the circle's edge. She spits, "Not you, you hapless excuse for a sorcerer. I should twist your heart into a pretzel and give it to the Ibwa. *She*"—she waves in my direction—"summoned me!"

She turns on me now. Her form seems to grow even larger as she screams, "Where is the key?"

While part of me wants to run in terror or tell her what I know, I stand my ground. My hold on the ribbon of light remains firm. I hope it will keep me safe like other protection circles. I stare straight into her serpentine eyes and answer, "I don't have the key."

"Liar!" Long, black, razor sharp claws erupt from her fingertips. She threatens, "You will give me the key or I'll shred your puny body into tiny pieces and feed it to the creatures of the River Styx." She lunges at me.

I flinch back and throw more of my light into my circle, raising the edges until I'm enclosed in a shimmering blue cylinder. Lilith rams into the light and bounces back.

A puzzled expression crosses her face. She angles her head. "What is this? A circle of light?"

While I've caught her off guard, and frankly because I don't know how long my circle will hold, I demand, "I summoned you, and I want to bargain."

Her whole demeanor changes. She seems to pull back into herself to consider my words. Her eyelids drop as she scans me from top to bottom. "Really? You want to bargain with me? You know what I want. I want the key. What does the Lady of Light want, I wonder?"

I clench my jaw in determination, shoring up my courage. "I want you to lift the curse from the Vampires—but only the part of the curse that binds them to you."

Lilith responds with a caustic laugh, "You want them to remain strong without paying the price of an eternity on the Plane of Fire? But what fun would that be? All those tasty little souls have been coming my way by the droves lately, it seems."

I square my shoulders and lift my chin in what I hope comes off as convincing. "That's what I want. You lift the binding off their souls, every last one of them, so they're no longer destined to the Plane of Fire."

Her eyes glow red. Having never seen a Demon before, I don't know what that means, but what I feel is excitement and greed. She really wants that key.

But her expression swiftly changes to one of anger again. "No, I won't accept this bargain. I won't undo the curse that will end mankind. Either give me another offer, or I go back." Her mood switches yet again to feigned nonchalance. "You interrupted me at an inopportune time."

I knew she would never agree to that. It was just a distraction, a bluff. I swallow nervously and ask for what I really want. "Then I want you to tell me all the benefit you get from taking souls. If you do that, then I'll tell you who holds the key."

Lilith throws her head back and laughs, a long malicious cackle that bounces off the walls of the cavernous space. Then she shines with triumph in her eyes and says simply, "Done."

I feel a snap in the air as the bargain binds us, and a heavy shadow falls over my soul. I don't understand it, but I know I'm tied to her and trapped by this bargain. Somehow I instinctively know this cloying feeling won't leave me until the exchange is complete.

In my peripheral vision, I see a guard slip silently into the room. Praying that it's Jack in disguise, I daren't look over there to draw attention.

A bright light flares outside, and a shimmering, iridescent glow seeps into the room. Vash, Emmet, and Shadow Man turn as one toward the doorway.

Lilith cares naught for the goings-on outside. She turns to me, an evil grin about her lips. A gleam of anticipation shines from her viper eyes. "The benefit, little girl, is that they give me substance."

The figure in the shadow starts to creep up behind Vash on the edge of the altar, and hoping it's Jack, I try to divert Lilith's attention.

"Sustenance?"

"No, imbecile." She advances on me. "I said *substance*!" she roars.

I flinch backwards as far as I can within the circle of chalk.

The rapid firing of automatic weapons sounds from just outside the door. At that moment, the figure in the shadow steps into the light, and I realize my mistake. It's Dean Schmidt. But too late, he grabs the Grimoire off the altar.

Lilith shrieks, "Get him!"

Vash turns around, grabs his arm, and holds him while Shadow Man starts chanting some spell.

Lilith's neck snaps toward Schmidt, and she screams, "You dare try to take the Grimoire? Give him to me!"

Vash shoves him toward the circle where Schmidt trips and falls flat on his back over the chalk line but the Grimoire flies from his hands and lands by Vash's feet.

I scream, "No!" But it's too late; they've broken the circle.

Lilith sees this immediately, and she lunges for Vash and the Grimoire.

I throw out another circle of light, this one large enough to catch her. It snakes around her and the chalk circle. In mid-lunge, Lilith is stopped, blocked by my light. She turns to me with fangs gleaming and eyes of death. Worse: eyes of endless torture.

It takes everything in me to maintain two circles of light at once. One misstep will mean my death, and worse. Lilith would be running around the world unrestrained. I know this but the force of concentration pounds at my head. My light grows weaker as I can't pull more light into me at the same time as I push these two ribbons out. I've never done it before.

But I must. I cannot fail.

Somehow, a little part of my mind is able to separate itself from what I'm doing and search for the light in the heavens above me. Its glorious warmth slides down the filament into my soul, but it's too slow. I yank at the light again and pull with all my might. This time it fills me easily. But it's too much. My mind stretches to its limit. Like it's tearing. Breaking. Ripping at the seams. A splitting pain slices through my skull. Then, shockingly, I feel my consciousness fracture into pieces. One fragment maintains the defensive circle around myself while another maintains the outer circle restraining Lilith. Yet another pulls more light into me, giving me strength, spooling into me to shore up my reserve. And the last portion of my consciousness keeps an eye on the room.

I almost wish I couldn't see the room. Lilith, head thrown back, spine arched like a bow, screams her fury. She can't get to me through my circle of light.

Schmidt stares up from the floor in frozen terror and whimpers softly. Lilith's eyes fly to him. He's caught in the circle with us, but he's unprotected.

Lilith jumps on him and pins him down. She leans over his face, and a click sounds as her jaw unhinges. A great sucking noise fills the room. It's the sound of Lilith inhaling his soul. His essence pulls out of his skin, resisting, but slowly, inexorably, it gets closer and closer to the abyss of her mouth.

Dean Schmidt of all people. I should let her have him, but my conscience protests. This isn't a fate I would wish on my worst enemy.

I watch in abject horror as his soul is about to be consumed, and despite myself, I scream, "No!"

I break off another piece of my consciousness and shoot another ribbon of light outward, wrapping it around Lilith. It twists its way between them, forming a barrier between Lilith's gaping mouth and Schmidt's dirty soul. Then, with a pull from the energy in the air in front of her mouth, I create a vacuum as Maev taught me, neutralizing Lilith's sucking force.

Her entire musculature turns rigid. She rotates her head completely backwards to glare at me. Her fury at being thwarted by me again seeps out of her very pores. She's still pinning Schmidt to the floor, but she's all but forgotten him. Black horns pop out of her skull, and red ridges form along her spine. Slowly, languidly, she rises, her spine bending and curving with an unnatural grace. Her eyes vow vengeance.

"You puny bitch," she spits. "Where's the key?"

Red light flares outside the building in two short bursts. The air fills with screams of pain and shouts of terror. But blessedly, I hear a familiar growl getting closer and closer.

Lilith ignores the noise and advances on me. "Where's the key?" She lifts her arm up, forming a ball of fire in her palm. With a mighty throw, she whips the ball at me.

I push every bit of light I can out into my protective circle, thickening the wall around me. The fireball meets the wall, sending sparks shooting in all directions. I'm safe for now, but the spot she hit has thinned, and dangerously so.

I reach up for more light, willing it to flow into me more quickly.

Broad shoulders fill the doorway now, and this profile is unmistakably Jack. Next to him, Varg vocalizes his malicious intent and takes a mighty leap toward Lilith. Vash turns to Jack and starts muttering a curse while Emmet hurls glowing green balls. Jack has no time for curses and sidesteps the spell while pulling out his sword.

In mid-flight, Varg disappears at the circle's edge and reappears on the inside. The circle holds as though he traveled through a different plane. He continues his airborne course until his mighty jaw is wrapped around Lilith's thigh. She lets out an angry screech of surprise and gouges his flank with her razor sharp claws, ripping through his fur. He releases her leg and lands on the ground, circling her, seeking an opening even as blood flows freely from his wound.

I look toward Jack just as he swings his blade through Emmet's neck. Blood splatters across the wall. Emmet's head separates from his neck, and his body, spurting blood like a fountain, falls to the ground. His head lands next to his body, bounces once, twice, and rolls sickeningly before coming to a rest at Jack's feet. Jack advances on Vash in a blur, easily dodging the electric balls being thrown at him in rapid succession.

I turn back toward Varg, who circles Lilith with incredible speed. He finds an opening and leaps, his body twisting in midair, and he lunges for Lilith's jugular. In the background, Vash's screams fill the air. Varg catches Lilith's neck in his powerful jaw and Lilith slices into his injured flank again with brutal efficiency. My heart stops as I watch and I drop my outer circle.

Jack sees my circle down and rushes her just as Varg drops to the floor, soaked in blood. A six inch flap of skin hangs from Lilith's neck, and black goo seeps from the wound.

Swiftly, I form the circle again while Jack attacks her. He lunges for her neck, hands grasping her head. But there is no way he can beat the creator who gave him his power. Lilith creates two massive fireballs and slams them down on his back. His black robe catches fire.

I involuntarily drop my shield and step forward, horrified, gasping. I must end this. How do I end this?

"No one!" I scream.

Lilith wrenches Jack's arms from her head. Bone snaps. She swings him away as though he's nothing more than a babe. Her eyes register disbelief. I scream again, "To my knowledge, no one holds the key!"

Jack tears off his robe, but still, smoke rises from his back.

Lilith eyes move from me to Jack and from Jack to me. Fear creeps into my soul, as it's clear in this moment she knows what Jack means to me. Her eyes blaze in fury as she turns to me again.

Why isn't she gone? The bargain was fulfilled. I felt the heaviness lift.

Then it dawns on me. I have to send her back. I yell, "I command you back to the Plane of Fire."

Lilith lifts her head, bellowing a vindictive laugh. The sound of it echoes off the walls of the chamber as she slowly dissolves to black.

CHAPTER 73

AFTERMATH

BLUEBELL KILDARE

JULY 21, 2022, RED AGES

Wash and Emmet's bodies and heads lie by the doorway, and Varg rests on his side in a pool of blood. Jack has stopped smoking and circles the room with his sword raised, still searching for enemies. His left arm hangs awkwardly at his side. I'm torn between worry over Jack's and Varg's injuries, but Varg seems far worse off.

I run to Varg and kneel down next to him. He's panting heavily, and his eyes are glazed. I've never seen him take a wound like this before. Blood still seeps from his side, and his skin and fur are in shreds where Lilith's claws sliced through them.

"Jack," I call out, "your arm! And your back is covered in blood."

Some of his rage seems to dissipate as he takes me in with hungry eyes. "I'm fine. This will heal within the hour."

"We've got to get Varg to Alexis."

Jack says, "No need. Dragomira's here and she's skilled with Demon wounds." He steps outside and bellows Dragomira's name. When he returns, Oliver is with him, and the two of them lift Varg onto the altar.

Using Guardian, I cut the robe off Vash's body and use it to put pressure on Varg's wound.

Just then, Dragomira appears at the doorway, her eyes wild with excitement. Her nostrils flare the moment she enters. "I smell my enemy. Lilith was here."

"Dragomira, Varg is hurt. Can you help him? Lilith wounded him with her claws."

Dragomira steps up to the altar, waves my hand away, and uncovers the wound. She flares her nostrils again and sucks in her breath. "The stench. I haven't smelled it in such a long time."

Jack stands next to me and places his hand on my waist, pulling me against his body. For the moment, I don't think about where things stand with us. I just welcome the warmth of his frame against mine as I softly stroke Varg's fur. Varg's intelligent eyes settle on me as he rests his muzzle on my forearm. Tears fill my eyes as I whisper, "Don't worry, boy. We'll get you back in shape." I only hope with all my heart that I tell the truth.

Dragomira begins her magic, and her chanting permeates the room, wild and beautiful. It speaks of deep forests and savage winds. Images of still nights and lush grasslands flash through my mind. I'm swept away by raging seas and ghostly mists. Her voice echoes off the chamber walls, gossamer notes, exquisite notes. Insistent. Unyielding. She commands the poison out of his wound. And still she sustains her song.

Maev and Ammon fill the doorway, then Maev rushes over and pats Varg's head, standing out of Dragomira's way. The wounds under Dragomira's dancing fingers slowly pull closed, one rip at time.

She steps back, and Varg presses his nose into my palm. I see the wound is completely sealed. Oh, the relief. A smile breaks over my face.

I turn to Dragomira. "Thank you so much. I'm in your debt."

Dragomira smiles. "You fought Lilith and survived?"

"Yes, I did."

"Then my price is paid."

Though I hate to burden everyone with more, I must. I step back so I can see everyone's face and say, "This group was the Order of Lily. The leader brought me here with the intent of summoning Lilith so she could question me about the key. Instead, I summoned her so I could have some control."

A grin breaks across Maev's face, and Dragomira gives a little huff of pleasure. Jack, though, tightens his frame and clenches his fist as though he's in pain.

"I don't know the leader's name, and he kept his face hidden, so I'll call him Shadow Man. He had the Grimoire."

A collective gasp fills the air.

"Dean Schmidt snuck in and tried to steal the Grimoire. Lilith caught him and tried to suck his soul out, but I blocked her with my light."

All eyes are pinned on me now.

"Then when all the fighting happened, I lost track of Schmidt and Shadow Man. And now both are gone, and the Grimoire is gone as well."

Dragomira says, "The question is, who has the Grimoire?"

CHAPTER 74

REFUSING TO RELINQUISH

JACK TANNER

JULY 21, 2022, RED AGES

When we arrive home, I watch Blue's soft form snuggled into the seat. She was so exhausted by the time we left the amphitheater, she drifted off to sleep as soon as the car warmed up.

After letting Varg out of the car, I open the passenger door and pull Blue into my arms. She snuggles her head into my chest and sleeps on, her soft mouth parted. My left arm aches a little from where Lilith broke it, but the bone has set, and it's almost back to normal. Even with a broken arm, her weight is a burden I gladly bear.

When I reach the landing between our apartments, I consider waking Blue up so she can unlock her door. But when I imagine setting her down in her bed and walking away . . . I just can't do it.

This time . . . This time almost broke me. I need her with me a while more.

So I push my door open and bring her into my apartment. I settle her gently on the sofa. Carefully, I remove her boots, tuck a pillow under her head, and lay a blanket lightly over her. And by the glow of candles, I watch her as she sleeps.

Unfortunately, I'll have to wake her all too soon. In just a few hours, the Sun Flare Celebration will start, and I have no idea what Ernesto has found. While she sleeps, I need to check on the case.

The chimerator would be too loud, so I pick up the phone instead and dial Ernesto. Whispering into the receiver, I say, "Ernesto, we got Blue out safely, and she's resting now. What's happening with the case?"

Ernesto whispers back, "There was only one vendor out today, and he didn't have any red balloons. I followed him to his house, and

Marian tracked down his information. His name is Sam Turner, and he lives with his wife Edith. I've checked around, and it seems there's only been one vendor out each day to advertise the festival. He's just been moving his cart to different parks downtown. Marian called the city and found out they're expecting eight balloon vendors tomorrow in the park. Sam's cart was empty when he left, so he must replenish his stock in the mornings."

"Where are you right now?"

"I'm behind his house. He and his wife have been sleeping since around midnight."

"Do you need me to relieve you? Have you had a chance to drink?"

"No, no, mi amigo. I'm not letting this guy slip away from me. I drank on my way over yesterday, so I'm fine."

"All right then. Call my phone when he's on the move."

"Si, si. I will."

Blue turns and mumbles something incoherent in her sleep. The blanket gets caught up under her leg, so I straighten it out, making sure her toes are covered. A strand of her hair is caught in her mouth and I carefully pull it away.

Then I walk into the bedroom to call Gambino. He can't hear my whispers like Ernesto can, and I don't want to wake Blue, disturbing these precious few hours of sleep.

Gambino answers with a rough, drowsy voice. "This better be good."

"It's actually bad. This is Jack."

His voice picks up a little. "What's going on?"

"We think we know how the fires are getting started. We think the balloon vendor that's been downtown by the parks has been handing out red balloons to the Gifted children. We speculate the balloons are filled with a gas and charmed to explode at midnight."

He curses loudly. "Jesus, Mary, and Joseph!" Some slamming sounds come through the receiver from his end. "The festival!"

"Yes, we've got the only balloon vendor who was out yesterday under surveillance. We'll track him in the morning when he picks up the balloons, but the city says there'll be eight carts out tomorrow."

"Holy Mother of Grace! They're trying to massacre every Gifted kid in the city!" Gambino curses.

"Yes, we know. We're going to follow the vendor to where he makes his pick up and try to stop him, but I'd like you to have your men at the festival just in case."

"Of course. Do you know when this is going to happen?"

"Well, the festival gates open at ten a.m."

"I'll be out there by six. I'll start rounding up my team now."

"Thanks, Gambino."

After hanging up, I pull a warm bottle of Bloodvine from my hot box and relax in the living room chair again. Varg is curled up on the floor near Blue's feet, sleeping lightly. He cracks an eye open every so often to let me know he's still on the job.

My eyes soak up the vision of Blue, warm and sleepy. The soft, pink edge of her lips. The elegant way her hand lies on the pillow. The curve of her hip. Just being with her in this room gives me immeasurable contentment.

Thinking back to how I felt when she was abducted today, I know things have to change. I can't go on like this anymore. There is really only one choice. I'm going to have to tell her the truth. Everything. And then somehow, some way, I'm going to have to convince her to love me anyway.

I rub my brow and think about how that scenario might unfold. It's going to be ugly, messy, and shocking. She'll hate me. Still, I must do it. This is just too painful. When things like today's events happen, I need to wrap my arms around her to convince myself she's real. That she's okay. This separation, this loving from a distance is killing me.

Enough melancholy. She's here now, and I'm going to enjoy just being with her for these few stolen hours.

CHAPTER 75

VIOLENT BURN

BLUEBELL KILDARE

JULY 22, 2022, RED AGES

I wake to the sound of whispering. Whispering? I crack open my eyes and see Jack talking on the phone across the room. Jack? Disoriented, I sit up, trying to remember where I am and how I got here. Last thing I remember, after Dragomira healed Varg, we searched the building for signs of Schmidt, Shadow Man, or the Grimoire, and all we found was their probable exit route. Then we got in Jack's car.

Jack hangs up the phone, so I ask, "Jack, how did I get here?"

He leans forward, resting his arms on his knees. "You fell asleep in the car and I didn't want to wake you to get your key. I'm glad you're awake now, though because some things have been happening."

"What?"

"We got your signal last night—brilliant idea to use Morse code, by the way—and I sent Ernesto to tail one of the balloon vendors. He's been watching him all night, and now the guy is getting ready to leave. We're hoping to track him to where he picks up the balloons. Gambino has men at the festival already in case we don't have any luck."

I stand up. "Give me five minutes to get ready. Can you walk Varg in the meantime?"

He agrees, so I rush to my apartment, do the bare necessity to freshen up, throw on a new shirt, and grab my backup gun and a bottle of water. I'm out the door in four minutes. On the five-minute mark, we're sliding into Jack's car and taking off.

"Where are we going?" I ask.

"The vendor Sam's house. We're hoping that wherever he picks up the balloons is where we'll find Joe and Becky."

Just then Jack's phone rings. "Yes," he answers. "Jesus Christ! Of all the days to get a conscience. Is he going? Okay, we're almost there."

Jack snaps the phone shut, his profile rigid and stressed. "Our guy, Sam, who Ernesto's been watching, has been arguing with his wife about going to the festival. Ernesto says he wants to pull out. His wife insists he follows through. Apparently they had a big row about it, but it seems like he's going."

"Jack, I want to get these guys so bad, I can taste it."

"I know. So do I."

We drive on in silence for a while, and Jack heads west of downtown into a residential district. Eventually he pulls over and calls Ernesto again. "We're here, just in front of your car. I'll let you pass first and tail you, while you tail him."

After a few minutes, a lumbering truck backs out of a driveway about a block away. Ernesto comes ripping around the corner, then jumps in his car and takes off. Jack pulls out behind him.

We drive to the north end of town, tailing Ernesto closely. Then Sam's truck pulls into a fast food joint.

I turn to Jack in amazement. "What in the Plane of Fire? He's on a mission to murder countless kids, and he stops off to get coffee and donuts?"

Jack pulls over behind Ernesto and murmurs, "If this guy's really had a change of heart, maybe he's purposefully trying to miss the drop."

"Cripes!" I curse. "I never thought I'd wish for someone to break the law, but this guy's conscience is going to get a lot of kids killed. If we miss that drop . . ."

Jack reaches out and strokes my arm soothingly, which only adds to my turmoil. Isn't he supposed to be all distant and aloof? I peer at him suspiciously.

He must misinterpret my thought, because he reassures me, "If he misses the drop, then Gambino's men and the rest of our team will be there to get the balloons when they arrive."

Sam finally comes out of The Dappled Donut, hikes his pants up over his portly belly, and hefts himself into the truck.

Jack pulls out after Ernesto. "Looks like we're back in business."

We keep heading north, and I begin to get a little inkling about where we're going. We take a right on Skull Cracker Highway, and the little niggle becomes pure intuitive sureness.

"Jack, we're headed toward the abandoned church where they tried to hold me before. Who searched the church again?"

"I asked Lazare and Gia to do it."

The farther we go up the mountain, the more the alarm sounds in my head. My mind drifts back to that first interview with Brigid when Becky gave me her drawing. The details of the burning church are still so vivid in my mind: the steeple on fire and flames shooting from the windows. A shiver goes down my spine and my sense of premonition only increases as we drive on in silence.

We turn off Skull Cracker Highway onto Sinners Hollow Road. Jack says, "You're right. This is the way to the church."

I never saw the outside of the church because I was blindfolded on my way up and running for my life when I left, but Varg apparently knows where we're going because a low grumble issues from his throat that gets angrier the closer we get. We wind back and forth on a narrow mountain road as we head farther up. The alarm in my head persistently rings until I can't remain silent any longer.

"Jack, I think you should call the fire department and tell them there's a fire at the church."

Jack eyes flit to me, staring intently for a moment. Then without saying a word or questioning me, he turns his eyes to the road and picks up his phone to call them. Thank goodness he trusts my intuition.

We make another turn onto Redemption Way and keep heading up, winding along. A break in the trees gives a breathtaking view of Crimson Hollow far below, but this is no time to enjoy the scenery. Finally we crest a hill, and the church sits directly before us. But Sam's truck is nowhere to be seen. Further, the church definitely isn't on fire, and I feel a bit like a fool. But a deep sense of foreboding still plagues me.

We all get out of our cars and Jack and Ernesto start scenting the air. Ernesto follows the driveway back past the church, then rushes back. "There's a dirt road leading up the hill behind that shrubbery."

My instincts scream at me to go to the church, though I have no logical explanation as to why. I step toward the building and ratchet my sixth sense up, allowing it to come into full power while my regular senses stay alert. I circle the church slowly, peering through the walls for a sign of life. When I come back to the front, I'm disappointed, but I only dig deeper.

I send my senses down below the church and spread my awareness out. There's only darkness until the small, familiar balls of life I recognize as rodents gleam at me. I recoil a bit. Then, taking a deep breath, I pass them up and continue farther. I run into two souls practically on top of each other. This must be Joe and Becky! They're somewhere hidden under the church, and they're still alive.

I snap my sixth sense off and turn to tell Jack. Out of the corner of my eye, I catch Ernesto's car moving up the dirt road toward whatever lies on the hill. Suddenly, a deafening boom fills the air, followed by a succession of blasts. Trees bend. Flames burst into the sky. Ernesto's car flies backwards. It flips three times. Then it lands upside down at the bottom of the hill where the road starts.

A large object flying through the air catches my eye. Sam's truck. It's flying off the hill toward us. A great force knocks into me, pushing me to the ground. I struggle to get up, but I can't. A shock vibrates the earth. I turn my head again and see the truck landing. Bouncing. Exploding! And then spinning until it comes to a violent stop, against some trees that border the church yard behind us.

A rush of wind. Burning heat. Jack's arms are on either side of me. He must be covering me. He lowers his head into my line of sight, and his lips move, but I can't hear him.

I look up and see the trees uprooted on the hill. Above them, a massive, glowing orange and black mushroom cloud hovers in the air. Dull explosions keep going off, but I can barely hear them. They sound as though they're coming through a long tunnel. The cloud expands and grows, taking over the sky and blocking the sun. Burning debris flies through the air like pieces of flaming confetti, landing all around us. Streams of smoke fill the air. Jack flinches. He's getting burnt as he protects me from the flames. Ahead of me a portion of the church steeple flickers with fire.

"Jack!" I scream. "The church! I saw their souls underground."

I struggle to get up, but I can't push Jack's weight off. He stands and lifts me in his arms. The world blurs, and the next I know, Jack's leaving me behind a slight berm on top of the hill opposite the church. I watch the surreal scene from my lofty position. Flaming debris continues to streak the sky, and small fires pop up all over the forest.

Ernesto. My eyes fly to his car. A fist punches through the window, and Ernesto curls his body out. I shout out to him, and point to the church. The roof is on fire now, and Jack has disappeared inside.

Where is the fire truck? Where is it?

The sounds of explosions have stopped. Ernesto appears by my side, and I shout, hardly able to hear myself, "Becky and Joe are below the church. I felt their souls. Jack went in to find them."

Then Ernesto blurs to the church's front door and vanishes inside.

Two fire trucks finally pull into the churchyard. Thank goodness. One continues up the small dirt road, and one comes to a stop in front of the church. Firefighters hop out, unroll their hose, and start blasting the church roof. I don't think they even see me.

Before I can stop to think, I'm running down the hill to the firemen, shouting, "Two people are trapped in the basement of the church. Two SIB officers are inside trying to get them out."

The fireman closest to me turns and winces. Then I see him yelling at the other men, but I can't hear what he's saying. He wraps me in a blanket and says something to me. I yell back, "I can't hear you."

The debris has stopped flying through the air now. All my attention is on the church as I hope with every fiber of my being to see Jack and Ernesto return. I bring out my sixth sense and check for their souls' light. The two souls I originally saw are still in the same place they were before. Jack's soul is below ground, moving toward them rapidly. Ernesto's soul is moving downward. Maybe a trap door?

The whole church is made of old wood plank, and the fire is eating it away. Underneath, Ernesto's soul catches up with Jack's, and they come to a stop near Joe and Becky. At least I hope that it's Joe and Becky.

My thought goes to Sam's truck and the balloons and the kids. Was it the balloons that exploded? I can't imagine that Sam is alive. Did he do it on purpose?

Looking over at the truck, I see the cab is in flames, but the firemen aren't doing anything about it. All attention is on the church.

Soon two more fire trucks roll onto the grounds, then four ambulances, and soon after, another fire truck. The first two trucks head up the slope. One stays in front of the church, pummeling it with water. Still, the flames grow higher. It now matches the picture Becky gave me. Flames shoot out the windows.

How will they get out?

It appears Ernesto and Jack are holding onto Joe and Becky now, carrying them away toward the back of the basement. Then I see their souls moving upward again on the other side of the church. A cellar door? I start running toward the church, but one of the firemen grabs me. Instinct kicks in, and I lift my leg to kick him, but reality sets in just in time. Instead, I shout, "My men are bringing the victims out from the back."

He starts shouting commands. A number of men move toward the church just as Jack and Ernesto round the corner of the building, covered in dirt and ash. Jack holds a man in his arms, and lays him gently on the ground by one of the fire trucks. Ernesto holds little Becky, who's sobbing for her daddy. She's all wriggling arms and legs, and she fights like a hellcat to get to her father.

As soon as Jack's arms are empty, I run to him and throw myself at him. He wraps his arms around me and pulls me in close. I hug him for all I'm worth, squeezing him tight until the reality of his safety sinks in. Jack pulls back and says something to me. But I shake my head and point to my ear. He frowns, then lowers his mouth to mine. His lips brush mine gently, coaxingly, searing me with his heat. His hand moves up to the back of my neck and strokes it gently. Confused as to why he's kissing me, I respond slowly at first, but before long I'm lost to his persistent enticement, and open my mouth to his. He sweeps his tongue in boldly, hotly, and pulls me closer, leaving me breathless.

Then he slowly leans away, catching my eyes. He purposefully bites his lip and a fat drop of blood forms. And he sweeps in for another kiss. Lost to everything but his offer, I take his lower lip in mine and suck it gently, feeling the tingling sensation start in my mouth and spread through my body. Just as the heat starts to burn through me, Jack pulls away. Frustrated, bewildered, I step back too.

Jack says, "We have to check what burned up on that slope. I'll be right back."

And I heard him. The drop of blood. My face flushes with embarrassment as my heart clenches in devastation. He didn't kiss me because he wanted to. He was trying to fix my hearing. With a curse, I turn away from him.

Jack and Ernesto move up the drive at Vampire speed again.

I scan the scene and see that the paramedics have Joe on a stretcher. Another paramedic holds Becky next to him. I ask the paramedics what hospital they're taking them to, and then I call Rubalia to have an escort bring Brigid there.

The church fire is almost out now, and one of the fire trucks puts out the last of the flames from Sam's truck. Smoke still pours over the trees on the hill, but the small forest fires have all been extinguished or contained.

I walk over to Becky. She seems calm now, but her small fists, white from the force of her grasp on the paramedic's shirt, tell a different story.

"Hi, Becky."

Becky's solemn eyes turn my way.

"Do you remember me? I'm the lady your mom went to see when your dad went missing."

Becky's little eyebrows are clenched together in concern.

"Well, we found both of you, and you're safe now. The paramedics are going to take you to the hospital to make sure you're both okay, and your mom is going to meet you there."

Becky demands, "I want my mama!"

"I know you do, sweetie. You'll see her soon. I just wanted to thank you for the drawing you gave me that day. The one of the burning church. That drawing really helped me find you."

Becky digs her head deeper into the paramedic's chest, but her forehead smoothes and she smiles shyly.

When her eyes widen in surprise, I turn to see Jack and Ernesto standing with us. Jack says, "There's a small warehouse up there. That must be where they were keeping the balloons. It looks like Sam was in the warehouse when the explosion happened. His was the only truck there, so all the other trucks must be on their way to the festival."

A dry, cracked voice breaks in. "It's the red balloons. They made me do it. They threatened to kill Becky."

We all turn to Joe, who's getting an IV inserted into his arm. He's hacking badly, making me wonder how much smoke he was exposed to. As soon as his coughing quiets down, he says, "But I tricked them on this last batch and charmed all the balloons to explode at ten a.m. instead of midnight so it would happen before the festival started."

My jaw drops in horror. Of course, Joe didn't know the mayor moved up the opening time. Jack curses, "Goddamn Mayor."

I turn to Joe. "How can we stop them from exploding?"

Joe says, "You can't. If you pop them, they'll explode."

"What can we do?" I ask.

"Release them at least five minutes beforehand. They'll explode on their own when they're high enough, and they won't be dangerous." Joe starts coughing again.

"Who was behind all this?" Jack demands.

Joe's gets a nasty gleam in his eyes. "Otto Cromwell of the Dilectus Deo. He tried to shoot us just before you came. He didn't need us anymore."

Jack asks, "Was that the body I saw outside your cell?"

"Yes."

"Jack," I interrupt, "we've got to call Gambino and get downtown."

Jack checks his watch. "It's 8:56 a.m. We have one hour. Let's get moving."

CHAPTER 76

REDEMPTION

BLUEBELL KILDARE

JULY 22, 2022, RED AGES

Ernesto's long frame is crushed against Varg in the backseat of Jack's car as we speed down Skull Cracker Highway, siren blaring. The tension is thick as we all silently cross our fingers that the balloons are managed safely.

Jack is topping ninety miles an hour, swerving around cars as nimbly as Varg jumps over brush on a run. Hating to break the silence but too curious not to, I ask, "So how did you get below the church?"

Ernesto answers, "There was a trap door under the podium. Joe and Becky were being kept in a cell below."

"What about this Otto guy?"

He laughs darkly. "He was nothing more than a mess of charred bone when we found him. Joe must have set him on fire. He's been on my watch list as one of the more radical members of the Dilectus Deo, and I think this is a fine end for him."

"Poetic justice considering he's burning families. How did you get out? Was it a cellar door?"

"Of sorts," he says. "It looks like a cellar door from the inside, but when you stepped through it, the other side was a massive cement drain pipe. I think this is how they transported the balloons up to the warehouse."

"Maybe if I hadn't escaped so quickly, they would have brought me down there and we would have solved this case days ago."

Jack makes an unhappy grunting noise. "Getting abducted by the perpetrator is not the way to solve cases."

A wry smile crosses my lips. "You have a point. But at least it explains why Lazare and Gia didn't find them."

His eyes flash dark and his lips tighten. I have a feeling he'll be having an unpleasant discussion with them soon.

I ask, "So what did you find at the warehouse? Did you see any sign of Sam?"

Jack's mouth furrows into a deep frown. "The warehouse doors were open, and the blast came from inside. The force of the explosion blew Sam into the forest. He couldn't have survived the heat anyway, but the impact of the trees killed him immediately."

My stomach sickens as I remember how he tried to delay making the drop. "Do you think he tried to kill himself?"

Jack shakes his head. "Maybe he thought he could pop the balloons and dispel the charm on them without them exploding. I doubt we'll ever know."

We slow down to fifty as we head through the residential district of Crimson Hollow. The festival is being held at Memorial Park, right smack in the middle of downtown, and the streets become more congested the farther we go.

We turn onto Shady Gallows Court, and Jack turns off his siren. After a few blocks, we come to a traffic jam, and I check the clock. It's 9:23 a.m. We made good time.

Jack calls Gambino. "Did the trucks arrive?"

I hear cursing on the other line.

"They look like food trucks with a side flap that opens," Jack says.

There's more cursing and more yelling from Gambino's side. I make out the words, "Every Goddamn . . . "

Jack says, "We'll be there in a minute. We're stuck in traffic, but we'll come on foot."

He snaps the phone closed and does a U-turn, then slides into some street parking on the right. While maneuvering, he explains, "Gambino says there are about a hundred trucks there, all built about the same. It's a typical carnival design. We'll have to figure out which ones carry the balloons."

We get out, and I say, "Jack, you and Ernesto go ahead. You're much faster. I'll catch up with you in a few minutes."

Jack studies me for a moment, reluctant, but the clock keeps ticking.

"Go, Jack. I've got Varg."

Jack and Ernesto blur out of sight while Varg and I start jogging toward city center. Jeez, the traffic is horrible. Cars are backed up on every road we pass. Pedestrians are hurrying with their children in tow. Store wares litter the sidewalk as small business owners try to make the most of the increase in pedestrians. Somehow, in all this business, a profile catches my eye from across the street. A man watches me for a second before he slips into an alley.

Cripes, that looked like Schmidt. Should I go after him? Between Jack, Ernesto, and Gambino, they probably have things covered with the trucks. I can't imagine that I'm really needed there. Making a quick decision, I dart between the cars and run into the alley, pulling my gun.

A few buildings in, Schmidt steps out from a dark alcove. I aim my gun at him. Varg advances with a menacing growl that echoes off the buildings.

Schmidt holds his hands up. "I just want to talk."

I move forward until I'm about ten feet in front of him, gun aimed at his heart. He looks like crap. The scar on the side of his face certainly does nothing for his appearance, but dark circles cradle his eyes, and his skin is sallow. His gaze darts to and fro as though expecting an enemy to jump out at him, yet I stand directly in front of him with a gun pointed at his chest.

"Where's the Grimoire, Schmidt?"

"I don't have it. The guy with the mask does. I swear."

His feelings are in even worse shape than his body. He churns with anger, regret, and pain, but most of all, he twists with confusion. His emotions are so heavy and volatile they fill the air like a tornado whirling debris about. The whole alley reeks of his turbulence.

"Why did you try to take it? Who are you working for?"

"I didn't want the Grimoire in the Order of Lily's hands. I'm not with anyone anymore. I quit the Dilectus Deo because I don't agree with hurting children, even your kind."

His eyebrows furrow, and his body shakes like a drug addict in need of a fix. "Plus, you saved my life. You could have left me on that cliff." Now the confusion overwhelms every other emotion as he asks, "Why didn't you leave me to die after all I've done?"

"You weren't an immediate threat to me. I don't go around killing people willy-nilly, Schmidt. My job is to bring about peace among the breeds."

His head snaps back so violently that he has to take a step back to balance himself. Then he demands, "Why did you save my soul from Lilith?" His eyes give away how deeply troubled he is by this question. Sweat pricks from his forehead and runs down the sides of his face.

I laugh wryly. "Schmidt, I didn't save your soul from Lilith. All I did was delay your arrival in the Plane of Fire. Don't worry; you'll be joining her soon all on your own at the rate you're going. And she won't take kindly to your attempt at stealing the Grimoire."

Desperate fear fills his eyes as this grim truth assails him. He shocks me with his next, quietly spoken question. "Am I redeemable? Can I be saved?"

I'm surprised he cares. Curious, I use my sixth sense to peer into his soul. It's tainted by evil rooted deep in his center, but on the outside, there's a golden light, a glow, perhaps of what used to be. Maybe he was once all good, but not now. Who knows if he's gone too far?

I pierce him with my eyes. "You fouled up Jason's case by not treating it like a kidnapping. Jason might still be alive if not for you. His parents will never forgive you. Then you tried to rape me. And when my wolf defended me, you reported him, knowing full well you deserved what you got. I'll never forgive you for either of those things. And you topped that off by abducting an innocent little girl."

I see him flinch and shame unfurls around him.

"Oh yes, we know about your involvement in that. Becky's family will never forgive you either."

Schmidt turns aside, his face wincing with the impact of every accusation I hurl at him. "So there's no hope for me?"

"I don't know, Schmidt. Your soul hangs in the balance, and the decision isn't mine to make. It's based on the whole of the light that you bring to life compared with the whole of the shadow you cast. The black taint of Lilith is strong on your soul. It's eaten half your light already."

His eyes widen in fear. But I'm not done.

"If you want to save yourself, you have to decide to change, and you need to follow it up with action. So, you tell me. Are you redeemable?"

He swings his eyes toward me and whispers, "Yes."

With that answer, his soul lightens a tiny bit. A small fragment of the black, seems to collapse into the light. It's tentative, but it's a start.

"Good. Then redeem yourself."

A feeling of relief sweeps the alley and perhaps a tiny bit of optimism, where before there was only misery.

I must admit I enjoy bursting his bubble. "Don't get too excited. For now, I'm arresting you. Put your hands against the wall."

Schmidt's eyes shift toward the alley entrance. "You don't have time. The Balloon Vendors are giving red balloons to the Gifted children, and they'll explode at midnight."

Of course he doesn't know Joe changed the schedule. "We already know that. We're confiscating the balloons now."

Schmidt's face contorts with alarm. "What about the bombs?"

"What bombs?"

"The trucks have PIN code locks, and if you don't use them and just bust the doors open, the trucks are wired to explode."

Holy cripes! "Where are the bombs, Schmidt?"

"Strapped underneath the trucks. The drivers don't even know about them."

Lady of Light! And I haven't replaced my phone or chimerator yet. I look desperately around for something I can cuff Schmidt to. All I see is a rickety handrail going up a cement stoop. It'll have to do. I nudge my gun toward the railing. "Move to that railing over there."

Understanding fills Schmidt's eyes, but he moves to it without protest. I slap one side of the cuffs on his left wrist and the other around the banister. Then I give him one more hard stare and take off as fast as my feet will carry me, thanking Yao and Wang the whole way.

CHAPTER 77

UNEXPECTED FIREWORKS

BLUEBELL KILDARE

JULY 22, 2022, RED AGES

I run past the sidewalk sales and wend around jugglers, dart between cars, and jump over cones. I reach the park, but keep going, circling around it until I come to the back entrance where a line of carnival trucks stretches out as far as I can see.

I start shouting as loud as I can, "Gambino! Jack! Ernesto! Stop!" and keep running down the line of trucks.

Jack comes to me first, worry engraved deep in the lines of his face.

"I saw Schmidt on the way here," I pant.

Ernesto appears at Jack's side now, and I continue. "Schmidt says there are bombs strapped beneath the trucks. The vendors have to open the trucks with the PIN code, or the trucks are wired to explode."

Jack's face turns to granite. "We've identified the balloon trucks, and Gambino's team has corralled them to the side." He flips open his phone and calls in the bomb squad. He gives the location and snaps the phone closed.

"How much time do we have?" I ask.

Jack checks his watch. "Sixteen minutes. Ernesto and I can disconnect the bombs, but the bomb squad will need to make sure they're completely deactivated."

"Go!"

Varg and I follow Jack and Ernesto to a blocked-off side road where a small fleet of trucks sits. Our team has a line of men handcuffed and arranged against the wall while pedestrians line up on the other side of the yellow tape. Many seem to find the arrests more exciting than the promised entertainment for the day. Necks crane and gossip flies. Gambino's men position themselves at the blockade, ensuring the public's safety.

Two blurs move from under one truck to the next so fast that I can't tell which is Jack. They quickly disconnect the bombs and set them toward the middle of the cordoned off area. After removing each bomb, they wrench open the truck door and tear apart the lock before moving on to the next truck. The seconds tick by, each one too fast, and yet each one seeming to last an eternity. Three trucks stand with their doors open, then five, and finally seven. A cluster of seven small bombs sits in the middle of the road.

A great motor sounds in the air, accompanied by a rush of wind. A helicopter hovers over the empty street ahead of the trucks and slowly lands. Two bomb neutralizers get out and immediately get to work casting their spells. They ward each bomb against fire and heat and then encapsulate it in a force field.

Meanwhile, Jack and Ernesto blur from truck to truck, pulling the balloons out and letting them drift away.

I jump into the last truck and pull my knife. The balloons, tied by ribbons to small weights, crowd the truck. I start cutting ribbons, grabbing armfuls, and stepping out of the truck to release them. One armful after the other, again and again, moving as quickly as I can. A shadow appears in the doorway of the truck as I grab another armload. Jack yells, "Get out of the truck. Now!"

Startled, I ask, "How much time?"

"Two minutes. This is the last truck. I've got it."

I look to the back of the truck and see it's still half full. Conceding that I can't do it, I step down. How I curse human speed sometimes.

Within one minute, Jack has released the rest of the balloons, and they float up toward the sky. The bomb neutralizers load the encapsulated units into strongboxes, which are warded containers that can absorb explosions. Somehow, seeing the bombs disappear within the gray metal containers, now triple-protected, gives me some ease.

I step back and watch the last of the balloons floating up to the sky. The air is filled with the innocent-looking red and blue globes, thousands of them floating gently up and over the park.

Jack stands next to me and pulls me against his side. "Sorry I yelled. You scared the shit out of me."

I pull strength from the heat of his body next to mine and feel somehow comforted. "I know. It's okay."

The pedestrians are shouting and laughing, amused at the balloons filling the sky. Kids are exclaiming over the sight. Babies lift their hands as though trying to catch them between their pudgy fingers.

The balloons float higher and higher, the circular shapes peppering the bright blue sky and making polka dot designs against the fluffy white clouds. A group gets caught in an eddy of wind and swirls in a delightful circle. Then a breeze seems to catch them, and they dance merrily in the air, their ribbons waving back and forth.

We stand there together on the street, Jack with his arm around me and both of us with our heads craning up, hoping the balloons rise quickly enough.

The first balloon explodes in an immense fireball, its bright yellow flare stretching fifty times its original size. Ribbons of dark smoke rain down around the burning core of gas like a starburst heading for earth, but the smoke trails burn out before they get anywhere close to the crowd.

After the first one dies out, another explodes. And another. Soon the staccato of rapidly exploding balloons sounds like the finale of a fireworks show. The air is ablaze with flaming fireballs, and smoke ruins the pristine color of the summer sky. But a few blue balloons seem to evade the carnage and keep rising higher until they appear as tiny dots fading against the azure beyond.

When the last of the red balloons explode, the crowd thunders their applause and graces the street with laughter.

Jack says, "Finally, it's over."

"Not quite yet. I left Schmidt handcuffed in an alley off Hangman's Court a few blocks away."

Jack's eyes gleam with excitement. "Excellent. Let's go get him."

We make our way through the congested streets until we reach the alley. I can see the stairs where I handcuffed Schmidt, but I can't believe my eyes. He's gone, and so is the entire railing. Its match stands in solitude on the other side.

I point to the spots where the bannister has been broken off. "I cuffed him to this bannister. He must have bent the railing over until it broke."

My eyes and senses sweep the alley, searching for any hint of him, but I come up with nothing.

Jack's nostrils flare as he picks up a scent. "I don't smell him here at all. I do smell you and Varg, though."

I kick the stoop in frustration. "Shoot. I bet he's carrying a scent-concealing charm now that he's on the run."

Jack's eyes soften and he lifts my chin with his finger, rubbing my jaw gently with his thumb. He says, "Let's go home."

CHAPTER 78

GOOD INTENTIONS

BLUEBELL KILDARE

JULY 23, 2022, RED AGES

Sister Mary Benedetto of gentle smiles and shy eyes escorts Varg and me to Father O'Brennen's office where I tap lightly on the door. She scuttles down the hallway as soon as the door swings open. Father O'Brennen's face lights up when he sees me.

"Oh, hello Blue. Do come in and have a seat." He indicates a pair of chairs on either side of a little table in the corner.

"Thank you, Father." I take one and he takes the other. It's so like Father O'Brennen not to talk to me from across the desk but to want to be on equal footing.

Father O'Brennen's concerned eyes turn my way. "How are you doing Blue? You're looking . . . " He trails off.

"Tired. I'm looking tired. The last two days have been grueling."

He asks, "Is there anything I can do?"

"I have to tell you about something that I did, and I want your opinion on it. I'm not sure, but it could be very bad."

He frowns and asks gently, "Do you want a confessional?"

"No, no. Nothing like that. I just want your opinion."

He slaps his knee. "All right then, give it to me. I've heard it all."

"You have not heard this. Trust me. Remember when I told you that I was prophesied to destroy Lilith?"

Father gets very serious now. "Yes, Indeed I do. I pray over it daily."

Of course. I knew he would.

"Well, I was captured by a secret organization that tried to summon Lilith so she could question me about something she wants.

Something I can't tell you about beyond that it would be very bad if she got it. They put me in a circle so I would be stuck with Lilith and she could do as she would with me. To gain some control of the situation, I copied their summons and spilt my blood on the altar first, so it was actually I who summoned Lilith."

Surprise fills Father O'Brennen's eyes. "You actually summoned Lilith?"

"Yes, then we bargained, and after that I sent her back."

Father crosses himself and says a quick prayer. Then he looks at me. "What did you bargain for?"

"Well, I asked for a piece of information that I thought might help me destroy her, and I promised to tell her who had the thing."

"Did you tell her?"

"Yes, I tricked her, because no one had the thing at the moment as far as I knew."

"Ahh." He puts his hands together and leans his forehead on them, pondering the situation.

I take a deep breath. "But either way, I still summoned a Demon even though I was forced into the situation. And I bargained with her. How bad is that?"

He purses his lips and furrows his brow. "What were your intentions when you did this?"

"Well, when I summoned her, my intention was to get control of the situation so I could save my life, but when I bargained with her, my intention was to get some of the information I need to destroy her and hopefully save the souls of the Vampires."

Father O'Brennen sighs in relief. "Blue, I believe that we are judged by two things only. One is our actions, and the other is our intentions. Your actions were understandable given the situation and your, er, prophecy. And nothing you've told me points to you having bad intentions."

He reaches over and pats my hand comfortingly. "Intentions do matter."

CHAPTER 79

PETUNIAS

BLUEBELL KILDARE

JULY 23, 2022, RED AGES

When Maud opens her door, the first thing I notice is how her eyes practically sparkle. Then I notice her flushed cheeks and the aura of happiness surrounding her. She's wearing a green and rose floral garden dress with a pretty, white, ruffled linen apron tied around her waist. Her hair is rose-colored today and pinned back with bronze barrettes. The whole ensemble reflects the sense of joy emanating from her.

"Blue!" she scolds. "You're late. I can't wait to show you what we did to the garden."

She grabs my arm and practically drags me in with a strength I wouldn't expect from a woman of her age. If I didn't know her, that is. Varg rushes ahead, and I kick the door closed behind me because the arm she isn't dragging is holding a bag.

"Come on, Chicky." She eventually releases me and stands in her living room, looking back and forth from the garden to the kitchen as though unsure which way to go.

"What's wrong?"

She says, "I almost forgot my manners and didn't offer you a drink. We're having Salty Dogs today. Hold on."

I can't help bursting out laughing as I follow her to the kitchen. She doesn't think dragging her guest through her home is bad manners, but failing to offer a drink is the gravest of sins.

"What's so funny?" she asks as she dips the rim of a footed beer glass in salt.

"You and your drinks, Maud. I promise I'd think no less of you if you didn't offer me a drink."

She huffs. "That isn't the point. I'd think less of myself."

She pours the concoction into the glass and practically shoves it into my hand. "Let's go!"

Her exuberance is certainly intriguing, so I eagerly follow her through the patio doors. And I must say I'm rather shocked.

"You did all this work in ten days?"

Maud beams, and Harry, who had been lounging in one of the new lawn chairs, comes to join us.

Maud says, "First Harry tilled the path all the way around the garden." As she says this, she touches his arm affectionately. "Then he tilled under the swing so all the weeds were gone. But we were careful to keep the clematis on the arbor. We edged the entire walk with glow stones and filled it in with sand and pebbles. We did the area under the swing too. We even planted the petunias around the swing."

"I see!" I exclaim. "They're lovely."

Maud's excitement continues to spill over. "Well, we kept needing to go in the house for breaks, and Harry pointed out that a little seating area out here would be nice."

Harry breaks in, "We were tracking dirt in the house, and Maud was having a fit."

I laugh. "I can imagine."

Maud slaps my arm. "Hey!"

Then she says, "Anyway, so we dug out a separate area for the flagstone patio. Once we installed that, we thought about how it would get chilly in the evenings, so naturally we needed a fire-pit."

I grin at this bit of good sense. "Plus it practically doubles the amount of time you can spend out here," I say.

I follow the path around to the patio and admire the fire-pit work. "Who did this masonry? It's excellent."

Maud gets very quiet and looks away from Harry.

"Did I just stumble on a secret of some sort?"

Harry clears his throat. "Well, the truth is, I'm Gifted with stones."

I appraise Harry. "Really? What can you do with them?"

He puckers his lips as though he doesn't like to brag. Finally he says. "Oh, I can move them and shape them and such." He waves his hand in the air like that is no big deal.

Actually, shaping and moving rocks is an incredible talent. It means he commands them. That's a massive power, but apparently he doesn't like to talk about it. To put him at ease, I let it blow over. "Well, the work is gorgeous. And I love the grill. So now you can have cookouts."

Maud says, "Yes, and we already had a ward specialist out to spell the patio against insects. The chairs were just delivered today. What do you think of the pattern?"

Six sturdy, cedar chairs with thick, multicolored striped cushions surround the fire-pit. "They're bold and bright. Perfect."

Maud beams. "Well, let's sit down and relax a bit."

I take the chair closest to me and sink in. Maud walks over to me with twinkling eyes and flips a little tray up on the side of the chair. "For your beverage."

I set my Salty Dog on it gladly. "I love it."

Maud takes the seat next to me and Harry next to her. Varg climbs on the seat on the other side of me, apparently deciding that outside furniture belongs to him just like yards do.

After a few minutes of idle chitchat, Maud turns a serious gaze toward me. "So Maev came to see me. She told me she'd introduced herself to you already."

"Yes, she did. She told me she sent Varg to me while she was off traveling in Christendom."

Maud tightens her lips. "After all this time I thought she was dead by now. She was always getting into scraps with her magic when she was younger. The least she could have done is written her own sister."

"I know. I feel the same way, but I'm trying to give her the benefit of the doubt. Surely she had a good reason for staying silent."

Maud huffs, making it clear that all is not forgiven between the sisters. Then she clears her throat and changes the subject. "Harry thinks we should add a pergola with a retractable canopy."

My eyes light up. "That would be perfect. Then you could read out here in the rain."

Harry says, "We'll probably work on a few of the beds first. I think the asters are in good shape, and the irises just need to be thinned out."

Maud and Harry start talking about all that needs to be done and arguing over which order to do it in. I watch them with a smile on my face, sipping my Salty Dog. It really doesn't matter what they do. They're doing it together, and I hope they do things together for many years to come.

Chapter 80

Setting the Stage

Jack Tanner

July 23, 2022, Red Ages

With a twist of my wrist, I shake the tablecloth out on a small dinette set I've arranged near the veranda's sliding doors. Through all my years, I've rarely played the romantic. But our situation needs to change, and I'm convinced this is an important step.

The rose petals come next, pink and red sprinkled in disarray on the tablecloth.

She's right. I keep going back and forth with her, and it isn't fair. I try to push her away, to do the right thing, but I can't stay away. So the next right thing is to give up on giving up.

Next come the candles. Fifty of them. Perhaps it's excessive. With a shrug, I place the wax-filled glass cups around the apartment on every available horizontal service. Each wick is dripped in a charmed lighting fluid, set to go off with a word. But I don't light them yet. I can do that when she arrives.

I'm still twisted up inside about this move. She just doesn't see how selfish my being with her is. I'll spell the moral conflict out to her before things get serious so she can play her card. That's the right thing to do. She should have a choice. But a choice made in the face of roses, candlelight, and a good meal might be more likely to sway her my way.

Who am I kidding? This is more than just a moral issue. I'm going to devastate her when I tell her the whole truth. I look at the apartment in frustration. It's not nearly enough. I'm not sure anything is enough.

In the kitchen, I pierce the vegetables with a fork. They pass the test. It's time for the thyme. A good palm full of fresh thyme leaves falls out of the bowl and into the rich Irish lamb stew made with potatoes, leeks, carrots, and onions. It softly simmers while I set the table. Two wine glasses come next. I set my media console on soft jazz and slip into the bedroom. A quick look assures me I haven't splattered stew on the white of my shirt. I rub my hand over my smooth jaw, wondering if she prefers a five o'clock shadow.

Well, that's it. The only thing to do now is wait. Wait and hope.

CHAPTER 81

Vile Hope

BLUEBELL KILDARE

JULY 23, 2022, RED AGES

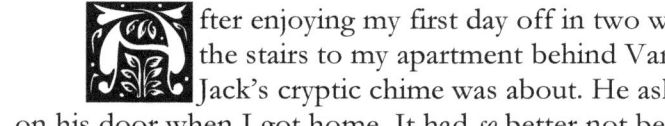fter enjoying my first day off in two weeks, I bound up the stairs to my apartment behind Varg. I wonder what Jack's cryptic chime was about. He asked me to knock on his door when I got home. It had *so* better not be about work.

"What's gotten into him, Varg? He sounded so . . . nice. Abrupt as always, but nice. Maybe even cajoling."

Varg tilts his head at me. "Yeah, I know you can understand me, you demigod, you. I hope you're happy about this little gig you've got with me."

When I reach the first landing, my phone rings. "Hola, Blue speaking."

"Hello, this is Counselor Redblood. I have some good news. Is this a good time?"

"It's always a good time for good news."

He says with no small amount of pleasure in his voice, "Well, it seems the case has been dropped. The complainant withdrew their complaint."

"What?" I'm shocked. "Are you saying that Dean Schmidt actually withdrew the complaint or someone made him withdraw it?"

The counselor hesitates, "Well, he has to sign the form, but his counselor submitted it."

"Really?" Maybe he's trying to redeem himself. How interesting.

"Yes, now remember, we still need to get Varg registered as a defense weapon."

"Oh, I know. Please start that paperwork as soon as you can."

"Very good. Have a nice evening."

When I reach the hallway, Jack opens the door, blocking the entrance to his apartment with his tall frame and broad shoulders. And is that a shy smile on his face?

"Jack."

"Blue."

I gaze at him expectantly.

"Blue, I've taken to heart what you said the other day. You're right; I haven't been playing fair with you."

Shock! Awe! I imagine a round of applause in my head. But I'm a bit leery still.

I search his eyes and shift on my feet. "Come again?"

Jack's voice softens, "I'd like to have an honest conversation with you tonight where I'll declare my intentions and share with you all my concerns. Dinner is ready, and I'd be honored if you would join me."

Is the room spinning, or is my mind twisting? Because the rules of physics, seem to have just changed. I hold on to the wall for support as the breath whooshes out of me.

I'm not sure if I'm ready for declared intentions. Undeclared intentions would be just fine. Even flying-by-the-seat-of-your-pants intentions would do the job nicely.

But I recognize this sick feeling tightening my body. This is the feeling of hope. Terrible, frightening, mind-blowing hope. Hope that twists in your gut because you're so afraid of it. You don't trust it. You don't believe it can live. And you know the cost of hope. You pay for it in every wretch of pain you feel as the fragile hope slowly dies and melts away. But I'm not letting this vile, miserable, despicable hope scare me away.

Despite the threatening gloom of hope, I allow a small smile to surface. "Jack, it would be my pleasure."

CHAPTER 82

FOUR TRUTHS AND A LIE

BLUEBELL KILDARE

JULY 23, 2022, RED AGES

ack ushers me into the center of his dark apartment. And by dark, I mean no lights. "Uh, Jack. I don't have Vampire sight."

Jack places his arm around my back and commands, "Light!"

And light they do. Beautiful, twinkling candles light up the whole room. Flames shimmer on the living room accent tables and on the café set. My eyes catch on the rose petals covering the table and on two small bowls with floating roses sitting to either side.

I sigh happily. "Jack . . . "

Jack smiles, and his eyes sparkle in the light. The shadows on the planes of his face make his cheekbones and strong jaw stand out. He takes my backpack and hands me a glass of wine. "Would you like to sit while I bring in the food?"

"Can I help you?"

Jack shakes his head tightly and pulls out my chair for me.

I slowly sip my wine as I watch him set a covered tureen, a bowl of crusty bread, and a delicious smelling orange salad in front of me. The salad is dotted with coconut flakes and laced with honey and lime. "Jack, where did you learn to cook so well?"

Jack tops off my glass with merlot and fills his own from a bottle of Bloodvine. He sits down across from me. "My skills run to rustic fare since I learned hundreds of years ago." He shrugs. "I don't cook often enough to advance my skill to the modern era. But with our enhanced sense of smell, Vampires seem to do well at cooking."

Jack uncovers the tureen and ladles some thick, meaty stew into a bowl. Its scent rises with the steam, rich and enticing.

"It's a shame you can't enjoy it."

Jack breaks off a hunk of bread and sets it on a plate for me, indicating the butter. "Oh, but I do enjoy it. It's a pleasure to watch you eat."

My cheeks heat up a bit, and I focus on my plate for a moment. First I must try this tender meat. I spear it and pop it in my mouth, and it falls apart in an exquisite goodness. "Oh, this is sooo delicious. You must cook for me more often."

Jack smiles, and I make a good dent in my dinner. Between bites, I manage to ask, "So why would you cook at all if you don't eat?"

"Well, you have to remember, I'm very old. When the Great Pact was first made, we didn't have blood banks, so local villages would loan us young adults for a year at a time."

I cough on my food, and Jack looks at me in concern.

Waving my hand furiously as I clear my throat, I gasp, "Don't stop there. Keep telling the story."

"The villages would usually have a lottery, entering any children who had just reached what they then considered adulthood. Typically two of their young would be given to us at a time. In trade for feeding off them, we would feed them. Well.

"We hunted, learned to tend gardens and grow herbs. It became a point of pride to keep our attendants plump and healthy. By doing this, we ensured the villages would continue to entrust us with their young. The poorer families might even volunteer a family member during lean years when they had trouble feeding everyone."

A quick swallow of water sets my throat straight. "So was this just a blood and food sharing thing, or were you lovers? Did the person have a choice?"

"The expectation was that they wouldn't deny their duty to feed us given the Great Pact. But anything more wasn't strictly required. As with all things, that depends on the individuals involved. I'm sure every scene under the sun played out, if you take every one of these relationships into account. Of course, in return we had to keep the village clear of Dark Vampires."

Fascinating. When my most pressing hunger is sated, I look penetratingly at Jack. "May I have some fruit salad and some declarations now?"

Jack scoops some of the honeyed oranges into a small bowl for me. "Yes, but I'd like to offer some truths before the declarations."

I peer at Jack through the veil of my lashes and fully take him in. He's leaning over the table in a crisp white shirt with folded cuffs tugged up to his elbows. Two—no, three buttons of his collar are undone. The planes of his face look chiseled in the candlelight. His expression is determined and wary.

I think a vile hope attacks him as well.

"What are your truths, Jack?"

Jack reaches across the table and lightly traces the creases of my hand with his fingertips. "Blue. You're apparently the person who's supposed to save the Vampire souls. Redeem us if you will. Let me state that personally. I know that you are destined to save my soul. Can you imagine what it would feel like if you knew that it was my job to bring you to the Plane of Light?"

"You feel beholden to me?"

"I feel exactly as though I owe you my very soul, because I do."

Jack tugs lightly on my pinky and starts stroking my finger up and down in a rhythmic motion. That little tiny action heats my blood. That small touch.

"But there's more. Now, in order to save my soul you have to die three times. You've already died twice. But you have to die once more." He pierces me with his eyes. "You have to *die*, Blue. To save my soul."

"Okay, I see where you're coming from. That's a lot to owe a person."

Jack catches my eyes. "Yes, It's a lot. Now imagine why I would struggle at the thought of taking something else from you, like your affection, your body, your blood, your pleasure. If I made you breakfast, lunch, and dinner every day for the next seventy years of your life, the scales would still not be even. Not in the slightest."

This is starting to make a little sense now. It clicks. It fits with his personality. How many times has he saved my life? How hard does he try to protect me? This rings of truth.

"Let's take this one step further, Blue. You have to die one more time. Twice you have died, and twice you've come back to life. How do we know it'll happen again? What if the third time you die is the last?"

Tendrils of fear lace through my gut. That's been my worry as well.

Jack pulls his hand away from mine for a moment. "Now, how much do I owe you? You are destined to redeem my entire race. Save my soul. Die another death. And perhaps lose your last life. What right do I have to ask anything of you or take anything from you? And yet I'm your boss, sending you out into danger every day."

Jack slams his hand down on the table and stands up, knocking the chair over. "The exact opposite of what I should be doing. I hate it!"

With abrupt movements, he picks up his chair and sits down again. He stares at me quietly for a moment. "I have one more truth for you now. On top of all of that, I am always aware—*always* aware—of the pure radiance of your light compared to the dark smut covering my aura. The evil chain of Lilith's hold. Why should you sacrifice anything for me? For us? You are much more valuable than I."

This strikes into my heart, and I won't listen to it. I whisper fiercely, "That last one is not a truth. That's a lie. Don't tell that lie to yourself, Jack. I am not a holy being. I am not without faults and sins. In fact, I'm regular. I'm just as good as the next person, and no better. The scales are even."

"I don't feel like they're even."

"Well that's your battle. But you battle with a lie."

I stab an orange with my fork for emphasis and take another delectable bite. Then I stand up with my glass of wine. "Shall I help clean up?"

"No." He beckons toward the sofa. "Come sit with me."

CHAPTER 83

DECLARATION OF INTENT

BLUEBELL KILDARE

JULY 23, 2022, RED AGES

fter filling his glass with Bloodvine and hastily drinking the entire contents down, Jack stretches his long legs out on the ottoman and pats the sofa next to him. I sit down on the edge of the sofa, stiff and nervous.

Jack wraps his arms around me and shifts me to his lap so my back leans against the arm of the sofa and my legs dangle over his thighs. I look at him in surprise, but a satisfied smirk rests on his face.

"Do you think this might be sitting a bit close for declarations?" I ask.

"No, it's perfect."

"Well, then, declare away."

He seems as nervous and tense as I feel, and it cuts my heart. He leans in and softly kisses my temple, three little kisses, chaste and sweet. He buries his nose in my hair and drags the smell in deeply. I thrill that he enjoys my scent. He shifts me again so that I'm gazing straight into his eyes. The powerful force of his gaze captures mine, even as tendrils of shame and determination curl around him.

"Blue, I have more truths to tell you, worse truths. But despite it all, I can't stay away. Despite the fact that I owe you everything, I can't help taking more."

His large hand traces the outline of my fingers as though memorizing their shape. Even this small touch lights my senses on fire. He turns my hand over and slowly brings my palm to his mouth. His eyes, green as grass after a summer rain, hold mine hostage. The tender and seductive feel of his lips burns into my hand. His lips whisper over my skin as though devouring this one part of me is his sole obsession. Craving swells around us.

In a clear voice, low with need, Jack says, "I want you in my life. Entirely. Completely." And he punctuates that with a soft bite on the meat of my thumb.

Desire shoots straight to my core, even as my heart stutters and fills with a tentative joy. But I'm unsure. My terrible hope has done its damage, and I'm afraid to expect much. I lift my hand to trace the outline of his jaw. My fingers, with a will of their own, find their way to his mouth and stroke his lips. "What do you mean by that? You want to date me? You want me in your bed?"

He lets out a low, dark laugh and swoops in for a tender kiss before pulling back. One hand lightly traces a fiery path up and down my arm as he speaks. "That and more. I want to be the one you turn to when you need help. To protect you and care for you." He kisses the tip of my nose and smiles. "I want to know everything about you, all your thoughts. Your hopes and dreams." His lips brush gently against mine. "And I want to know everything you've been through. The happiness and the pain." He drags his lips up the curve of my cheek and softly kisses my eyelid. "I want to know you so well that I carry your memories as well as I carry my own." He tenderly kisses my other eyelid. "Until we are so close we don't know where one of us ends and the other begins."

As he speaks and shows me what he means, my heart swells, and the hope doesn't feel so vile anymore. It feels almost . . . possible.

He runs his thumb down the curve of my cheek. "And I want to hold you." He groans. "I need to hold you." With that, he pulls me tightly into the circle of his arms. I welcome his warmth.

His lips find mine gently, brushing lightly, tenderly. Our breath mingles in an open-mouthed kiss. Bliss. Can this really be happening to me? The wonder of his declaration overwhelms me.

His large hands grasp my head and tilt it to accommodate his wants. Light little kisses, breathy and tender, travel across my jaw. My hands graze his strong arms through his shirt. Soon I feel his hot breath in my ear, and a shiver runs through me. I cling to his shoulders, an anchor in a wild tempest. One luscious suck at my earlobe and he travels down my neck.

Already, my body burns for him. My nipples bud and tighten. Stretching and yearning, they push through my thin shirt. And they ache. Oh, they ache for him. His lips travel down my neckline, and his hand slips up to lightly brush my nipple. I push my breasts forward, begging for more.

Jack's mouth, wet and hot, closes over mine, and he kisses me hungrily. A starved, open-mouthed kiss, that speaks of endless wanting and eternal desire. My fingers thread through his hair, trying to deepen the kiss. But he keeps it teasing. Tormenting. I moan my despair.

Still, his hands tease my nipples, lightly flicking each bud, gently pinching, and flames of desire lick at my belly, luscious, sweet, and agonizing. I find myself growing wet and hot and even more ravenous. My hands explore the strong muscle of his shoulders and enjoy the strength of his arms. Our hot breath joins together again, rapid and shallow.

Jack shifts me again so my legs sit on either side of his lap, and the hardness of his cock through his trousers presses exquisitely where I need him. I open my eyes. He looks at me with such a controlled hunger, his dilated black pupils set against the spinning, deep green of his irises.

His expression turns unsure. "I want your shirt off. May I?"

"Oh, yes, you may."

His pupils dilate even more, practically swallowing his irises. Grabbing the hemline, he lifts my shirt in one sure pull, and I sit before him in my black lace bra. His eyes fly to my cleavage, and he reaches out one curled finger. He slides it with slow deliberation down the inner curve of my breast. My breath hitches as I watch him. He drags his finger up the opposite side and then down again, tugging lightly at the center of my bra where the two cups join.

"Jack, you're killing me."

He chuckles, but I've had enough. I reach for the buttons on his shirt, releasing them, exposing the curling, golden chest hair that tapers down his torso and disappears into his trousers. All the while, he teases my breasts with little light touches that drive me insane. I tug at his sleeve and demand, "Take this off."

He does, and I skim my fingers over his chest, delighting in the feel of him under my touch. I don't think my fingers have ever been so happy. I stroke his sides and reach around to caress his back as much as I can. Coming round to the front, I tentatively run my thumbs over his nipples. Jack jumps and grunts, then pulls me away from him, bending me over backwards. His hot, wet mouth captures my nipple through my bra, nibbling and sucking.

His arousal, hard against my belly, tempts me. I rub myself against him, wanting more—oh, so much more. With a small snap, my bra falls loose. Jack pulls at the shoulders and takes if off. Then he stills.

I raise my head and watch his face. His molten eyes adore my breasts, and his low voice breaks. "You're so beautiful."

With one hand supporting my back, he cups the underside of one breast in the other and slowly raises it, lowering his mouth at the same time. Every fiber of my being is focused on that one nipple as his mouth, fiery and moist, descends. Closes over it. Sucks it, tugs it, pulls it gently before finally letting go.

I push against his cock with desire. I need him closer. Then he moves to my other breast, lifting it tenderly, giving it the same devastating care until the peaks of my nipples are pebble hard and warm moist heat floods my burning core.

I can't take it. I lean my head on his shoulder. "Jack, I want you so much."

Jack pulls me back and tilts my head up to meet his eyes. Regret and pain live there. I hurt for his hurt. "I want you too, Blue. But there are still ugly truths for me to tell you. The worst, really. You may regret even this."

I can't imagine regretting loving him like this. Letting him love me. Like a child begging for a sweet, I plead, "Tell me after. I promise I won't regret it. I just want you so much."

With that, Jack stands, holding me still wrapped around him. His low voice whispers in my ear, "Then let me pleasure you." He carries me into the bedroom.

CHAPTER 84

ALL AND NOTHING

BLUEBELL KILDARE

JULY 23, 2022, RED AGES

He gently lowers me to the comforter and lays pillows beneath my head. He pushes my jean legs over my knees and slowly removes one boot and then the other. With my torso propped up on the fluffy mound of pillows, I watch him undress me. The candlelight gleams off the planes of his broad chest. The ripples of his muscles entrance me as he moves.

His jaw is fixed in a rigid line, as though restraining himself. Next, he slides his hands up and peels my socks down my calves, caressing my leg as he goes. All the while, his eyes burn into me, pinning me to the pillows, a violent green storm, a massive pool of contained energy. He drags his hands up my legs and rests his fingers lightly on the button of my jeans. His gaze turns questioning.

"Yes," I breathe. His jaw tightens further.

He releases the button and leisurely pulls down the zipper, then grasps the edge of my waistband and pulls it down, kissing my belly, inch by inch, as it's revealed.

His mouth travels over the soft part of my belly. When he approaches my dark curls, he detours to the left and travels down my hip. He's too far away. My arms ache to hold him. All I can do is run my fingers through his hair, teasing the golden curls. I want to hold him, pull him so close to me that I can't feel the difference between his skin and mine.

His lips travel down my thigh, and his hands lightly caress the backs of my naked knees. As he scoots down the bed, he pulls my jeans off little by little until he's finally at my calf, where he tugs them off completely.

"Jack," I say breathlessly.

Here, with him. This is where I'm meant to be. Every nerve on my skin cries for his touch. Aches for his kisses.

Jack slowly looks up at me from his position at my feet, raking my flesh with his eyes until he reaches my face. He smiles, a beautiful glorious smile that surely I'll remember for the rest of my life. The candlelight spills a warm glow over the planes of his face and bounces off the edges of his short curls. He looks like a fierce angel swathed in golden light.

He lowers his mouth and presses warm, moist lips to the arch of my foot. Open mouthed. He licks. Devours. I've never felt so loved in my entire life.

"Come to me," I whisper. "I want to hold you. I need to feel you in my arms."

Jack does come to me. He lays himself over me, covering me, holding himself up by his elbows. I wrap my arms around him and stroke his back in long, hungry movements. His lips lower to my neck again, licking and nipping along the side of my jugular. And I know he's hungry for more than just my body.

"I could do this forever," he breathes in my ear. "I will if you'll let me."

Then he lowers his mouth to mine, and I'm lost to his heat and his passion. His lips envelop my lips, searing me. His tongue dances in and out as he rocks his body softly against me. My legs wrap around him as I urge him closer, but he's like a burning flame, wavering, dancing away in teasing delight. I'm so wet and so hungry. I want more. I want it all.

Jack trails a molten path of open mouthed kisses down my neck and over my cleavage, where he latches onto my breast. I arch back. Incoherent moans escape my lips. He sucks my nipple in a timeless rhythm in accord with the rocking of his body. Hungrily, he moves from one engorged nipple to the other. I dig my nails into his back, desperate for more. Electric desire sets my core aflame, and wanting floods my body.

Jack's nostrils flare in response, and he drags his kisses down farther, setting off an inferno inside me. His tongue briefly delves into my belly button, then continues on, kissing a path toward the edge of my panties.

He lowers himself between my legs, and I watch as his mouth

descends to the apex of my thighs. He presses his nose into my soaking panties, running it up my cleft, and follows by licking the outside of the silk fabric right over my clit.

"Oh, Jack." I throw my arms over my head and turn to the side, unable to watch anymore. Unable to think anymore.

I feel the soft silk of my panties drag down my legs and the rough calluses of Jack's fingers leading them.

Then Jack calls my name, low and raspy. "Blue."

I flutter my eyes open to see him sitting there on the bed next to me. His chest muscles strain with his control, but his eyes caress me reverently. He moves toward me and lies down by my side, curling his body around mine, trapping one leg between his and pulling my thighs apart.

"Blue," His voice breaks, "I'm going to touch you now."

I turn my face toward him on the pillow and get lost in the depth of his eyes. When his breath falls softly on my lips, I say, "Yes, Jack. Please."

His eyes, so dark, so bright, invade mine as he pulls my thighs gently apart until I feel the cool air of the room brushing at my liquid heat. Then his hand whispers over my swollen flesh, parting my folds further. His fingers glide, warm and rough, slick and wet over my cleft. My inner walls stretch and widen. My body arches for him.

"Jack," I breathe, unable to control my mounting desperation. My lips part in urgent appeal.

He rests his cheek against mine and soothes me. "Shhh, it's okay. I've got you." He pushes himself up on one arm so he can watch where he touches. His finger climbs and holds still, pressing lightly on the center of my clit.

"Jack," I moan again as I try to push up. But his thigh traps me. The pleasure sits just out of my reach, and I can't get close enough.

"Shhh," he whispers again as his finger lightly taps my clit.

I open my mouth, panting, and try to find his mouth for a kiss. I need more. But he's too high above me. My mouth finds the flesh of his arm, and I suckle it, biting down softly. He growls his pleasure in response. And still his finger teases me.

Jack taps my clit again and again, pausing after each time. Keeping my legs locked. Keeping the edge of ecstasy just out of my reach.

Torturing me.

I twist in his arms, until I'm facing his chest, and pull his whole areola into my mouth. Another growl rumbles from his throat. Pleased by his response, I copy him. I nibble my teeth lightly at his nipple, feeling it harden into a tight bud. He groans again.

Then where there was warmth from his body is only cool evening air. And I ache for him.

I lift my head to see him sitting between my thighs, watching me hungrily, patiently. With his eyes pinned to mine, he runs both hands up my thighs. One hand parts my folds, and in excruciating slowness, he inserts one long finger, pushing his way in. My body instinctively clenches around him. The other hand travels up farther until his thumb rests firmly on my clit, and he strokes it ever so lightly. I watch him watching me, and I arch up, pushing against the rough pad of his thumb.

"Yes," he says.

He slips his finger out of me and pushes in again, the glorious pressure so satisfying and yet not enough. I arch and push up against his thumb again. "Yes, again," he softly encourages as he slips his finger out and this time presses two fingers deep inside me.

All the while Jack pins my eyes with his and watches my face. I hold his eyes in this intimate embrace.

"Sweet Blue," he whispers.

A wildness takes over me, and I find myself pressing against his thumb to a raging beat as he glides in and out with the other hand.

"You're the most beautiful woman I've ever known," he says. And his eyes drive into me that he truly believes it at that moment. My thighs fall wide open, and I push up with all that I have, the wanting growing stronger, rising to a fevered pitch.

I close my eyes, as my whole world is the feeling of Jack's hands on me. Nothing else exists except for this moment in time.

Jack demands, "Look at me."

I do look at him. I see dark green eyes and the sensual expression on his face. I see his body rocking gently as his fingers slip inside of me and then back out, his parted lips flush and swollen, his gaze hungry on my face.

My muscles stretch further at the sight of his desire. My thigh muscles tighten. Reaching. Imploring. Just when I'm on the edge, just when paradise is around the corner, Jack withdraws his hands.

Aching, throbbing, emptiness. Devastation.

"Jack," I demand in a breathless, gravelly voice.

But instead of leaving me, he lowers his head between my thighs and licks in one teasing motion from the bottom of my cleft up to my clit. Then he suckles me. I buck my hips off the bed. He releases me and places my ankles over his shoulders so I'm spread wide, laid out like a feast before him.

"You're exquisite," he murmurs as he gazes at my most intimate of places.

Both hands trace over the contours of my swollen pink flesh. Then the stars must align because he places his tongue over my clit and slips his fingers inside me again. I rub madly against his tongue.

My fevered body sets an ascending rhythm, rocking against him while Jack groans his pleasure, impelling me to continue. With each luscious invasion of his fingers, with each magnificent press of his tongue, the desire burns hotter, blazing and wild. I feel myself reaching the edge of the precipice, but I hang on. Then thousands of electric points of light seem to explode in my body, and I topple over the edge. My thighs go rigid and my inner walls clench, as liquid heat flows out of me. My whole body arches off the bed in white hot pleasure.

I weep with pleasure.

But Jack keeps pressing my clit with his tongue and keeps pushing into me, controlling the rhythm where I cannot, until he rips everything from me. Until he pulls every tremor out of me. Until he drains me. Destroys me.

Until I am nothing without him.

CHAPTER 85

THE UGLY TRUTH

JACK TANNER

JULY 23, 2022, RED AGES

Blue's eyelids flutter closed, and her arms lift weakly in invitation. I gather a blanket from the closet and slip down by her side, laying the covering lightly over us. Then I pull her sweet body into my arms and give her a tender kiss on the forehead.

"Jack," she whispers as she twines her arms around me, "why didn't you . . . " She blushes, then says, "I want all of you. You didn't even take off your pants."

Then she asks in a small voice, "Don't you want me that way?"

I groan, because I want her so much my cock feels stretched to the limit and my balls ache. I wanted her before when I watched her flesh turn rosy with desire, her mouth parted in pleasure. And I want her now, all warm and sleepy. A day, a week, a month, a year of having her—none of it would be enough to stop wanting her.

I kiss her temple. "Yes, I want you." There's nothing at this moment that I want more—except her love. Yet we have a storm to weather before I can have either. But Lady of Light, how I want her.

"Then why?" she asks sleepily.

I pull her tightly against me. "Because we still have things to talk about. It wouldn't be right."

She opens her intense blue eyes, filled with concern. "I'm ready to listen."

"Not yet," I murmur. "Let me hold you for just a few minutes. Then we'll get dressed and finish our conversation."

Blue sighs and buries her head into the crook of my chest. Her hand caresses my back in small, languid strokes. I wrap my arms around her waist, pulling her forward until her breasts crush against my chest and her leg wraps around mine. We lie thus while our bodies calm down and our breathing evens out. And I hope desperately that this isn't the last time I'll ever get to hold her.

As inevitable as the rising of the sun, even this moment of peace must end. Eventually Blue stirs and sits up. "I have to use your bathroom."

I point to the door on the other side of the room. She awkwardly covers her body, so new to lovemaking her shyness is still prominent. I smile at that. She grabs her clothes and darts to the bathroom.

With a sigh, I get up and find my shirt. I pour another glass of merlot for her and some Bloodvine for me and wait for her to join me in the living room.

She emerges from the bedroom fully dressed and wearing a soft smile. I pat the sofa next to me, inviting her to sit down. When I offer her the glass, she takes a good gulp of the wine. It seems to bolster her courage because she comes at me with her inspector voice, sharp and assertive. "Okay. I'm ready. What is this big mystery that I'm sure you're making into too big a deal?"

I smile wistfully at her. "I wish I were, but I'm afraid I'm not."

She chews her lip. "Well, then . . . I guess just tell me."

I sit back a bit to give her space. "Blue, what were you told about the death of your parents?"

She frowns deeply. "Father O'Brennen told me that Dark Vampires were hunting when they happened upon the alley my parents were in and killed them. He said I was with them, that my light killed one and scared the rest away. But it was too late. My parents were already dead. Then a Daylight Vampire found us and brought me to Father O'Brennen. He placed me in the orphanage."

She looks at me then, and a little light goes off. "You were the Daylight Vampire."

"Blue," I say looking her squarely in the eyes. "I didn't just happen upon you in that alley. I was hunting those Vampires. I didn't know your family was there, but I'm the one who drove the Vampires down it. It's because of me that your parents died that night."

Her eyes darken and her smile drops, but I'm not nearly done yet.

"And when I saw how your light killed one of the Dark Vampires, I thought you might be the Illustrissima. The one we were looking for.

So I brought you to Father O'Brennen."

Blue stiffens and scoots away from me a bit. "So after you accidentally killed my parents, you picked up your prize and hid her away in the orphanage? Have I got it right?"

I lower my head in shame, then lift it again, as she deserves to see my eyes for the rest of it. "Yes, I've been the primary benefactor for that orphanage since it was built. I brought you to Father O'Brennen knowing that if you had no relatives, he would put you there. It was easy enough to demand regular reports on you. But I didn't watch closely enough. Every atrocity that occurred to you in that orphanage is my fault because I put you there."

"And the reason that I was never introduced to a family as their potential child? Not even once?"

"I didn't know that, Blue. I swear. Matilda must have done that on her own, but I should have questioned it. I thought they were good to you there. But I've recently found out how Matilda really was. How she punished you."

Her head jerks back and her eyes darken.

"I forced her out. I know it doesn't erase what happened to you, but I truly didn't know. It's too late to prosecute her, but we can bring a civil suit against her if you want."

Blue stands up, her eyes flaming hot. "And my job?"

"I knew you were close to Maud, so I told Walter I needed an investigator and described your skill set. Then, predictably, he recommended you to me. But you must believe me, you're the best investigator we have. Your intuition is incredible. I never expected you to be so good, and I wouldn't trade you for the world."

"So, Jack," she snaps, her eyes flashing deep blue and her aura pulsing brilliantly with her fury, "what part of my life is my own? What part wasn't managed and manipulated, all because I'm supposed to be 'the Illustrissima'? Not my family. Not my childhood. Not Maud. Not my job. You pretended I was a stranger when you interviewed me. You've deceived me my entire life."

She holds her hands clasped against her breast as she says this. Pain and rage fills her eyes. "What about us, Jack? Is this all because I'm some fantasy savior of yours?"

I stand and reach out to her, but she flinches away. Still I persist.

"Blue, at first I knew that you might be the savior of the Vampire souls, so I wanted to watch over you and protect you. And I thought I was doing that by getting reports from the orphanage and keeping you close on the job. But then you came to work for me and I began to know you as a person, your amazing strength, your gentle grace, your ferocious independence. And everything changed. My priorities shifted. So much so that I started to convince myself you weren't the Illustrissima. I didn't want you to go through this. I'd rather see you alive and damn all our souls. My feelings for you are the most real thing that's ever happened to me."

Her eyes flash in disbelief or perhaps simply rejection. "And what are your feelings, Jack?"

Everything in me cries out to tell her, but I can't. If she has to ask, then it's pointless. I say the only thing I can so she knows what to expect. My voice cracks as I answer. "Blue, I know you hate me right now, but I'm not giving you up. I'm going to earn your trust again."

Her eyes, wide and tragic, shine with an unnatural brilliance, but her voice . . . It whips like a knotted lash. "Good luck with that, Jack."

Then she spins on her heel and calls, "Come, Varg."

I watch, helplessly, hopelessly, as she slams the door behind her.

CHAPTER 86

SHATTERED

Bluebell Kildare

July 23, 2022, Red Ages

As soon as I enter the apartment, I slam the door behind me and then collapse against it. Pain slices through me and my body slides on weakened knees down the length of the door. Wretched, heaving, ugly sobs erupt from my breast. The image of my parents, who I barely remember, flashes in my mind, and I think of all the lonely, terrible years at the orphanage. The cruelty and violence. The aching emptiness. Jack was watching over me the whole time. He could have helped me. He might have made sure I went to a family who loved me.

Tears flow as I think of what my life could have been. I might have been happy. Instead I was kept there, under Matilda's thumb and Jack's cold and distant eye.

Then I think about my first days on this job. It's the one thing I've been most proud of all my life: that I got the job at all, and that I was good at it. But all the while, Jack would have kept me on if I was the worst inspector in the world. All so he could keep watching me.

He says he cares about me. He says he wants me. I'd like to deny it, but I know it's true. I can feel it.

But what does it matter? He's deceived me. He's manipulated me. I feel like I just found out I've been acting in a play, and all the while I had thought my life was real.

I curl into a ball on my living room floor, helpless to stop the tears flowing from my eyes. Varg whines softly by my head and lies down next to me. I grab his fur and rest my head on his neck, thankful for his comfort. But even Varg is here because of the prophecy. All these people, all these relationships just revolve around me being the Illustrissima.

Why can't they care about me? Just me?

All the love I have for Jack, for truly I still love him, sits like a sour ball in the pit of my stomach.

"Oh, Jack," I whisper through my tears, "how will I ever trust you again?"

CHAPTER 87

GLIMMER OF HOPE

JACK TANNER

JULY 23, 2022, RED AGES

The reverberation of her slamming door echoes through the hall as the memory of her pain-filled eyes rips me apart. But that isn't the worst of it. The worst is when I hear her sobbing on the other side of her apartment door. I sit down next to my door, as close as I can get to her, listening to her shatter into pieces.

I'm so angry, I want to crush skulls, crush bones, tear out hearts, and bring death and destruction to the one causing her pain. But I can't. Because it's me.

I hear her whisper in her apartment, "Oh Jack, how will I ever trust you again?"

I want desperately to go to her, to hold her, to erase the pain and kiss her sorrows away. But I'm the one who's hurt her, and she doesn't want me. I clench my hair in my fists and let my tears fall as they will while I listen to her breaking heart.

Now she knows everything. There are no more secrets. There's no more manipulation or deception. At least now, any honor she gives me or scrap of affection she throws my way, I can honestly accept without knowing I'm tricking her.

But what chance will there be of that?

I must try to make amends. I must earn her affection and her trust again. But how?

I'll tell her everything I know as it happens. That's a start. And I'll seduce her if I have to. I'll seduce her mind, body, and soul.

I'll find a way.

And with the thought of a fresh slate, I see the first shaky path toward a future with her and the first faint glimmer of hope.

WANT MORE?

Thank you for reading *The Light Who Binds*. The excitement in the City of Crimson Hollow will continue in *The Light Who Burns*. Be sure to sign up for release news at: www.liloabernathy.com/sign-up. For those who would love to hear the voices of their favorite characters, audio versions are available. If you would enjoy some history on Varg you can check out the Kindle ebook short story, *The Binding of the Wolf*.

Please take a moment to leave a review. They help me so much and I promise I read everyone.
Amazon: amazon.com/author/liloabernathy
Goodreads: goodreads.com/Lilo_Abernathy

Support
For those inclined, here are some other ways you can support this book and my future work.

- Recommend it to friends on Goodreads.
- Vote for it on the Goodreads lists.
- Recommend it to your Goodreads groups.
- Post about it on Facebook.
- Tell your circles about it on Google+.
- Recommend it to your book club.
- Tell your friends about it!

Connect
I love when readers connect with me on social media.
My Site: www.liloabernathy.com

Thanks for helping spread the word!

AUThOR AUTOBIOGRAPHY

I'm currently forty-four, but that could differ depending on when you read this. Unless some fundamental laws of nature change, I expect that number to only get higher. I'm half Italian and half Irish. Well, the Irish side is sort of an Irish/German/English/French/Scottish mix, but since I believed I was truly half Irish until my mother's foray into genealogy, I'm sticking to that story.

I live amidst the Smoky Mountains and can sometimes see cloud shadows lying on the mountainside from my front porch. I am not yet snobbish enough to call it a veranda, but time will tell. Sometimes my young adult daughter joins me on the veranda . . . err, porch . . . to admire the view. Often, my Australian Shepherd runs around the veranda chasing off the thieving birds who attempt to steal food from the bird feeders we leave out. What would we do without him?

I started working full time while in high school and haven't stopped since. My illustrious career began with a smattering of service experiences at various fast food and restaurant chains, went on to fine jewelry, slipped into property management for housing projects, morphed into corporate real estate, then ended up in mergers and acquisitions. Please don't ask how that happened as it's still a mystery to me.

My home is a modestly sized ranch with living-room walls of boring light beige, which make the perfect backdrop for my brightly colored Klimt and Van Gogh canvas prints. Van Gogh and Klimt would like to move into my dining room and bedroom next, but their expansion will have to wait on the success of my latest story. All things in due time.

More importantly than all the above, you absolutely must know my favorite color is purple. Not Barney purple—no offense to Barney—but more of a medium eggplant purple. I like to think of it as a "mature" purple, but deep down I know it's really just purple.

www.ingramcontent.com/pod-product-compliance
Lightning Source LLC
Chambersburg PA
CBHW070153260626
47160CB00002B/337